Maleficent

Cover Design: Francesca. C.S.
Illustrations: Saikotik
Memory Break Art: Kole
Book Design and Typesetting: Enchanted Ink Publishing

The text type was set in Garamond Premier Pro

ASIN: B0FD8VDXQJ (E-book)
ISBN: 979-8-9992626-0-8 (Paperback)

Thank you for your support of the author's rights.

WWW.CASSANDRAMDAUTHOR.WEEBLY.COM

This tale is not for tender love or soft hearts. It is for those that know the devastating effects of love and the insatiable hunger wanting brings from the experience of being left out to starve.

What would you give for power, control, love, life?

Everything.

You will give everything as you stand like a lone lighthouse in a raging storm, battered by every violent break of wave across your surface as you witness these characters give everything.

And it will all be taken from them.

Again.

And again.

And again.

BREAK GUIDE

Skips in time. Present day.

No longer present day.
Back into a memory or exiting one and returning to present day.

TRIGGER WARNINGS

Malicent is a dark fantasy, horror genre. Due to the nature of it's content, many of the themes and scenes are intentionally disturbing to read. Your safety and enjoyment is paramount. Please be aware this is a list of triggers that may be found but truly nothing is off limits in this dark world. Please stop reading at anytime you feel triggered.

Abuse including physical, emotional and sexual assault, sexual violence

Potential CNC, Dub Con

Bullying, vulgar language, crude humor

Detailed scenes of child abuse

Death and dying, including suicide, murder, and death threats

Mental illness, PTSD, trauma

Sexually explicit scenes

Graphic depictions of violence, torture, gore

hateful language, classism, racism

Drug and alcohol use

Potential religious references and suggestions

Proceed with caution. Viewer discretion is advised.

Cassandra
M.D
Malicent

CHAPTER 1
Millicent

R AIN COURSES DOWN MY ARMS, MIMICKING THE SHEER, silver-streaked markings branching toward my wrists. A blinding white flash chases a monstrous boom that rattles my ribcage. The vibrations run down my bones to my knees, buried deep in cold mud. No. This can't be right. Rain isn't red, yet I'm covered in it. There's no silver on my arms, only red. As I inhale, the taste of ash fills my throat, constricting my lungs. For a moment, it jolts me back to the present, my awareness sharpening as adrenaline courses through my veins.

"Little star," my mother croaks on the ground, curled around my knees, cradling me even as she feels far colder than usual. Mama is never this cold. She is warm. She is the sun, and I am the stars. "You need to go." Her hands push against my stomach, trying to thrust me away. An inhumane sob escapes from my chest.

I clutch her shirt, trying to form words through my panic. "Mama, come! Get up!" My voice cracks with desperation. Each word tears out of me in a screeching plea. I jolt from shock as lightning strikes again. The sound silences the screams around me for a moment. The brief stillness is shattered as the screams and snarls surge back in a cyclone of echoes. I don't want to look. I just want Mama to get up.

She shakes her head, her voice trembling but firm. "I can't get up. You must go. They're coming." Her tone grows more commanding, urging me to obey. The witch markings on her arms begin to glow faintly, a soft white light creeping along her skin. I shake my head, a desperate plea for her to stop trying to push me away, to not use her magic against me. A gentle arc of white light pulses from her hand, the force knocking me back. The warmth of it tingles my skin and momentarily lights the area, if but for a second. It's her last attempt as she tries to send me away with what little strength she has left.

I dig my knees deeper into the mud, anchoring myself down against her push. What small magic I possess stirs, my eyes beginning to glow—a defiant light that not even the gold and red flames from the burning buildings can penetrate. The blackness suffocates the light as though it is the true threat, a malevolent threat that needs to be contained rather than the beasts that prowl within it, the beasts that are claiming my sisters' lives one by one.

I crawl to her, clutching at her dress. "Up! I can't go without you! Mama, up!" My body trembles with sobs. My eyes blur with a mixture of warm tears and cold rain. She's crying, too. Her tears are red, crimson streaks run down her face. A flash of lightning strikes bright and white, illuminating her for only a moment. Red stains everything—her dress, the ground, and the air around us. An ocean of red engulfs her and me. Desperation drives me to claw at her dress, tugging with what strength I have left. Weak. My frustration ignites my magic. Thick obsidian clouds pour down my legs. They seep into the ground, draining life from the grass under my feet.

"My little star, I love you so much. You are so brave. But you must go. You can't win this."

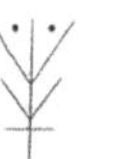

I shake my head fiercely, refusing to accept the idea of being apart from her. "Where I go, you must follow! You promised!"

She coughs, a terrible, wet sound, and more red spills from her lips. Her breaths grow shallow, each one labored and wrong. I tug at her again, desperate. The arms that moments ago pushed me back now fall limp. Her left arm slips into the mud. I lunge forward, grabbing her arm with my small hands, clinging to her. The blue depths of her eyes, the very ones that mirror my own, dim as the light of her magic flickers and fades.

Finally, she isn't resisting. She will help me. "Mama!" I scream, standing and pulling with all my strength. But she doesn't respond. She doesn't even blink to acknowledge me. I freeze. My fingers tighten around her cold wrist.

For the first time, I feel utterly alone. A void fills my heart where her presence has always been a steady rhythm as constant as my heartbeat. Now gone, it settles, as if it were never there. My chest caves inward. I collapse to my knees, hunching over and heaving to fill lungs that suddenly feel void of any air.

My hands claw at the ground, desperate for something solid to anchor me. My heart fractures, and the scream that tears from my throat burns and cracks, but the sound is masked.

The deep rumbling roar, guttural and otherworldly, from a creature I have never heard sounds. My ears ring, and I'm briefly deafened. Even in the darkness, the outline is unmistakable. A monstrous horned head emerges from the crumbling walls of the nearby cobblestone temple. The structure collapses under its immense weight. Debris flies from the roof as two leathery, black, clawed wings burst free. Shards of stone and dust are sent spiraling into the air. The wings unfurl, massive and terrifying, its veins stark and black as lightning flashes in the distance behind the creature. My eyes widen in utter shock, my mind unable to fully comprehend its size at such a close distance.

The creature lowers its head, and I can make out jagged horns running down its massive skull. Its large jaws gape open. From within

 3 

its throat, a torrent of silver flame erupts, engulfing five of my sisters in an instant. A sickly wet warmth trickles down my leg as the acrid stench of burning flesh fills the air. My stomach churns violently, and I double over, retching. I narrowly miss vomiting on my mother. Anguish twists my insides, bringing more tears to my eyes. My body shakes uncontrollably—from fear, from adrenaline, and now from the force of heaving sobs.

The leathered lizard—I have seen it in only books—draws my attention as it makes way onto the grass. Its massive hind legs crush the last remnants of the crumbling building. Stones tumble down as it descends to the ground in its full, terrifying length.

Its shadowed, scaled tail drags behind, equipped with immense spikes that slice through the air with each movement. The earth trembles beneath the heavy, deliberate steps. Each one reverberates through my bones.

The lizard completely ignores the hellish chaos erupting around it. The monstrous shadow creatures that are ripping the coven to shreds, that tore Mama apart, don't even seem to exist to the beast.

Keeping my eyes on the beast, certain it will come for me next, I notice someone perched on its back. My gaze locks with silver eyes—piercing, unnervingly bright, capable of penetrating the oppressive magic suffocating the air.

Confusion whirls in my mind as I recognize him. *Him.* Of all people, he is the one riding this monstrous creature. A cold understanding settles into my bones, heavy and unshakable. It brings with it a violent fire, a hatred that ignites deep in my very soul, scorching everything it touches.

Our eyes remain locked, but he doesn't move. He doesn't try to help Mama. His beast lunges forward. Its gaping maw consumes another of my sisters in a flash of silver flame.

A guttural snarl rumbles nearby, and I feel the oppressive gaze of a shadowed beast shift toward me.

He did this.

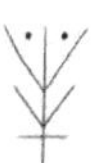

He turns away, never looking back as the creature—now unmistakable, a dragon—takes flight. Its wings carve through the open night, leaving behind echoes of cries and a hell he created. He rides to safety, soaring above the chaos he unleashed.

I am left behind, surrounded by death. Rage consumes me as my heart falters, its rhythm ceasing in tandem with hers.

I close my eyes.

I PEEL MY EYES OPEN, ADJUSTING QUICKLY TO THE DARKNESS OF my room. I'm inside, in my bed. Not outside. Not real. *It wasn't real.* I repeat the thought endlessly, grounding myself to the present and trying to soothe the panic. The room is still cloaked in shadows. Night lingers. I sit up, running my hands through my obsidian curls. The unruly thickness and endless kinks tangle around my fingers. I never sleep well anymore. My memories are hell-bent on replaying themselves over and over, whether I'm awake or asleep.

I feel him before I hear him, the faint, scratchy squeak of the wheel that is Oliver's voice. His presence is as intrinsic to me as the awareness of my own arm. I don't have to see it to know it's there. *Ollie* is the same. I always know where he is without needing to look.

Shadows gather on my bed near my thighs, coalescing into a small, pudgy blue imp.

He stretches his tiny bat wings, wiggling his stubby toes. "Me Misses!" *Ollie* squeals, his tone almost surprised, as if he wasn't expecting me.

Whenever I'm in distress, the bond we share pulls him to me. It requires no conscious thought. I have learned that much by now. His shiny eyes scan me, no doubt taking in the deep circles under my eyes and the sheen of sweat on my skin. He knows the drill already.

Ollie patters his way up to my side, settling next to me with a plop. His distended belly, round and heavy, spills well past his knees as he sits.

"Just a bad dream," I mutter, leaning back against my headboard. A full explanation is not necessary for Ollie. He is fully aware of what haunts me.

"I don't dream" he says simply, looking up at me with black voids for eyes.

I can't help but entertain my little familiar. "Ah, shall I become an imp then? Maybe I'll rest." I offer him a smile, one I've shared with no one but Arcadia. Yet even then, my love for Ollie is something entirely different. He's a part of me both figuratively and literally.

Ollie flashes me a toothy grin. I swear it reminds me of a feral, elderly dog. "Me Misses is perfect! She just needs wine!" His small, chubby three-fingered clawed hand pats my leg in what he must think is reassurance.

I raise a brow, teasing, as I point out the flaw in his solution that came far too often. "You'll make a drunkard of me."

He looks at me, completely confused as to why this would even be an issue. I can't help but chuckle, amused by my imp's silent judgement of my lack of enthusiasm.

I yawn, and instantly, Ollie responds. The confusion on his face disappears, replaced by a determined focus. He's ready to help me recover from my nightmare. Ollie rises, pushing up on his knees, and motions for me to turn my back to him. Our bedtime routine takes hold like a well-worn habit. I lie on my side, facing away from him, and out of thin air, he conjures a brush.

He begins combing through my tangled hair, humming a soft tune, the same one I often hum to myself. Each stroke of the brush is gentle, soothing, as if he is trying to brush away more than just the knots in my hair.

My gaze wanders across my room, settling on the aged bookshelves lining the walls. The books are a disarray of frayed pages and worn spines telling stories of their own.

I'm half tempted to read until I grow drowsy again, but Ollie's ongoing war with my tangles assures me I won't be leaving this bed any-time soon.

My gaze drifts to the large window at the center of my wall. The moon hangs high, its silver light spilling across the room. It feels as though she's watching—*always* watching.

A prickle runs down the back of my neck, an awareness that makes me inhale sharply. Then, it comes, a hauntingly familiar voice that I know better than my own.

Her words slip into my mind, a sensual whisper that seems to echo with an impossible duality. How can one speak so softly and sweetly yet so hoarsely and deep at once?

"Sleep, my star," she sings, her voice a chilling caress that sends shiv-ers down my spine.

It's only now that I notice the tremor in my hand and the pause in Ollie's brushing. She releases me, her laughter trailing behind. It is as much a mockery as the name she calls me.

I swallow the pain that the affectionate nickname stirs deep inside me. My star. A name once filled with warmth, a name that my mother used for me. Now, it is a reminder of what I've lost.

I've read that some animals must consume rocks to digest their food. Bearing that weight is what allows them to survive. Pain has become my stones. I consume it in gluttonous amounts to help me stomach this world from the ache it brings, to let me survive.

As Oliver resumes brushing, each stroke of the bristles glide over my scalp, soothing me deeply. The tension drains from my body, mus-cles loosening with every gentle pass. My eyes grow heavier until, at last, they slide shut.

G ROANING, I PULL A PILLOW OVER MY HEAD TO BLOCK THE offensive sunlight streaming through the oversized window. The window feels far too large for this small room. I hate early mornings. The sun's rays are relentless in its pursuit, ensuring I don't get another minute of rest. Today is a sleep-in day, I decide, as the exhaustion in my body agrees after yet another restless night.

A knock at the door ruins my great plan.

The sweet, singsong voice of Arcadia floats in as the door creaks open. "Good morning, sunshine! Rise on up! Elanora wishes to see you," she chirps, clearly for no other reason than to piss me off.

It is working.

"Lovely. I can't wait," I say, sarcastically rolling onto my back and finally sitting up.

Cadia smirks, leaning casually against my doorway. "Oh, yes, my queen. Duty calls."

The teasing nickname pulls a reluctant smile to my lips and warmth to my chest, the kind only she can manage. There was little that could dampen her mood. She's sunshine personified, with her tight white curls—thick, wild, and untamed—contrasting with the deep, rich tone of her skin. It reminded me of the soil in the gardens after fresh rain, dark and full of life.

Golden witch marks shimmer on her chest, climbing from beneath her breasts, swirling up her sternum and across her cleavage in intricate swirls and dips. If the sun could be melted into paint, then it was used to draw every mark on her skin. Her almond-shaped eyes hold the same brilliance, the golden hues swirling with vibrant life.

To showcase her marks, Arcadia had to dress rather exposed, choosing gowns designed specifically for her. The necklines of her custom coven attire plunged into deep, daring V-cuts that reached her navel, orchestrated deliberately to flaunt the intricate beauty of her markings. Despite her warm and inviting presence, her power was anything but. Arcadia was a curse user, a rarity in our coven. Her mother had fled her own coven and sought sanctuary here, an extraordinary request that *Nora* only allowed because of the devastating power her mother possessed. That same power now lived on in Arcadia.

I slide from bed, unsurprised that Ollie is already gone. The little imp is always somewhere, doing something, and never sticks around for very long.

Grabbing a casual black gown from my wardrobe, I quickly slip out of my nightgown, tossing it aside, and shimmy the gown over my hips and bust.

The coven gowns were all identical, for it is customary in many covens to match or at least follow a shared theme. Ours were made from lightweight and comfortable fabrics that draped loosely on our hips down to our ankles. Each gown had a built-in bodice to keep our chests secure and waists cinched and, of course, short sleeves to display our witch marks.

I catch sight of mine shimmering in the mirror, silver networks of intricate lines that stretch from my shoulders to my wrists. The number of markings reflected one's power, a fact Nora insisted we highlight. To outsiders, they served as a show of force within the coven. They established rank.

When I was younger, it was exciting to watch my marks come in. Power develops slowly, and it isn't until one's first bleed that

the true strength begins to fill us. My journey into power was even more complicated.

I was told since I was little that I was rare, not just in the loving way my mother would say it but in the harsh, exacting way Nora would remind me. If I played too much with the others, if I stepped out of line or didn't study as long as she deemed necessary, I'd hear it. As I grew older, I learned what they meant by "rare."

I possess blood magic and dark magic, a potent combination not seen in centuries. I am the only witch to possess two forms of magic. Such power comes at a cost.

Ancient texts speak of power in cryptic whispers, their pages worn and their words faded. They all ask the same question: *What would you give for power?*

Anything. I have given everything, and they have taken it.

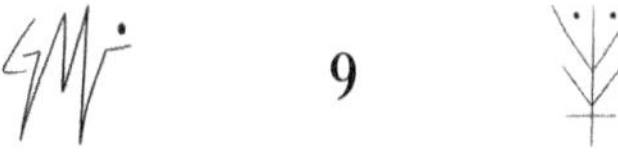

"Going to stare at yourself all day?" Arcadia snickers from the door, pulling me from my thoughts.

I roll my eyes as I cross the room toward her. Her jab about my vanity is almost laughable coming from the most vain woman I know. "Well, when my marks and tits look this good, how can I not?"

The comment transforms us both into simple giggling girls. As soon as I realize I'm laughing, I stop myself, wiping the feeling away and replacing my smile with the emotionless mask I always wear.

Arcadia's laughter fades, understanding softening her expression as she offers me a gentle smile. She doesn't press me, doesn't need to.

Arcadia got to play with others as a child, free to laugh and love. She was ignored by Nora, cherished by her mother, and once she reached the age to leave the coven, she took the opportunity without hesitation. Now she's always on the move, tasting and touching everything the world has to offer.

I wasn't so lucky. I lost my mother, was taught isolation, the rules stacked high against me. My life is defined by limits. The simplest one of many: I cannot leave the coven walls without Nora's instruction.

I was Nora's fixation, her project. We were so different. I knew I couldn't let myself be seen laughing or bonding, especially by the elders. It would violate one of the most important rules she taught me—isolation.

My magic is volatile, tied tightly to emotions. When they rise, my power endangers everyone around me, friend or foe. For everyone's safety, including my own, Nora has drilled isolation into me since I was young. Her lessons were clear: if I wasn't close to anyone, they couldn't hurt me, and my meltdowns could be avoided.

Still, I hid my relationship with Arcadia. The shameful truth is that I longed to be close to others, to feel more than the numbness Nora demanded of me. Nothing is more shameful to me than my own desires.

We part ways, and I make my way toward the tall, spiraling tower to the east side of an academic wing, where Nora's office resides. The cool air of the hallway is a welcome reprieve from the morning sun.

Guided by memory, I walk down the hall, turning left and climbing the winding, dark steps lit only by slivers of sunlight slipping through small windows. At the top, I stop before the wooden door. Anxious nerves bundle up low in my stomach, the knot forming there solidifying. I knock and wait for permission to enter.

"Enter," a cold voice calls out, snuffing out any traces of warmth Arcadia had left behind.

Pushing open the door, I quickly take inventory of Nora's office. Pristine and orderly as always, not a book out of place on the shelves lining the walls. Even the quills on her dark oaken desk are precisely arranged. She sits behind her desk, her hands clasped, expecting *me*, of course.

I close the door behind me and step toward the small green leather chair across from her. The morning sun filters through the large green-paned window behind her, tinting the room in an eerie emerald glow.

In the corner, her owl familiar perches motionless. Its unblinking eyes are locked on me. Its unbreaking gaze is unsettling, like a second Nora, always watching. They say familiars represent some part of their witches, and in her owl, I can see it—the cold precision, the endless vigilance.

The thought makes me wonder about Ollie. Am I so depraved that the very darkness in me is reflected in his hellion existence?

"Millicent, I have a new assignment for you." Her sharp features remain almost motionless as she speaks.

Her long white hair is pulled back into a tight ponytail, accentuating the severe angles of her face. She looks ancient, though her appearance betrays little of her true age. A few faint crow's feet frame her eyes, and her face has a more mature set to it. If you squint and stand close, you might catch a faint line or two on her forehead. Even as she speaks, her face barely moves, her expressions restrained. It's almost unnatural.

Witches age the way Felix's prized mead collection does. Their features only refining and ripening with the passing of centuries. By the time a witch appears truly old, she could easily be two thousand years old.

"You will travel to the Southern Continent, to the kingdom of Galderia under the rule of king Felix Tyran."

I stare at her. It is all I can do. We never interact with mortals unless it's for sacrificial purposes. *Why would I work with vermin?*

"What is the purpose of this?" I ask, working to keep my tone steady and mask the irritation rising within me at the idea of helping mere mortals.

Nora doesn't so much as blink at my question. Her voice, already cold, hardens further, like steel cutting through the air like a blade. I am reminded of my place. "The purpose is for me to know and for you to follow the order given by your superior. Questioning an elder? You have been raised far better than this, Millicent Le Strange."

Her sharp correction scrapes against my pride, leaving a sting that spreads across my skin. Shame and stupidity rise, pushing to the forefront of my mind. I shouldn't have questioned her.

"There are things in that castle containing great power, artifacts you will inquire into. The king will also allow us to move about without persecution. I've been informed that the seer there, Luna, has foreseen the North, awakening something dark. Tyran wants our involvement for protection."

A devious smirk pulls at her lips, betraying the true nature of the "protection" she's offering, protection that serves only her interests.

"Didn't know you cared so much about protecting mere vermin," I snap. My tone sharpens as my irritation flares again at the thought of being paired with mortals.

She chuckles, the sound light and artificial. "Come now, you're smart. I don't care for the king and his petty issues, but if the North uncovers new power...the Le Strange coven will be the ones to claim it."

Of course, she wants a front-row seat and hands-on access to any power Tyran is foolish enough to hand her. I don't bother asking why. I already know. This is what I'm trained for, what I was born for.

I am rare. To mortals, I am cursed, diseased, a blight that only death can cure. To my coven, I am a weapon, lethal and deadly, the one who will deliver death.

"When am I to leave?" I ask, not bothering to ask for how long. She wouldn't care about the duration of my absence. She wouldn't care how long I was gone, so long as she got what she desired.

"Tomorrow. Tyran will send transport, but it will meet you in town. They do not dare enter the woods."

So the mortals had some sense. I rise, bowing slightly out of respect. The movement is second nature after nearly 200 years of practice.

As I turn to leave, her voice stops me mid-step.

"Do not disappoint me. You are to be perfect. Less than perfection is not tolerated. You will report to my familiar and follow all instructions. Do not disobey the king. I will know if you do."

Her words hang heavy in the air. The unspoken threat of failure and disobedience presses down like a weight on my chest. I'm not surprised she wants constant reports. I'm not foolish enough to think she trusts me. Nora knows what lingers inside me. She's the one who put it there in the name of power. And gods, am I powerful.

"Understood," I say coldly before leaving her office.

I descend the winding stairs, step by step, until I finally breach the open air. Stopping outside, I take in the view of my home, the coven I had never left for more than a day, let alone overnight. Well, not when I was aware of it. Now I would be living somewhere else.

I inhale deeply, letting the smell of moss and grass fill my lungs, committing it to memory. The breeze shifts, carrying the scent away.

With a final glance at the world I've always known, I make my descent downhill, heading to visit my mother's grave one last time.

CHAPTER 2
Cage

Twist at the hip as you punch. *Momentum* makes the blow far more effective." The words leave my mouth with a heavy, irritated sigh. For the third time today, my patience grows thinner explaining the basics to the same inept guard. This time, I draw out the word "momentum," slow and deliberate, as if the concept might finally penetrate his thick skull and we can avoid a fourth lesson on a simple proper punch.

I snort, not bothering to hide my amusement as he attempts to follow through but his focus on the movement leaves him wide open. His opponent seizes the opportunity to nail him in the face. A crack echoes as blood spurts from his now broken nose, twisted grotesquely. Amazing. Serves him right.

I step past without a second glance, letting my attention drift to the next sparring match. I know it's hot, and I can feel their resentment burning as much as the sun and them cursing me for adding another hour to their training. Their thoughts seep into my head, unbidden, as natural as air. The power thrumming beneath my skin never lets me forget it's there, always searching for an outlet. Sometimes, it's found in their minds.

Without warning, I step into the ring and sweep a guard's legs out from under him. He crashes on his ass with a sharp curse. I lean in, peering down on him like a storm cloud.

"You lean too much on your left leg," I say, brushing a piece of lint off my shirt before turning sharply on my heel. My retreat is swift and deliberate, cutting off any chance for a response, not that I would be entertaining any discussions. This is a damn training yard, not a chow hall for idle banter.

The captain had insisted he couldn't oversee this himself, his excuse wrapped in whatever duties he claimed to have. It annoyed me then, and it still does. The real weight of my frustration presses into the hard set of my jaw, lacing every command I bark to the guards in the punishing midday sun. Not a flicker of guilt stirs in me, not even pity, as they sweat and stumble.

Surely, Kalix is off doing gods knows what or, more likely, gods know who. Meanwhile, the mages needed work. I need to be there with them. I'm their leader, not a drill sergeant for these bloody guards. Mages are coming from across the realm to train under me now, their numbers swelling by the day, not that anyone is complaining. King Tyran is overjoyed. His defenses have never been so strong. Every new recruit is just more fresh meat for me to whip into shape.

As if the thought of Tyran summoned the man himself, his snooty messenger emerges from the edge of the yard, scurrying straight toward me.

"Master Black," he says in that tight little stuck-up voice that I don't particularly enjoy.

I slowly raise a brow in question just to grate his nerves. For my own entertainment, I decide to use his first name. "Loric," I drawl, running a hand through my raven hair. The sweat helps to slick some back—for all of three seconds—before the messy strands flop into my face once again.

Loric's lips press into a firm line of distaste. I can't help but smile in response, to add fuel to the fire of his dislike.

"King Tyran is requesting your presence at once," he says, chin held high and undeterred.

I give a dramatic wave of my arm. "Then by all means, lead the way. Can't keep Tyran waiting."

Loric quickly hurries from the training yard, carefully weaving around the sparring bodies as if afraid one might touch him. I almost hope someone knocks into him—or at least kicks some dirt his way—just to see him squirm as his pristine outfit gets soiled.

Keeping pace is effortless. He can't be taller than five feet, I imagine, while my six-two frame eats up the space between us with ease.

We make our way through the stone palace halls lined with gilded chandeliers and ornate paintings depicting long-dead kings and their victories. Servants pause to bow in respect as we pass. Guards offer simple nods of acknowledgement. The courtesans and ladies of the court, however, are much more entertaining. Their thoughts did not need to be read. The way their eyes seemed to devour me says enough. Everyone knows I don't commit, but my bed was by no means empty.

At 206 years old, my lifespan feels endless. Mage blood keeps me looking no more than thirty, and I'm well aware that my features are considered attractive. When you're nearly immortal, attachments lose their meaning; the world is plentiful. The world is mine to take, and I hunger for more. I refuse to limit myself.

Finally, we reach the massive golden doors, a garish testament to King Tyran's excessive tastes. They swing open revealing the king himself, perched on his throne like a dragon atop his horde. He's dripping in gold—robes, jewelry, even the hefty crown atop his head of cascading golden curls that flow down to his shoulders. His bright blue eyes lock on me, lighting up like a child's.

"Cage!" His grin stretches wide, rounding his cheeks as he clasps his hands and leans back into his throne. "Thank you for coming."

I smirk, raising a brow. "I had an option not to?" My tone is playful as I step deeper into the room.

Loric bows and slips away, a signal that this isn't just another of Tyran's casual summons.

"No, of course not. I am being polite." Tyran replies, his grin never wavers.

"Ah yes. What a shining example of royal decorum, Your Highness," I say, my voice dripping with sarcasm as I cross the room to the empty throne beside him, the one that's been vacant for years.

He's only twenty-eight, thrust into power when his father died, and the weight of the crown hasn't done a damn thing to curb his appetite. An heir was needed soon, but the man can't seem to settle—or keep his dick in his pants long enough to make it happen.

Tyran doesn't even try to hide the dramatic eye roll my retort earns him. Not that he could. Felix did everything with a flair for theatrics. *Diva.*

"Now, Black, we have business to discuss," he says, rubbing his hands like a scheming rat. It's exactly the kind of gesture he makes when he is up to something.

"You mean you're scheming?" I lean back in the chair, propping my elbow up on the armrest and resting chin on my fist as I cross my ankle over my knee.

"Why are my plans called schemes but yours and the commander's aren't?" he asks, looking genuinely affronted, like he's about to pout.

"Because we actually plan. There are steps, clearly defined, and we have a goal," I say, staring him down. "We don't drink so much wine that we grab a quill and come up with a master plan to take over the continent while calculating how many bastard sons we can produce in a week by impregnating every woman we meet."

Tyran huffs in protest, "I get drunk one time and have a master plan, and now it's thrown into my face! Gods above! Live a little!" He sinks into his chair, sulking like a petulant child before mumbling, "I could impregnate so many it is not...illogical...just give me rest breaks."

Suppressing a laugh, I wave a hand to redirect the conversation, "So, what's this business?"

Tyran perks up immediately, turning to face me with the kind of enthusiasm that makes me brace for whatever absurdity he's about to unleash. "We're at war with the North. They're annoying. I've been thinking about power, how we get more of it. So far, more mages have been a huge help."

He pauses, dragging it out far too long for my liking. I know better than to interrupt. He'll start over from the beginning. I truly do not have the patience for both training guards and Felix's theatrics today.

"Witches," he whispers, as if the word itself is forbidden. "For centuries, we've hunted and burned them, but they're strong. What if we could bridge the gap, find something they want and use it to get them to comply? Think about it, Cage. They're half fucking demon!" His eyes light up filled with exuberance.

My chest tightens, burning from the fury that is spreading like wildfire inside of me. I tense. My hand flexes against the cool golden armrest.

"Iris has made herself at home here just fine," Tyran continues, oblivious to my growing anger. "Her skill set has been incredibly useful, especially in our current situation."

"No," I say, my voice sharp and final. The word leaves no room for argument.

Tyran's grin falters, but only for a moment before he recovers, "Well, I'm the king, so...yes. I will want you to train and keep an eye on them."

Like hell I will. "No." My interruption is sharp, cutting him off mid-sentence. "You sit here reading texts and hearing stories about what they used to be. I lived with them—for a time. They're insanely powerful, lethal, and they do not care for human life."

Memories flash behind my eyes: the fucking white-haired bitch tying me to a stone altar, her knife running over my flesh, unzipping my skin until my blood flowed freely. I was weak.

Tyran raises his hands in surrender, his palms up like white flags. "Look, I know you were with them for a time, but—"

"But what, Felix?" My voice is low, dangerous. "I trusted one witch—one—and she's here in these very walls. The rest? They follow their own fucked up moral codes. They're abominations. That's the truth, ingrained in me as deeply as the scars left on my body and the lies I believed for years."

Tyran shifts in his seat but presses on. "The North is up to something. I do not know what, but a seer came to me. Call Luna crazy all you want, but she's predicted everything."

Gods above, he's actually listening to that lunatic.

The North is a cold, dead land, shrouded in snow and mystery. Our spies haven't been able to penetrate their ranks since Tyran's grandfather. Entering the land ensures certain death either by the cold, creatures, or the company.

Mountains and sea help keep our lands safe from the maleficent magic that has reigned there since the dawn of time. It's the region where the tales claim that the most wicked of things went to rest.

World enders.

Their sons.

Their servants.

"We'll need witches for what's coming. It comes at night. We'll need creatures of the night," Tyran says, his tone uncharacteristically serious. "And before you argue, witches would never agree to this, but they have. That alone is a huge feat for us."

The shock of witches agreeing hits me like a slap to the face. "They agreed?" Witches don't make deals, especially not with mortals. This reeks of wrongness. A trap, plain and simple.

"Yes, they agreed, which tells me they know something, too. In return, they get free rein and won't be hunted. And yes, I know the damn risks," he adds. Irritation flashes in his eyes. "But there's nothing to protect if what Luna warns us about comes true."

For once, real worry etches itself onto Tyran's face, carving lines into

19

his youthful features. It makes him look older, more drained, finally showing a sliver of the true weight of carrying the crown.

"What is Luna predicting, exactly?"

Tyran shakes his head, frustration clear. "I'm not allowed to know it all—fates above—but something dark, something strong and capable of wiping out the South, is being brought in. And with what we have right now, we'll lose, even with you."

The words land like a stone in my chest.

"No moves have been made yet," he continues, "but they will come. I'm just trying to prepare."

How ominous. Luna couldn't even manage to specify if it's an army, a god, a new fun power, or witches teaming up with the North. No, just "something dark" that "could kill the South." Brilliant. Thank you, Luna. The night sky is black, you mental ward patient. Truly narrowing it down for us.

I sigh, rising to my feet. Rolling my neck and shoulders, I try to shake off the tension coiled in my muscles, but the weight of this unwelcome news refuses to leave. "What coven agreed to help?"

"The Le Strange," Tyran says, all too proudly. The fucking idiot.

The shadows beneath my skin stir like restless tides, the inky onyx coursing over my neck, chest and arms beginning to writhe. I feel the silver in my eyes churn as his words settle like poison in my veins. It evokes a wrath like no other from deep within. That name, the one I swore would never pass anyone's lips again. Tyran just made a deal with the devil to save us from some new hell.

The young king would learn the devil comes when you call but it's no friend to anyone.

The scars on my back burn again, echoing the memory of when they were fresh. Rage wells up, thick and suffocating, as the hate I've buried for years claws its way to the surface, constricting my throat. They should have all died that night, every last one of them. Of course, the Le Strange survived.

Cockroaches always do.

CHAPTER 3

Millicent

TODAY MARKS THE DAY I LEAVE THE COVEN. MY TRIPS beyond its borders have been few and fleeting, only ever for sacrificial rituals, and I have never ventured overnight, let alone this far. Nora forbids it. Standing at the edge of the tree line, I hesitate, my next step weighed by thoughts of Cadia. I hadn't said goodbye to her, a selfish attempt to shield myself from the inevitable hurt and pain our parting would bring. My attachment to her always made me feel so weak. Swallowing the lump in my throat, I force my legs to walk forward.

"Oh, yoo-hoo!" Cadia's voice rings out, growing louder as her footsteps close the gaps between us. Before I can react, her body slams into mine, nearly knocking me off my feet. Her arms wrap tightly around my waist, pulling me into a fierce hug. "No goodbye to your favorite person in the universe? I'm insulted, you bitch," she teases, her laughter bright and unrestrained as she releases me.

I turn to face her, and my resistance crumbles at the sight of her radiant smile. She's glowing with excitement, her joy contagious and bittersweet. Throwing my arms around her, I squeeze her tightly, not caring if Nora might catch us. I was leaving anyway. A smile tugs at my lips as I lean back, taking in her face, drinking in her features as if indulging myself in the memory. "Isn't it odd I'm the one leaving this time, not you?"

"I am overjoyed," Cadia says, her voice brimming with sincerity. "For well over a hundred years, I've been desperate for you to see the outside world. Millicent, you'll love it—if you embrace it." Her golden eyes gleam knowingly as she offers me a pointed look, one that makes me roll my eyes in return. *In what world would I love this situation?*

"Love it? I'll be living with vermin. What's there to love about that?"

Cadia snorts, undeterred. "Oh, come on. Humans are fun. They make great mead, entertaining stories, fun trinkets...and let's not forget, plenty of them know how to pleasure a woman." She wiggles her eyebrows mischievously, grinning at my discomfort.

"I *will* not be having any of that, thanks." My reply is sharp, though her teasing pulls a faint smirk from me despite myself.

"Lame ass," she mutters, but her tone softens. "I mean it, though. Embrace it, and you'll love it. That whole 'vermin' bullshit is old news. Out there, there's no Nora. No suffocating expectations. No endless lessons. Just...you. Who is Millicent without all of that? You might finally figure it out. Just promise me one thing. Write to me. I want updates."

Cadia is different from the rest of the coven. I've always wondered why. Maybe it's her bloodline. She's a curse user, something unique among us. Or maybe it's just who she is. Unlike the others, she doesn't mind humans. She even talks about them with something close to admiration, recounting stories of men waiting on her hand and foot. Cadia never endured the lessons I did. Her curse magic did not require the blood or sadistic rituals mine does. Yet, for all she faced, her spirit has never been broken, her morals never warped to match the darkness of our sisters. Perhaps it's because she escaped. At twenty-one, she ran from the coven, exploring the world for years, returning only for fleeting visits. That freedom shaped her into someone I envy and admire in equal measure.

"I'll write," I say, a spark of hope warming my chest. The thought of seeing her again, of having some tie to the familiar in the unknown, steadies me. "Maybe, if it is not horrendous, you could even visit."

Her smile widens as she cups my face, pressing a kiss to each of my cheeks. "Count on it. I can never stay far from you." Her gaze glints with mischief. "And when I visit, I'll expect wild tales and a proper adventure, and a *good* time. Don't disappoint me, darling."

"Oh, *absolutely*. A blast, Cadia," I reply, my voice dripping with sarcasm.

We share one last embrace before I turn toward the forest, my heart feeling heavy. As I step into the shadow of the trees, I glance back just once. Cadia and the coven stand in the distance. I take it all in, a final snapshot of the only home I've ever known.

Then I keep walking. What lives in these woods will not bother me anytime soon. Their instincts warn them of what runs in my veins, what has consumed my soul. I can't give my patron all the credit for rearranging the very particles of my being. My heart ceased to function a long time ago. A string, invisible and tight, pulling on my heart, urges me to return to Arcadia to ensure someone I love is safe, to feel *affection*. I continue to push forward, each of my steps purposeful and confident. The thread snaps, and I feel the familiar nothingness flourish through my chest, growing like untamed vines.

I hear *her* cackle growing so loud I stop hearing the forest around me. *What heart? What soul? You lost those long ago.*

Her words don't rouse me. She doesn't lie, and in a way, the Nightmother is me, her presence sewn into the fabric of my being, woven tightly. If undone, the entire canvas of my skin would split and cease to exist.

I continue, and she accompanies me into the darkness of the woods.

Malicent

I PERCH ON THE ROUGH, GRAY STONE LEDGE OF A FOUNTAIN ON the outskirts of Ravenfell, the bustling town just beyond the dense forest surrounding my coven. The mortals move in predictable patterns, their lives small and meaningless. Vermin. I scan the crowd, and my eyes catch what can only be my escorts.

A golden carriage cuts through the rabble like a shard of sunlight, its opulence screaming luxury that only a king can afford. The sun's reflection off the polished surface nearly blinds me, and I squint against its brilliance. I have a feeling I will tire of gold long before my business there is done.

The crowd parts instinctively, murmurs rising when the carriage halts a few feet from me. Golden banners flutter from its sides, matching the polished white mares that pull it and the gilded armor of the knights escorting it. The entire display reeks of importance and ostentation. *Just as I thought, my ride.*

The door swings open, and a guard steps out, his expression stiff but controlled. "Lady Le Strange," he says with an air of forced respect.

I'm surprised he's bothering with courtesy though I don't show it. Most mortals fear witches. Some even fancied themselves brave enough to hunt us. At least this one has the sense to keep his composure.

"We are to escort you to the castle. It is a three-day trip. We must make it to the first stop before nightfall," he continues, his tone carefully neutral.

The men surrounding him remain silent, but they don't need words for me to hear them. Their thoughts slip into my mind, as clear and loud as if they'd spoken aloud.

For a demon, she sure is attractive. I thought witches were hideous.

Her eyes...what kind of blue is that? Are all witches' eyes so vibrant?

Damn, look at those marks. She has to be even stronger than Lord Black's mages. Gods, let's hope she doesn't cause any issues.

Diseased bitch. We'd be better off burning her to ash.

What is the king thinking, inviting this thing? He's never lost his family to her kind.

The last thought draws my attention. I find its source easily enough—the guard to my left, his clenched jaw ticking with concealed disdain. He's trying not to look at me, but his hatred radiates like heat from a flame. I meet his gaze and grin obnoxiously wide, savoring the flicker of unease that passes over his face. Let him stew.

The guard in front of me speaks, pulling my attention to him. "Let us depart." His voice is steady, but his eyes flick nervously toward the dark forest behind me.

The Twisted Hollows looms in the distance, a labyrinth of ancient, gnarled trees with branches that claw at the sky. Their bark is rough and scarred, with knots and twists that resemble faces frozen in agony. Tales say the souls of the lost are trapped within those trees, condemned to an eternal descent into madness. I've always dismissed such stories, but the unease in his thoughts betrays his belief in them. He isn't worried about the trees themselves, though. It's the creatures lurking within the untamed wilderness that haunt him. He has right to fear them. The Twisted Hollows are teeming with life and magic after nightfall.

I follow him into the carriage, relieved to find it free of the garish gold I'd expected. *Thank the Nightmother.* Instead, the interior is red and white. I sink into the leathered seat across from him, grateful for the ample space that keeps me out of reach. No other guards join us. The one seated across from me remains silent. Good. I don't particularly care to know anything of him. Men are much more tolerable when they keep their mouths shut.

Stretching out my leather-clad legs, I cross my ankles and arms, leaning back as the carriage lurches into motion. My training leathers are a second skin, the black material flexible enough to move with me yet durable enough for battle—sleeveless, of course, to flaunt the silver witch marks that swirl from my shoulders to my wrists, a testament to my power. Across my back rest two dual crescent moon-shaped blades,

their edges lined with red runes I meticulously carved myself. Each rune siphons my magic into the blades, imbuing them with deadly precision.

Magic, though powerful, always demands payments. Witches can only feed it for so long before exhaustion sets in. When the energy runs out, magic turns on the body, devouring organs to sustain itself. Internal bleeding inevitably follows, forcing us into a period of stasis, a deep healing sleep that lasts anywhere from three to five days depending on how much damage was done. Blood magic, however, gives me an edge. It lets me have fun. By feeding during a fight, I can recharge, keeping my magic from targeting my organs. That strength, however, comes with a cost. Once the bloodlust takes over, my magic takes control. Friend or foe, it makes no distinction. I've been told I transform though I remember none of it. I only know that I wake up days later disoriented and confused as hell. It's a vicious cycle—feeding, losing control, collapsing, stasis. Always the same.

The carriage jolts over uneven terrain, the motion pulling me from my thoughts. Outside the window, the bright green trees of the countryside sway in the wind, a stark contrast to the darkness of the Twisted Hollows. I let my senses stretch outward, brushing against the faint auras of any magical creatures lurking nearby. Even without sight, I can feel their presence.

The stronger your magic, the more you can sense. Everything with even the faintest magic leaves a trace, an aura, if you look closely, a distant presence within range, and sometimes even a scent. Mortals, despite their lack of power, have an instinctual ability to detect strong magic disrupting an area. It's a survival mechanism, but it is useless against weaker forms.

I catch the guard's nervous glances as his eyes flit between me and the window. His fidgeting is almost endearing, though. I can feel his unease prickling at the edge of my awareness. He has been working up the nerve to say something. I call it a fun little game: *Will he grow the balls to ask or not?*

Finally, he clears his throat and clasps his hands, his knuckles white from tension. "You...you don't look like a demon," he blurts, his voice quivering. "Forgive me if that's rude. I've read books on witches."

I let my eyes settle on him, taking my time as I look him over. He's young, perhaps twenty-two, with sandy hair in an unruly mess and sun-kissed skin. His honey-brown eyes hold a certain warmth, but his nerves make them dart nervously. Judging by his unscarred face and the slight hesitation in his movements, he must be new to the command and unlucky enough to be put on witch duty.

I tilt my head, studying him like one might examine an insect pinned to a board. "These books sound like tales," I say, my tone dripping with disinterest, "but they may not be wrong. It depends on the witch."

"The Le Strange coven is documented in historical texts," he begins, his voice faltering as he fidgets with his fingers. "Maybe not the inner workings, but...its actions—and what resides there."

"And what do the historical texts say?" I ask invitingly, just enough to encourage him.

He swallows hard. "That the Le Strange coven is the closest to demonic in nature. That you're the ones who partake in human sacrifices the most. Th-that you...regularly travel to the underworld and...and repopulate it with devils," he stammers, his words tumbling over one another in his rush to get them out.

A chuckle escapes me, low and sharp, as I lean back against my seat. "We are the closest," I admit, letting my words hang in the air before adding, "Shall I show you?"

Before he can react, I release a thread of my magic, letting it coil through the carriage. The air thickens instantly, an inky black cloud seeping into every corner, blotting out the light. The temperature plummets, and the faint warmth of the sun is replaced by an icy chill. The guard stiffens, his breath coming in shallow gasps as he presses himself against the far wall.

"No, please!" he shouts, his voice cracking, filled with panic.

I laugh—a full, delighted sound that echoes through the suffocating darkness. With a flick of my wrist, I reel the magic back into myself, the inky cloud dissipating as quickly as it appeared. The sunlight floods the carriage once more, and the warmth returns. The guard remains frozen, his wide eyes staring at me with pure terror.

I smile, savoring the delicious fear radiating off him. A simple lamb, like all the others. *I hope he pissed himself.*

He doesn't speak again, nor does he meet my gaze. I keep my eyes locked on him, my grin growing wider as I relish in his discomfort.

The Le Strange coven is indeed the most demonic in nature, though not in the way mortals imagine. Our magic doesn't come from portaling to Hell or mating with devils. If the ancient texts and stories passed down are to be believed, our origins stretch back countless millennia to the Estrela.

The Estrela, beings of cosmic beauty and life. One Estrela in particular was said to have unparalleled beauty and stars woven into her hair, but she fell into something forbidden. They say it was a devil who ensnared her, but he was no ordinary devil. He was a world ender, created to balance the fabric of the realms, where creation must coexist with destruction. Captivated by her radiant power and ethereal kindness, this world ender tempted her, drawing her from her path. From their union, seven daughters were born—a fusion of creation and destruction unlike anything the world had seen.

The Estrela raised her daughters alone, but it wasn't long before their powers became apparent. Each daughter embodied a unique branch of magic, creating the foundations for what witches are today: blood magic, necromancy, summoning, curses, dream walking, manipulation, and black magic.

Blood magic is both a blessing and a curse. Witches who wield it can feed on life to restore their power, their

strength, and triple their speed in battle. Their bodies heal almost instantly, making them nearly impossible to kill. But this power comes at a cost. Once lost in blood-lust, they can no longer distinguish friend from foe. Their bodies become self-sufficient killing machines, sparing nothing with a pulse, not even those they love.

Necromancers are reclusive and obsessed with creation. They taxidermy creatures into grotesque forms, bringing them to life as tireless servants. Forever toiling in their labs, they often fall into maddening obsession crafting abominations that nature never intended.

Summoners excel in commanding entities from hell with natural ease. Whereas most magic users fail—or find themselves devoured by cunning hellions—summoners thrive, creating packs and bonds to fuel themselves with power. Hellions instinctively submit to summoners, their power sensing an inescapable dominance.

Curse users are dangerous even in their youth, often causing harm before they understand their abilities. A curse requires no incantation or study, only intent. A word, a touch, or even a thought can unleash devastating effects, regardless of distance. Until they learn control, the amount of accidental destruction they can cause is staggering.

Dream walkers are the reasons the mortals hang dream-catchers and bells around their beds—*as if that would work.* These witches can slip into dreams with ease, manifesting nightmares that bleed into waking life. They prey on the emotions that lie between consciousness and sleep, feeding on fear and despair as they twist reality into something horrifyingly surreal.

Manipulators don't read minds. They don't need to. A glance is enough to ensnare their victims, a white haze glazing over their eyes as they become prisoners of compulsion. Manipulators take what they desire, leaving their covens filled with servants who cater to their every whim, from feeding them to bathing them. They wield power effortlessly, preferring to let others do the labor.

Black magic, the rarest and most destructive, allows its wielders to command shadows and shape them into tangible forms. Beasts born of darkness obey their creators while mental attacks and shadow flames devastate enemies. At its strongest, black magic can summon black lightning, repel attacks, or create impenetrable shields.

The Estrela's daughters became legends, their powers leaving chaos in their wake. As they grew stronger, so too did the death toll. They destroyed mortals other Estrela cherished, sparking a war between creation and destruction. To counter the witches, the Estrela joined with mortals, creating the first mages, warriors imbued with magical power to protect humanity and eventually bring the witches to extinction.

The mother of the witches still ached for her daughters, so she took them deep into the forest and infused the land with magic wild and fierce. Her powers warped the woods into a realm of shadows, a sanctuary for her children. Like all things, such potent magic comes at a cost. The darkness spilled into the surrounding lands, birthing creatures twisted and heinous, leaving mortals to fear what they could no longer control.

So, the witches remain with their covens, shackled to the forests and mountains, far from mortal lives. This is why we are feared, why sacrifices are made, and why the hatred between mortals and witches endures. It is also why mages were created: to hunt us, the predators, the hunter, and the hunted.

Over time, witches have refined their bloodlines, our powers growing sharper, deadlier, more honed with each generation. We are not like the mortals, soft and fleeting. We are the predators. And predators never forget their place.

I suppress a smirk as I look at my *prey* across from me. He doesn't realize how much I can hear in his silence—the tension in his jaw, the way his hands twitch on his lap—savoring his discomfort. *Prey*, I think, my amusement curling at the edge of my lips.

My thoughts drift to what awaits me at the castle. *Mages*. I have never liked their kind—arrogant, self-important, and always eager to flaunt their moral superiority. I know they'll be there, and I am already steeling myself to endure their pompous asses.

Still, I won't be like this guard, shrinking into silence. I'll have my way, as I always do. I'll work alone, answer to no one, and bend them to my demands if they stand in my way. Let them try to hunt me. My fingers drum lazily against the leather seat as the carriage bumps along the road, my smile widening just slightly.

They have no idea what they've invited into their gilded halls.

CHAPTER 4
Cage

A LE STRANGE WITCH IS COMING TO THE CASTLE. WORSE, I'm expected to work with her.

My stomach twists at the thought of it being Nora or one of the other insufferable elders slithering into the castle. I don't trust their kind. I don't like their kind. Soul-sucking cunts, the lot of them, but *Nora*? If she stepped foot in this castle, Vyraxis would manifest and rip this castle to shreds.

Tyran doesn't even know which Le Strange they're sending. He only knows she's valuable. Nora's chosen protégé. Only the "finest selection" was promised to him, whatever that means.

Nora part two?

The very idea of it sits like a knife in my gut.

I know how Nora thinks. I *know* what her "favoritism" looks like. I was nothing but a toy when I was younger, power dangled before me like bait on a hook. She would never limit any of her own kind the way she sought to control me. This prodigy of hers, she'll live and breathe Nora's gospel. A devoted disciple to the fiend herself.

And I'm expected to work with her.

A sharp flick against the rim of my wine glass draws me from my thoughts. I don't need to look up to know who it is.

Kalix.

Mismatched eyes, one sage green, the other flaxen yellow, stare at me. They're filled with mischievous intent. He's waiting for a reaction.

"Distracted, Black? I'm hardly getting any attention," Kalix murmurs, feigning disappointment.

"How will you ever survive?" I smirk, lifting the silver chalice and taking a slow sip, letting the bitter wine coat my tongue as it slides down my throat. Kalix leans back in his chair, his eyes drifting lazily across the room. His posture remains tightened. His voice drops just enough to ensure privacy. "He has not shown yet."

"He will," I reassure him. "It's his damn ball. The bastard will show."

Leaning back into my seat, I observe the layout of the ballroom. We've positioned ourselves well, tucked into a secluded corner near the open balcony doors. We have a clear vantage point over the gathering. To our right, the balcony doors frame the moonlight, its gleam spilling onto the polished floors. To our left, the dance floor stretches wide. Steps leading up on all sides to the elevated rim where the nobility linger, a bowl-shaped design meant for display, power, and hierarchy.

Unlike Tyran's estate, where gold drips from every surface, the Duke's tastes run the colors of deep green and red. Every tablecloth, every curtain, and every sash adorning the guests present tonight reflect his chosen colors. Even the white marbled flooring, streaked with black veins, matches the elite who tread upon them. However, It's the walls that I can't help but admire. Polished dark oak is lined with portraits of the Duke's family lineage, each face meticulously rendered in oil, purposefully displaying their claim to power. Yet, the Duke himself is absent.

His portrait tells me what I already know. He's short, round, and

insufferably smug. A man of his status should be swarmed by admirers and opportunists alike.

But where is he?

Tyran sent us here for a reason. A spy confirmed that Duke Leving has been in contact with the North. And traitors, particularly those of high status, cannot simply be dragged in for questioning without igniting some political backlash. So here we are, the lovely Captain Kalix and I, masquerading as honored guests, playing Tyran's game.

Kalix whistles, tilting his head to the right.

There. An exact match to one of the portraits. Duke Leving's daughter steps into the ballroom. Her presence turns heads. As expected. Long, sleek blonde hair, a striking frame, and wide, bright blue eyes. She's just like her father. She wears a deep-red gown tailored to perfection, its fabric hugging her curves while proudly displaying her family's colors.

"I believe her name is Annabeth." My voice remains low just enough that only Kalix can hear.

A slow grin spreads across his lips. "That is how we find dear old daddy."

With a smooth practiced motion, Kalix rises to his full height, a living wall of muscle draped in dark green and red. Towering over every man in his vicinity, he moves through the ballroom with confidence and purpose. The crowd parts instinctively out of respect, out of wariness, or simply to avoid being trampled. Women glance up as he passes, their thoughts spiking briefly with lust.

Kalix approaches Annabeth. He dips into a courtly bow. He doesn't need to, but that's precisely why he does.

Though I remain seated, their thoughts flood into me, keeping me attuned to the entire interaction. Kalix could block me if he wanted to. I taught him how. He knows better. He knows I want the intel.

He towers over her, his sheer presence enough to tilt the dynamic in his favor. She must look up to meet his gaze, and Kalix makes sure she does.

"The infamous captain of the guard," she says lightly. Yet the nervous flutter in her mind betrays her. *Gods, he's enormous. And those eyes—*

Kalix offers his hand, adorned in a collection of rings. Annabeth hesitates a fraction of a second too long.

"Kalix, Lady Annabeth." He greets her smoothly. "Thank you and your father for having us."

He is using her first name on purpose. A subtle trick I've watched him employ more times than I can count. He's trying to make her feel closer to him.

The more you give, the less they guard their hearts. Soften the defenses, and that's when the real fun begins.

He's going through his process. It's a game he plays well.

Annabeth is already a blushing mess. Amusement tugs at the corners of my mouth as I take another sip of wine. I'm thoroughly entertained. Kalix has always had a gift for charming ladies.

The women at the castle whisper about him, as if he were a marble statue brought to life, with his strong jaw, captivating eyes, and thick lashes that shouldn't belong to a man his size. His shaggy dark brown hair is always worn the same, swept to the side and just unruly enough to make him seem untamed rather than unkempt.

It's his size that holds their attention. He trained since childhood and grew into a frame too large to be anything but imposing, even now. The black tunic stretches taut across his broad shoulders. Annabeth notices.

Of course she does.

"Certainly, Captain," Annabeth replies sweetly, releasing his hand.

Kalix's smile doesn't waver. His tone remains friendly and almost... effortless. "I was hoping to speak with your father. He was expecting me, but I can't seem to find the man of the hour."

Annabeth's lips curve into a deliberate smile, but her fingers twitch at her sleeve, smoothing out a crease that isn't there. "Oh, I'm not sure. I'm sorry. I haven't seen him."

Father is not to be disturbed.

"You must be preoccupied," he muses, his smile shifting, teasing her. "A beautiful lady such as yourself has better things to do than keep track of her father."

Before she can respond, he invitingly extends his arm. "Would you allow a poor fool like me, who has already *wasted* your time, to waste some more over a drink?" Kalix's eyes glint with amusement.

Smooth.

Annabeth pauses but slips her arm into his, "Of course, Captain." She nods shyly, her voice softer and blush deepening.

As Kalix guides her to the wine table, he flicks me a quick glance. A silent cue. We are moving to stage two in this plan.

I rise, adjusting my trench coat, and wander to the patio doors, pretending to need some fresh air before slowly drifting to the wine table. Keeping my distance, I station myself at the opposite end and casually observe.

"A wine for my lady?" Kalix asks, his voice light and charming as they arrive.

Annabeth attempts to focus, but the heat of his presence is impossible to ignore. "I don't drink very often, Captain...perhaps something sweet?" she manages, her voice just a touch unsteady.

Kalix leans in, one hand pressing firmly against the table, the other reaching for a bottle of wine. Caging her in without touching her, he pours it into a glass.

"Don't drink very much? What a good girl," he says, his voice low, indulging her. He lifts a glass to her but doesn't offer it just yet. Instead, he lowers his lips to her ear, close enough that she nearly shivers. "Try this for me," he says, his voice smooth and coaxing. "It's sweeter, with notes of peach and jasmine."

She reaches for the glass, but he doesn't let go. His fingers remain curled around the stem, a gentle but calculated motion.

"Personally, I prefer something with a little more depth," he continues, carrying just enough weight to make the words linger. "Something... fulfilling."

She swallows hard.

I read every thought racing through her mind. *For a virgin, she certainly has a vivid imagination.*

Annabeth reaches for the glass, but Kalix clicks his tongue.

"Allow me," he whispers, bringing the rim to her lips himself.

His other hand lifts from the table, his fingers trail along her jaw, tilting her head back.

"Open."

The single command sends her heart into a thrashing rhythm, each beat pounding against her ribs.

Annabeth obeys. She sips the wine.

"Good, yeah?" Kalix smirks, holding her gaze with every sip. He doesn't let her look away, doesn't let her focus on anything but him. When he finally pulls the glass back, she exhales sharply as she blinks up at him.

Her eyes drop to his lips, so close, drifting just above hers.

"Thirsty for something else?" He murmurs.

Her breath hitches as his fingers shift against her jaw. He grips firm enough to remind her of his control.

No one notices what happens next. But I do.

Kalix places the glass down. With movements both subtle and fluid, his thumb finds the side of his silver coin ring. As he presses against it, a near invisible compartment clicks open.

Inside, an odorless, tasteless powder.

He doesn't pause, doesn't hesitate. With barely a whisper of motion, the contents disappear into the wine. The ring clicks shut, and by the time he picks the wine glass up, poor Annabeth is already lost in him. Kalix brings it to her lips again, and this time, she drinks greedily, fueling the fire burning in her stomach.

Kalix chuckles, amused at her eagerness. "Such a greedy girl."

Her pupils dilate. The shift is subtle but unmistakable.

I move to their side in an instant. "Let's get her somewhere quieter," I say smoothly.

Kalix sets the wine down, taking Annabeth's hand.

Always so easy.

The drug in her system is working fast, her body loose and her mind pliant. The thoughts are easy to sift through.

And, damn, she actually thinks Kalix is a suitor.

Sitting in her thoughts makes this job even easier. Poor girl is lost in some fairy tale. I think the Abyss would turn into a land of sun and rainbows before Kalix settled down with anyone.

Kalix doesn't mix work and personal life. Never has. He's emotionally unavailable, drowning in an obsession hole over someone just as emotionally unreachable. I don't question it. Who am I to demand Kalix make sense of the situation for me?

I'm not one to judge. Obsession? Love? Whatever they were, I'd never felt them.

As we walk, I glance at Annabeth again. Cute. Soft. Easily Led. I have no doubt she'd obey anything I asked her, but she's not my type. Too fragile. Too breakable.

I don't make love. I don't cuddle or coddle. Sex is a release, nothing more, and I have plenty to release.

Outside of some chick bouncing on my cock, what else was there? My lovers were one-night things, rarely revisited, because they couldn't handle the darker side of me.

A short time later, we guide Annabeth through the crowded room, her steps light and unsteady. She doesn't question us or give any resistance. The drug is still working. Good.

The cool night air greets us as we step onto the patio. The garden stretches out into seclusion. Perfect. No unwanted eyes.

Kalix leads her down into the path, the distant hum of music fading as we traverse the shadowed gardens. A stone bench waits beneath a trellis, vines curling over the frame like grasping fingers. We sit her down. A precaution.

Kalix squats in front of her, casual and relaxed. I stay standing next to him, arms crossed over my chest. Watching.

Annabeth lifts her gaze, and the moment her eyes find me, her entire body stiffens.

Fear. Pure, instinctive.

Nearly as tall as Kalix, I know what she sees. Bright silver eyes, unsettling and inhuman, are set in a face that offers no warmth. Black ink crawls up my throat curling over the edges of my tunic. My shoulder length hair falls in shaggy, unkempt waves, just unruly enough to hint at disorder.

Kalix smiles up at her. His expression still holds traces of amusement, but his eyes are sharp now. Focused.

Me? I don't smile. I don't need to.

Kalix places his hands on her knees—firm, steady, careful not to wander. He likes to make them flustered. It makes his job easier, just another part of his method.

"Annabeth," he says, the charm gone from his voice, replaced by something colder, sharper. "Where is your father?"

She flinches. Her breath stutters. She tries to speak but chokes instead. Coughing, struggling, her body resisting the words forming on her tongue.

Her frantic gaze flicks between us, realization dawning on her in a slow, creeping horror.

She can't lie.

Annabeth gasps, throat tightening like a noose. She claws at her collarbone, desperate for air.

"He is at the guest house," she chokes out.

Kalix doesn't let up. "Doing what? Why the secrecy?"

Her body convulses with another attempt to resist, but the drug doesn't allow for hesitation. Her lungs constrict.

Annabeth is learning quickly.

Her face turns a deeper shade of red. Panic arises with every shuddering breath until—

She breaks.

"He will not tell me exactly what he does," she blurts, the words

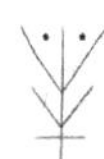

spilling out in desperation. "But there are times, sometimes hours, when he disappears there. He doesn't always come back the same."

Her fingers tighten in her lap. "Sometimes he seems...off. Shaken. I worry about him, but I'm supposed to tell no one!"

The realization of what she said hits her all at once.

"That's enough." My voice cuts through the night air.

Annabeth flinches.

"You did well, Annabeth." I take a measured step forward, silver light flaring in my eyes as my power bleeds into the air. Shadows shift—thickening, stretching, responding to my call. "Forget this conversation. Forget our faces—*or else.*"

Kalix rises. His voice, sharp and commanding, leaves no room for argument.

"Off with you now."

Annabeth bolts from the bench, nearly tripping in her haste. Her fear is now a tangible thing in the air. She won't stop running until she's back in the safety of the ballroom.

It would be of little consequence if she told someone, anyway. Even if she told someone, what could they do?

I am the black mage. The title alone demands fear, commands silence. The strongest mage of our time. The only one who has a bonded dragon.

No one would *dare* challenge me.

The hunger stirs.

A familiar voice—a whisper, a temptation, a need.

Unstoppable. Take it all. Have it all.

Use it just one more time.

The darkness coils through me like a drug, sliding over my skin as if waiting to be fed. Just one hit, one pulse of power, and I'd feel it again.

Raw. Consuming. Limitless.

The idea is intoxicating.

The need unbearable.

Power always comes at a price. And you never truly know the cost until it's too late.

A sharp finger snap slices through my thoughts.

Kalix.

He must sense the monster in me awakening. His eyes are on me, steady and unyielding.

"Put it on a leash. We have a job to finish," he warns, his voice low and firm. No patience for argument here.

He turns on his heel, cutting through the shadows of the garden, boots grinding against scattered cobblestone. The path ahead leads to the guest house, looming like an omen in the distance.

I shake my head and follow Kalix, pushing the hunger back down. Burying it.

Black mages were never part of creation.

Our origins are unclear, lost to time and half-truths. The old texts claim that we were never meant to exist. It's accepted that our magic formed as a response, an answer to the ever-growing power of witches. An evolutionary necessity.

Maybe that's true; maybe it isn't.

But I know this: there is something inside me.

It wakes, restless and starving.

What am I?

I've never had a single apprentice complain of a presence in their veins, whispering of its hunger. They call me Cage, Lord Black, or the first mage to the king of the South. A respected warrior. Protector of people.

If only they knew this is just a mask, a skin, I wear.

What would they think of what dwells beneath if they knew the truth of what I am?

The evil within has surfaced countless times. It drove me to wander, to destroy, to seek power. And no matter how much I took, it was never enough.

Nothing was ever enough.

I hungered for more. Fuck, I was starving for more. Always more.

Even now, restraint is a daily battle. Time has made managing the monster easier, but it was very much still alive.

It's still there. Watching. Waiting. Tempting.

And, gods, it is ever so tempting. Sometimes, when I spiral too deep into the depths of my being or when I become the *thing* that lurks down there, I wonder if Nora was right.

Maybe the Coven was *right*.

Maybe their lessons, their punishments, their chains really did protect people from me.

For a time, I believed it.

Then I sober up. And I remember the manipulation and the hours of torture. Every "special" lesson, every scar, served one purpose: for Nora to gain control.

Not to help me. Not to save me. To own me.

I fall into step behind Kalix, watching the tree line and the rooftops, waiting for the first sign of a new player in our game.

My vision is sharper in the dark than most. A gift from whatever dark force sired my magic. The night is clear and sharp, nearly as visible as if it were bathed in sunlight. But distance is my limit. The further away I try to focus, the more the details blur.

A shift. A whisper.

Something stirs ahead, not seen but felt. My magic awakens of its own will, coiling at the edges of my skin, recognizing a darkness I cannot yet see.

The guest house looms in the distance. The small, forest green cottage is almost black under the cover of night.

Then I reach the door.

Awareness slices into me. A sharp pull. A whisper of instinct.

A warning.

"You are going to want to cover as much skin as possible." My voice

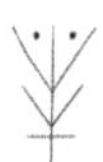

is a low growl, almost lost in the thickening air. The argent glow of my eyes intensifies, bleeding silver light into the dark.

And the house changes.

Its true color reveals itself beneath my gaze.

CHAPTER 5
Cage

THE MOMENT WE STEP INSIDE, THE AIR TURNS HEAVY.

Sulfur lingers in the air, thick and acrid. It burns the back of my throat. There's no light, not even the faint flicker of a candle.

The wood beneath our feet groans as we move deeper into the entrance. Kalix silently closes the door behind us. His hand moves to his sword. The scraping of steel against leather is barely audible in the silence. I do the same, mirroring his movements as my eyes sweep the house.

The first floor is undisturbed.

To the left, the kitchen is shrouded in shadows. The only light filters through a moonlit window, casting sharp silver outlines across the counters.

To the right, the living room sits in eerie stillness. A lonely clock on the wall. Its rhythm beats far too loudly. White sheets drape over the furniture. Untouched, frozen in place, I surmise the house hasn't been used in some time.

So why the hell is the Duke here?

My fingers tighten around the hilt of my sword, keeping the blade raised in a defensive position across my torso.

The wood creaks above us.

We freeze, listening. Silence follows.

I tilt my head toward the staircase and push forward, taking two steps at a time to minimize the sound of my boots on aged wood. Kalix follows.

The second-floor splits into two parallel halls, both lined with closed doors. Shadows stretch long and still, unbroken by candlelight.

Something isn't right.

"Should we flip a coin?" Kalix whispers.

His tone is light, but I hear the restraint beneath it. A joke, yes, but not without tension.

I don't answer. Instead, I reach outward with my magic, trying to latch on to any viable mind. Nothing. Just static. A void where thoughts should be.

Then, a choking rasp.

The sound scrapes against the silence, coming from the final door at the end of the hall.

I move. *Steady now*. Kalix flanks me, guided toward the sound.

The presence I sensed earlier outside of the house waxes and wanes. There, then gone. It slips through my awareness

Odd.

My fingers brush over the cold steel doorknob. I push it, and the hinges groan as it swings open.

Inside, the room is swallowed in nearly total darkness. Only a single window to the right allows enough moonlight to carve a faint silhouette through the gloom.

In the center, a figure kneels, hunched in on itself. The faint silver light catches on fabric, revealing the Duke's insignia stitched into the back of his overcoat.

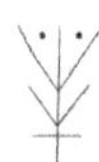

"Duke Leving," I call, my voice low but firm. I ensure he hears me clearly.

Nothing.

I never sensed his consciousness when we entered. And even now, I can't read him. He is a void, an absence.

That shouldn't be possible.

Leving isn't a mage, nor does he have one in his ranks. He shouldn't be capable of mental shielding. Even if he were, I'd be able to sense the resistance.

Mental shielding is something beings with magic in their blood can perform more easily than those without. A mortal can still do it, but it takes extensive training by someone who is an expert on the topic, typically someone with mind magic.

There's nothing. It's not silence, it's absence.

He remains frozen in place. Not even the subtle rise and fall of breath disturbs him.

Kalix and I step forward, slowly and with measure. The air feels even heavier now.

Something isn't right.

He smells wrong. Kalix's thought slips into my mind.

"Sir," Kalix says, his voice firm, trying to get his attention.

Nothing. Not even a flinch.

Leving remains locked in place, hunched forward. We're close now, barely a foot away.

Cautiously, I extend a hand. Maybe physical contact will snap him out of whatever this is. My fingers brush his shoulder.

The door slams shut.

A gust of air rushes past, like something stepping back into the room.

The presence I felt outside is here.

Leving jerks violently. His body convulses. His spine bends back with a wet, sickening crack.

Then he freezes. His head snaps back. Suddenly, arms fling outward, fingers twitching and stretching as if trying to grasp at something.

A second of silence. Then his breathing changes.

Shallow. Ragged. *Wrong.*

"What the fuck?" Kalix curses, his voice sharp. He instinctively steps back and tightens his grip around his sword.

Then bones snap. The sound is wet, a series of horrific cracks.

Leving's arms contort, twisting at impossible angles. His fingers break, then reform, the bones shifting in deformed angles.

His neck jerks violently to the side—too far, too fast. A killing angle. Yet he doesn't fall.

Instead, his feet slip underneath him in a series of sharp, disjointed movements. His spine bends, folding him backward into a grotesque bow.

Pushing off the ground with deformed arms, his body rises. His head twists, cracking and turning, until our eyes meet.

Gone is the brown from his portrait. Only white remains—glassy, empty, and soulless.

His jaw unhinges. Yellow foam bubbles at the corners of his mouth, spilling between his teeth.

Then he screams a sound that isn't human or natural. It splinters the air.

Then his flesh tears open.

From within, inky spikes spear outward, punching through muscle and bone.

They burst from his back, his arms, and his chest, ripping through him like blades from the inside out.

Blood spills in thick, violent bursts. Each fresh wound sends sheets of crimson splattering onto the floor.

"Well, let's not wait for it to finish transforming, yeah?" Kalix quips, his voice strained as he chokes on the thick sulfur air. He tugs at his tunic, making sure to cover every inch of exposed skin.

It's likely some type of hellion capable of possession. Not a common pest but a far worse breed.

And if I'm right, its blood will eat through human flesh like acid, down to the bones.

Kalix lunges. His blade glints in the faint moonlight.

Steel arcs through flesh.

The Duke's head falls, plummeting to the ground with a thud. It rolls before coming to a stop. His body collapses after it.

It's silent again for a moment. Nothing moves.

Then his chest rises.

Not breathing. It's something else.

Something worse.

"You've got to be fucking kidding me." Kalix's displeasure seeps into his features.

I take a cautious step forward. My fingers grip tightly around my sword. My eyes sharpen, trying to make sense of what I'm seeing.

This thing is fighting its way out.

The body twitches, then convulses.

A wet, tearing sound rips through the room.

My mind barely pieces together what's happening before long, black claws, tips red as rubies, punch through his chest, ripping it open from the inside out.

The force splatters our clothes with blood.

The thing inside him sinks its claws into the wood, anchoring itself. And then it begins to pull free.

A head emerges first, covered in long black hair that falls forward like a curtain that conceals its face.

Below it, its rib cage gapes open, filled with organs in all the wrong places. It's wrong, *twisted*.

I have never seen anything like it.

What the fuck is this thing?

I move.

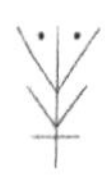

My blade drives forward, spearing through its gaping ribcage, straight into the twisted mass of organs.

The thing lurches, screeching. Its free arm snaps out toward me.

A flick of my wrist.

A razor-thin arc of magic slices clean through its limb, severing it mid-motion.

The howl it releases is deafening. Raw agony laced with fury. A sound too sharp and layered, like a chorus of things screaming at once.

My ears hurt.

My blade stays buried, pressing deeper, searching for what I hope is its heart.

Kalix moves.

His blade swings in a deadly arc.

The head separates cleanly, sent rolling across the now blood-slicked floor.

The creature writhes, convulsing—then, stillness. I hold my stance, taking controlled and measured breaths.

A few seconds pass.

Nothing. It doesn't reanimate.

Kalix exhales sharply, nudging its decapitated body with his sword.

"Should we take it to Iris?" he murmurs reluctantly.

Neither of us want to touch the damn thing.

I exhale, dragging my hand down my face before re-sheathing my sword. "This is a problem."

I glace at what's left of the Duke. His body is ruined, but the bigger question remains.

"How the hell did this get inside him?" My voice is quiet, more to myself than Kalix. "If he was dealing with the North...what the fuck are they dealing with?"

We need answers.

Kalix mutters a string of colorful curses, something about Iris owing him for this. I smirk.

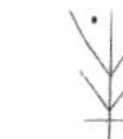

"As if you could command her of all people," I jest. Kalix snorts but doesn't argue.

I pull on a pair of black leather gloves, noticing Kalix doing the same. He gags dramatically at the stench, shaking his head.

"Gods, this thing smells worse than it looks."

He reaches inside his coat, retrieving a row of vials, and tosses a few toward me.

We get to work, methodically harvesting what we can—dark, slick tissue, unfamiliar organs, anything. The smell is rancid, thick with rot.

Neither of us speak, but we don't need to.

We both know.

Iris will have to settle for samples this time.

There's no way in hell either of us is carrying this damn thing tonight.

CHAPTER 6
Cage

I MARCH DOWN THE HALL, MY JAW IS LOCKED, AND MY PATIENCE wears thin.

I tug at the cuff of my sleeve, fixing, fidgeting—giving my anger something to do.

"So," the younger guard beside me starts, "D'you think she'll be ugly?"

A quiet snicker follows.

Some fools still believe witches are hags, withered things covered in warts and wrinkles, the magic in them rotting them from the inside out.

In truth, it's the opposite.

"Witches are exceptionally beautiful," I say flatly. "Their beauty is a deadly trap, a lure for men who are too ignorant to recognize the danger."

The guard's smirk fades slightly. I catch the tensing of shoulders in my periphery.

Better they be uneasy than snickering when a Le Strange witch is being brought onto castle grounds.

The guard's hand moves to the hilt of his sword. "What...what are they, then? If not human?"

I allow the silence to stretch a moment, letting the weighted question settle.

"Half hellion," I say at last. "Demon, some claim. Others argue something else entirely."

I glance at them, smirking at their growing discomfort.

"All the stories agree on one thing: they're also half Estrella."

The guard swallows hard.

"The tale says a world ender raped an Estrella, forcing her to conceive seven daughters. Each one became something...new, variations of the same terrible thing. Some favor their Estrella blood. Others?" I exhale sharply. "They take after their father."

The guard's thoughts are almost entertaining, a brief distraction from the murderous urges plaguing the edges of my mind.

What if Nora is here?

Or worse, she's the one escorting the witch?

I don't know how I'll react if I come face to face with her. Hell, if it's any of the elders, I don't know if I can do this.

I don't want a new witch here.

I don't want a *Le Strange* here.

My mind races, sifting through a catalog of witches' faces—the ones I knew, the ones I killed, the ones that might still remain.

That's the problem.

I've slaughtered too many to know who even survived.

Anyone I once knew could be a memory now. The witchlings from back then would be grown now, but I never met them.

Maybe it's one of them.

We breach the entrance to the castle, descending the stone steps toward the carriage waiting below. Guards stand in stiff parallel formations, lining either side of the vehicle. One steps forward, gripping the handle, and pulls the door open.

The moment she steps out, magic slams into me, rivaling my own in intensity. The force is strong, potent. It scrapes against my senses.

Dark magic user. For sure.

The dark knows its own, and mine writhes, awakening beneath my skin in recognition.

Then I see her.

Black hair drinks in the sunlight, swallowing its warmth. Pale skin glows in contrast. It's almost...ethereal.

And then, her eyes.

Wide. Oceanic. Drowning me in an instant.

I sink.

I descend, a willing victim to the blue depths, as a ghost from my past stares back at me.

I DON'T THINK I'VE EVER SEEN EYES THAT BLUE.

She's staring up at me, small but unafraid. She has been dragging a stuffed bunny by its arms all over the coven. The thing's a mess, missing a button eye and covered in a hefty number of frayed patches. It's probably been dragged through enough dirt to have lived a dozen lifetimes.

Her dress isn't much better, hanging loose off one shoulder and streaked in grime.

And her hair...

Dark and wild, it sucks in the sunlight without giving an inch of its color back.

I glance down, finding her bare feet pressed into the grass.

"Where are your shoes?" I ask curiously.

She plants her hands on her hips, her bunny being thrashed in the process.

Sassy.

"I like the feeling of grass on my feet," she declares. Then she taps her foot against the ground as if she's testing it, debating something.

I wait.

She caves.

I can't help but smile as she gives in. She's the most animated person I've ever met here. The only other one who actually speaks to me.

"Why are your marks already in?" she blurts, pouting as she glares at her own arms. "It is not fair!"

I glance at the dark ink swirling in intricate patterns down my arms. "Uh..." I hesitate, my voice quieter than I intend. "Elanora says I'm very strong. It might have something to do with my magic or...my bloodline."

I'm still not familiar with talking to people. The words feel strange to me.

She does not look impressed.

Millicent jabs a finger at me. "Mama says I'm strong, too! And I'll have big marks! Bigger than yours!" The fire in her eyes alight with the hottest blue flame.

I blink, caught off guard.

I pause briefly before replying, "Yeah, I'm sure they will be," I offer, trying for politeness.

"They will," she insists, cocking her head in another sassy dramatic flourish. Then, with absolutely no hesitation, she asks, "Where's your mama and papa?"

The words stabs like a blade slipped between my ribs.

How do I explain this? How do I tell a child, a five- or six-year-old girl, that I killed *all* of them, that Nora found me and took me in because I slaughtered an entire village?

I can't.

"I lost them."

She gasps, eyes wide. "I can help you find them! I'm *real* good at the 'finding things' game!" she announces proudly.

I shake my head. "I lost them permanently."

Her small brows furrow. She doesn't quite understand, but she frowns anyway.

"...Is that why you have no friends?" she asks, tilting her head. "No one is allowed by you."

Smart girl. *And too damn forward.*

Her words are innocent even if they carve deep.

She doesn't know—couldn't know—that my power isn't something I can control, that I can't have people close because being near me means dying.

I tighten my fist, gripping the emotions she has stirred within me before they take over.

"Well, **I'm** Millicent Le Strange!" she declares proudly, holding out her tiny hand like she's offering me something far more important than an introduction.

I stare for a second, then shake it.

"Cage Black."

She snickers.

"My name's cooler."

I smile again.

Her words are playful, innocent. She doesn't mean to insult my name. She's just a child, certain hers is better. I have a feeling Millicent thinks a lot of things she has or does are better than others'.

"It is very pretty."

She beams, glowing from the compliment.

"Call me Millie! My friends do."

I blink.

Friends?

"I'm sorry you lost your mama and papa and have no friends," she says simply, like this isn't the most obvious, tragic thing in the world. Then, *with absolute certainty*, she adds, "We are friends now."

She thrusts her bunny toward me. I stare, realization dawning on me. She's giving it to me.

When I don't immediately take it, her little brows scrunch in frustration, and she starts shoving it toward my chest.

"Millie, this is very kind, but he seems important to you. I can't take him."

She shakes her head, her curls bouncing wildly. "We can share!"

A voice calls from the courtyard.

"Little star! Come!"

Millie turns her head at the sound, her mother waving to her from beside the well.

Her smile drops when she sees me.

Nothing new.

I sigh, relenting. I take the rabbit from Millie's hands, if only to stop her ramming it into my chest.

Satisfied, she grins one last time before skipping off, her curls bouncing as she runs to her mother.

I watch.

I watch as her mother takes her hand without hesitation, swinging arms, making Millicent laugh.

My chest tightens.

My fingers curl around the rabbit's worn fabric, gripping it like something fragile. Something I shouldn't be allowed to hold.

Footsteps.

The distinct clicks of heels echo in the air. Measured. Cold. Familiar.

Nora.

I barely have time to shove the rabbit down my coat before her voice reaches me.

"I can sense your magic up in my office."

She stops in front of me. I don't lift my head.

"It is time for your session. Come."

A cold sweat breaks out at the base of my neck.

I go.

I always go.

Because it is necessary.

Seven Devils

As I scream, I repeat it.
It is necessary.
As I pass out from the pain, I repeat it.
It is necessary.

CHAPTER 7

Millicent

I CANNOT BEGIN TO FATHOM WHO STANDS BEFORE ME OR WHY Nora would even align with a kingdom harboring the one responsible for killing half of our coven.

He is no longer the boy I remember. The power he once wielded was but a drop in the ocean compared to the force he is now. He has grown into something formidable. He's handsomely broad-shouldered and muscular. His leather vest is laced tightly against his frame.

The silver eyes that haunt my dreams are sharper in reality. They penetrate me like daggers, framed by dark lashes. Black marks coil up his arms, extending over his chest and neck.

A clear display of his power. I have never seen such dark, plentiful marks.

A raw, untamed anger ignites in the pit of my stomach. I could end him now. I *should*. My gaze flicks to the guards positioned behind him, then to those stationed at the rise upon the entrance to the grounds. If I fed while fighting, I could take them all out. I would only need to be fast. And lethal.

Then I hear Nora's voice in my mind.

What family I have left expects more of me. There is no room for sentimentality. I was trained for control, conditioned to suppress emotion. Even as I sobbed over my mother's death, Nora forbade anyone from comforting me. Arcadia had to sneak into my room just to hold me as I grieved. It was Ollie, of course, who carried me through it.

Isolation. Detachment. These were drilled into me until they became second nature. Yet now, standing before my mother's killer, detachment is slipping from my grasp. I try focusing on the space just past him to cool my emotions. My magic stirs and picks up in a flurry of explosive tingles along my skin.

"Le Strange," his voice rings out, firm and commanding. He crosses his arms. The movement makes his biceps and chest flex beneath his vest. "Living here will be simple if you make it simple. You are not to harm anyone within these walls or in the surrounding areas unless instructed. You will train under my supervision for proper handling. Today, you will meet with your king and be shown your living quarters. You are not permitted off grounds without an escort."

His face remains unreadable, giving nothing away. *Does he recognize me?* Surely, he knows the coven's name. But we were children then, and nearly two centuries have passed.

My eyes narrow slightly. Who does he think he is, commanding me?

Nora told me to behave, so I will, not because of this mage or his king. He is certainly not *my* king. Witches have no place for men in our world. The very idea of any man assuming authority over me makes my hands itch to claw out his eyes.

"Lovely," I say, my tone dripping with sarcasm. "Shall we get this show on the road?"

Cage turns without a word, motioning for me to follow. As we ascend the steps, guards fall into step around me, six behind, six ahead, and a mage at my side. The sheer number is almost laughable.

Are they truly this afraid of me?

Their unease rolls off them in waves, seeping into my awareness. I revel in it. A sick thrill runs through me at the thought of how much effort they're putting into keeping their precious castle safe—from me.

As expected, the halls are teeming with vermin, their movements like those of ants skittering about. Yet something unexpected catches my eye. They're bowing to the mage.

Interesting. Someone is of high rank.

So he's more than a glorified guard.

I almost want to provoke him, just to see what power keeps these people in line. To know what, exactly, I will face at the end of all this.

But I am not here for them.

I'm here for the North.

I'm no stranger to crowds—the coven life is also full of movement and energy—but the sheer luxury of this place is unfamiliar. The castle halls gleam with wealth, their walls lined with intricate carvings and polished stone. Above us, massive golden chandeliers hang like suspended suns that cast a warm glow across the corridor.

Unlike the chandeliers, the rest of the décor is more restrained, giving my eyes a break from the overwhelming shine of gold.

That reprieve ends the moment we reach what I can only assume is the throne room.

The towering golden doors swing open. My gaze glides over the soaring white stone pillars, rising from floor to ceiling, before settling on the thrones. Two massive chairs of gilded opulence. The king sits atop one.

Younger than I expected.

His features are striking, as are his sharp, sky-blue eyes. He's the kind that artists would immortalize in paintings of the sun gods. Golden curls frame his face, catching the light in a way that makes his sun-kissed skin glow.

The guards bow. So does Cage.

I do not.

Hands clasped in front of me, I stand my ground.

The king smiles at my defiance, seemingly amused rather than insulted.

Cage straightens, turning to face me. **"Bow."** His tone is absolute, leaving no room for argument.

I like to argue.

"I do not bow before vermin," I say plainly, locking eyes with him. A challenge. A dare.

Make me.

Cage's jaw tightens. He moves.

Marching toward me, his hands twitching at his sides. He wants to strike me.

And I—I would welcome it. This is a perfect excuse to lay the bastard out—right now. Nora never said I couldn't defend myself.

"Cage, enough."

The king's voice slices through the tension, filling the throne room. "I do not expect something raised in the woods to bow to me. No offense, Miss Le Strange."

His words drip with amusement, but I hear the arrogance spewing beneath them.

Cage halts. His jaw is clenched so tight I half expect his teeth to crack. He exhales sharply, spinning away from me, retreating up the steps to stand beside his king.

King Tyran leans forward, propping an elbow on his throne, resting his chin against his fist. "I assume Elanora has told you why you are here?" he muses.

"The threat in the North. You want the expertise that a witch of my blood can offer in dealing with it." My voice is monotone, betraying nothing. I refuse to let my thoughts show.

The king nods. "I am unsure of their exact plans. Strange events keep occurring. Something is not right. And so far, the signs link them to it." He pauses, "The seer here has foreseen their involvement. Her visions only confirm what we are already discovering."

They have a seer—here? Most interesting.

Seers are rare, but most are useless frauds. If the king puts faith in her words, she must be good. She must have proven herself.

"I believe you may understand what we have uncovered," he continues, his boyish features hardening. "And when the time comes, I believe we will need you to win."

My curiosity is piqued. "What exactly have you been finding?"

The king's expression darkens. With a flick of the wrist, he dismisses his guards.

I raise a brow, watching as they stride past me. They close the heavy doors behind them.

Cage remains still, watching me like a hawk, as if expecting me to make a move. He's prepared to strike if I so much as flinch in the king's direction.

The king meets Cage's gaze. A silent conversation passes between them before Cage speaks.

His voice is rough, deeper than the king's. "We've found traces of some darker magic, both known and unknown. Sites where unnatural creatures have appeared. The disturbances are spreading. And something is...changing." He exhales. "We've seen an increase in what we're calling possessions though we don't yet understand the source. It's evolving—into what, we don't know."

I listen intently, my mind turning over the possibilities. Darkness is afoot.

And it is far worse than I expected.

"People accused of ties to the North are disappearing. And when we go to confront those who remain, we find...something else." Cage's voice is steady. "Magic I can't explain. A presence warping them, birthing new entities I've never encountered before."

New entities?

I tilt my head. "And the seer?"

The king sighs, shaking his head. "She is limited—or she refuses to share more. Fates and balances and all that." His voice carries a thread of disappointment, convincing me he isn't lying.

My gaze flicks toward him as I extend my mind into his, brush it, testing the edges of his thoughts.

I hit a wall.

My breath stills for half a second. My eyes widen.

He did not notice my attempt.

I wonder who taught him.

Slowly, my gaze drifts to Cage.

Does he have an ability like mine?

I race through the possibilities, and instinct pulls my defenses up. If Cage can read minds, I will need to ward my room and my subconscious against every crack that could be used against me.

I will not allow myself to be exposed.

"Cage will explain the arrangements to you," Felix says smoothly. "You are a guest here, Millicent, and my kingdom needs your help. There are rules, of course. History has made them necessary. But you are no prisoner."

His smile is warm, disarmingly so.

"If you need anything else, please come to me. I am king Tyran, but you may also call me Felix,"

I meet his gaze, unmoved. "Noted," I say flatly.

A guest? As if I would ever subjugate myself to their hospitality. Do they truly believe I would walk in and submit?

Cage descends the steps, pausing only to offer Felix a brief bow.

Felix chuckles at my dismissal. He's unfazed. "I think having a new witch around will really stir things up!" He claps his hands, pushing himself to his feet.

A new witch?

My spine stiffens. Was one already here? His words are casual. I did not expect this.

Why would a witch live amongst vermin and mages?

This I have to see.

Felix sighs, rubbing the back of his neck as he steps down from the throne. "Cage will show you the rest. Being king unfortunately means

63

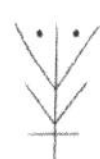

I am needed elsewhere." He exhales heavily, clearly unenthused by the prospect of whatever duty awaits him.

With a snap of Cage's fingers, guards reenter the room, falling into formation around their king. I watch as they escort him from the chamber. His golden curls disappear through the towering doors.

I turn to leave, but Cage moves to block my path.

He steps in close, lowering his voice so only I can hear.

"I know who and what you are," he murmurs. His silver eyes darken. "He thinks it's a good idea to have you here. I disagree." His breath, steady, controlled. "Prove me right and you will be disposed of."

A threat.

I whip my head toward him. My glare is sharp enough to cut. "Lay a finger on me, and I will shatter you—along with anything you hold dear." My voice is like venom, hate lacing my words. "You clearly do not know who or what I am to threaten me so openly. Your insolence is noted."

Cage's breath deepens. His eyes gleam with anticipation.

"I will welcome the day, little witch."

His tone is calm. Too calm.

He strides past me toward the door.

"Come."

The single command cracks through the space like a whip, as if I were nothing more than a dog.

I grind my teeth. My nails dig into my palms, the sting keeping me from unleashing my magic and blasting him through the wall.

"And here I thought mages were well mannered and pampered." I sneer, stepping in behind him.

The rhythmic click of my swords against my back fills the silence. Let him hear it. Let him remember that even without my magic, I am still a threat.

Cage doesn't turn, doesn't even slow his pace.

"You are inhuman," he says, his voice as cold as the steel on my back.

"An insult to life. You deserve to sleep in the dungeons and eat scraps. Manners should be the least of your concerns."

I stare at his back, fantasizing about impaling him on a row of shadowed lances.

Hell, I would mount his head on a spike outside my door as a trophy.

Instead, I smile.

A slow, sharp curve forms on my lips.

"Ah, and yet, here I am. A guest." I let my voice drip with malice. An insult wrapped in truth.

Cage doesn't respond.

I feel the shift in his posture, the flicker of restrained rage that coils beneath his skin.

Lovely.

We continue down the hall, our steps echoing in silence.

CHAPTER 8
Millicent

MY COVEN IS BY NO MEANS SMALL, BUT THIS CASTLE dwarfs it with ease. The sheer scale of it is absurd. Some halls are teeming with people while others remain eerily empty. Such wasted space. That's all I can think of as Cage points out yet another meeting chamber.

"Why so many?" I ask, peering into what he calls the war room. A fitting name given the swords and shields lining the walls, framing a massive oak table in the center. Maps are sprawled out across its surface, littered with small figures I can't quite make out.

"Can they not conduct all their business in one?"

"There are a lot of people here," Cage replies. "Meetings happen simultaneously. It keeps things organized. Helps remind you of the type of meeting you are in. This one, obviously, for tactics and war." He gestures toward the weapons displayed along the walls. "The last room? That was for trade—merchants, taxes, imports, all that."

His explanation certainly is...practical, but his voice lacks warmth. Still, at least he's stopped glaring at me over the past hour. A minor improvement.

His footsteps retreat, and I move quickly to keep pace, twisting my head to study the art along the walls. All elegant and well kept, a complete contrast to the paintings slowly tarnishing with age at my coven, the paint flaking away as each year passes.

Cage raises a brow, eyeing me like I've grown a second head suddenly. "Don't get out much, do you?"

I meet his gaze with a deadpan look. "I'm simply looking at art," I grumble, crossing my arms.

There are a lot of things I want to say to him. I could remind him that I don't spend my days wandering gilded halls like some pampered noble, that I have not felt freedom breeze through my hair while I explore the world on a dragon to see, taste, and touch everything each continent has to offer. I *could* snap at his condescending attitude.

I hold my tongue.

Because I don't yet know how to say any of it. Not without bringing at least this wing of the castle down when I inevitably lose control of my emotions.

Slaughter him now.

The voice slithers into my ear, a whisper that is impossibly distant, stretching down an endless tunnel of shadows. A breath against my skin, delicate as silk.

It's soft. Too soft. The kind of voice that soothes a child to sleep. The kind that murmurs lullabies beneath moonlit cradles. But the words it weaves are laced with malice and bloodshed.

You want this. You always have.

My fingers twitch at my sides, the air suddenly too thick. It would be so easy, so gratifying, to obey.

To let her in.

To let her out.

I fix my gaze on the stairs, forcing each step forward, shutting out the whispers curling in the back of my mind.

The winding steps are eerily familiar—too familiar. The grooves beneath my feet mirror the path to Nora's office. The memory settles like ice in my spine.

Is she watching me even now?

An unwelcome thought. Her familiar could be lurking somewhere beyond these walls, spying on me, recording every step I take.

A final turn brings us to the top of the stairs where the space opens into a long, singular hallway.

Surprisingly, the space is well lit. A row of tall, arched windows runs along the outer wall. Beyond the glass, the view is beautiful. The forest stretches endlessly, a vast sea of green shifting with the wind.

It should be beautiful, but it's nothing but a cage.

Cage.

He stops at the first door on the right. His hand rests on the handle before pushing it open. "This will be your room."

Then, without looking at me, he points further down the corridor, at the dark door at the end of the hall.

Twisting vines, deep green and engraved into the wood, crawl over its surface.

"That is my room," he says plainly. "We are the only ones permitted on this wing."

"Going to sleep well being this close to a witch?" I ask, tiling my head slightly.

Does he fear me? Does he believe himself above me? Or is he simply arrogant, thinking he can best a witch like me?

Curiosity gets the best of me.

I reach for his thoughts, stretching my senses toward him—seeking, pressing, testing.

I hit a wall.

Not just a wall, a steel fortress, locked tight. Impenetrable.

My breath stills for a moment.

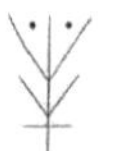

Cage's silver eyes narrow. He knows what I just tried.

Slow, deliberately, he lifts a finger.

"One," he counts, his voice flat. "I do not fear you, little witch. You are in this wing to ensure you don't run around at night. This room is warded. I will know every time you step in or out of it."

I scoff internally. Yeah, totally not a prisoner.

"Two," he continues, his eyes darkening, "do not ever try to get into my mind again."

The air between us seems still now.

"A part of me is half tempted to let you in," he murmurs. His voice changes to something almost...amused. "Just to watch you squirm like a rat in a trap. To let you crawl inside, only so I can crush you the moment you do."

He leans in slightly, the silver of his eyes sharpening like the edge of a blade.

"I would enjoy digging through the rot inside you."

The words aren't a threat. They're a promise.

I lift a finger, mirroring his condescending gesture. Now my voice drips with sweetness.

"One," I begin, unable to contain the sass bleeding into every syllable, "don't be mad at me because you got stuck with babysitting duty. Because that's exactly what this feels like."

I tilt my head further, feigning concern.

"You will train me? Watch me? Ward my room? Take me on little adventures? What's next? Tuck me in? Dress me? Wipe my ass? If you plan to feed me, I prefer my food fresh."

His lips part to snap at me, but I cut him off mercilessly, lifting another finger before he can get another stupid word out.

"Two," I continue, my smirk growing, "if you think you will ever get in my mind, you are truly delusional. Your arrogance must be stifling. I am not a mage. I am not some vermin. I am—"

The bastard rolls his eyes and then, before I can finish, shoves his fingers against my lips, silencing me.

"You know, Millicent, you're grown now, but you're the same little brat you were back then, aren't you?" His voice is casual, but there's a venom laced beneath it. "I don't want you here. I'm following my king's orders, but given the choice, I'd burn what's left of your coven. I'm surprised you even made it out."

A slow, sly grin spreads across his face, watching for my reaction.

So he does remember me. He knows exactly who I am.

His words boil my blood. My instincts take over before my mind catches up.

I snap.

My teeth sink into his fingers, hard, like the feral beast he thinks I am.

Cage jerks back with a sharp "Fuck!", shaking out his hand. But instead of showing anger, he actually laughs.

Laughs.

And I'm the insane one?

I glare up at him, seething, before spinning on my heel and storming into my room.

The moment I step inside, my pace slows, my anger momentarily eclipsed by surprise.

The space is larger than I expected, larger than anything I've ever had. A four-poster bed, its frame deep mahogany, sits against the left wall, swallowed in a thick pine-green blanket. Across from it, a red velvet sofa rests before a gray stone fireplace, its hearth empty but grand.

The balcony doors are wide open, letting the crisp air rustle the edges of the heavy curtains. Golden light spills across the floor, cast by a massive chandelier overhead, its arms curling like gilded branches.

My footsteps are muffled by the handwoven wool rug covering most of the space. Intricate designs of red, yellow, green, and blue are stitched into the fabric.

I take it all in, my mind already set on one thing: I'm going to drag that sofa out here.

"Maybe we should muzzle you."

Cage's voice is a poison, laced with amusement. I hear the smirk in it before I even turn.

I ignore him, stepping onto the balcony and gripping the railing, staring out over the vastness of the forest below. The treetops shift in the wind, dark and stretching far beyond the castle's borders.

At least out here, I can breathe. I will be out here a lot.

"King Tyran has arranged an introductory dinner for you," he says, his voice dropping into that infuriatingly detached tone. "You'll meet others involved with the situation in the North."

I turn, finding his silver gaze already on me.

He will always be watching, just like Nora's owl.

That will be a problem. Once we know what the North is up to, if I am to get what I came for, I'll have to learn how he fights, how he thinks, and what he fears.

Because one day, when they realize I was never here to help them, I will kill him.

Just like he killed my family that night.

Cage's smirk sharpens. "Do try not to bite anyone at dinner, yeah? Who knows what diseases you might pass."

With that, he pushes off the door frame and strides away, leaving me alone in my room.

I flip him off.

Muttering curses under my breath, I shut the door, rubbing my temples.

For my first day, he sure is testing me, and restraint is not something I practice often.

A prickle runs down my spine.

A presence.

I lift my head and freeze.

There. Perched on the iron railing of my balcony, its gaze fixated on me.

Nora's owl.

Its copper eyes reflect the light. Its gaze is unrelenting as though soaking in every moment. It sees everything.

She sees everything.

"Ah, there you are. I'm behaving," I murmur, cocking my head at the owl.

It doesn't react. It simply watches, recording, absorbing, and transmitting every movement, breath, and thought Nora might find useful.

I wave lazily, flicking my fingers at it, before turning away and plopping down on the sofa. The velvet cushions soften my landing, but the weight of the owl's gaze still presses against my skin.

I want to ask it. I want answers. Does she know Cage is here? Has she been watching him, too? Does she know what I know?

I don't ask because Nora is not to be questioned.

A familiar chill slides down at the edges of my periphery. Shadows coil in the farthest corner of the room. It pools, spills, and slithers down the walls. They creep across the floor and stretch toward the low table in front of me.

Then, they twist.

A spiral of darkness spins itself in a small cyclone, whirling in a tight vortex, before the shadows abruptly snap inward.

And Ollie materializes. He twirls with the shadows, his body spinning like a giddy little tornado before he finally skids to a stop.

"Haha WHOO-ahahahahah!" He giggles and then strikes a dramatic pose, his stubby fingers snapping into the form of small sling shots aimed at me.

"Me Misses! Wow! Upgrade!" he gasps, his round black eyes glistening with wonder as he takes in his surroundings: the plush furniture, the oversized bed, and the fireplace. Our room is simple back home. Small and cozy, well-aged with time. This room alone must seem like a palace to him in comparison.

I smirk. "Welcome to the Southern Kingdom, Ollie. We'll be living here for a while."

Ollie's wings flutter while his tiny feet kick off the ground as he flings himself at me.

"Me Misses in a castle? My QUEEN!"

With a wail of adoration, he throws himself onto my lap, nearly making me laugh before his pudgy weight knocks the wind out of me.

"Keep your voice down," I whisper, still happy to see him.

I cup his chubby cheeks, tilting his head up until his beady black eyes meet mine. "They do not know I am the heir, and I want to keep it that way."

Ollie immediately salutes. His tiny claws click against his forehead.

"I SEAL AND HAVE NO LIPS!" He declares proudly, puffing out his chest, but, in reality, it's just his stomach bulging even more.

I snort, shaking my head. My frustrations—my lingering emotions with Cage, Nora's damn owl—fade away, swept aside by Ollie's erratic personality and his poor language skills.

Ollie always does this. There's no one else like him.

He speaks in broken, absurd English but refuses to learn anything. Yet, he sees the world in the most unfiltered, unhinged way imaginable. To him, *we're* the strange ones, bound by ridiculous rules like "you can't drink wine all day," "you can't run around naked," and "you shouldn't screw whoever wherever."

It never made sense to him.

And I love him for it.

"Very good." I lean forward, peppering kisses on his cold, soft skin. He dissolves into a fit of giggles, kicking his stubby feet in the air.

Ollie is—gods, what is he?

A mix of a child, a dog, and that one friend who'd waste no time giving you secondhand embarrassment.

But he is also mine.

He has been with me since I was only five. My closest companion outside of Arcadia, my best friend.

And despite everything—despite the chaos, despite the commentary, despite the fact that he humps things when he likes them—I wouldn't trade him for anything.

Ollie climbs off my lap, wobbling dangerously before his chunky three-toed feet find purchase. He sashays across the room, his tail flicking behind him as he pokes at everything.

I let him roam, his giddiness infectious as I set about arranging my room the way I want it. With Ollie's help, if you can call it that, I slowly settle into my new space.

The sun begins to dip below the horizon. Dinner should be soon.

As if on cue, a knock on wood echoes at my door.

CHAPTER 9

Cage

WHEN THE DOOR SWINGS OPEN, I EXPECT THE WITCH who nearly bit my fingers off earlier to be standing there. Instead, for the second time today, I'm surprised by who or what stands before me.

I blink, scanning the doorway before finally looking down. And I find myself face to face with a creature both ridiculous and bizarre.

A chunky, blue-skinned thing—an imp. His plump belly protrudes so far forward that it completely swallows his toes. His arms are stubby and expressive, one black-tipped claw resting on his hip, the other drumming impatiently against his thigh. A long, rounded nose dominates his face, sitting low between two enormous, beady black eyes void of any apparent intelligence. Behind him, a thin blue tail sways, ending in a fine-pointed tip.

"Me misses thinks it's dinner time," he declares, his tone carrying a distinct nasal whine.

I arch a brow, placing my hands on my hips. "It is, in fact, dinner time. Who are you, exactly?"

The imp sniffs the air dramatically. His grimy claws twitch, and his expression twists to disgust, as if my scent is terrible and insulting to his senses.

"**Oliver** to you," he says, his voice tight and snooty, as if his name is a sacred privilege bestowed upon me.

I crouch down, entertained despite myself. I have never encountered an imp before, only read about them. Familiars are created from their witch's soul, a reflection of their witch. Of course, Millicent's familiar is stuck up, sassy, and dislikes me.

"Hello, Oliver," I offer, cocking my head to mirror his posture and observe his reaction. "I am Cage."

A flash of sharp yellowed fangs, some chipped, others missing, gleams back at me as his lips curl into a toothy grin.

Oral hygiene, it seems, is not high on an imp's to do list.

His actions and words come off as almost playful, his exact mood is hard to pin. His body language is tense, his wings spread in defense, and he hasn't allowed me into the room. However, he is smiling at me and still offered his name, and the door hasn't been slammed in my face.

Then, from within the room, a softer version of Millicent's voice—something I did not think possible—floats to the hall.

"Ollie, don't talk to strange men."

Oliver huffs, crossing his arms.

"This one **stinks** of magic, Misses! **BAD** business!" His tiny nostrils flare as if confirming this assessment. "I will keep him at bay! No **boys** allowed!"

A spark of wild magic whirls in the air around him, erratically zigzagging toward the door in a frenzied streak of blue lightning. The wooden slab slams shut, or at least tries to.

My hand shoots out, stopping it with a sharp thud. My fingers brace against the wood.

Oliver scowls, his features scrunching into what I assume is an attempted glare. But with his misshapen features, it looks more like a confused pout.

Then he pounces for my gut.

I don't bother moving. What damage could something this small possibly do?

Before I can find out, Millicent scoops him up, catching him mid-air with ease.

She pulls him flush against her chest, her arms banding tightly around his waist to keep him in place.

Oliver writhes, snarling, pouting, and kicking like a feral beast or an upset toddler.

"Lemme at him, Misses!" he howls, wings flapping in protest.

It's clearly doing nothing, but I'll give him this: the little guy's got heart.

"No, you are too strong for him, and I need him alive," Millicent murmurs, her lips brushing against the imps' large, floppy ear.

Ollie stiffens, his tiny claws twitching against her arms. Apparently disappointed, he crossed his stubby arms tightly over his stomach, pressing them into that round belly of his.

I tighten my lips, suppressing a chuckle as he louts out a long, dramatic huff.

The feral little thing actually wants to maul me.

"Leave now. I will see you later," Millicent says softly, pressing a kiss to the ugly thing's cheek.

I watch, making a note of it in case she ever decides to risk anyone's life or harm anyone.

The Le Strange has a weakness.

A rather blatant one to say the least. She's not so different from the others.

They all grow up the same way, replicas of one another, molded in their coven's fucked up belief system.

I know what she is.

Intimately.

A small plume of smoke poofs in the air as Oliver vanishes, leaving us alone.

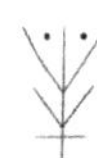

"You know, I've heard familiars are like their witches in some ways." I muse, tilting my head as I watch Millicent closely. "Is he also a little bitey?"

I'm not really asking. I just want to get a rise out of her. If I have to suffer her presence, then she won't be at peace either.

Millicent doesn't hesitate. "I will make sure he gets you next time and you can find out." Her voice mimics mine, down to the same inflection.

I arch a brow.

Little witch.

Still, knowing we actually have to make it to dinner without attempting to kill each other, I decide to be the mature one.

I step out, assuming she will follow. And sure enough, the heavy thud of her boots trail behind me. Even in silence, I can feel her distaste clinging to me, pressing against me like acid on the back of my tongue.

We walk for the longest ten minutes of my life.

Then the royal dining hall looms before us.

Gold. Everywhere.

The sheer sight of it's blinding as light reflects off the dinnerware, statues, and even the intricate carvings on the massive dining table.

Servants weave around the space setting out platters of rich meats, steaming breads, and fruits so vibrant they almost don't look real.

The room is designed to be a spectacle, the elongated table capable of seating twenty guests. Tonight, though, it is reserved for only a select few.

Guards stand rigidly in the corners of the hall, their gold-plated armor gleaming under the chandelier's glow.

Everything about this room demands attention.

Felix is already seated at the head of the table, his infamous golden curls catching the candlelight.

"Ah! Welcome! Come, sit, Millicent," he says warmly, rising from his seat and pulling out the chair beside him.

I nearly laugh at the look on Millicent's face as she approaches. One would think manners insult her.

Felix, of course, doesn't bat an eye.

That's the thing about him. He's the type that doesn't need to be mirrored or returned. He's a rare type of man—a rare type of king— even he was forced into the role at such a young age.

Felix was my first true friend here—before Kalix, before anyone else. I would *dare* say my best friend.

I was young when his father welcomed me into the castle. Back then, I didn't care about my position.

I only cared about two things: food and stability.

After the Le strange incident, I was always moving, always going somewhere new. Vyraxis was my only constant.

Those years were easier with her. She protected me. Our bond transcends the material world. Our souls intertwined the day she was created.

Felix is different.

He isn't bound to me like Vyraxis. He isn't a creature of magic or some part of me made whole. He was simply there. A tangible force. A tether to something real.

The sun illuminates the darker parts of us and brings them to light.

Felix did that for me.

He was my first ray of sun after so many years in the dark. He saved me from the self-isolation, from the loneliness that gnawed at me, from the addiction to power that threatened to consume me whole.

Yet, the hunger is still there—still stirring, still whispering, still wanting for more.

The "more" that I chase now is different.

More laughter. More time together. More training to protect *them*.

I don't think Millicent has ever felt this.

I glance at her, the little hellion sitting stiffly beside Tyran.

She wouldn't understand.

"Please, it's Felix while we have dinner. I insist!"

Felix settles back into his seat, preening over Millicent, ensuring she finds everything to her liking.

The familiar weight of Kalix's footsteps resounds from the entryway.

I turn to greet him, but before I can, something flickers in my periphery. A flash of red, vivid and striking, cutting through the room's golden glow.

Iris.

Her fiery curls bouncing as she overtakes Kalix's presence although he dwarfs her, so much so that it is almost comical.

Kalix may be the captain of the guard, a commander used to leading entire battalions, but it doesn't matter.

Because Iris bosses us all around.

Eyes locked on Millicent like she's never seen another woman before, Iris boldly slides into the seat beside her.

Kalix, as usual, plops into the chair with all the grace of a collapsing wall. His weight slams into the seat so hard the wooden legs groan under the impact.

Felix, who has been in the middle of one of his long-winded rambles, pauses long enough to extend a warm hand toward Iris.

"Millicent, this is Iris. Iris, this is Millicent Le Strange," he announces, his tone as inviting as ever.

Iris turns to Millicent, her full attention fixed on her, her eyes alight with curiosity and amusement. "A Le Strange witch! I am shocked one of you even came out here."

Millicent remains composed. "Strange times," she replies smoothly. Then her eyes sweep over Iris, assessing, searching. "You have magic, yet I see no markings? Are you a mage?"

Her gaze flicks over the slivers of exposed skin, visible from where Iris's dark green overalls dip at the ribs and shoulders. If Iris were marked like witches, Millicent would have already seen the evidence.

Iris throws her head back and laughs, her body shaking with amusement. Her laughter lightens the room. It always does.

"Goddess above, no!" She exclaims, pulling her hair forward and twisting, sliding her straps down to reveal her back.

I already know what Millicent will see.

Across Iris's back, an intricate tree, its sage-green swirls shimmer like winding patterns of living energy. It coils from the center of her spine before branches extend toward her shoulders.

The sight of it snags my chest.

An urge.

I can't stop my gaze from dropping, tracking every swirl of the design, every curve of her bare skin—

Wait.

No, that's not mine.

Kalix.

I flick a glance at him from the corner of my eye, already knowing what I'll find.

He's staring, completely unblinking. His entire focus is pinned on Iris's exposed back.

Ignoring his attempt at burning the image into his mind, I return my attention to the two witches.

Millicent trails her eyes over the markings, her expression shifting to something close to awe and intrigue. "These are impressive," she acknowledges, her voice carrying an edge of respect. "What is your magic?"

I'm surprised Millicent is even being civil. Then again, Iris is another witch. That must make her worthy of respect in Millicent's fucked up hierarchy of human worth.

Iris slides her straps back up, securing her overalls once again. Her smile widens, beaming under the compliment.

"Necromancer," she announces, as if that alone explains everything, "Here, I mostly work in the lab as more of...a biologist—a chemist of sorts! The boys bring me specimens, and I test them."

Felix leans back, smirking.

"She dissects them."

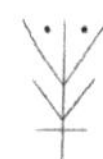

Iris waves a dismissive hand, ignores him entirely.

"I'm trying to figure out what the North is up to, what exactly they're creating, and what the source is."

She speaks faster now, her nerdy excitement creeping into every word.

Millicent's brow lifts. "A necromancer? Do you have a bunch of beasts hidden somewhere?"

Iris's eyes light up, and she nods enthusiastically.

"Once upon a time, yes, but not so often anymore. I mostly help with tragic accidents when animals are hurt. I still get the itch to make creatures, but they need to be fed, and that's...not practical here."

Felix clears his throat.

"Yes, we definitely don't need your man-eating abominations roaming the castle."

Iris barely acknowledges him, still grinning, until—

Tyran ducks just in time as a grape sails past his head. His grin widens.

"We appreciate your restraint, you closeted psycho."

Iris rolls her eyes but doesn't argue, instead leaning back and reaching for her wine.

"Now poor Kalix must feel neglected. You two can chat forever after dinner."

Kalix snorts and rests his elbows on the table, turning his attention over to Millicent.

"I am Kalix, captain of the guard. I work in the field—creature killing, location investigations, and interrogations."

The light from the massive chandelier above glints off the silver rings adorning his fingers as he laces them together.

Millicent's expression shifts instantly, her face morphing into an impassive, dismissive stare.

"No magic, then?"

Her tone is flat, uninterested, like she's already decided he has no worth.

I feel my jaw tighten.

Typical.

Her kind has no care for humans outside of breeding or blood sacrifices.

Kalix, however, does not miss a beat.

"No, suppose not." His smirk curves slow and deliberate. "If Cage and I both had magic, what use would *you* have?"

His condescension sinks into the air.

Millicent's eyes narrow, the sharp retort already forming on her tongue.

Felix, ever the peacekeeper, throws his hands up like a man warding off an angry bear.

"You both are exceptional in your own ways!"

Across the table, Iris stifles a giggle behind her wine glass. The tension still lingers, but I seize the moment to regain control.

"We will all need to work *together*. Out there, bickering will get one of you killed."

I let the words sink in, my gaze sweeping across the table before I finally settle on Millicent, thrumming my fingers on the table.

"Each player here has a role and a purpose, Millicent."

My eyes find hers, pinning her in place. Her shoulders tense.

Good.

"Between trips, we prepare. You will assist Iris. Or Kalix."

Her posture stiffens further. Someone must not like being told what to do.

That will change.

Dinner continues around me, Kalix pestering Iris, occasionally lobbing strawberries at her like some child. She throws half-hearted threats between sips of wine.

Felix, now deep into his third glass, snickers, inserting himself into whatever conversation catches his attention.

I let the noise fade into the background, as I'm focused on her. Between bites of food, I study Millicent. I cannot quite place her.

 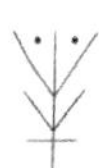

It's instinct to categorize people, to define them by what they were and where they came from.

Yet, she doesn't fit, not yet. It feels like I've known her for years. This is the same way I once knew Nora—the same way I knew the dungeons beneath her beloved coven.

I can still smell them: the damp earth and copper tang of blood saturating the air the deeper I went. It was an odd scent, a fusion of decay and ritual, of history and horror, thick enough that it clung to your skin long after leaving. I swear I still inhale it sometimes when I wake from memories that chased me like desperate souls clawing their way from judgment at the gates of hell.

Now there's her: devoid of emotion one moment and running her mouth the next. And then silent.

Fitting.

A Le Strange witch would only know how to feel hatred and anger.

Iris kicks Kalix's shin under the table.

His knee jerks instinctively, slamming into the underside of the table. Dishes rattle, silverware clinks loudly against porcelain, and Felix and Millicent jolt.

Felix lets out a sharp yelp as his bottle of wine wobbles dangerously, nearly tipping.

His entire body lunges, hands outstretched. He manages to catch it.

After a deep sigh of relief, he cradles the bottle to his chest, clutching it like a mother nursing a child. The moment is so absurd that under different circumstances, I might have smirked.

Instead, I take advantage of the small window the chaos has created.

She's off guard. I know it's wrong, but the need to get inside her mind is too strong. I need to figure her out. I need to learn who she really is. Who is she beneath this emotionless mask?

Or is this who she is now?

I don't like surprises, and it aggravates me that this is the first time in my long life I have been unable to read someone. She isn't

the girl I knew. The smiling, laughing, expressive Millicent from years ago is gone.

Dead.

I had mourned her. I had believed her lost forever: the Millicent I knew and loved, my very first friend. This thing sitting at the table, carrying her face, her voice, her form...

She is not her.

I focus, reaching for her mind. I imagine peeling back the layers, pushing past the barriers, sifting through the void.

And I strike a fortress of ice, sharp and jagged. I've seen mental defenses before, but the emptiness shocks me.

Somewhere in my focus, I realize I'm staring at her.

And she knows. The black widow herself has caught me in her web. Across the table, her cavernous ocean eyes lock on to mine, flickering with realization. She isn't just blocking me. She's watching. Waiting.

And then...a squeeze. It's subtle. It's not an attack or a violent expulsion from her mind. It's uncomfortable.

A warning.

There's something in it, something that lures me instead of repelling me. A sensation just on the edge of pain, like the pull of a hook lodged beneath my skin, drawing me into the depths of her gaze.

I understand now. I understand why moths fly into fire and perish: because it is beautiful. Even knowing the danger, the warmth still calls.

A breath.

On the inhale, my spine bends backward, too far.

On the exhale, I'm bent even further, my body arching unnaturally over the chair, my muscles shaking violently.

Kalix shoots to his feet.

"What the fuck!" His voice cuts through the room. His gaze immediately snaps to Millicent.

I hear his chair scrape, feeling the shift in the wind as he moves toward her.

I'm still shaking off the last remnants of her hold. Her power coils around my body like an anaconda, tightening until my nerves fire off erratically. My muscles jerk beneath her influence.

She does have some bite to her.

I'm done with this performance.

My mind recoils from her grasp, and in a single breath, I shatter the connection and break free from the tangles of her web. My consciousness snaps back into place, and my magic settles inside me once more.

I roll my neck and shoulders, stretching out the last of the tension as I sit up. I keep my expression blank.

If she's expecting fear, awe, or even grudging respect, she won't get it. And that's what annoys me.

Not seeing her disappointed reaction frustrates me more than the struggle. Irritation gives way to curiosity and then amusement.

Iris is wrapped around Kalix's legs like a damn koala, half-seated on the floor, arms and legs locked around him in an effort to keep him from lunging.

Felix chuckles, finally pushing to his feet. His crown tilts slightly from how long he's been lounging.

"Well, I am now too drunk for this circus of idiots."

His heated red cheeks betray the effects of an emptied wine bottle.

"Can we not assault one another?" He sweeps a look around the room like a disappointed father addressing his unruly children.

"The bitch started it!" Kalix sneers, jabbing a finger at Millicent.

Iris pinches his leg, hard.

"**Ow.** You little—"

Kalix hisses, glaring down at her.

Annoyed with her antics, he reaches down, yanking her off his legs with ease. She lets out a string of expletives, thrashing in his grip, but he hauls her over his broad shoulder like she weighs nothing.

"Kalix, put me down!"

Her roar is fierce, except it sounds more like an angry lion cub challenging the alpha of the pack.

Kalix's hand comes down in a sharp **smack** against her rear.

"Adults are talking, Rainbow."

Iris lets out a startled squeak, freezing for half a second before resuming her flailing.

Eventually, she gives up, pouting like a child as she pushes, propping herself up on his back, chin resting on his shoulder. She waves lazily at the rest of us.

"Well, goodnight, guys! Millicent, come by my lab anytime! Nice to have another witch around."

She smiles warmly despite her predicament.

Kalix scoffs, placing his free hand on his hip.

"Yeah, so nice. I'm honestly so overjoyed." His voice is drenched in sarcasm.

Felix steps in beside him, beaming.

"I knew you would be!"

He reaches up, brushing a few strands of Iris's hair out of her face.

Kalix's attention shifts immediately, eyes narrowing on Felix.

"What, are you a hairstylist now?"

His grumbling is still audible as they finally leave the room. Felix's smirk lingers. He knows how to get around him.

I exhale slowly, finally returning my focus to Millicent.

She stands, unbothered. "I believe I can find my room on my own."

Her confidence doesn't miss a beat.

I rise as well, mirroring her.

"One can only hope your brain isn't so rotted that you're capable of such a small task. If I had to take you everywhere, I really would truly be babysitting a grown woman, wouldn't I?"

The irritation slips into my tone, sharper than I intended. I don't wait for her response. Instead, I turn and leave, letting the conversation end on my own terms.

I know where she goes. I've warded the castle's key points, my magic laced into every entryway, every hallway, and every room.

Malicent

I don't need to physically follow her to track her. Let her try some-thing. I welcome the excuse to crush her under my boot—to shatter that self-righteous attitude.

I'll wait.

CHAPTER 10

Millicent

THE DAYS PASS, BORING AND REPETITIVE. NOTHING ENtertaining happens, so I make use of the time mapping my surroundings and learning the movements and routines of those within. I feel more in control when I know where everyone is, what they do, and when they do it.

Cage, surprisingly, isn't as ever-present as I expected. Despite his claims of "supervision," he keeps to himself. His routine mirrors Kalix's, with meetings, training, and more training. The only difference is that Cage operates in a warded wing, a fortress to keep intruders out. Mages slip in and out, drawing runes upon the door to pass through the barrier. I can't help but linger nearby. Are the artifacts Nora desires hidden in those very halls?

Breaking wards tends to alert the owner unless they have a massive number running and several are disrupted, are inebriated, or are consumed in battle. Simply entering it only alerts them if the ward only allows certain people entry. Too many enter this one for it to be selective.

Right, left, half square.

Years of doing this procedure have made the mages not guard their process with their bodies, exposing the patterns they draw to me.

Iris, on the other hand, might as well be stitched to her lab. I'm half convinced she sleeps there. The fact that another witch is here—and willingly so—baffles me. At this point, I wouldn't be surprised if she beds these mortals willingly.

How repulsive.

Sure, we witches always used mortal men for breeding, but we tend to kill them after. Eating the liver blesses the baby with good health, or so the tradition goes.

The cold stone beneath my fingertips grounds me. Its rough grooves leech the warmth from my skin. I savor the feeling, letting it anchor me as my thoughts spiral. The cold reminds me of dinner the other night, when Cage had the audacity to pry into my mind.

I wonder what he found: a *frozen abyss? A void darker than even his own nightmares?* My body may be warm, my appearance full of life, but I am something else entirely inside.

Yet, I am still confused. He didn't even fight back. He let me push him out. Why? A trick? A test? I do not trust him; I never will. He plays with life and power like a child, teetering on a tightrope. How long has he been this way? Since we were children? Since before? I wish I had seen it sooner—if someone had—maybe he could have been stopped. Maybe Mama would still be alive. Maybe my sisters wouldn't have perished. How many more has he killed? Cage seems to be doing great despite the blood on his hands.

He thrives while I hardly get to sleep, tormented by the nightmares he carved into me. My fingers curl, my nails scraping and ripping against the stone; I let the sharp sting ground me. I welcome it, feeding the rage simmering beneath my skin.

What is it like, I wonder, to grow up here after slaughtering those who took him in? To trade their blood for a silver spoon? To rise in a golden palace, first hand to the king, and be granted more power— more power he so clearly craved while mine was taken away.

So much has been taken from me, hollowing me out until I clawed at the void, desperate to be whole again. The coven made me whole—no easy claim to power, no golden path to comfort. The coven taught me the burn from flame forges an unbreakable blade, and suffering sharpens it; I have never been sharper. Typical of a mage to seek such luxuries, to drown in softer pleasures while he calls himself strong.

I am not bitter, no. Comfort breeds weakness. I have stared into the abyss, endured its torment, and emerged anew. I am no lamb.

I am a wolf.

A slow, predatory smile curves my lips as my steps become firmer. When I can take what the North holds, blood will rain down on Cage, painting his skin as it did mine that night.

I will repeat history.

And I'll make a damn show of it.

I nearly collide with the smug bastard as I round the corner quickly, blissfully unaware that I've wandered into the west wing, where the mages reside. Instinct kicks in. I recoil, my body demanding distance between us.

He isn't wearing his usual long black coat. Instead, a loose black tunic hangs from his frame. Its deep neckline exposes the carved lines of a muscular chest and the black swirls of his markings creeping up his neck. He smells of sweat and earth, his hair is damp and unruly. His trousers sit low on his hips and hug his thighs. The weight of his large black sword tugs them lower. My gaze flickers to the dragon-carved handle and the embedded red jewel catching the dim light.

He crosses his arms, his shirt riding up to reveal a deep cut of muscle running down his waistline and a thick patch of hair following its descent.

"My eyes are up here, witch." his voice is gruff, laced with amusement.

My eyes snapped to his face, "I was looking at your sword—the handle, specifically."

His smirk widens. He's far too pleased with himself. "Yeah, you sure were looking at my sword." His tone was far too suggestive for my liking. He's pouring fuel on the fire of my already festering rage.

The desire to carve that stupid smirk off his face is overwhelming. If he wants to look at me in such an insolent way, perhaps I should just make it a permanent look for him.

"I would sooner gouge out my own eyes before looking at the sword you're so obviously proud of," I say flatly, crossing my arms to mirror him.

Cage shrugs, completely unfazed. "Go for it." He steps past me, deliberately keeping his distance as he disappears down the hall.

I welcome the distance. My control only goes so far, and my impulse to sink into his flesh and mar it grows with every footstep of his that echoes on stone.

My fury boils. The sconces lining the corridor flicker violently before snuffing out, plunging the hall into shadow.

The darkness twists, writing, spilling from the ceiling like ink. It moves with me, feeding off my anger, crawling down the walls like a swarm of spiders.

I take a sharp breath. Exhale.

Control.

The shadows retreat as I turn, forcing myself toward my room.

The night concludes as it always does. I remember the day to Nora's eerie little owl. The thing perches, unblinking, absorbing my every word. This is the routine now. If Nora has a message, its beak will part, and her voice will slither through the silence, like a prophecy, reminding me of who truly pulls the strings.

Even once the lights extinguish in my room, the faint white eyeshine of the owl penetrates the dark.

Always watching me.

CHAPTER 11
Millicent

I. Temptation
*"Entity can access the host's imagination, attack
perceptions, and infuse thoughts into their minds.
The beginning of the fall from grace."*
-The Wretched Sacrament

I TAKE MY DINNERS OUTSIDE NOW, SEATED ON A WORN STONE bench half-consumed by moss. The garden is quiet here, untouched by the castle's endless movement. The willow trees drape their limbs low, like thin fingers trailing in the cold breeze. I prefer this part of the garden—it's undisturbed, and the hush of the wind is my only company.

The air has sharpened with the season's change. It feels crisp and refreshing. I welcome the chill, it keeps me present. Grounded. Setting down my bowl of grapes, I pull my knees to my chest, tucking them beneath the folds of my dark blue gown. Beyond the hedges, the night thickens like a dark expanse swallowing the garden. My thumbs graze the soft cotton stretched taut over my knees as the evening begins to breathe.

"Millicent."

The whisper drifts through the wind.

Nightmother.

Darkness stirs in response. It seeps across the grass, twisting around the brush, and slithering up the willow trees. The garden wilts beneath its touch, dulling into a barren landscape where life is devoured by the void.

The hollowness creeps outward, until it reaches me...fills me.

Echoing the hollowness, my next heartbeat feels distant, as if my pulse is no longer mine. I inhale deeply, letting the cold air flood my lungs.

I EXHALE, WATCHING MY BREATH COIL INTO THE COLD AIR. Another breath—haaa—the sound rolling out like a firebreather's conjuring, as though I might summon warmth from deep within.

Snowflakes swirl around me, gathering in my cupped hands. I lift them closer, marveling at every snowflake. I try to memorize each unique shape. I wish to paint them for hours, but the moment warmth touches them, they vanish—a quiet loss. I forget within a moment what they looked like.

Suddenly—impact. A burst of cold against my coat.

Arcadia.

She grins from behind a low stone wall, her white hair blending into the snow. She's peeking at me through snow-dusted air.

I laugh—wild, untamed—and crouch low, my hands already working to pack my own snowball. She won't win this fight.

"Arcadia!" I laugh, rising to launch a snowball straight at her head.

She yelps, narrowly dodging as I take off after her, giggling. The snow fights back, dragging at my shins and climbing to my knees, but I push through. Arcadia's laughter echoes ahead, so light and free, like it belongs to someone untouched by the world.

Out of all the girls our age, Arcadia is my best friend. We always said we were soulmates of a sort. Opposites in every way—her white hair, deep mahogany skin, and golden eyes are stark against my black hair, pale skin, and ice-blue eyes. Yin and yang, we call it. A balance only we understood.

Then, the crunch of footsteps behind me draws my attention.

I stop short, my breath still caught in a laugh. Turning, the cold air stills my lungs.

"Nora."

I bow deeply, the weight of my skirts pulling snow into the folds of the fabric. The sight makes me smile—for once, the black I wear like all the other girls is marked by something else. Something uniquely mine.

I rub my cold hands together, trying to coax warmth into them. I cup them close when that fails and blow hot air over my palms.

Nora's smile is tight, but that is just how she is. Mama used to say not to mind it, so I never do. Arcadia is long gone; I don't blame her. The other girls avoid the elders unless summoned. They are busy. We're not to waste their time.

Nora steps forward, reaches out, cupping my face. "You are freezing, little one." She strokes my skin softly, so tenderly that my heart melts. I drink up every ounce of affection I can get. I miss Mama every day. Grief is a living, breathing creature inside me, a beast that never truly sleeps.

"How about you come inside?" Nora murmurs, her thumbs smoothing over my cheekbones. "Warm yourself."

Nora says not to cry. Crying is a weakness, and it will not bring Mama back.

I still cry.

Alone, in the dark. With Ollie curled against me, or Arcadia's hand in mine.

Nora is right. Crying does nothing.

And yet, I cannot stop.

She takes my hand. Her grip is firm—final—like she has decided something for me again. I let her lead me across the main yard, toward the building that houses her office. This time, she does not take me upstairs.

She leads me down.

A door I have never touched: red wood, forbidden to all but the elders. She opens it without hesitation, and I step inside before I can think the better of it, before I can give action to the deep tug in my gut attempting to force me to back away.

Soon, the air begins to change.

What little warmth the world had above vanishes as we descend. The stone steps spiral downward to an underground system of tunnels.

The scent of iron. Damp Stone. Still water.

The tunnels stretch ahead, lined with flickering sconces that cast long shadows against the tan rock. I wonder who carved these halls, who dug through the earth to shape them, how old they are, and why they even exist.

We take the left fork, and the air grows heavier.

The passage widens into a cavern, its ceiling jagged with large amethyst crystals jutting down like fangs. Thin rivulets of liquid seep into the stone, dripping into a pool of dark water. As I stare at the water, pin-like prickles of awareness spread across my body.

Not right, not natural. My magic stirs, awakening in response.

Nora does not stop.

She leads me past the water, past the crystals, toward something... out of place. A living space?

I see a deep-red rug, circular and worn at the edges; a dilapidated stone fireplace; an old loveseat, its leather flaking like dried skin; and a low wooden table, dark and squat and thick with dust.

Still, something is wrong here; I feel it in my bones.

"Elanora...I thought we were going to get warm?" My voice is barely a whisper, my fingers tightening around hers as unease prickles up my spine.

This chamber is certainly not warm. The winter months have frozen the ground above, but here, beneath the earth, the chill feels...unnatural.

Nora's thumb caresses the back of my hand, coaxing me to press on.

She leads me to the circular red carpet, its surface marked with strange runes, symbols I do not recognize.

This is not a place for warmth.

She sinks first, then she gently tugs my hands, guiding me to sit before her.

"I will make you warm," she murmurs, her voice softer than I've ever heard. "You will never go cold again. Never go hungry. The only hunger you will know is the drive to be more, to do more, to go further than anyone else you encounter."

"You are so rare Millie."

Nora's fingers glide across my cheek, tucking a loose curl behind my ear.

"I know Mama is not here and I'm so sorry."

Her voice stirs something deep in my chest. My throat tightens. My eyes sting with tears I try not to shed.

"That mage will pay for what he did to our family. You may even be the one to make him pay one day. Who knows?"

A tear finally falls. My weakness exploited in front of my elder just as it was exploited the night the mage took everything from me.

For Mama and my sisters, I would make him pay.

"For now, we must focus on our future. You are a big part of that."

Her tone shifts, as if this isn't a choice but a fact.

"Only fifteen, and you are extremely strong." Nora cups my face, "Not since your mother has our coven seen such power. And even she was not nearly what you are. What you will become."

Her eyes gleam with intensity, locking onto mine. As she speaks, I understand the desire in her eyes. Not unkind, rather, it's an expectation.

Purpose.

Her pride in me means everything. And in these moments, I feel worthy.

"I will help make you stronger. You trust me, yes?"

Her voice weaves through me so easily. Silken. Coaxing.

I nod before I even think.

"Of course, I love you," I squeeze her hand trying to reassure her.

"Of course you do," Nora smiles warmly.

She releases my hands, raising one toward the ceiling.

Beneath the amethyst crystals, the water stirs with a ripple, a shift. It rises.

A single tendril spirals up from the pool, slithering through the air like a living thing. I watch, until it coils into her palm.

It changes. The liquid solidifies, stretching its form and revealing a base, a stem, and then the cup.

It's a chalice born from nothing. Yet, there is something awful about its surface.

I trace the engravings—a faceless creature with a mouth open wide. There are no eyes. Its arms—four of them—are clawed and jagged. The depiction is craved in jagged scribbles. The lines are too faint to form a clear image in the chaos, but a chill crawls up my spine.

The stem is bone. The base is a fragment of a human skull.

Slowly, the cup fills. The liquid is thick, black, and slick as oil. My breath tightens. My heartbeat pounds.

Everything in me screams—run. Like a ship's horn in the fog blasting in my head.

Something in here is wrong. Deeply, irreparably wrong

The tendril retracts, sliding back into the pond. The water ripples and then stills, as if nothing had disturbed it at all.

Nora lowers the cup to my lips.

"Drink," she murmurs. Her voice is smooth and unshakable. There's no room for argument.

"Drink to never go hungry, to never go cold, to never let your coven die again—"

"To avenge your Mama."

Her eyes do not waver.

I do not want to need for things.

I do not want this emptiness.

I do not want to be weak ever again.

I do not want to let Mama down.

With a shaking hand I reach out. My fingers brush the chalice stem; it's deathly cold. A grimace twists my face as the chill bites deep, sinking into my bones. Even the snow outside—the mounds of snow gathered with my bare hands—could not compare.

"Your mama would be so proud of you." Nora whispers.

A kiss presses against the crown of my head. Tears fall down my cheeks; I do not wipe them away.

The icy rim of the chalice presses to my lips. I drink.

The moment the thick sludge slides down my throat, my body revolts. It is filth—rot and decay. My stomach heaves, my throat constricting as nausea slams into me.

Swallow.

I force it down.

The weight of it settles in my gut like lead. For Mama. She would be proud. Nora will be proud. The mantra hammers against my skull. My throat constricts, the bile rising in my throat.

No. *I am worthy.*

I swallow the vomit that burns its way up, choking on it as it mixes with the tainted liquid already inside me.

My body betrays me.

My legs and arms tremble. Everything shakes.

The chalice slips from my fingers.

Nora catches it.

Her grip finds my jaw, tilting my head back, and forces my lips apart.

She pours, and the rest of it floods in.

My body seizes, convulsing against the floor. My shoulders jerk, my spine arches, the air burns in my lungs.

Nora's grip tightens on the back of my head, holding me still as the last of the sludge slides down.

She covers my nose and mouth.

"Swallow. Do not dare spit it out," she commands.

Her eyes shift but I cannot understand how.

I swallow—but I do not mean to.

I need air, I cannot breathe.

The moment my throat bobs, she releases me.

I gasp, sucking in breath too fast, too sharp, and the world spins. My limbs collapse.

I hit the floor.

My head cracks against the thin carpet, the impact sending a shock of pain down my spine.

Heat.

Something warm and sticky spreads beneath me.

Blood.

The pounding in my ears slows.

My heart...slows

Why?

Why...slowing...?

...heart...?

slow...

I kneel in the blood-soaked ruins of my home. Red rains down on me. Thick, warm—endless.

My mother lies beneath me, unmoving. She's still warm. She can't be gone.

"Please get up."

The copper tang of blood chokes the air. The crackling of flames devours the silence.

Beasts linger in the shadows around me. Fangs flash. Claws tear. Screams cut short,

They are feasting.

I lift my head, panic clawing at my ribs.

How am I here?

This happened before. Yet, I'm here again.

The massive beast crashes through the temple roof, the impact rattling the ground.

Cage sits atop it.

This is where fear should take me, where despair should shatter me.

Something is different this time.

Power courses through my veins.

As I rise into the air, a slow, wicked smile spreads across my lips. A voice purrs up my spine like a whisper wrapped in silk.

It does not belong to me, nor anyone I know.

"Kill him."

Dark and thick with pleasure, her voice purrs seductively and I feel compelled to obey.

And I will. Gladly.

I raise my hand, feeling the power expand and consume me.

The fabric of the sky rips apart at my call. A jagged tear in the heavens splits open like a wound.

Tendrils of light spill from it—not golden, not warm, but raw, searing destruction.

Lightning obeys me.

It slams down mercilessly, burning white-hot as it tears through Cage's body. The thunderous boom roars in triumph, echoing like laughter.

My laughter.

I watch with utter delight as he burns—cremates—his form, crumbling into nothing but scattered ash, and his dragon dissipating along with him.

I laugh maniacally, my chest rising and falling with exhilaration.

This is what power feels like.

I turn, my gaze seeking another target.

The beasts. They still tear everything in sight. My rage knows no bounds as I bring light to the place.

Light does not always bring life.

It can be death.

And tonight, it will rain down upon those who hurt the ones I love.

I throw my arms wide, spinning in circles, letting the red rain soak my skin.

Their snarls warp, stretch, and twist.

Screams replace them.

I stop.

I stand—not on a war-torn battlefield, but in a village torn through by flame and horror.

The bodies are not beasts...they are people—a charred ocean of corpses—blackened by my own lighting. The scent of their burnt flesh clogs my throat.

Shouting rises above the storm. Villagers—the ones who still stand—brandish weapons, their screams filled with raw hatred.

Slurs. Curses.

They see me as a monster. I am one.

The priest steps forward, leading them with his cross held by trembling hands. His voice, however, does not tremble, but the quiver in his bottom lip hints he is not as unaffected as he pretends to be. He holds his ground, shouting prayers and wielding holy water. His faith fortifies them.

Fools. I am already in your minds.

Their fear and anger are thick, curling through my senses. It feeds me. Fuels me.

A wild laugh bubbles from my throat; the sound has a dark cadence.

Not mine, or is it?

The voice is there again. It's feline and silken, rubbing against my mind like a cat arching into a touch.

"Vermin, livestock." Her words slither through me, curling into every crevice of my thoughts.

"They were made for you. To be consumed. To make you stronger."

The chanting begins as a single murmur and then as many.

A chorus. A roar.

"They kill your kind. They have always killed your kind."

"Cage is one of them. A mage stole what you loved. Mages love humans."

"Take, Millicent."

"Take."

The moment snaps.

I lunge.

Sickle blades—black as hunger, sharp as a whisper—curl into my hands, though I do not remember summoning them.

I know intrinsically they are mine.

My body moves before I think, like a predator finally unleashed.

I rip them apart.

One: a body split at the waist.

Two: a head rolling into the dirt.

Three: ribbons of flesh unwinding from bone.

I am unstoppable. Wading through the blood, I bathe in their screams.

The hunger begins as a slow, gnawing ache, which soon becomes an unbearable thirst. My mouth feels dry, and my gums ache.

I can hear them. Their hearts. Beating. Calling.

"Feed," she coaxes

I know what she means; the words are inside me.

I move without thought, without hesitation.

A grin spreads across my face. The last of them scatter, but one remains: the priest, clutching his cross like the wooden prop will save him.

Fool, your gods have abandoned you.

He sees what I am; he knows.

He lunges, pressing the cross to my chest.

It burns. Not life fire—deeper. As if something inside me writhes beneath it.

Odd.

I hiss, recoil, but I do not retreat.

The wooden symbol is nothing. He is nothing.

I grab his wrist, twisting and bending until the bones snap and his tendons tear.

His cry—his *chorus*—sings to me.

I loom over him, instinct guiding me. My grip sinks into his hair, forcing his head back. His pulse flutters against his throat, rapid and weak.

Begging.

I smile.

And I bite.

Fangs—I have fangs—sink deeply, rupturing his artery and splitting his flesh.

Blood rushes into my mouth and down my chin, covering me in warmth like a soft blanket against my skin.

The hollowness is gone.

I feel right. I feel whole. This sense rises deep within me until...pain.

My shoulder suddenly contorts, convulsing as though it were not mine, and suddenly the world tilts.

Darkness crawls at the edges of my periphery, and the chanting fades into static.

And then...nothing.

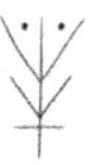

CHAPTER 12

Cage

W E RECEIVED INTEL FROM THE PERIMETER GUARDS on the eastern side of the city—near Briarmere Forest—that those cattle had been found slaughtered. Kalix was the first to get the news and had already geared up to investigate.

I set out through the halls, searching for Millicent. She had taken to eating her dinners outside, and I knew exactly where to find her.

Stepping through an open archway, I emerge into the crisp night air, and the garden unfolds before me in moonlit silence. Sure enough, my guess is correct. Obsidian-black curls spill over the back of the stone bench. The unruly depth of their darkness is unmistakable.

"Up, little witch. Dinner is over...we need to go." My voice is firm, loud enough to carry over the bench as I approach.

She does not move. She doesn't snap at me.

Odd.

We have been avoiding each other, and I welcomed the reprieve while it lasted. But there was work to be done, and she had a purpose here—whether she liked it or not—whether I liked it or not. We cannot afford to dance around each other indefinitely.

"Le strange," I call out louder, my voice cutting through the stillness as I move around the bench.

No response.

My irritation sharpens. "Quit playing games," I snap, stepping in front of her.

Then I see it.

Her hands clutch her knees so tightly that her knuckles have turned bone white. Her eyes—normally burning with defiance—are empty voids locked on the darkness ahead.

Expecting to see something, I follow her gaze into the garden.

Nothing.

"Well? What the hell is it, witch?" My impatience flares. Crouching to her height, I snap my fingers in front of her face.

She jerks back, her eyes suddenly sharpening into focus, back to the ice blue I'm familiar with from years ago. A sharp inhale rattles her chest as she gasps for air, like someone resurfacing after being held underwater too long.

Panic.

A raw vulnerability flickers in her eyes, something I didn't think possible before. A crack in the iron fortress that she wears like armor. It's fleeting, as in the next breath; rage floods in, swallowing the fear as her defenses snap back into place.

Before I can react, she shoves me hard.

I stumble back, landing unceremoniously on my ass.

She points a finger at me and yells, "What the hell!"

Her cheeks are flushed, but whether it's from anger, embarrassment or something else entirely, I can't tell.

"I said your name three times!" I snap back angrily. "What the hell was that—spacing out like some crazy bitch."

Millicent blinks, the last traces of confusion flickering across her face before she wipes it away, masking herself once more. She does this

constantly, removing emotions like discarding a worn cloak. It makes me wonder...

What does she really feel?

Nora never felt anything. Is her spawn the same?

"Forget it," I huff, brushing the grass from my clothes, as I rise. "There's been a string of cattle slaughtered. We need to investigate. Lately, creatures have been stirring up trouble as they have been pushed out from their natural territories." It's admittedly becoming more prevalent and a larger pain in my ass. The horror scenes these things leave behind are becoming more gruesome and are putting the South more at risk with each passing week. "Every time, we've found something— some magical marker, deformity, or twisted evolutionary trait. Iris has been cataloging the changes." My voice lowers slightly, "Whatever the North is doing, it's corrupting nature itself."

The weight of my words lingers between us.

Millicent slides her feet down from the bench, standing in a single fluid motion. She smooths the skirts of her gown, the moonlight catching on the silver swirls of her witch marks.

"Well then, why are we standing here?" She says decidedly, "Lead the way."

I let my eyes trail over her attire; it's practical in some ways. The black gown clings to her bust before loosening into a flowing fabric that drapes down to her ankles. My eyes glaze over the slit that exposes her leg, revealing a dagger strapped to her thigh. *Smart girl.* My gaze continues upward, assessing critiquing. Of course, she'd leave her shoulders bare, displaying her markings like a challenge to any passerby.

"My eyes are up here," she says dryly, throwing my own words from just a few days ago back at me.

I smirk. "Simply noting your dagger," I reply, matching her tone. "And the fact you are wearing a dress to combat. If these creatures are hellion in nature—" My voice dips low, daring to take a step closer to her, "—their blood will burn off all this pretty skin of yours. But, by all

means, if that is your plan, go ahead. Wear your pretty little dress. I'd be quite entertained."

Her expression darkens, suspicion narrowing her eyes.

I lean down a breath away from her face, letting my smile shift.

Then, without warning, she moves.

Her leg hooks under mine, her body slamming into my chest with surprising force. The world tilts and I hit the ground hard, knocking the breath from my lungs. Before I can recover, cold steel presses against my throat. She straddles my chest pinning my arms down with her knees, she leans into the blade, warning me.

"You dare talk down to me?" she hisses. Her voice like a venomous whisper dripping onto my skin, "You forget yourself in this golden little castle. This is right where you belong—beneath me." Her eyes burn with fury, a raw delicious rage. "Actually, I wish you were six feet deeper."

Her breath is warm against my face. My own fury stirs, like an old hunger whispering at the edges of my mind.

I almost want to smile.

Clever little witch.

She should know better than to think she has the upper hand.

A slow hunger stirs deep within me, whispering demands like an old addiction. If I could just kill this witch and drain her power, I would. I could take more. Be more. The thoughts coil around my mind, its grip tightening with every passing moment.

Aggression hums through my veins; instincts sharpen. My hands move before I can register it, sliding beneath the hem of her gown, trailing up toned legs to thick thighs. I grip hard, digging into her flesh, feeling the heat of her smooth skin. An anchor. A claim.

A challenge.

A slow smirk pulls at my lips. "I appreciate a woman who takes initiative," I murmur, my voice steady, unwavering, even as her blade kisses my throat. Her eyes burn into mine, unyielding, daring.

This little witch might actually do it.

The steel presses harder, biting into my skin. My smirk spreads wider.

"I will cut your tongue out, mage," she hisses.

I roll my eyes. "How original."

Her muscles tighten around me like a silent threat. I am not one to be intimidated. No one has challenged me in years.

She is like a fun little mouse, and I am ever a patient lion.

"Hearing you drone on with empty threats is getting boring." My voice is flat, unimpressed. She thinks a dagger will keep me at her mercy. Laughable.

We have more pressing matters, and I've entertained this delusion of hers long enough.

With a single shift of my weight, I push up, making her gasp. My grip remains firm on her back as I maneuver her beneath me and press her back against the earth. Her previous position leaves her legs spread against my chest. Her knees bend, and her legs hang over my shoulders despite keeping the dagger pressed to my skin.

I cage her in, forearms braced beside her head, suffocating the space between us with my presence.

She glares, but I don't miss the slight heat rising to her cheeks. *Interesting.*

I lean in, my lips grazing the shell of her ear as I whisper, "I was looking at your dagger." My voice is deliberately smooth. "It's exquisite."

Cruelty pulls at my lips.

"You, on the other hand? What is there to look at?"

I let the words settle, waiting for them to cut.

"You are nothing but an empty husk, surviving off the harm you bring others. Nora's favorite, I hear." My silver eyes narrow as my old hatred stirs. "You bitches deserve to burn in the pits of hell you were created in. Hell—go lower. You probably are abysmal." Burning her and Nora, what an eventful show that would be.

I wish to capture their cries and play them back like a sweet melody, soothing me into sweeter dreams and sweeter situations than the one I currently find myself in.

Millicent's body coils beneath me, her muscles tensing as she prepares to strike.

Such a predictable, murderous little creature.

Before she can act, I grab her arm, twisting before she can drive the blade into my throat. The dagger tumbles from her grasp, and I chuckle darkly.

"Bad girl." I pin her arm over the other and lean onto her, trapping her, enjoying the fury flickering in her eyes.

My other hand rises, plucking the dagger from the grass. Slowly, I trace the cold steel over the bare skin of her chest, watching as goosebumps rise in its wake. Her breath shudders, but her glare never wavers. The heat from her gaze would surely set me on fire if she had such capabilities, her mind ripping mine into ribbons if a crack in my shields occurs.

I press the flat edge of the blade lower, following the delicate line of her sternum.

"Fuck you, Cage." Her voice is low, growling from the back of her throat. Rage thrums beneath her skin, and I sense her magic stirring to life. Her eyes flickered like the first embers of a fire. "In the end, I'll make sure you all burn."

Well, that will not do.

I continue my path, tracing an idle pattern against her ribs, pausing just over her heart. I could end this little game with a slight push through the fabric. Bury the blade deep and let the devil bleed out beneath me, just as I am sure she has done to hundreds.

"Behave, little witch." My voice drops low. I click my tongue, the same way I do when correcting a hound that doesn't know its place. I decide it is time to stop messing with her.

She stiffens.

I am already bored with this.

Sighing that our game is over, I let the dagger slip back into its sheath on her thigh and secure the strap.

My fingers work through the leather, glancing over the inner curve of her leg. I don't miss the way her breath catches, just for a moment. A small shiver runs through her muscles.

Oh, this was delicious. She fights so hard, as though she revolts at my touch, but her body betrays her. She must loathe herself for this.

A slow smirk curves my lips. Good.

My voice lowers to something thick and taunting, a husky whisper that brushes against the small space between us. "Tell me, Millicent— have you been properly fucked? Or does no one dare? Asking a Mage to, low bar for you, yeah?"

Her face flushes crimson, yet fury still burns in her eyes.

"I don't want to sleep with you!" Her words snap like a whip. She pushes against me, her thighs flexing against my waist as she struggles, her hands shoving at my chest in a futile attempt to knock me off.

Too easy.

I manage to seize both wrists with one hand, pinning them above her head. Her arms are stretched taut, halting her escape; her body writhes beneath me, cementing her helplessness.

I chuckle, low and dark, leaning in. "Oh, but little witch, you're fighting too hard for something you claim not to want."

I drink it in.

"Tell me," I purr, my hand gliding lower, tracing the inside of her thigh. "If I slide my fingers between these pretty little thighs, will I find you dripping in need?"

Her body reacts before her words, her muscles tensing beneath my touch. My hand slowly slides up her inner thigh.

I continue, like a drunk eager for more.

Her pupils dilate, and she holds her breath, just for a second.

There it is.

Satisfaction curls deep in my chest as my fingers skim the thin fabric of her panties, feeling the wet heat beneath. A sharp inhale escapes her lips.

"Lace," I smirk. "My favorite. Did you wear this for me?"

"Get the fuck off me." She squirms viciously, trying to get free, but it is useless.

I slide one finger to the center of the lace, applying just enough pressure to make her squirm.

"Just as I thought," I taunt. "You are weeping for me to stretch and fill you."

I hook a finger into the fabric, pulling it down just enough to make her think—just for a second—that I might touch her.

Then I release it.

The fabric snaps back into place, earning a sweet little gasp to breach those full lips of hers she was attempting to keep sealed shut. Her body wants, even if her mind does not.

Before she can lash out and actually begin using her magic, I deliver a quick, teasing slap over her needy mound.

I grin down at her, savoring it.

She can fight. She can spit, curse, and claw all she likes, but cannot lie to me.

"Now go change, unless you plan to let the beasts fuck you. I hear witches are into that."

I wink and remove my hand from her heart and release her arms.

The slap comes fast and hard, the sting spreading across my cheek before I fully register the impact.

A sharp little thing.

I rub my jaw, amusement curling in my chest even as I rise, finally giving her the space she craves.

"No more games. We need to go." My tone slips into my calm, collected mask. The demon sneering up at me is only one of the many plaguing these lands.

Millicent's breathing is ragged, her fingers tremble before clenching them into fists. "If you ever put your hands on me again, agreements be damned...I will incinerate you."

I don't chase after her; the truth of her words is settling. Some great beings remake the world; others burn it. A split second of dread runs up my spine, chased by an odd sense of knowing. An instinctual certainty—like how one knows their heart will beat without thought, or their next breath will come.

She will burn it all. She will be the end.

I exhale a low chuckle. "Say that when I can't still smell you on my fingers."

Her stride falters—for a moment—before she disappears into the darkness.

Control and dominance come in many forms. She shows her weaknesses so easily, handing them to me like weapons.

I find it comical.

Since she arrived, I've been studying her, compiling her traits, learning her character, and tracking her every reaction. She can wield hate, anger, and violence like second nature, but she cannot handle touch, softness, or herself.

Even as the sting of her slap lingers, I know I made my point.

Her words only confirmed what I suspected: she is like Nora. And I will not let another Nora exist.

When all of this is over, she will burn. I will make sure of it.

<h1 style="text-align:center">CHAPTER 13</h1>

<h1 style="text-align:center">Millicent</h1>

I CHANGE, SO I DON'T HAVE MY SKIN ROTTED OR BURNED OFF. As if I'd ever fight in a dress. The very notion is idiotic, and his presumption just pissed me off more than I care to admit.

Sometimes, my memories pull me under. They washed over me not as passing thoughts but as living, breathing moments. I feel them, see them, and hear them as if I never left. I had been drowning in them, lost in the storm of a day that reshaped my life.

The first necessary step to power.

I never heard Cage call my name or noticed his presence. I recall only the sharp snapping of his fingers in my face, dragging me back. The vulnerability of it—the thought of him watching me, observing my mind fracture in real-time—makes me want to puke.

His hands on me evoked a mix of nausea and feelings too shameful to name. It's not that my darker sexual appetites shame me. It's that he baited them out. I don't want to feel any lust when he is around.

Shoving the feelings down, I slip into my usual combat attire: my trusty black bodysuit, form-fitting and practical, paired with a harness for my sickle blades. My fingers work through the motions, tightening straps and fastening buckles. My hair is pulled into two tight braids.

I follow the unmistakable sound of Iris's shrill, high-pitched giggle. It leads me to a room that feels more like a lavish sitting area than a meeting room: plush red couches, a golden bar gleaming under warm light, and a grand fireplace. Kalix sits at the bar, his posture impatient as he swirls whiskey around in his glass. Iris, ever excitable, hops off the couch and bounds toward me the moment she spots me.

"There you are! I've been waiting to explain some things to you," Iris exclaims, her green eyes sparkling with excitement. She swings the satchel off her shoulder, delicately pulling out an array of tools: a vial, a syringe, a shallow dish, surgical blades, and some other implements I don't recognize.

"Use the syringes to collect any gooey or bloody samples—drool, slime, I don't care!" She holds up the vial next and a dish. "Vial for liquids, dish for solids. You can use the blades to scrape off anything useful. The more samples, the better, since we're still figuring out what matters most." Her eyes flick to my hands. "I'd advise wearing gloves. If you don't have any, I brought extras; they're on the table."

She shoves everything back into the satchel and hands it to me. Adjusting the strap so it won't hinder my movements, I nod my head toward the table. "Gross. Will do...and thanks for the gloves."

As I glance to the side, I notice Kalix is completely absorbed in his whiskey. A question rises unbidden, pressing at my lips before I can stop it.

"Why are you here?"

Iris stills for half a second before offering me a small, knowing smile. "It's honestly a long and boring story. I wasn't brought here against my will. I chose to find my own happiness." Her tone is genuine and sincere, but something unspoken flickers in her eyes—a sadness buried beneath her practiced ease.

She keeps her voice low, as if reluctant to invite the weight of the conversation in the room. I appreciate it.

"You are a witch? Your coven? And these are all humans?" I ask in disbelief. The very idea of leaving one's sisters—to live among vermin—is unfathomable.

Iris meets my eyes and doesn't hesitate. "I am a witch," she says steadily. "And a proud one at that, but I choose my family. My coven, they're not my family." Her tone hardens like iron beneath silk. "Cage, Felix, Kalix—they're my family. You may not understand, but I hope, for your sake, that one day you do. Our covens are not all there is. What they do is cruel. We can choose our lives. We can choose our family... shit, who we love even!" Emotion thickens her voice, threatening to spill over. "And, for once, Millicent, I get to decide what I wear, where I go. And no elders control me here."

I fold my arms, and my tone is colder than I intend. "I could never betray my family like that."

The words are a reflex, ingrained through years of devotion. A coven is sacred. You live and die for your sisters. You give everything for them.

Iris's expression hardens, but there's still something flickering behind her eyes, raw and unguarded. "I wish they felt the same about us." Then she excuses herself, sighing. Her exit is heavy. She's frustrated. At the doorway, she pauses just for a second. When she glances back at me, there's something in her gaze.

Pity.

I don't understand it. The thought burrows under my skin. I refuse to acknowledge it. Instead, I walk to the table, slipping on a pair of gloves. The silence lingers a little too long before Kalix's voice, rougher than Cage's smoother cadence, cuts through the air.

Kalix pauses, running a hand through his hair as he swirls his whiskey. "Iris does not need me to protect her, but my baby is a crier. If you make her cry, it won't end well for any of us." His voice is gruff but carries an air of affection. "You don't know her story, and she doesn't know yours. She wasn't always like this. She had dark days; her coven life was hard."

He swirls the amber liquid in his glass before downing it in one swift motion. Setting the empty glass onto the bar, he rolls his shoulders, relaxing his muscles.

"I don't hate witches, Millicent. Hell, not even the Le Strange ones." His gaze flicks toward me. "I've seen girls like you. Hardened into weapons, until there's nothing left. I'm not saying I know your story, but I will say, I don't hate you for it. Because we have all been in dark places and done even darker things."

My eyebrows pinch together, not understanding why we were still on this topic.

"I haven't been in any dark places," I state, as a matter of fact. "Not outside of what others have inflicted. I don't know about other covens, but mine's the best. The strongest." Pride settles deep in my chest. I turn to face him.

Kalix huffs a quiet laugh and shifts on his stool, crossing one ankle over his knee. Leaning back against the bar, he props his elbow up. His posture is loose, but his smirk is sharp. "Okay, denial, we don't have to talk about it." He speaks smoothly, but there's something teasing in it— like he knows something I don't.

Then, without missing a beat, "Now tell me, have you really fucked a guy and eaten his liver to have a baby?"

I choke on nothing. His tone takes me off guard. "What the hell? Do I give that kind of aura off?"

Kalix snickers, his grin widening. "I've heard that witches do it. Gotta make sure we're safe. It's just a general screening question."

He lifts an imaginary notepad and pretends to write something down. "Next one. Do you turn into a pig on a full moon?"

I snort at the foolishness of his question, "Yeah, totally. I grow wings, too," I mumble sarcastically.

"Uh-huh. I see." Kalix pretends to scribble more notes. "Terrible news—you're delusional. I'm afraid you suffer from pig-related hallucinations. When did this desire to be a pig first start? Is it a fetish? This is a safe place." He nods solemnly, like a concerned doctor.

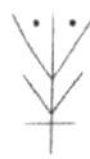

I can't help the laugh that escapes me, masking it with a cough as I smooth my expression back into its usual blank canvas. Kalix catches it anyway, his smug smile widening just as Cage strides into the room, looking ready for a fight.

His presence shifts the mood entirely.

My eyes flick to his armor, and I'm curious whether his attire is made from the onyx scales of his dragon. The plating covers his torso and legs, bound together at the seams with thick leather. The same dark material extends up his neck and down his arms, clinging tightly to his frame and leaving little of his skin exposed. His sword, ever present at his hip, gleams under the lamplight.

"Let's head out," he commands, turning on his heel without waiting for acknowledgement.

I grip the leather strap of my satchel, falling into step behind him with Kalix close behind.

Outside, three horses await us, each a varying shade of brown. I step up to the smallest one, judging it to be the fastest and, more importantly, the easiest to mount. Slipping my foot into the stirrup, I swing my leg over the saddle in one fluid motion. I shift my position with a firm grip on the horn.

Beside me, Kalix and Cage mount their steeds with practiced grace. Without a word, Cage urges his horse forward, and we follow. The heavy gates groan as they rise, and, trading glances, we ride into the night.

Exiting the castle under cover of darkness is bleak. The plains stretch out before us, dotted with sparse trees swaying in the breeze. We cross a small bridge and the landscape changes; scattered houses soon give way to a dense cluster of towering apartment-style homes. Even at this hour, the city is alive. Tavern music spills into the streets, mingling with the laughter of drunks and the distant clatter of hooves on cobblestone.

As we ride deeper, the houses become smaller, the spaces between them widening. The noise fades. The air thickens with the scent of

damp earth, hay, and livestock. My horse snorts. A sharp, acrid scent—fertilizer—makes my nose wrinkle just as my mount rears. It stomps its hooves in protest.

Cage reins in his own agitated steed. "We go on foot from here. The animals won't get any closer. They know something isn't right."

I glance at him, then at Kalix's horse. Both are equally unsettled.

"Shhhh," I murmur, running a soothing hand down my horse's neck. She exhales sharply, but her body relaxes under my touch. Slipping from the saddle, I land lightly, bending my knees to absorb the impact. I lead her a few steps back and leave her to graze.

Cage and Kalix do the same, their whispered words of reassurance barely carrying over the thick silence.

I inhale deeply, focusing. My senses extend outward, seeking, but there is nothing. Nothing beyond the presence I've come to recognize as Cage's.

Something is out there, and the horses know it.

Not trusting what my senses fail to detect, I move toward the pasture. A flaking wooden fence marks the boundary. The cattle were likely grazing when they were attacked. The moon provides just enough light to see, and my dark vision sharpens the shadows. Still, I keep my awareness stretched, reaching out to avoid any surprises.

It's too quiet.

No bird. No rustling in the trees. Just the ceaseless drone of crickets, blissfully unaware in their small world, oblivious to what has taken place.

Bracing a hand against the wooden plank, I vault over the fence, landing in tall grass that sways against my shins. Boots thud behind me—Kalix and Cage are following.

Then I see them.

A cluster of dark mounds. Six, at least. I beeline toward them. Whatever the horses sense, I don't feel it yet. Is it too faint? Waxing and waning in and out of range? Or is Cage's presence drowning me out, his magic saturating the air like ink spilling in to water?

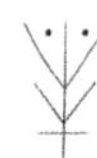

"No sulfur smell this time. Looks like an animal got to them," Kalix observes, stepping up to the first carcass.

The cow lies on its side, its body torn open. Its internal organs are missing—sucked clean out. Only shattered bones and torn flesh remain, as if something with a massive maw took a single bite and hollowed it from the inside out. Its eyes are glazed over, flies buzzing hungrily around the exposed tissue. Some preen themselves on its brown coat.

I crouch beside it, narrowing my eyes as I study the remains. There's nothing left but the ligaments and tendons that hang loosely like ribbons against torn muscles. "Does it usually smell of sulfur?"

Kalix kneels next to me, slipping his satchel off his shoulder as he retrieves a silver dish. "Honestly? There are so many variations, we still don't know what's consistent. Maybe you'll have some insight, dark girl." He wiggles his eyebrows, smirking slightly as he flips open the dish and unsheathes a surgical blade.

Rising to my feet, I cross another cluster of bodies moving in the opposite direction of Cage. My eyes scan the ground for clues. The field has been walked over by farm animals and workers. No distinct prints can be made out.

My mind riffles through bestiaries, piecing together what little I know. Many creatures prefer organs for their high nutrition value, but the method of extraction here is unnatural.

I crouch again, my fingers ghost over the sheared flesh where the body was torn apart. The angles of the wounds suggest multiple creatures—or our lovely beasty has multiple mouths, tearing from various parts at once.

Hell, it could even be something worse. Something with a maw that unhinges, swallowing its prey from the inside out.

That leaves a bigger question.

How did no one see or hear this?

The farmstead is distant enough that the owners were spared the

sight, but I can't believe that cows were silent when they died. They cry. They thrash. They fight.

So why was there no struggle?

My gaze drifts past the farmhouse, across the open land, to the tree line Cage had identified earlier—Briarmere Forest. It isn't nearly as menacing as the Twisted Hollows that surround my coven. There, magic of that magnitude warps nature into something unrecognizable. There is no such magic here.

Or is there?

The North is up to something. Cage mentioned mutations—evolutions—that have begun reshaping creatures into things he has never encountered before.

They still don't know the full extent of what's happening, and they certainly haven't explained everything to me.

That needs to change.

Pondering this, I move toward the forest's edge. My eyes adjust swiftly to the darkness, sharpening the details of the towering trees. Their trunks stand far enough apart that I can see between them, unobstructed by dense brush.

I summon Ollie with a thought. A moment later, he materializes onto my shoulder, kicking his little feet in the air.

"Me Misses! Midnight stroll?" His screeching squeak rings in my ears as he twirls a lock of my hair around his finger.

"Ollie, something killed those cows," I tilt my head toward the mutilated corpses then gesture to the woods. "Find it."

"Of course, Me Misses!" He giggles, rocking himself forward before tumbling off my shoulders and vanishing into the dark.

I follow at a leisurely pace, though I can't see him. I don't need to. Our bond pulses in my mind, keeping me acutely aware of his location. His wings may be small, but he is fast (and lazy).

His movements erratic, Ollie is teleporting from space to space in quick bursts, covering a vast amount of ground at an incredible pace.

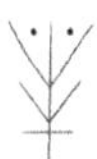

Lazy, but effective.

Then I feel it—a spike in his curiosity. His voice pushes through the link like a whisper against my thoughts. "Me Misses, come look."

The eagerness in his tone pulls at me, his insistent tug on our bond pushing me to move faster.

Something's there.

CHAPTER 14

Millicent

DODGING SOME FALLEN LOGS AND TWISTED ROOTS, I push forward until, eventually, the forest thins to a clearing. Ollie perches on a stump, his dark eyes darting toward the ivy-cloaked cave nestled on the hillside. It's nearly invisible against the moss-covered stone.

"There are two men in the fields. Go get them," I order, waving him off before turning to the cave.

As I push aside the emerald ivy, a wave of something dark and decrepit slams into me. *There you are.* My fingers tighten around the steel hilts of my blades as I unsheathe them from my back, my muscles tense in preparation. Within, the darkness is absolute. No light filters through the dense earth, but it doesn't matter. I don't need it.

As I descend on my mission to find the beast responsible for the massacre, the temperature plummets unnaturally quickly. Frost creeps along my boots like the thin tendrils of ice spiderwebbing across the stone walls. The soil beneath my feet is firm, solid enough that each step echoes faintly.

Then comes the smell: thick, rancid, and clinging to the air like grease. The scent of death. I bring a hand to my nose, but it does little to block the stench.

Something crunches on my next step.

I glance down. Bones—some still clothed in rotting flesh, others stripped bare—litter the floor. With every step, more splinter and snap under my weight.

Still, I press on.

Then, I hear it, a faint broken sob.

A child? No. That's impossible. There's no way a girl wandered down here.

Which means this is either a trap, or this is something that likes to keep its victims alive. A slow-feeding creature, perhaps, but that doesn't fit. Not with the carnage left behind in the fields.

Is this the same beast?

Or am I missing something here?

The passage begins to narrow, the walls tightening around my shoulders. The space shrinks further as I push forward, forcing me to turn sideways to slide between the stones. Dirt breaks loose in dry clumps, flaking into my hair and coating my arms. I take smaller breaths, trying not to inhale the dust.

The sobs grow louder.

The sorrow in them is visceral, each cry drawn out with an aching loneliness.

My arm slides through an opening in the rock, and I pull myself forward, and I find myself in a massive cavern yawning before me.

Immense and sprawling, it dwarfs the passage I just escaped. Five tunnels gape like mouths, stretching into the darkness. The crying spills from the center tunnel. I mark the one to my left mentally as the first tunnel and note the center one as three to help direct myself.

I step forward, quickening my pace, ignoring the brittle crunch of bones. I follow the sobs down the third tunnel, navigating another narrowing passage. Suddenly, I squeeze through a tight gap only to end up in another open chamber.

It's the same one.

The tunnels still gape ahead. The sobs still come from the third.

My grip tightens on my blades. There was no shift—no flicker of runes, no distortion of magic—that I could sense. And yet I looped.

I try the fourth and fifth halls. Same result.

I retrace my steps along the cavern walls, sheathing my blades to run my hands over the stone, searching for hidden runes or markings. I already know this is not practical. The chamber is circular, endless, stretching so high that even my sight cannot pierce the darkness above.

Stalactites hang like jagged fangs, dripping slow streams of cool water from their tips. Below, stalagmites rise in sharp, uneven clusters of miniature mountains, carving out obstacles across the cavern floor. If there are runes, they could be anywhere.

My frustration mounts. I leave the wall, kneeling beside one of the larger stalagmites and running my fingers along its rough surface. Nothing.

Taking a slow breath, I try the first and second tunnels again.

The loop repeats.

How long have I been in here? Something is fraying at the edges of my awareness.

The presence I felt at the mouth of the cave has been shifting, waxing and waning like the ebb and flow of the tide. Has it been an hour? Longer? Losing track of time is never good, especially now that I'm certain:

I'm in something's domain.

There's no curse. No illusion.

Only the most evolved creatures—those whose very existence is steeped in magic—can create a domain like this. Within these domains, reality bends to the creatures' will. They can manipulate space, summon illusion, and distort time itself. The strongest can do even worse: inflict poisons, insanity, curses, compulsion, the list doesn't end.

To test my theory, I turn, scanning the cavern for the hundredth time. Then I see it.

The entrance is gone. Only smooth stone remains.

"Ah, so you know I'm here," I call out—not just to the dark but to what is lurking unseen. My voice echoes through the cavern, swallowed by the silence.

"Come now, don't be shy," I sigh, rolling my shoulders as my patience wears thin. The bones scattered across the floor suddenly make sense. If this thing lures, traps, and simply waits for its prey to starve, that would explain the remains.

Something doesn't add up. A creature capable of controlling a domain this vast shouldn't rely on such a weak method of hunting. This is too...passive.

I spin the ring on my thumb, thinking.

Then the crying grows louder, and so does the sound of footsteps.

I freeze, my eyes snapping toward the third tunnel. Small, shuffling steps grow louder. Slowly, she emerges.

It's a little girl—she couldn't be more than five. Her blonde hair hangs in tangled clumps. A torn brown dress clings to her tiny frame. Her bare feet are blackened, flecked with dried blood, the wounds fresh from the jagged bones underfoot.

Red-rimmed blue eyes stare up at me, filled with tears.

"I w-want m-my m-m-mommy," she stammers, breath hitching between words. "Are you going to take me to her?"

Her voice wobbles, eyes widening with sorrow.

My fingers flex at my sides, but I don't reach for my sickles. Not yet.

"How did you get down here?" I gentle my voice, but my body remains cautious, ready to strike.

The cries I heard earlier didn't sound like a child this young. They were deeper, more developed. Now they've...changed. Adjusted. As if they're guessing what her cry should sound like.

She sniffles, tears spilling down her dirt-smeared cheeks. "Please, I-I'm l-l-lost," she hiccups, clutching her chest as if struggling to breathe. "I'm st-st-stuck, I'm h-hungry. I w-want my m-mommy."

Her small feet shuffle forward toward me, eager for help. She nearly stumbles as her left ankle rolls sharply. Oddly enough, she doesn't react. Doesn't flinch.

She just keeps coming.

Now inches away, I see her clearly. The hair is wrong. Not just tangled or filthy. It's lifeless. Strands grow at unnatural angles, spouting from her scalp like weeds.

She tilts her head, peering up at me. Doe eyes are rimmed with silver tears.

White-glazed. Hollow.

Not hu—

I react instantly.

My fingers reach around the hilt of my crescent blade, pulling it forward in one fluid motion. The steel flashes as I bring it down—aimed at her neck.

My blade never lands. She catches it.

One small, filthy hand clamps around the steel like a vice. My shoulder wrenches as she yanks the weapon from my grip, the sheer force popping the joint out of place. I suck in a sharp breath, but before I can react—

She flings my sickle behind her, treating it like a common dagger.

The steel vanishes into the darkness, clattering against the stone. She doesn't even blink at the gash in her pam where the blade sliced deep.

The crying swells.

Her mouth widens and she lunges, fingers outstretched, nails sharpened and seeking flesh.

I narrowly dodge, twisting to the side as her hands swipe through the space. My boot digs into the packed earth, grounding me as I unsheathe my second blade.

She halts mid-motion.

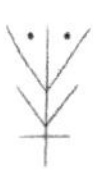

A scream of frustration rips from her throat, and she starts changing. Her arms snap outward, flaring at her sides like the spread of a winged creature ready to take flight.

Joints pop. Bones stretch. Skin tears. Her arms lengthen, skin splitting over the shoulders as new bone pushes through. Her legs follow, ripping open at the calves and quads, the muscle warping—expanding—shifting into a form built for speed.

She drops onto all fours.

Long clawed fingers dig into the stone, locking into the earth. Blood pumps into the spaces around bones as her entire skeletal structure shifts, stretching and adapting for explosive movement. Her spine arches, vertebrae snapping into a more canine-like posture. The monstrosity before me carries the face of a child, but its body now resembles something canine— Lycanthropic in nature.

There are creatures that can mimic human form, some that can change their bodies.

But not like this.

This is something else—an evolution. A forced one.

The same kind of corruption Cage has spoken of. The same kind they still don't fully understand. Of course, Nora desired whatever the North has—it is capable of creation.

Gods create.

The creature lunges, using its new form to close the distance between us instantly. Her cries still echo around the cavern, but I don't run. Instead, I sprint forward to meet her head on, blade aimed straight for the skull.

The impact is sickening. Steel drives into the bone. The curved steel cuts deep, splitting down into the creature's neck.

A shrill screech erupts from her throat. Its front arms thrash violently, trying to dislodge me.

It can't touch me. Every blow lands against a conjured shimmering black orb shield, faint streaks of blue crackling along its surface as it encases me.

I smirk and twist my blade.

The creature's neck gives.

Muscle and sinew shear apart as I shift my weight, bracing my bicep beneath the hilt before wrenching the sickle sword outward in a brutal twist. The maneuver slices cleanly through her neck.

A pool of onyx spews from the side of her neck, bursting in thick, viscous waves after my final strike. The blood sizzles. It splatters against my shield, hissing as it trickles down the barrier. Pieces of her esophagus slip from my blade, and the heaps of tissue hit the ground with a sickening splat.

Her form wavers, as if deciding whether or not it should fall. Then she crumples. No final twitch. Just a hollow collapse.

I let out a slow breath. It's done. My shield retracts. The air shudders as the energy dissipates, leaving only the stink of corpse. I crouch, reaching for my satchel, ready to clean off my blade before the corrosive blood can do any lasting damage. Then—

A loud cry splits the cavern.

Deafening.

The shrilling cry makes the walls shake violently. Dust rains from the ceiling as loose stones crack and drop, shattering upon impact.

My head snaps upwards.

Between two stalactites, something stirs, and I should have seen it before.

Long, deep-violet bat wings unfold from the darkness. Clawed fingers, capable of shredding through reinforced steel, anchor its massive frame.

It was watching me the whole time.

Muscles ripple beneath ashen, scarred flesh, coiled tight beneath its leathery hide. Even the long hairs across its back, when suspended in stillness, mimicked stalactites blending it seamlessly into the cave's canopy.

It moves.

The snarl it releases rattles my bones.

Its gaunt, skeletal face tilts downward, sunken feline-yellow eyes locking on to me with malicious intent. A mouth—too wide, too jagged—parts. Countless rows of needle-thin, yellowed teeth drip with saliva.

This is a Crepitus Vox, but this one is wrong. More advanced. Mutated.

I set my blade down, the threat of corrosion keeping me from sheathing it. Rolling my neck, I loosen the tension, letting the movement travel down to my shoulders, into my arms, and into my fingers.

The air crackles—a whoosh, then a hiss—as onyx and blue flames combust at my fingertips. Flooding the chamber with flickering light.

A chittering pulse fills the air.

It slams into my mind like a hammer. My mental shield shudders, rattling like an earthquake determined to bring the foundations down.

I grit my teeth. Hold strong. **Focus**.

Flames burst from my hands, a violent surge of blue and black. My arms chase the creature's form as it vaults from wall to wall.

It responds instantly. The pulsations increase in frequency, vibrating through the cavern like a war drum. My bones rattle, my arms, my legs going numb.

I persevere. Even mutated, advanced, I can take down a Crep. I've faced worse. Fought worse, and in greater numbers.

I step forward, tracking its movements, and my boot knocks something.

The girl's body.

A wave of cold crashes over me.

No. Something is wrong.

A jagged tear rips through my mental shield. The pulsations flood in, wave after wave. Raw alien pressure slams into my skull and I feel as though it's splitting.

Hunger, so hungry. The thought floods repeatedly to me making my stomach cramp and my mouth salivate. My flames flicker, then extinguish.

I gasp, clutching my head as the world tilts, spins, and distorts. The force digs deeper, wreaking havoc in my mind.

"Dost thou hunger?"

The voice hisses into my mind, a deep and unnatural baritone that slithers through my thoughts like oil. The shock of hearing it—understanding it—nearly drowns out the pain.

Nearly.

Agony slams into my bones. The pressure feels like it cracks my skull, and all at once the pain of a thousand needles pushes through my mind like a pin cushion. My body locks up. Every muscle stiffens, a slow, creeping paralysis spreading through my limbs. My knees buckle. I drop, hitting the ground hard.

"Sweet lamb."

Its voice coils around me, suffocating me, tightening my muscles. The words are mocking, indulgent, as if it's savoring its meal before taking the first bite.

This...

This is worse than I thought.

The mutations are more than what I imagined—far beyond. Telepathy? An entire domain? That shouldn't be possible. How did it even get past my wall?

The girl. Something about her.

I don't have time to figure it out. The Crep moves.

I fall forward, my body completely unresponsive. My vision blurs, but I can still hear it.

The claws scrape against stone as it dismounts from the wall. The ground trembles beneath me. I can feel it approaching. It's coming to feed.

The beast purrs, sniffing the air with great satisfaction. "Lamb for slaughter," it murmurs, inhaling deeply, savoring my scent. "For thee to feast. Born of dark, but not like thee."

I need to move, but I cannot.

Then—

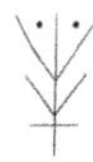

Something else shifts in the shadows. A second presence.

A growl, then the eyes. Sapphire pierces through the darkness, and the Crepitus Vox stops. It sniffs the air. A low, guttural clicking vibrates from its throat in a warning.

It knows.

A new predator is near.

The rotting stench thickens as the Crep steps over me. I want to vomit, but I do not wretch. Its massive weight shifts above my frozen body, pausing as it takes in the new arrival. Not to shield me, but rather to guard its meal.

The shadows suddenly ripple. Oily waves of black smoke twist into a solid form, pooling into the shape of a massive panther. Six long, sinuous snakes protrude from its back, their bodies coiling and flicking as they taste the air.

Its sapphire eyes remain locked on the Crep, sizing up the bigger threat.

Muscles coil.

It pounces, and the Crep lunges to meet it. They clash in a flurry of claws and fangs. Exploding in a flurry of movement, bodies slam into stone, and snarls and screeches tear through the cavern.

I cannot see them anymore. Only the sounds remain.

I lay frozen, staring at the cavern wall, waiting for the victor.

CHAPTER 15

Cage

THE STENCH OF DEAD FLESH HANGS THICK IN THE AIR. The cattle long since dead, their carcasses are now a haven for a magnitude of insects. Flies buzz and burrow into the decaying tissue.

I snap the lid on the final sample dish, sealing away the unnatural blue tissue I've collected. Slipping the dish back into my satchel, I hoist the leather strap onto my shoulder.

A few feet away, Kalix is gagging. His sleeve is pressed against his nose in a futile attempt to block some of the smell. His enhanced sense of smell makes it worse for him, though I can't bring myself to feel sympathy. If anything, the sight of him struggling almost makes me smile.

"If you hurl on the samples, Iris might actually turn you into a common dog," I yell out, watching as he retches again.

Kalix shoots me a scowl, "So she threatens time and time again, yet here I am—man of flesh!" He winks and chuckles, but his amusement is cut short as he gags after inhaling another lungful of decay.

I shake my head, exhaling sharply. Enough distractions. Scanning the area, I motion around us. "Where the hell is our witch?"

Kalix, still regaining his composure, lazily flicks his wrist, pointing a small surgical blade toward the tree line. "She went wandering that way."

I freeze mid motion, deadpan.

"And you did not think to follow her?" I say flatly, but irritation coils beneath my words. "Or even mention it?

Kalix shrugs, still unfazed.

"You simply let her saunter off for a midnight stroll in the woods?"

Kalix begins the tedious task of cleaning his tools, wiping each blade before tucking it into his bag. "She's no prisoner, Cage. Her coven is here to help. And yeah, I question why as much as you do." He throws me a knowing look. "She's cooperating. She has not done anything wild."

He straightens, sliding the satchel onto his shoulder.

I roll my eyes, crossing my arms. "She bit me." I retort. The words come out sharper than I intended, but I don't care.

Kalix smirks, and that damn smirk sees right through me. "I bet you deserved it." His voice is light. "You can be bossy. And an arrogant prick." He pauses, grinning wider. "Who I love, of course!" He raises his hands innocently, but I narrow my eyes, unamused.

"I know the Le Strange coven, and I know your history with them. Hell, I know how mages and witches have always been at odds. I'm just looking at her the same way I did with Iris." He sighs, his voice lowering. "She is not some bloodthirsty creature. Her coven is insane, sure, and Ed—"

The words die in his throat. I catch the flicker in his expression— the way his jaw tenses, his gaze slipping.

Iris.

That name, the one he won't speak for Iris's sake, weighs on him like an iron chain.

The name that keeps her up at night. That makes her sleepwalk, wandering halls in search of someone who isn't there.

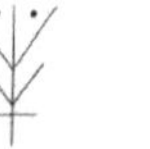

Magic always takes its toll. It's never free.

And we always pay the price.

"Iris is nothing like Millicent," I argue, my arms crossing tighter in defense.

Kalix shakes his head. "No, she's not," he admits. "But her coven? It's just as dark and twisted as the one you have endured. Think, for once, about what Millicent may have gone through there."

His voice lowers. "Iris was favored, too. And you know what that means. What do you think it meant to be favored in her coven?" He pauses. "You were favored once, Cage. By the elders."

The words settle like lead in my chest. The pain resurfaces like a ghostly echo, mirroring the sound of my own screams. My hands clench, nails biting deep into my palms—anything to replace the violent rage clawing its way up my throat.

I force my jaw tight, steadying my voice, "She could just be Nora number two," I snap. "Someone will have to replace her. And she is already on that path."

Kalix sighs, rubbing a hand over his face. "Well, if Millicent is the next Nora and this goes to hell, I'll help you kill her myself." His voice is blunt, but there's no humor in it.

He straightens, rolling his shoulders back. "In the meantime, we all have to work together. I'm not babysitting, and I'm not breaking up fights. Let the damn witch wander. Let her do whatever to find answers." He huffs. "Because we sure as hell haven't found any on our own. And whether you like it or not, Iris has been a huge help." He hesitates. "Millicent might be, too."

The word "help" does not belong in the same sentence as a Le Strange witch. Nora used to call it that—help. She proposed everything to me under the guise of guidance. I am extremely familiar with what their help looks like. It comes in chains, in pain disguised as purpose.

Millicent is no different. Kalix doesn't understand. His weak spot for Iris has blinded him, made him think Millicent deserves the same chance to prove herself. I open my mouth to argue further, but before I can let my emotions get the better of me, Kalix yelps.

"What the hell!"

He stumbles back. His wide-eyed shock is locked on a small blue imp standing patiently, impossibly on top of one of the cattle. Oliver balances perfectly atop the carcass's exposed ribs, swaying slightly with the movement of his tail.

Kalix looks from me to the imp, half expecting an explanation.

Oliver ignores him. Instead, he straightens to his full, unimpressive height and amplifies his voice—a grating, high-pitched screech that scrapes over my eardrums like nails against slate. I resist the urge to cover my ears.

Barely.

"Me Misses requires you now. Follow me." It isn't a request. It isn't an informative gesture. No, it's a command.

Then, without a word, his small bat-like wings begin to extend. They flap furiously, carrying him into the air. Oliver hovers just long enough to glare at us before darting toward the woods with surprising speed.

Kalix stares after him.

I nod once, confirming we're going.

I break into a jog, keeping up as Oliver disappears between the trees. Kalix follows a step behind me as we push forward, and soon, the forest swallows us. Branches whisper overhead as we move.

Thankfully, Kalix's eyes are just as adjusted to the dark as mine. I don't have to worry about leading him; he keeps pace, ducking branches, leaping over fallen logs, and stepping around roots looking for unsuspecting prey to entangle.

The cave's entrance is nearly invisible, camouflaged beneath thick ivy and moss that blend into the rocky incline. If not for Oliver hovering impatiently by the opening, we might have missed it entirely.

He's been grumbling the entire way, throwing dirty looks at my legs and muttering faint complaints about the inconvenience of traveling with wingless creatures.

"Me Misses is inside, so is eater of cow." His voice is a peculiar mix of a screech and squeak, quieter now that he is not booming it across a field. With a small, clawed hand, he pulls back the ivy curtain revealing the cavern beyond.

Kalix exhales sharply beside me. "I don't fancy whatever is down there," he mutters in distaste. The singing of metal cuts through the night air as he draws his sword from his sheathe.

I follow suit, gripping my hilt. The red gem embedded in the handle pulses softly beneath my palm.

No sounds come from the mouth of the void.

Nothing stirs within the shadows.

The stench that rolls from the entrance is unmistakable. Thick, putrid—the same sickly rot that clings to the cattle, slithers into my nostrils.

I wrinkle my nose, "Cow eater, huh?" I mumble more to myself than anyone else. I reach out with my magic. Nothing. No aura. No magical marker. It's becoming a pattern. Whatever the North is meddling with, it either knows how to cloak itself, or it's something else entirely. Either way, it makes me uneasy.

There is something I can feel, a familiar storm of chaotic energy like a raging wildfire that swirls in blue and black. It churns deep within the cavern.

Millicent. She's active.

"Our witch is down there," I whisper as the weight of the cave presses down on us, "And she's not alone."

Kalix's grip tightens on his sword.

The cavernous hall opens before us as we begin our descent. Its vastness swallowing the dim light from behind. The deeper we go, the more the space changes. The walls tighten, the ceiling lowers, and the passage shrinks.

Soon, we're forced to shimmy through a narrow corridor, the rough stone scraping against our chest and backs. I hold my breath, trying to avoid inhaling the dirt and debris crumbling around me, but it's useless.

The grit stings my eyes, blurring my vision. I blink rapidly, forcing the irritation away. I can't afford to lose focus. Not down here.

Then, beneath my boots, I feel them.

Bones—not just scattered fragments but piles of them. The further we go, the more they gather. This isn't just a cave; it's a feeding ground.

The narrow corridor expands into a vast, dark chamber. I drag myself free from the constricting passage. My muscles tense almost the moment I step forward. My instincts flare, and I scan the room for movement, for any threats lurking in the shadows. The air in the chamber is thick, saturated with the familiar energy that clings to Millicent. If I focus, I can see it: a thin, flickering veil of black and blue power.

I take another step forward, then freeze.

A panther the size of a horse prowls from behind a stone outcrop.

My pulse quickens. That is no ordinary beast. Atop its sleek, dark body are six massive anaconda-like snakes that coil along its spine. Their heads shift, tongues flicking the air in unison, but their eyes burn with a familiar, piercing blue.

The beast snarls, stepping fully into view. Its muscles ripple under the black sheen of its coat, but my gaze is locked on its face—on the way it moves. Its jaw unhinges, not just wide, but too wide, splitting apart with a sickening pop. I watch with a mix of curiosity and slight horror. A second row of fangs glistens behind the first, lining the cavernous opening of its throat.

Then both its cheeks open. Like gills, they flare outward, revealing even more rows of jagged, predatory teeth. Its tongue flicks, serpentine, ending in a needle-like tip. It moves like the snakes on its back, mirroring their eerie synchronized motion.

I don't breathe.

Behind me, Kalix swears. "What the fuck—?"

He moves forward, but I throw out an arm, stopping him from getting closer. The beast watches us, sapphire-blue eyes gleaming with hunger—with something else.

Something intelligent.

Something familiar.

That color—that glow—I know those eyes.

From the shadows, Millicent steps forward—calm and unbothered. She walks alongside the beast as if it's nothing more than a house cat, her hand running smoothly over its side.

"Nyx, down," Millicent commands. Her voice is steady and controlled. Nyx obeys immediately. Its grotesque cheeks seal as if they were never split open in the first place. What was once a nightmare of fangs is a simple, oversized predator again. It rubs its massive head into Millicent's palm like a domesticated pet.

Kalix stiffens beside me, his thoughts a tangled mess of disbelief. Millicent doesn't wait for us to gather our wits.

"About time you guys got here," she says, tilting her head toward the carnage sprawled across the chamber. "We will need to collect a lot more samples."

I follow her gaze to the true culprit. A Crepitus Vox, its body shredded, is sprawled across the cavern floor, but my eyes don't linger on it.

I see a torso, small, childlike. Or it had been, once. The grotesque twist of its unnatural limbs is a mutation. Something wrong. Millicent had killed it, and judging by the half-missing head, it hadn't gone down easily. The head, rolled to the side of the body, shows a disfigured, mocking attempt at a female. I point toward the remains.

"Her...?"

"This Crep is advanced. It created an entire domain." She exhales sharply, rubbing the bridge of her nose. "They're too territorial to share areas, so when I killed...whatever that is, it must have pissed the Crep off. That's when it came out to attack."

I blink, "A domain?"

She nods, her hand absently scratching beneath the panther's chin, as if this entire conversation isn't horrifying. The beast leans into her touch, nearly knocking her off balance with the force of its affection.

"I don't know how that's even possible," she mutters. "If a Crep can make a Domain, perhaps it was playing host to something. Somehow these two creatures are connected."

Something cold coils in my stomach.

That's impossible. Creps don't host anything. They kill. They use their pulsing waves to paralyze and disorient their prey, luring them into a slow, helpless death. They're not advanced. They do not build domains.

Millicent sighs through her nose, as if resigning herself to the conversation. "It was able to penetrate my mental shield," she admits. "But only when I touched the girl." Her fingers tighten around her panther's fur. "We need to take the entire body for Iris to study. However, touching her may be risky."

I stare at her, unblinking. "Truly?"

The look she shoots me is flat. Unamused. "Truly."

Her glowing blue gaze pins me in place, a slow frustration simmering in their depths. She thinks I'm an idiot. I break the stare first, dragging a hand through my hair as I walk over to the dead Crep and nudge it lightly with my boot.

Kalix, however, has not moved. His gaze is still fixed on the panther.

"So...Nyx?" He asks hesitantly, "Is this...? What the hell is it?" He blurts, unable to help himself.

She smirks, a rare glint of amusement flickering across her face. "This is one of my shadow beasts." She runs a hand down its spine, her tone casual, almost bored. "Shadow work to create living beings can be simple or complex. Nyx is something I've worked on since I was little, so he's...rather complex."

Kalix points a cautious finger toward Nyx's still-closed mouth.

"So, you made it?" His voice is skeptical. "Snakes and all? By all, I mean the mouth. Definitely the mouth." I glance between him and Millicent, watching as the corner of her lips tugs upward—not quite a smirk, but close enough.

"I suppose," she muses, running a hand over Nyx's thick fur. "I never planned it this way. It just...formed. Kept forming." Her fingers trail along the panther's spine, thoughtful. "They say the caster shapes the beast. Personality, need—it all determines the form." She exhales, her voice dipping into something reminiscent, almost nostalgic. "Nyx has been with me a long time. Now, he shifts only when needed."

She glances up then, her smile sharpening, a flash of something wicked and teasing in her gaze. "He has a twin, you know." She pauses. "Shall I summon Twyx?

Wonderful, the insult to life herself has a whole army of beasts.

Kalix sheaths his sword so fast I hear the metal scrape against leather. He shakes his head, adamant, stiff. "No. Nope. Nooope. I am so good." He takes one deliberate step back, then another. "I'm more of a dog person, anyway. Sorry to your...kitty cats." He walks away quickly.

Millicent lets out a soft huff of amusement before turning back to her shadowy companion. She runs her hand over Nyx one last time, murmuring something too low for me to catch, and he dissolves. Shadows churn where he stood, a thick black fog that seeps downward like smoke pulled by gravity. It spreads, slipping between cracks in the stone, vanishing into the darker corners of the cavern. Gone.

Kalix stiffens slightly, watching from the corner of his eye. His grip on his sword tightens before he forces himself to look away.

I exhale. We need to move. Kalix pauses near the corpse of the grotesque, malformed child-thing, pulling his cloak from his shoulders. Silently, he crouches and begins rolling her body up. Meanwhile, I kneel beside the shredded Creptius Vox, beginning the slow, tedious process of collecting samples. To my mild surprise, Millicent joins me. She lowers herself to the ground, placing her satchel beside her.

Kalix is right. We are working together. We have to work together. If I am to survive this, I need to be stronger. Letting emotion dictate my actions—rising to every taunt, every challenge—is a weakness. One I refuse to succumb to.

Malicent

Millicent is here willingly, but not for the reasons Nora claims. I do not believe, for one second, that this has anything to do with Tyran and wanting to avoid persecution.

No, she has a reason. A plan. And, for now, I will use her. I will let her fight, let her teach, let her reveal what she can do. I will watch and wait, and one day, she will slip. That will be her downfall. She will show her true colors, and when she does, I will strike. She flaunts her power because that is what her coven demands. She shows everything because it is in her nature to be seen.

I will not make the same mistake.

I will hold back. I will learn everything she is. And then, I will crush her with it.

The thought settles in my chest like a slow-burning ember, and I almost smile, even as the rancid stench of the Crep's rotting flesh fills my lungs.

I continue collecting samples.

CHAPTER 16
Millicent

I HAVE NEVER BEEN INSIDE IRIS'S LAB, BUT AS A NECROMANCER, I expected some grim space filled with carcasses. I'd heard tales of Necromancer covens—how their god-like egos made them insufferable, their creations prowling the grounds like extensions of their will. Their buildings were rumored to have towering steel rods spiraling into the sky, calling lightning to fuel their twisted experiments. I imagined blood-streaked floors, air thick with decay, and instruments with purposes I couldn't even begin to name.

The wooden door slams open with a resounding thud as Kalix kicks it with enough force to send it crashing into the stone wall.

"Classy as always," Cage remarks, shoving his hands in his pockets. He strolls past Kalix like someone who has been here many times before.

Kalix lets out a disgruntled huff. "I carried a rotting corpse through half the damn castle. I'll kick open whatever door I damn well please." He stomps inside, the bundled body still slung over his shoulder.

I take a step back, observing the ease with which he carries the thing. Kalix is a large man, all strength and brutal efficiency, but his endurance is what impresses me most. He's carried that weight all the way from the horses, through the winding halls, and up the stairs without breaking a sweat.

The lab is nothing like I imagined. Instead of the dim, blood-soaked dungeon I expected, light floods the space, casting warm hues of yellow, green, and red across the atrium. The ceiling is formed by massive, circular windowpanes with colored glass that filters the sunlight into dancing patterns along the stone floor.

Shelves line the vast, circular room, stacked with glass bottles in every shade imaginable. Between them, potted plants spill their vines toward the ground, weaving through the space like living decoration. The air hums with energy that feels alive. It's warm. Bright. Full of vitality. The air is fresh despite the corpses around—almost sterile with hints of herbal notes from the multitude of plants. It's the complete opposite of what I had prepared myself for.

At the center, Iris stands hunched over a steel table, sawing into a carcass. She doesn't seem the least bit disturbed. A record spins in a wooden player beside her, its golden flower-shaped speaker pouring out a gentle, rhythmic melody that feels utterly out of place.

Hearing us enter, she pauses mid-cut and lifts her head. Her peculiar goggles—bulky and strange—are fitted with at least ten rotating lenses. She tugs them up onto her forehead, revealing sharp green eyes that glint with curiosity. It's almost absurd, the way she butchers a carcass in a room bathed in colored light and the scent of fresh plants.

She's dressed in deep-moss green overalls, the fabric speckled with dried stains; whether they're from blood or something else, I can't tell. Her fiery hair is pulled back into a loose half-up style, allowing a few wild strands to tumble freely down her back.

"Back already? And you brought a gift?" Her eyes lock onto Kalix as he makes his way to an empty steel table.

"A whole mutated corpse—your favorite," he grunts, hauling the bundle off his shoulder. The body lands with a dull, wet thud on the metal surface.

Iris wipes her hands clean on a rag, then pushes her goggles up, placing them on her forehead, tucking them just above her bangs. "Oh, goodie!" She beams, her excitement almost childlike. She might be an oddity among Necromancers, but her fascination with the dead is on brand.

Cage drags a stool closer and plops onto it, leaning back against the table behind him. He motions to the corpse, "We brought samples too—another specimen. Millicent killed both, so she can give you the details."

Iris claps her hands together. "Ah, the first day out, and you're already handling it all! How exciting." Her voice is warm, strangely delighted given the circumstances. "I'll need a full report, but be warned, I'll write down everything you say." She hums as she reaches impatiently for the cloak covering the body, her fingers curling around the fabric, ready to peel it back.

Before she can, Kalix's hand shoots out, catching her wrist.

"Slow down, Iris." He says firmly with no room for argument. "Millicent said there's something wrong with this one when you touch it. I'll do it." His thumb brushes over her wrist before releasing her, and she hesitates only for a moment before pulling her hand back. Her gaze flicks to me.

"What happens when you touch it?" Her curiosity sharpens along with her tone.

Kalix begins unwrapping the body, his hands are ironically careful despite his brute strength.

I step forward, finally moving deeper into the lab. My eyes adjust to the way the daylight hits the corpse. Under the warm glow, it looks more unsettling than in the cave.

"A Crepitus Vox was present." I say steadily, but my mind is still reeling. "No one can break into my mind—yet when my foot touched this girl, or whatever she was, it just...let it in."

I stare down at the corpse, still puzzled, replaying the event in my mind. Now fully exposed under the daylight, it's even clearer that this

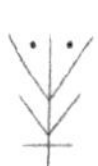

had once been a girl—somehow reanimated, twisted into something terribly inhuman.

Iris absorbs my words in silence, her eyes flicking between mine and the body. Then, as if I had just handed her the most exciting puzzle of her life, she grins. "I am *most* intrigued." She pivots on her heels, her boots clattering from all the buckles strapped across them. "I'll get to slicing and dicing right away."

She strides toward a workbench, retrieving an array of tools. The room is lined with metal tables, each holding something different—glass beakers, swirling vials, distillation equipment, and stacks of surgical instruments. Others, like the bone saw, are far more...intense. There are other devices I don't recognize, ones covered in barbs and coils that I don't *want* to recognize.

"How hard is your mind to break into?" Iris calls over her shoulder, lifting a spiraling drill with a wooden handle. Kalix moves to her side, extending his hands as she starts stacking tools into them. He watches her with an amused smirk.

"Pretty damn hard," I reply, crossing my arms. "I've been trained to shield since I was young, and I am two hundred years old." I don't often dwell on my age, but right now, I feel it. The reminder gnaws at me; today, something managed to breach my mind. A space I had guarded viciously. A feat no one had ever accomplished, but one.

Kalix snorts, "Shit, you are old."

I hear him yelp before I even look up. Iris has pinched him, hard, mumbling under her breath, "I'm one hundred and twenty. What does that make me, little mortal?"

Kalix grins, flexing his arms as he clutches her tools tighter to his chest like a prize. "A cradle snatcher. A cougar mama, if you will. Little mama." He leans obnoxiously close trying to nip at her cheek.

Iris swats at him but with a smile tugging at her lips. "Down!" She corrects, smacking him lightly on the nose as if he is an unruly pup. Kalix's laughter fills the room, a deep, rich sound, warm as aged wine, reverberating through the bright space.

Cage watches them with a bemused smile of his own. "I am two hundred and six. I suppose that makes me the ancient one here."

Kalix, still following Iris like an obedient pup, nods without looking back. She carries nothing but a simple rag, while he is loaded down with her supplies. The contrast is almost comical—his burly frame towering over her as he hauls her tools like a dutiful pack mule.

"It's true," Kalix muses, placing the instruments down with exaggerated care. "Which is why I kick your ass when we spar. Your old blood just isn't up to par." His grin is full of smug confidence.

Cage rolls his eyes. "Right. That's definitely why you occasionally win. Has nothing to do with other reasons."

A silent exchange passes between them, one of those wordless conversations built from years of familiarity. Cage's silver gaze narrows ever so slightly, assessing. Kalix's smirk deepens, his posture relaxed but knowing.

Iris, either uninterested in their silent game or deliberately ignoring it, turns her attention to me. "It's not that I doubt you're skilled," she says lightly, but there's a thread of calculation in her tone. "For measurement and documentation purposes, I just need to understand the extent of your defenses ..." She trails off as her gaze flicks between us, hopeful, her bright grin an attempt at reassurance.

"Would you be open to letting Cage attempt to break into your mind? It would help me gauge where the strength lies. Ultimately, the hope is that it will help us understand how this girl let the Crep in. Certain magics and curses have their own weaknesses. If I can identify what it is, I might be able to counteract it."

I revolt at the very thought. Letting him in—even attempting it—is unthinkable. There is too much in my mind he is *not* allowed to see. It would leave me vulnerable, leave an exposed nerve ready for him to exploit. I would be a fool to allow that so willingly.

"No." My voice is curt, final. My muscles tense at the suggestion, the finality of my answer resonating down to my bones. I place my hands on the steel table, forcing my attention to the corpse. A

distraction. I study the body as if it holds answers, as if I haven't already looked it over a dozen times.

I feel Cage's stare before I even glance up. He's dissecting me without even reaching into my mind, his focus pressing against my skin like a blade. I lift my eyes, locking onto his.

"If your ability to keep others out is so strong," he muses, his voice carrying a dangerous undercurrent, "why are you worried? Maybe you're not as powerful as you claim, little witch."

A challenge. A taunt, a dare. My fingers drum against the table, slow, measured. I won't bend under the pressure of a mere mage—especially not him. I scoff, tilting my chin up in defiance. "Give it your best shot then, little mage."

His satisfaction is instant. He leans back against the table behind him, utterly relaxed. His smug expressions sets a spark against my temper. His silver eyes darken, churning with flecks of white as his power begins to unfurl.

The air shifts.

A cold pressure seeps into my mind, like water suddenly flooding into a sealed space. My awareness sharpens as the sensation ripples against my defenses—like waves lapping at the edges, testing me. Like a shark, his magic circles around me, hunting for a weakness.

He hasn't attacked yet, but I feel the strength of him. The water churns, swirling more chaotically as he ventures closer. I push back, fortifying my defenses. The walls in my mind rise—tall, reinforced, and unbreakable. Jagged spikes grow from them, forcing him to keep his distance. Still, his magic lingers just beyond.

Then, the water shifts again. Something moves.

Tentacles, massive and slick, unfurl from the depths. They slide along my walls, tightening their hold, to anchor them in place. More rise, coiling through the water like serpents, ignoring the spikes that dig into their flesh.

The first strike comes—not a brute-force attack but something more patient and calculated. The fine tips of the tentacles begin to twirl,

drilling into the wall at multiple points. I feel the pressure building against me and push back. **Hard.**

Iris's voice rings through the space like a distant warning. "Remember, he is simply trying to break your wall. Do not attack him. Cage, do not attack her. If you do break the wall, come out immediately."

Restraint, the hardest lesson of all. I seal up the cracks as quickly as they form, reinforcing my defenses, refusing to give an inch.

The water ripples again, and this time, something floats toward me. Alone, in the dark abyss of my mind, it drifts.

A stuffed bunny.

Its fur is matted, one button eye missing. Its body is stitched with a dozen mismatched patches from earth-toned fabric sewn together by unsteady hands.

A child's toy. A relic from a past I refuse to acknowledge, a ghost from a life that was stolen from me. And Cage is too close to it.

CHAPTER 17

Cage

ER ABILITY TO KEEP ME OUT OF HER MIND WITHOUT a countering attack is impressive. Unfortunately for her, I know a few tricks to slip past even the most ironclad minds. One of the most effective is using something personal, something tied to memory.

A single thread is all it takes. If I dangle it just long enough, a small seam will open into a mind. One weakness, and that wall crumbles. I picture the stuffed bunny she used to carry as a child—the one she gave to me. The moment a hint of recognition flickers in her eyes, I seize it. I grasp the thread, yanking it hard, and channel my magic into her mind with lightning speed.

A sharp thud echoes in my chest, my heart hammering against my ribs. My knees weaken, forcing me to grip the edge of the table to steady myself. Kalix is speaking beside me, but his voice is distant. My gaze is held captive by hers, and before I can resist, I am dragged under. Air abandons me as I am submerged.

The world dissolves. Kalix. Iris. The lab. Gone. Everything disintegrates as I am unwillingly pulled into something vast and unknown. I sink deep into the abyss of her consciousness, a place I was never meant to go.

When I finally blink, the atrium is gone.

A desolate landscape stretches before me. Black sludge clings under my boots, each step met with a sickening sound of suction. The air is thick with acrid smoke that curls in dense coils, and my throat burns as I instinctively cough, but then I see them.

The ground, once a field, is now nothing but scorched earth. The grass has since been reduced to ash. And beyond, through the shifting veil of smoke—bodies. Thousands of them.

I narrow my eyes, focusing past the haze. A vast sea of corpses are sprawled across the battlefield in the armor of their country and the blood of their defeat.

A figure moves. She saunters toward me, slow and unhurried. Her hips sway with grace. A deep, menacing laugh drifts through the air—rich, oily, and laced with something inhuman. As she steps closer, my stomach twists.

Millicent. Not as I know her. She's clad in black-scaled armor, the dark plating gleams like the hide of predator. And her eyes—

Twin voids stare back at me, a bottomless abyss that threatens to consume everything underneath her gaze.

"Do you not know how to bow?"

The command thrums through the air, thick with power, pressing against me like unseen hands. My knees falter as the force almost buckles them beneath me, but I resist. A wide, devilish smile stretches across her face, pulling her features too tight, too sharp. It isn't a smile of amusement. It's hunger. A predator savoring the moment before the kill.

Then...she moves.

Too fast.

 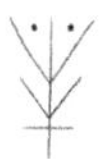

A blur of motion, and a jolt of force slams into my shoulder. My body crumbles beneath it. My knees crash into the ground as the impact rattles me to my core.

"Now, how did you get in here?" She tilts her head, the motion is jarring, disjointed, as though her body barely remembers how to mimic human movement. "Have you come home?" Blood slicks her mouth, dripping in slow rivulets down her neck.

"Home?" My voice is hoarse and unsteady. "What is this place? Millicent, I didn't try to pry into your mind. I want to leave. It was all just—"

I don't get to finish.

Her hand shoots out, fingers clamping around my jaw. Sharp nails pierce my skin, pressing deep enough to draw blood. She snarls, "Seems we are both stuck, but I see you now." Her grip tightens, her voice slithering over me like a curse. "Hidden from thee you have been, little sheep. Little lamb."

The smile returns, spreading too far, stretching up her cheeks, distorting her face into something monstrous. "You are stronger," she muses, her tone thick with amusement. "Good. You will need your strength."

Her fingers lengthen. The nails sharpen into wicked points and plunge deeper as pain erupts, hot, searing. One claw punctures the soft flesh inside my cheek, ripping the thin membrane of my mouth. My lips part in a silent scream, but no sound escapes. She lifts me effortlessly, toying with me like a cat playing with its food. I hang there, suspended in her grasp, choking from the blood pooling in my mouth.

"There is nothing you can do to stop what is done." Her voice lowers to a purr, "What is done has already happened."

My pulse pounds, erratic—the world tilts.

"Get stronger."

"Live deliciously."

Her hand tightens, and then—

She throws me.

The void swallows me whole. I plummet, disoriented, weightless. The darkness stretches endlessly below me, the world above shrinking until all that remains is the echo of her voice.

"Get out."

I slam back into my body violently, the force of it ripping me away from Millicent's mind like a drowning man being wrenched from the depths.

The moment I return, my stomach revolts. Doubling over, I retch onto the floor, my entire body convulsing as the remnants of my dinner splatters onto the stone. Kalix curses, barely dodging the mess in time. "Gods, watch it!" He stumbles back, shaking his boot as if that'll save him.

Iris rushes to my side, her hands warm and steady against my back. "Cage, you okay?"

I nod, sucking in deep, ragged breaths, trying to cool the fire in my lungs. The world tilts around me, disoriented and wrong, but I shove the nausea down. Iris straightens, her sharp gaze flicking between me and Millicent. "You weren't supposed to attack."

Her words slice through the air, but I barely register them. Millicent stands frozen, staring blankly ahead before she finally draws in a slow breath. Her eyes flicker as she blinks back to herself, becoming lucid.

She looks at me. Confusion. Something unsettled lingers in her expression, something that throws me off.

"Millicent," Iris says again, more firmly this time, taking a cautious step toward her.

Millicent exhales, rolling her shoulders as though shaking off invisible hands. "I think he got past my wall." Her voice is steady, but I see a flicker of unease in the way her fingers curl into fists. "What did you see?"

She is worried. Not just that I got in, but that I saw something I shouldn't have. That realization twists something deep in my gut. She

155

didn't know I got in? She's trained, skilled; she should have felt it. No witch leaves their mind unguarded without knowing. Yet, she's completely unaware.

Which means ...

I don't know what the hell I just walked into.

"She didn't attack me," I say, my voice gruff, still trying to piece it together myself. "It may have been her subconscious." They're empty words, but I have nothing else to offer.

Iris exhales, some of the tension leaving her frame. She turns back to Millicent, her voice softer now as if handling something fragile. "Are you okay?"

Millicent watches me carefully. Calculating.

"Yes, I'm fine." The answer is too quick. Too rehearsed. She turns the ring on her thumb, the only tell that she's rattled beneath her collected facade. "I was unaware he got in. I'm not sure what happened. Did you see anything?"

She's analyzing me. Waiting. Her apprehension confirms my suspicion that she has deeply guarded secrets. I don't know what I saw. One thing is certain—Millicent doesn't want me to know.

"A battlefield," I say shortly. "Covered in bodies. And you."

Her fingers still around the ring for half a second. Then, she forces an exhale, tilting her head slightly. "I've never been in a war," she muses, her voice light, distant. "My subconscious, you say? Maybe that was it."

The words are a deflection.

Kalix, who has been blessedly quiet for once, finally huffs a laugh. "That is a brutal subconscious. You need some sunshine or something, you little rain cloud." His teasing grin breaks the tension as he strides toward the exit. "I'll grab some cleaning supplies and water."

As he moves past me, I push off the table and call after him, my voice hoarse.

"My puke. Let me help."

He snorts. "Nah, you earned this one." I shake my head, following him out. Whatever happened in Millicent's mind, I'll figure it out later.

For now, I just need to steady my own.

CHAPTER 18
Millicent

MY MIND REPLAYS THE IMAGES OVER AND OVER LONG after Cage and Kalix depart, leaving Iris and I alone in her lab. Thankfully, she doesn't pry, too absorbed in the corpse they brought her.

I hear a sickening crack as she splits its chest open with steady hands. Her goggles magnify the details as she prods the tissue with thick leather gloves.

Seeing the rabbit from my childhood had shattered my defenses, allowing Cage to break through my mental walls. In that moment, I sensed an opening in his. My response—to exploit that weakness—was a matter of pure instinct.

CAGE FINALLY TAKES THE RABBIT AFTER I PERSISTENTLY SHOVE it at him. His intrigue is palpable, bright and sharp, popping like the bubbles in a carbonated drink. The moment my mother calls for me, I take off, skipping toward her. He watches, silent, his fingers curling around the rabbit as he tucks it safely in his coat. Even now, I can feel his envy.

He turns as Nora approaches, her commanding voice cutting coldly through the air. "I can sense your magic all the way to my office. It is time for your session. Come."

His nerves spike. Adrenaline floods his system, making his skin clammy. The memory is foggy, shifting in and out of focus as he follows her. Across the coven grounds, they move toward the place we call the temple.

One moment, they are stepping into a vast room, pews stretching toward a grand altar at the head. The next, the scene fractures, shifting to winding tunnels that coil beneath the earth. The scent of damp soil thickens, pressing against his senses. He shivers as the cold steals the warmth from his skin, but he keeps walking, driven by something fierce.

The images blur again.

His bare form is now chained—his wrists, ankles, and neck are bound to a circular stone altar. The air is heavy with incense. Hooded figures loom around him, their black robes pooling at their feet. Twisted skulls of antelopes and elks crown them, their horns curving like grotesque spires.

Nora stands above him. She slides on her mask. "Let us contain it." Her voice cuts through the chamber.

The cloaked figures step forward, their daggers gleaming under the dim light, each blade etched with pulsing red runes. They hover over Cage, surrounding him; their movements are methodical, and practiced.

The first cut is precise.

Then another.

And another.

Steel kisses flesh as they carve into him, slowly and deliberately. A cruel art. His skin splits open like a latticework of fresh wounds

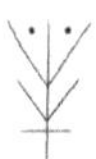

blooming across his body. His magic seeps from the gashes, mixing with the thick rivulets of blood cascading down the altar's surface.

The grooves beneath him drink it in, filling the carved channels that encircle his body.

The bloodletting continues. The runes carved into the stone flicker, drinking deep from the sacrifice.

The bloodletting continues. His screams shatter the air, raw and unrelenting, until his voice frays.

I feel it all. The pain shoots through me. My vision wavers from the sheer intensity that threatens to drag me under. And still, they carve. Still, they take.

Cage convulses, his body trembling under their hands. When his strength begins to wane, they force a thick belt between his teeth, silencing the agony burning in his throat. He does not last much longer, despite his focus on remaining conscious, on enduring. Darkness claims him, and the last thing he sees is Nora's sadistic grin of satisfaction at her work.

EMERGING FROM HIS MEMORY LEAVES ME REELING; SO MANY questions claw at my thoughts. I endured bloodletting, too, but mine had a purpose. It made me stronger. This...this was different. Nora mentioned containment, but what was there to contain? His reaction—his fear—was too hardened. Like this was normal for him. Had this been routine?

Great pain begets great power. That principal has been drilled into me since childhood, and I am living proof of its truth. What if Cage's suffering wasn't about power at all? I cannot help but wonder if something more was at play. Bloodletting also weakens the host. What would they be trying to control or contain with Cage—in Cage?

I don't have time to reach an answer. Iris's voice shatters my thoughts. "I still get the urge to bring these things back to life. Odd, right? Even knowing how horrifying they are, even knowing they'd attack, I can't shake the itch to reanimate them."

She holds a long pair of tweezers, guiding a blade along the thin muscular wall of the creature's exposed organs with expert care. Her voice is calm, almost absentminded.

"Odd indeed, but it is in your nature. There's no shame in that," I say casually, watching her work with precise delicate movements.

"I agree. I like who I am—when I am not reanimating everything in sight," She smirks, lifting a thinly sliced sheet of tissue with her tweezers and placing it into a dish. "The rumors about the god complex? All very true. I get a little...out of touch. Very preachy."

I huff a quiet laugh. "I know the feeling."

Her gaze flicks to mine; she's curious.

"When I fall into bloodlust, I black out completely. I don't even recall what happens or what I am like. It's rare that I let it happen, but when I do, my sisters are usually there to stop me." I pause, smirking. "Apparently, I get a little preachy and a bit insane. Allegedly, I try to eat everything in sight."

The memory of Arcadia telling me a theatrical story comes back to me—her frustration, her dramatics. She hadn't been overly pleased about facing me, but I found the story...amusing. *Let them all bear witness to my power.*

Iris smiles widely. "When you say sisters, I assume you mean coven. Do you have any blood sisters?" She switches out her tools for a syringe, focusing on larger arteries, testing multiple entry points to see if any viable fluids remain.

"No sisters," I say. "I had my mother. She was my only blood relation." The words settle heavily in my chest. My heart clenches at the mention of her.

Iris notices, her movements stilling over her work. When she looks up at me, she gives me her full, undivided attention. "I am sorry for your loss." Her voice is quieter now. "I had a blood sister, too. I lost her." A shadow flickers through her expression. "She was the other half of my

soul. I miss her every day. Grief never really goes away—you just learn to live with it. It lingers, like a presence in the room. A memory that haunts us, but in a sad, loving way."

Her smile softens, her eyes grow distant. "The grief reminds me she was real and I loved her—it is beautiful in that way." She shakes herself out of whatever thought threatens to pull her under and returns to her task.

I stare at my hands. "Haunting feels too tame a word for what it is," I murmur, the words flowing out before I can think.

Iris tilts her head slightly, listening.

"Not just haunting—watching. Waiting. Longing to devour me until there is nothing left." My fingers tighten around the edge of the table. "That's what it feels like. A curse I cannot rid myself of. If the price of relief is to erase her from memory, to carve her from my soul, I don't want it."

I lift my gaze. Iris's expression is unreadable, but her sadness lingers in the set of her jaw, in the way she exhales slowly through her nose.

"I will bear this," I say. "And I will long to see her in my dreams. Better to have had and lost than never to have had at all. That is what Arcadia always says." I sigh, forcing the thoughts away from my mother and from Cage, chained and screaming. "She is like a sister to me. The only one I'm truly close with from my coven."

I lean back slightly, letting the shift in topic settle. "I think she'd love the castle. Arcadia has a taste for luxury."

Iris perks up. "Maybe she can visit! Tyran loves playing host." She resumes her work, securing the final vial into its holder before grabbing a leather book and quill.

I smile at the thought of Arcadia here, surrounded by gold and finery. "Maybe. She doesn't stay in one place for long. As soon as she was old enough to leave the coven, she did."

Iris settles onto the stool beside a wooden table that is nearly empty save for scattered stacks of papers and unfurled scrolls. She pats

the seat next to her. "Come sit. I want to start the record of the events from the field."

I push away from the table where the creature's remains still lie and take the seat beside her. She flips open a leather-bound book, dating the page with a careful stroke of ink. "Did you ever venture out?" she asks lightly.

I shake my head. "I'm not permitted to. My elder has strict rules for me. I remain on coven grounds, and my training schedule is more demanding compared to the others."

Iris purses her lips. "Well that doesn't seem very fair. Awfully boring, really." She leans forward slightly, green eyes glinting with thought. "The world is massive, and our covens are so small. Did you ever wish to explore?"

I consider the question, tilting my head slightly. "Yes," I admit. "Especially when Arcadia began traveling, returning home with tales and trinkets. You don't defy the elders, as you know." I shrug, not overly bothered by my arrangement. "I also came to understand my role in the coven and why the rules exist."

Iris hums in response, jotting down notes as she speaks. "And what was your role?" She glances up. "I was one of the best Necromancers, so I was utilized for creation. To shape things that should never exist." She exhales, shaking her head. "Things that defy nature. Things made from power-hungry ambition."

Iris seems genuinely interested in me. It's...nice. Talking to another witch, someone who understands without needing constant explanation.

It eases a weight I hadn't realized I was carrying.

The pressure in my chest—the one that always lingers—lifts ever so slightly. It reminds me of late nights spent talking Arcadia's ear off. "I am considered rare, both in my coven and by power standards," I say, studying the grain of the wooden table. "I hold two types of magic— blood and dark magic." I pause. "To wield two forms is—"

"Exceedingly rare," Iris cuts in. "So rare I've never seen it documented. You may very well be the first." Her certainty sends an odd sense of validation through my chest. "Yes. Because of my rarity, I was a target from the start," I continue, propping my elbow on the table and resting my chin on top of my hand. "As I grew, I became something else—a source of destruction. My magic requires constant training and discipline. My elders made sure that I had both."

My breath slows. "Power comes at a price. Part of mine is freedom. The freedom to go where I wish, with whom I wish." My gaze drifts to Iris. "When this is over, I will return to my coven. I am here now, under Elder orders."

Iris takes a moment to respond. She dips the quill into the ink pot, hovering over the page as if collecting her thoughts. "I've learned that power can come from different places—your physical form, your blood, or the control you possess. To lack control over your own life and your own choices?" She shakes her head. "That is the greatest loss of power."

Iris's gaze meets mine. "I would give anything for freedom—to wake in a place where the sun warms my skin, where I decide where I go, who I speak to, who I share my life with. I have already paid the price for power." Her voice softens. "And now, I have paid for my freedom. I only hope that, wherever your path takes you, Millicent, you can find both."

She has no idea what I have paid. No idea of what pieces of myself I have given away, never to be reclaimed. Her ideals are different from mine, but I knew this from our first exchange. If I chose her path—if I abandoned the coven—I would not simply be free. I would be unbound. Untethered. Without discipline, without structure, without Nora's control, my power would consume me. I would not exist as I am now.

Iris is sweet, and I am not.

There is a world of difference between what runs in our veins and what we must do to keep it from destroying us. "It is different for me, Iris." My voice is steady, but my fingers betray me, idly spinning the ring on my thumb. "My elders are here to help me." A pause. Then, quieter, almost hesitant, "You can call me Millie."

"Millie is cute. I like it! I like your full name too." She rolls her eyes but gives the biggest grin. The sorrow lingering in her features is finally fading away. "The nickname around here for me is 'Rainbow,' but you'll notice it's rarely used—unless it is Kalix." She rolls her eyes at the mention of his name, but there is a smile behind them.

I grin mischievously. "Soo...Kalix?"

Iris groans, "Please don't even ask. He's a really good friend, that's it."

I arch a brow, believing otherwise. "So do all your good friends smack your ass often?"

Her face flushes. "Okay! Tell me about your night, gods above!" She squeaks, flipping open her journal in a dramatic attempt to change the subject.

I laugh but let her escape, settling into my recount of the evening. I start from the beginning, from the moment the horses were acting strangely. Iris writes furiously as I speak, keeping pace with surprising ease. Occasionally, she interrupts with questions to clarify details, ensuring she is recording everything in the proper order. She absorbs every word like a sponge, her fascination with the Crep evident in the way she leans forward, intrigued by its abilities.

Somewhere between recounting the battle and describing the creature's mutations, my stomach lets out a low grumble in protest. Exhaustion presses heavily on me now—the weight of the hunt, the fight, and restless nights settle deep in my bones. We had barely returned before heading straight here. I stifle a yawn as Iris finishes her final notes.

"Alright," she says, finally setting down her quill. "I'll get to work and let you know what I find. In the meantime, get some rest—you all need it." She leaves her journal open as she slips off the bench, flipping through her notes before turning back to her experiments. Music hums softly from the record player as she resets it.

I push off the stool with a deep stretch to soothe my aching muscles. The walk back to my room feels longer than usual. My feet drag with each step, the exhaustion weighing me down like lead. Finally, the noise from the halls blur into a quiet stillness. My room isn't far now.

Golden curls round the corner, catching the dim light as Tyran steps into view. Even with the hood of his dark sage cloak pulled up, a few loose strands escape to frame his face. He lets out a low whistle, eyes flicking over my bloodstained clothes and the dirt covering my skin. "Whoa there. You look exhausted."

I cross my arms. "Yeah. That's kind of what killing does." My gaze sweeps over his cloak. "No gold? Didn't know your vanity would allow for other colors."

His usual grin doesn't falter. "I'm being inconspicuous, Millicent." He sighs dramatically, rolling his eyes. "I like to not feel my crown sometimes. Sue me; I'm a man who likes to have fun."

"Uh huh." I step forward, intent on leaving, but he moves too—awkwardly—blocking my path. His hand reaches to grab my arm, but he quickly retracts it, realizing it is unwise.

His stance shifts, just slightly hesitant, if not a bit timid. I pause, arching my brow.

"You look hungry." Tyran's voice is low; he is careful not to let it echo down the hall. "At least let me have food sent to you. I'd offer to eat with you, but you don't look like you want company." His lips twitch into a small smirk. He's being playful, but there's sincerity beneath it. "I'm grateful for your help, and I'd prefer if one of my most valuable assets didn't pass out from lack of sustenance."

I scoff, crossing my arms. "Valuable? Can you drop the act? I am a bloody witch." My patience wears thin, and the thought of my bed nearly convinces me to shove past the smiling fool.

For once, his grin falters. He almost looks offended. "Yes, valuable," he says with a firmer tone. "Why would I strike a deal with a coven if I secretly hated witches? Also, hello, I practically made a deal with the devil to get your people involved because I needed you here. You're of immense value."

The soft edges of his face harden slightly. "For the record, your elder is terrifying. I'm beyond relieved it's our beautiful, vibrant Millicent here and not her." His chest puffs up slightly, like he's so pleased with himself.

I tilt my head and raise a brow. "So you don't hate witches—you just need me pampered and at my best because I'm the one who's going to kill the North for you, yes?" My voice drips with sarcasm. I shift on my feet, longing to get to my damn bed.

"Do I like witches? Depends on the witch, just like I don't like all humans." Tyran shrugs. "I love Iris. I've met some pleasant ones on the road. Historically? Sure, they can be a problem, but that's the past. I'm much more interested in the future." His grin turns mischievous. "Do you require pampering? I can arrange it. Perhaps it would bring a smile to your face if Cage was ordered by the king to rub your feet." He tugs his hood down as a servant passes, pulling his cloak tightly around himself.

I snort, clapping a hand over my mouth to muffle the laugh. Tyran's grin stretches widely and triumphantly. "I will inform him of his new duty first thing tomorrow!" He raises a pointed finger, his voice full of mock authority.

"Gods above, no Tyran." I shake my head vigorously.

"Please, it's Felix." He presses a hand to his chest as if wounded. "Tell you what, if you agree to eat, I'll resist the urge to assign Cage his new role as foot masseuse. Deal?" He extends hand.

"Fine, Tyran—"

He cut me off with a sharp shake of his head, "Felix."

I roll my eyes, huffing as I start over. "Fine, **Felix**. You can send food to my room. Happy?" I give him an exaggerated, fake smile of annoyance as I shake his hand.

His face mirrors mine perfectly, making my lips twitch with another chuckle. "Brilliant. I know your weakness now," he teases, dropping my hand and stepping aside. "Off to your room now, chop chop!" He claps his hands.

I arch a brow at him but don't argue, waving him off as I move past, resuming my walk.

Behind me, Felix slips into an archway leading outside. I briefly wonder where he's heading, shrouded in secrecy, but exhaustion keeps me on my path. I'm too tired to care.

The climb to the private floor feels endless, each step heavier than the last. When I finally reach my door, my hand pauses on the handle. I glance down the moonlit hall; Cage's door looms just ahead.

Does what I saw in his memories haunt him in his dreams, too? I have too many questions whirling in my mind about what I saw and the purpose behind it.

It was necessary. It always is. My grip tightens on the knob as my own memories of my necessary steps to power mix with what I saw. The thought lingers longer than it should. I shake my head, exhaling sharply, and push into my room, determined to let it go.

Ollie appears the moment I step inside—his timing always impeccable.

Wordlessly, he helps me out of my bodysuit, now clinging to me like a second layer of skin, sealed tight with sweat and fatigue.

As always, Ollie helps me through our near-nightly routine, assisting with my bath, then settling me into a fresh nightgown. The light fabric allows my skin to breathe, and the short hem, brushing mid-thigh, allows for comfort without restriction.

A knock at the door breaks the quiet. A servant steps in, delivering a platter stacked high with meats, cheeses, nuts, and fruit. The rich aroma fills the room, dancing up my nose. My stomach growls, demanding to be fed.

I sigh, shaking my head. Damn that golden-haired king. I hadn't wanted to accept his meddling, but now, with the scent teasing my senses, I find myself grateful for his persistence.

I crawl onto my bed, sitting cross-legged as I spread the meal out in front of me.

Having food is not odd, but having someone demand I eat and send food to me is. Le Strange witches are fiercely independent. We do not coddle one another. You take care of your own injuries, your own needs, and help your sisters only when they ask. Only Arcadia has tended to my wounds when I have lost consciousness. Only she has fed me when I could not feed myself.

Ollie plops down beside me, extending his little legs forward. They nearly vanish beneath the round swell of his belly, which now rests over his knees like a plush cushion.

Without hesitation, he digs in and shovels handfuls of food into his open mouth. I laugh as jam and cheese get on his obnoxiously long nose and remain there, hidden from his view as he continues digging in, wiggling his toes in pleasure. "Ollie, there's jam and cheese on your nose," I laugh.

His tongue pokes out, wiggling wildly as he tries—and fails—to reach the tip. After a few futile attempts, he gives and returns to his meal without concern. When we finish eating, I grab a rag and wipe his face. He chatters in that odd, insect-like noise of his, enjoying the affectionate act.

Once I am sure no lingering jam can end up on my sheets, I slide onto my side, letting him brush my hair. He hums softly—a song my mother would often sing to me. Ollie gently starts brushing the ends and carefully works upward toward my scalp.

My gaze drifts toward the open balcony doors. Perched in the shadows beyond, Nora's ever-present owl watches. I should give a report. That is my duty, but I'm far too tired. "Tomorrow," I mumble, my voice barely audible, unsure if I even managed to say the word out loud.

Sensing my unease, Ollie doesn't pause his humming. His chaotic magic stirs instead, bouncing in white shimmering streaks along the walls before slamming into the balcony doors. A barrier forms, white light crackling before settling into a deep gray, dark as storm clouds.

169

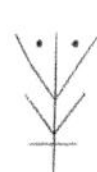

The curtain is nearly solid, save for speckled patches where faint light still peeks through. The owl disappears behind it, and peace returns. Oliver hums on, his fingers deftly weaving through my hair. My eyes flutter closed, his song pulling at memories long buried.

I hear my mother's voice singing the same melody. A lullaby from another life.

Sleep takes me, carrying me toward dreams of better times.

"It's late, little one. You must sleep now," my mother whispers against my temple, pressing a soft kiss there before peppering more along my forehead and cheeks.

I squeal in delight, wriggling in her lap. "Please Mama! Just one more time!" My wide eyes twinkle up at her, my best attempt at a puppy-dog face. I'm not ready for sleep—not yet. She laughs, the sound rich and warm. It's nothing like the dry practiced laughter of the other coven girls. *My sisters,* I correct myself.

"Okay, one more time," she concedes, the last traces of laughter fading into an easy smile. She pulls me closer, tucking me into the safety of her arms. I curl against her chest, my small hands tangling in her long black locks—the same depth of darkness as mine. Pressing my cheek to her heart, I listen to its steady thrum, letting it ease the restless pang still vibrating inside me from my rather adventurous day.

She hums first, a familiar melody that makes my own lips twitch with the urge to join in. Then, as she begins to sing, I let the vibration of her voice seep into me, my own chest echoing its rhythm, my heartbeats synchronizing with hers.

"Sleep and hush, time can wait.

My little star, the world is yours to create.

You shine so true, my precious one.

Your glow will last when the day ends, and the dark hath come."

Seven Devils

Her fingers trail along my back in slow, soothing circles, coaxing my body toward sleep. My eyelids grow heavy.

"Forever in your love I will stay,

To guide you home and light your way.

Never be truly afraid,

For my sweet little love is far too brave."

The words soften, fading into the haze of sleep. The last thing I hear is the steady rhythm of her heart—strong, unwavering.

A sound I once believed would last forever.

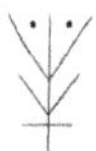

CHAPTER 19

Millicent

II. Vexation

*"Entity begins to torment the selected host. Abuse
includes physical and mental. Body is not yet possessed."*
-The Wretched Sacrament

ARCADIA TAPS MY HEAD WITH THE BACK OF HER BRUSH,
scolding me for moving too much as she works through my hair.

"You pull too hard!" I whine, resisting the urge to free my poor hair
from her ruthless grip.

"You're the biggest baby I know, Millie. Suck it up! Beauty hurts."
She's rolling her eyes at me; I just know it.

"I'm tender-headed! Maybe I don't need braids. I'm a hair-down
girl anyway. They might not even look good on my face."

Another sharp whack to my head. I whip around and grab the handle, fighting to rip that damned brush from her grasp.

"You're a baby, and that's a lame ass excuse! You're hot in everything! So at least come up with a better lie if you want me to stop, you conniving witch." She grunts as we wrestle for control. We're both sitting on our bottoms locked in the heat of battle. I stick my foot out against her stomach, pushing hard for leverage. The brush rips free.

"HAH!" I shout victoriously, holding it high.

My triumph is short-lived. Arcadia lunges, tackling me to the floor. I shriek, my laughter garbled as she grabs for the brush. I stretch my arm out, keeping it just out of her reach.

Arcadia freezes mid-grapple, her body tensing against mine. A split second later, she slips off me, shifting to her knees with her head bowed low.

"Elanora," she says, her voice quiet but steady.

My stomach drops; I hadn't noticed Nora enter the room. The shift occurs almost immediately. The laughter that once filled the space is strangled into silence, suffocated by the weight of her presence. The fire still crackles in the hearth to our left, its warmth now a distant thing, swallowed by the creeping cold that follows our elder like a second shadow. The red tapestries adorning the wall seem darker now, the worn fabric wrinkling beneath the sheer gravity of her scrutiny.

I drop my gaze to the floor and follow Arcadia's lead, lowering myself to my knees. I bow my head as a show of respect, though I feel the faint tremor in my fingers.

Nora steps forward, her heels tapping against the oak flooring.

"Arcadia," she says, her tone sharp enough to slice through the air, "what are you wearing?"

The air thickens with tension. I watch from the corner of my eye as Arcadia's hand curls into a small fist against the floor. "A gown, Nora." She keeps her head bowed and her voice steady.

Nora clicks her tongue in disapproval. "Not one of the gowns specifically tailored for you," she corrects coldly. "You are one of the few witches given custom attire. Do not be so ungrateful."

Arcadia straightens, she manages to keep her voice measured. "I just wanted to cover up today, is all. It's chilly." She explains quickly, as if hoping that it might soften Nora's retort.

I glance at her gown—similar to mine in its plain black corset top and flowing ankle-length panels. Unlike mine, the problem lay in the neckline. Too modest.

Arcadia's custom gowns are not meant to conceal. They are cut deep, plunging all the way to her navel, designed to bare the golden witch marks curling over her chest. A display of power, of lineage. A requirement. Nora tolerates no deviation. To cover one's marks is to hide strength. To hide strength is to be weak.

A sin.

"You will bear the cold." Her tone is flat, absolute. "If you cannot withstand a mere breeze, you will not survive beyond these walls. Far colder things await you in the world, child." The word *child* lands with the sharpness of a blade. "Change. Now," she commands.

Arcadia's jaw tightens, but she does not argue. She merely bows her head, rising swiftly to her feet. Without another word, she turns on her heel, striding toward the door. She does not slam it behind her. She does not look back. And then, it is just us.

The dull thud of Nora's heels against the wooden floor is the only sound as she approaches.

"Millicent, you've been excelling in your lessons," she says smoothly. "Today, it is time for another." She extends a hand.

I hesitate—only for a breath—before I place my hand in hers, allowing her to pull me to my feet. Her grip is firm, cool.

My nerves are already frayed. Inside, the chaotic energy I fight to keep contained stirs violently, like rats clawing for an escape. We follow a familiar path. Leaving the warmth of the residential wing behind, we cross into the Academic building. Our footsteps echo throughout its silent halls.

Then down.

The staircase spirals, the light from above thinning into nothingness. Soon, we arrive at the network of cavernous halls. I furrow my brow as we pass the chamber that houses the pool of that foul-tasting, black liquid. We always stop here. Always.

Not tonight.

"A new lesson today. The next lesson." Nora's voice resonates through the corridor. The torches flicker against jagged stone and earth, casting shifting shadows that seem to stretch and breathe. "In nature, Millicent, you can be a wolf or a sheep. Sheep exist to be devoured. They are necessary, but not all are worthy." Her steps are slow as she moves in circles around me.

"To remain strong, wolves select their prey carefully. They do not waste their time on the weak—the inadequate." She pauses, letting the words sink in, then asks. "Are you a wolf or a sheep?"

The question is rhetorical, yet I still answer. "I am a wolf." I keep my voice steady, but the confidence is a lie. We press forward. The corridor breathes a faint draft, and soon, a door looms ahead. A bitter chill seeps from beneath it. Nora pushes it open.

Iron grates against iron. The hinges groan in protest, but they do not deny her. In front of us is a cavern, but different from the one she typically takes me into. Beyond the threshold, the chamber's ceiling vanishes into the open sky. The full moon hangs above a ghostly twin reflected in the still lake below.

The lake glistens, its surface too smooth. The outlines of distant trees emerge in twisted forms warped beyond recognition. The bark coils in tight, wrung-out spirals that unfurl into unnatural, horn-like protrusions. They are barren, lifeless, as though they were never meant to bear leaves.

Nora's grip tightens around my wrist. Wordlessly, she commands me forward. The shoreline, an uneven bed of cold, smooth stones, crunches beneath my feet. Each step grows heavier, my body resisting—

The voice returns.

It's the one only I can hear—the one that has lived inside my mind since drinking from the black waters. "Come, my child."

It is a siren's call: soft, yet shifting, as though spoken by many voices at once.

"Come, sweet child, come."

Her voice slithers through the chamber—soft at first, coaxing, almost maternal. Then it shifts. The cadence distorts, deepens, as if layered with another voice beneath it. Something does not belong.

Nora drops my hand. I barely have time to process before she raises her hand to my back, unzipping my gown in one motion. The fabric pools at my feet. "We will see if you truly are a wolf, Millicent." She murmurs. "Walk into the water."

A tremor ripples through me. "That...that is all I must do?"

She strips my clothes from me, and I am bare before the cold can fully register. Goosebumps rise on my skin, sending a shudder that rolls down my spine as the air bites deep. My breath escapes in faint plumes, curling before me like smoke. The chill settles under my skin—into my bones. Yet, I do not argue; the chambers are always cold.

"That is all you must do, little star." Her voice softens—an old, familiar trick. A lullaby of control. And like always, it works.

Little star.

Mother used to say I would never be afraid. That I was too clever for fear. I cling to the thought.

One step. Then another. My bare feet meet the smooth, wet stones of the shore. The lake awaits me, too dark, too still. The water laps at my toes. The unsettling sensation is immediate. A slippery, *oil-slicked* cold seeps into my skin, coiling like something alive. It's the same feeling that slid down my throat when I drank from the chalice.

"Get in the water." The voice claws into my mind, its talons scraping. It doesn't shout—it commands.

My legs obey before I do. Each step feels less like my own. I am walking to *her*, I realize. *To it.* I stop. A tremor ripples through me as nausea churns in my gut, threatening to rise and burst out.

There's no time for that. Nora's voice cuts through the chamber like ice splintering against stone. "Continue. Do not hesitate. Wolves do not hesitate. You...your weakness is an infection. We will rid you of it." She waits—barely. "Does strength come from gentleness?"

"No Nora," I recite, the words spill out as a reflex. "Strength comes from enduring." A lesson that is seared into my mind—burned into my skin. A lesson I have bled for.

Her tone sharpens, slicing at me with a cold finality. "Great power begets great sacrifice. What is it to sacrifice fear? To kill the instinct of hesitation? You are to be perfect. Flawless. *Relentless*. A lamb has no place here." She pauses. I can feel it coming. "Your mother would be ashamed to see such weakness." Her words hit harder than the cold.

And I hate myself for hesitating.

My back is to her. The water stills at my ankles. Weak.

I was too weak to save my mother.

I will never be weak again.

Even in the dark, I will shine, I will not be lost; I hum her song under my breath—soft, fragile—an anchor as I finally take the next steps. The water climbs up my shins. My knees. Then my thighs. It's cold, each inch a new punishment. When it reaches my shoulders, I shudder violently. My teeth chatter and my breath forms broken clouds before me.

I stop. Centered—alone—in the moon's reflection. Silver above. Silver below. Then, something enters, and there's a shift in the air.

The lake ripples as something massive slips into the water from across the chamber. A distant splash, and a wave rolls outward, pushing water to my chin. I sway off-balance, bracing as the lake divides.

Something is swimming toward me. It's enormous. Its silhouette, a black shadow, moves with fluid grace. It is too smooth. Too purposeful. My night vision sharpens, but the creature remains veiled in the shifting darkness.

Too far to see. Yet far too close.

"You are rare, Millicent," Nora calls from the shore. "Your vessel can hold such power—but more than that...you are a lamb."

Terror rips through me. My chest tightens. My fingers curl beneath the surface forming fists that break the mirrored moonlight.

"A lamb who will turn into a wolf. That does not happen in nature. You will be the first."

I hear footsteps behind me. Nora is leaving. Her steps fade. She does not stay.

She never meant to.

When she walks away from me, my voice fractures as I whisper, "Nora..."

She doesn't respond.

The door groans closed, and the iron seals with a final, echoing *clang*.

And I am alone.

The mass slides into the moonlight, its form shifting like smoke in a storm of shadows. My eyes widen. It's closer than it should be, but it vanishes before it can get too close.

My breath hitches. Panic claws at my lungs. I start breathing too fast—shallow breaths—too sharp and useless.

I can't breathe.

No. That's not true. I am breathing.

My head snaps left and right, searching. The surface has gone eerily still, undisturbed like nothing was ever there.

Then...bubbles. I see a few at first and then more.

My mouth goes dry. My heartbeat pounds in my ears.

The bubbles stop.

Silence.

What game is this thing playing?

It strikes.

Within seconds of thought, long pale limbs explode from the depths behind me. The hands are inhuman—elongated and skeletal—with fingers tipped in jagged, hook-like claws. When they slap down onto my shoulders, one wraps around my neck, and the other clamps over my mouth.

I scream into its palm, but the sound is swallowed by water.

The thing yanks me backward with terrifying force. It drags me down deeper and deeper beneath the surface.

Water closes over my head.

Claws pierce into my skin. I scream, thrash, kick, and punch, and my lungs heave against its crushing strength.

Water seeps between its fingers, pouring into my mouth. I choke, and my breath vanishes. Fire ignites in my chest; it's burning and screaming for air. My limbs grow heavy, and blackness creeps into the edges of my vision.

My flails are wild and desperate.

I cannot die here.

I jolt upright, lungs heaving. The darkness in my vision is replaced by moonlight trickling into my room. I clutch at my throat, relieved from the air filling my lungs, and my skin glistens with sweat so that the sheets cling to me.

My head whips around my room as I scramble back, pressing myself against the headboard, as it feels safest there.

I clutch my knees to my chest, trying to ground myself as I scan the space.

I'm in my room.

Was it a dream?

I rake trembling fingers through my hair, rocking slightly.

No. I'm losing it. The visions. The voice. They're getting worse.

The rocking stops when I see the deep, sickly bruises blooming across my shoulders. In the center of each one is a clotted gash.

My hand flies to my throat and then my cheek. There are more wounds there.

This wasn't a dream.

How did I get back here?

The thought shatters.

The slow creak of my door slices through the silence—a high-pitch whine that scrapes down my spine.

"Arcadia?" I whisper. "Nora?"

No answer.

The sconces that normally line the hallway outside are dead.

Only a void remains.

I try to steady my shaking hands, clasping them together but failing. My fingers turn to the ring on my thumb, spinning it over and over like a lifeline.

Focus.

I call on my magic, reaching inward. My eyes ignite in a faint, flickering blue. A soft glow spills into the room, enough to see but not enough to feel strong.

The familiar swell of power is gone. In its place, there is only a sputter. A fizzle.

Panic claws up my throat. I reach desperately for Ollie.

Nothing.

I tug harder on the bond but still find nothing. I've never failed to summon him—not once since I was five.

I've blocked him before, yes, to spare him my emotions when things got dark. But I haven't blocked him now, and he's not coming.

"Don't worry," it whispers. "I'll take good care of your skin...until it tears."

The voice isn't in my head anymore. It's here at the foot of my bed.

The sound—no longer singular—shifts between four voices, layered and broken. Male and female. Young and old. All speaking as one.

Terror coils in my stomach as I press myself tighter against the head-board. My hands shake uncontrollably.

I open my mouth to scream, but there's no time.

A figure launches from the foot of my bed. It's a woman, if she can be called that. Her black hair hangs to her waist, veiling her face entirely. Below her chest, there's nothing but bone; her ribs protrude outward, skinless and slick.

She crawls like a spider, and she's fast. *Too fast.*

In the time it takes me to blink, she's on top of me.

Four arms—the same ones that dragged me under the lake—grip my ankles and wrists. She slams me flat against the bed with overwhelming strength.

I thrash, desperate to break free, but it's useless. My limbs barely twitch beneath her crushing grip, and my muscles scream...burn. Still, I am too weak.

Her exposed spine stretches beyond where her ribs end, lengthening unnaturally into a sharp, pointed tail.

It twitches.

"Little lamb, offered up."

She laughs—a fractured, maniacal sound that rattles through the air.

Then she darts forward. Her hair-draped face presses against my ear, her breath hot and sour.

"Long have we lingered," she whispers, her voice cracking. "Since the day you were born, you have belonged to me. A vessel waiting to be filled. Let me complete you."

Pain erupts violently across my stomach as she slams her ribcage into me. Bone pierces flesh.

I scream, but no sound escapes.

We are joined, bound by the grotesque merging of body and will.

Her face jerks, twitching unnaturally before her mouth finds mine.

She kisses me, but not with affection—with ownership. Her crusted, slime-coated lips seal over mine. A thick, putrid sludge floods down my throat.

The pressure is unbearable. My throat stretches too far—skin pulled taut around my neck as it bulges.

I convulse.

My eyes roll back and my knee twists sideways, breaking the joint under her force. Then my shoulder gives out, bones tearing from sockets.

And then...

Malicent

Darkness.
Not sleep.
Not death.
Absence...like someone has blown out the flame that fed my soul.

CHAPTER 20

Cage

I GROAN AS THE MENTAL ALARM RIPS THROUGH MY SKULL, tearing me from sleep. I'm still exhausted, spent from being up all night and half the day. Most of it, if I'm honest, stems from whatever happened in Millicent's mind.

Now this?

I curse aloud, shoving the blanket off my legs and sitting up. The wards on Millicent's room are flaring like mad. Lovely. She's up to something again. Does the wretched thing not sleep?

I don't bother changing; rather, I stomp into the hall wearing the same loose trousers I wore to bed. I sleep too hot for shirts anyway. Grumbling, I make my way toward her door.

When I arrive, I don't bother knocking before I push it open and walk in unannounced.

"Fuck," I groan.

Her magic is in full swing as chaos unfolds before me. Shadow imps bounce wildly across the room, tearing into anything they can get their claws on. Millicent is in bed, either dead asleep or pretending to be.

"Hey, witch." I stride toward her, swatting an imp out of the air as it tries to nip at my ear.

I shake her shoulders. Her brows pinch, and her breathing finally gives it away, shallow and erratic. Sweat glistens on her brow.

So, a nightmare, then.

With a sigh, I drop carelessly onto the edge of her bed. The mattress dips, causing her body to shift slightly.

"Witch. Up," I bark, louder than necessary. "Your magic's causing a shit show."

The nearby imps scatter like startled butterflies, tumbling through the air in frantic swarms.

She doesn't move.

I lean over her, my irritation simmering hotter. Gods alive, I just want to be asleep right now—not coming to tuck this devil in. With a growl, I slip my hand behind her neck, fingers threading into the thick curls at her nape. I try to pull her upright. Her body slumps, limp and unresponsive like a discarded puppet.

Still nothing.

My hand drifts upward, cupping her cheek. Her skin is incredibly soft—too soft. It's the kind of softness that whispers danger. Maybe she does bathe in blood. I honestly wouldn't put it past her.

She's not scowling at me, spitting venom, or snapping some smart-ass remarks. For once, her face is quiet, almost...innocent. It's strange how pretty something looks when it's not baring its teeth.

My thumb brushes the curve of her jaw, trailing across her petal-soft lips.

A hunger—dark and sharp—rises from the part of myself I rarely unleash, which used to rule over me in the past. That other half sees her now, this threat made vulnerable.

And it wants it.

My hand tightens reflexively in her hair.

My voice drops, rough with something I don't name. "Millicent,"

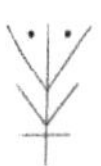

I whisper, tapping her cheek. "I'll come in there and pull you out. Not even dreams can keep you from me."

Her nose twitches.

Then her eyes snap open—wide, wild, and filled with pure terror.

She screams. The sound is so loud and raw, it pierces my skull, sharp enough to make me flinch.

"Shit," I mutter, clapping my hand over her mouth to muffle the sound. "Hey, it's me. It's Cage."

My thumb at the back of her neck shifts, offering small, steady strokes, meant to comfort her—anything to stifle the banshee wail echoing through my skull.

Her eyes stay locked on mine, and I can't look away from those deep, endless oceans.

She wears that damn mask, hiding behind sarcasm and scorn. Now I see it all: panic and fear. For once, nothing is hidden. Raw emotion flickers across her features, each one more revealing than the last. It only stirs the urge in me to see every emotion I could extract from her—experience how her tears taste, how her laugh sounds.

Then, the fire returns. The inferno I've grown accustomed to—the one that usually comes with insults or blades—is back.

Her hands shoot up, shoving mine away. "What the fuck! Why are you in my room?" she snaps, her voice sharp enough to cut steel. It's not really a question. She's demanding an explanation, as if I need one.

I roll my eyes. "Can you *not* scream? I can hear you just fine, thanks."

I gesture lazily to an imp dangling from her curtain rod. Its tiny claws dig into the fabric like it owns the place. "Is this a habit of yours when you sleep? Summoning chaos? Let me guess: a nightmare where you're forced to live among the mortals? Sorry...vermin, right?"

I sigh heavily, long and theatrical.

Her eyes narrow and glow. Suddenly, the room shifts. The imps all stop. One by one, they turn. Their beady eyes fix on me. Then they leap

with claws bared, teeth exposed. Shadows snarl through the air as they vault from the walls and furniture like rabid beasts.

"Seriously?"

I'm too goddamn tired for one of her little temper tantrums.

I raise my hand, palm up, fingers unfurling slow and deliberately—just so she can see what's coming.

The imps close in, but before they can reach me, my hand slips from the back of her neck...to her throat.

My fingers wrap fully around it—the column of her neck bared and delicate beneath my palm. She doesn't flinch. Of course she doesn't. The mask is back in place.

"Do you like these little imps?" I murmur, voice low, dangerous. A smirk pulls at the corner of my lips. "I know you care. You pretend you don't, but you do. They're yours, just like that cursed familiar of yours."

My magic stirs.

I reach, feeling along the threads of shadow that animate her imps. They pulse with her essence—a part of her in every one.

The first Imp lunges at me, teeth bared and ready to sink into my shoulder. I close my hand, and they freeze all at once.

Then the shrieking starts: high, sharp cries that echo off the walls as I twist their insides. They drop, convulsing midair, and their small forms writhe as if torn from the inside out.

Millicent's eyes flick to the closest one, crumpled on the bed. It gasps, barely alive and twitching.

She winces.

"Stop," she demands, her voice sharper now.

"Your wish is my command." My voice is dipped in venom.

My magic surges. A pulse of energy ripples from my hand, and every imp disintegrates in unison. Their bodies collapse into murky shadows, snuffed out of existence until nothing remains.

Gone.

The room stills.

The shadows obey me just as easily as they obey her—something she seems to forget far too often.

"As satisfying as that was," I continue, a slow smirk spreading, "I'm exhausted. And I'd rather not spend the night cleaning up after your emotional mess. So, try keeping magic in check, yeah?"

"You *willingly* came into my room just to clean up my mess?" she snaps, throwing my own words back at me.

I laugh dryly. "Believe me, I don't *want* to be in here. It's my job to keep things in order."

I yank my hand from her neck. The sudden absence sends her tumbling backward onto the bed.

I stand.

"I would rather swallow glass than ever be in your room—or your bed—outside of duty."

I move to the door and twist the handle. Locked.

I glance back. She's sitting upright now, her fists clenched in the blanket. Her posture is coiled like a blade ready to strike.

"You hate that I'm greater than you," she seethes. "You're a murderer, Cage. Just like me. Your blood may be arcane, your power sharp, but I've *never* killed without a purpose. I never butchered so many that a coven barely survived. Your hunger? Your destruction? It's worse than mine ever was."

She laughs, sharp and cruel, and the sound cuts through the tension like shattered glass.

Anyone can justify their sins. She just wrapped hers in pretty words. Her so-called morality is nothing more than a painted excuse.

Still, her accusation lands, causing me to pause for a split second.

"The villages you've pillaged—ripping people from their homes? The abusive cycle you feed within your coven—on the women you call sisters?" I snarl. "I pray to never have a family like yours.

I let the silence stretch, just long enough to sting.

"But you don't really have any family left, do you, Millie?"

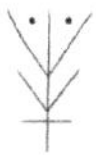

She tilts her chin, regal and unyielding. Defiant.

"No," she breathes. "You made sure of that. Even for yourself, am I right?"

Her smile is slow—too knowing. And when it lands, it lands hard.

My jaw clenches, and my grip on the doorknob tightens until my knuckles go stark white. Blood stops pumping; my hand tingles.

She's not wrong. I ended up in that coven because I obliterated everything that tied me to another life. My magic was volatile, raw, and unchecked. And I was young.

I still remember the moment it happened: obsidian spikes rising from the ground with the snap of my fear; and my mother impaled, gasping for the breath she couldn't catch. Even dying, she told me it wasn't my fault.

Five days.

Five days of my mother's cold skin against mine.

Five days of intimate education on how the smell of a human body changes as it decomposes.

I remained curled between their bodies for five days, my mother and father lifeless beside me. I didn't eat. I barely breathed. Every breath I took was drenched in the putrid rot of them mixed with the piss and shit their bodies expelled.

Every breath I took felt stolen, unearned. I was alive, but they were dead.

Because of me.

Then Nora found me.

She promised safety and to help me control the storm growing inside me. I believed her. Gods, I *wanted* to believe her.

She trained me, molded me. She said it was for my own good and that the chains were necessary.

And for a while, I believed it—that is, until the night my magic turned against her.

Until Vyraxis.

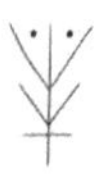

Only then did I escape, and only then did I realize it had all been a lie. I wasn't trained. I was controlled and abused. I was *used*.

Millicent? She's still in it, still drowning in that same indoctrination.

I doubt she's ever left the coven walls long enough to *know* who she's without Nora's voice whispering in her ear.

"Guilty as charged." I turn toward her, raising both hands as I lean back against the door. "Tell me, Millicent: have you ever actually *left* your coven?"

"Of course I have," she snaps—too quickly, too sharp.

I grin, cruel and tired. "You are a shit liar. If you ever did make it past those trees, you'd know the world isn't what you've been told."

Her eyes narrow. "You speak like a deserter. Weakness has tainted your mind."

She lifts her chin, reciting her words like a sermon: "In this world, you are either a sheep or a wolf. And here you are: clustered with your little herd of sheep. It's fitting for someone as low as you."

That old lesson.

I know it well. Nora preached it during our special sessions, always as the blade slid in.

Suddenly, I want to know if Millicent's back bears the same scars as mine.

"I know the price to be a wolf," I say, quieter now. "And I'm happy to be a sheep."

That hits hard.

Her expression cracks just slightly, her mask slipping as the words find their mark.

"Did you become a wolf, Mille?" I press, stepping closer. "First of your kind?"

She opens her mouth. Then, she closes it again.

She knows what I'm quoting. *She hears it.*

"Rare, right?" I murmur. "I was too."

I pause to allow the words to sink in.

"I wonder," I add, "if she would've ever looked at you if I'd stayed."

The silence between us goes razor sharp.

I've had enough.

I twist the doorknob and yank. With a mere thought, the ward cast on the room fractures whatever spell she threw up to keep me in. Nice try.

She's strong—no doubt—but she still hasn't shown me her teeth. The only one she obeys is Nora, which means some deal must've been struck—one that keeps her claws sheathed...for now.

I step out and slam the door behind me. With one final mental flick, my ward pulses, confirming it's still intact.

And then I'm finally free to go to bed. I trudge back to my room, too exhausted for any further bullshit from her. I could have stayed and argued. I could have asserted myself over her again, but she is not worth the time or energy.

Thanks to her, I know sleep will not be easy tonight, not that it ever really is.

I know that my parents will be in my dreams tonight.

And the smell of decaying flesh.

CHAPTER 21

Millicent

I WALK AROUND THE MAGE QUARTERS TAKING NOTE OF THEIR hands on the ward barrier again.

Right, left, half square.

That sequence will give me access to their wing, including the artifacts Nora wants. I let myself smile as the plan Nora's familiar has relayed to me turns in my head.

Cage will feel my revenge soon.

I don't linger. I walk the second floor of the castle, enjoying the solitude this hall provides. The entire right wall is a series of open arches. There is no glass, just carved stone allowing the lingering heat of the day to escape on the occasional breeze. Through the gaps, the sounds of the training yard drift upward: clashing steel, shouted commands, and grunts of exertion.

Below, guards and knights move through drills, sharpening their skills. On some days, the mages join them, practicing hand-to-hand combat and swordplay. When the vermin are out of sight, they spar with spells, weaving magic into tense standoffs.

I spent a portion of the morning with Iris, only to come up empty-handed. She still doesn't know what's mutating the creatures or how the morbid girl shattered my mental shield with just a touch. Still, I stayed longer than I meant to. I've started to enjoy our talks.

I don't do well sitting still. It gives my mind too much room to wander. The anxious energy inside me fizzes like carbonation with no release, so I pace the castle, waiting for it to pass.

Peering down into the yard below, I see no mages today—only guards running drills beneath the sun.

Kalix leads them through a series of evolutions, his voice booming over the clatter of steel. "Luca, switch sparring partners. Choose someone stronger."

The boy obeys at once, hurrying to find his new opponent.

Even among the dozens of men, Kalix stands out. He towers over them all, his shoulders broad enough to dwarf anyone beside him. Even from here, distance does little to hide the way muscle ripples beneath his tunic. He moves like someone born to command, but it's odd how graceful he navigates the space for a man his size.

He is captain of the guard after all; still, something about his strength feels...off, unnatural, too much.

Training has always helped with my anxiety back home. Movement gave my mind something to cling to. Now, with Kalix down there, I hesitate.

Living among vermin hasn't been as intolerable as I imagined it would be. That alone should terrify me.

There's a warmth between Iris and Kalix—a closeness I've never shared with anyone outside of Arcadia and my mother. How did she manage that...with a human? Are there other witches who've softened to mortals the way she has?

Cage's words echo in my mind; in hindsight, they're sharper now. I've never left the coven or seen what the world holds beyond the twisted woods of home. If there are witches out there who've fallen for mortals, I wouldn't know.

Arcadia always returned with fun trinkets and wild stories. She was happy when she told them. She was happy.

The thought claws at my chest, burrowing deep and hollowing me out, just like the trees we'd find, eaten from the inside by termites. I rub the center of my sternum, trying to summon warmth to press away the ache.

Disgust follows quickly. I curl my fingers into a fist.

This is weakness. My sisters would say I'm going mad. Nora would agree.

I yearn for comfort and the fondness of humans. I'm entertaining thoughts I can't even name. It's the newness of it all, a novelty that will fade. I will settle.

I know who I am, what I am. And I am not weak.

I invite the numbness back. I let it harden in my chest like stone— let it quiet the noise.

Iris's sweet voice breaks through my thoughts like a bird's song.

"Gawking at the guards?" she teases, her cheeks round with amusement.

I laugh dryly. "Absolutely not. I think being cooped up in that lab of yours is making you see things."

I turn to look at her. Her hair is a mess, frazzled and damp from hours of work. One strap of her overalls hangs loose against her ribs, the other barely clinging to her shoulder.

"Sooo," she drawls, sliding up beside me, "the clenched fists aren't from some desperate yearning for a man's flesh?"

She leans over the sand-colored ledge, resting her forearms on the warm stone.

I join her, mirroring the pose; my eyes drift to the sparring guards below. Repulsion balls up low in my throat at the suggestion I yearn for their flesh in any fashion outside of consuming them.

"How do you do it?" I ask, barely above a whisper. "How can you be around them so easily—sleep with them...for pleasure?"

"I can create life. I can bring things back, even if they're not quite

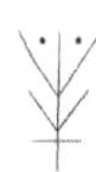

the same as before. That might be hard for you to understand, but to me, they're just like us. When I revive them, their heart beats the same as yours. As mine."

"Your father was human. So was mine. That makes us more alike than you think."

I frown. "I never knew my father. I imagine he's dead. My mother was a kind, soft woman. Sometimes I wonder if she killed him...or did as you do."

Iris smiles faintly. "I've met witches in love with humans. I found it beautiful. I believe all life has worth. Our differences make us interesting—make the world vibrant."

She glances at me, her voice gentle. "May I ask...why do you call them vermin? What did your coven teach you?"

I hesitate. I don't mention that the word came from the Nightmother herself, the first time she ever spoke to me. She doesn't like being spoken of to outsiders. Only her chosen—her children—can carry her name.

Instead, I offer a different truth.

"The rumors say we lure humans back to the coven to be slaughtered. We did perform those rites but only outside the coven grounds. Even those have mostly died out." The unnoticed tightness in my chest loosens as I sidestep any mention of the Nightmother.

I pause, chewing the inside of my cheek. The words catch in my throat. "We discovered our own blood works better in rituals."

My thumb finds the ring I always spin when such memories resurface; I need to ground myself. I twist it hard, chasing comfort while visions rise: the sting of a blade, the loss of strength, and the way my sisters had to carry me, limp and bleeding, back to my room.

"That sounds awful," Iris says softly. "But I'm not surprised. Power always demands a price, and most are willing to pay anything."

Her tone is carefully controlled—understanding—but held back. It's as if she's resisting the pull of her own memories.

What has she given up for power?

"I would apologize for prying," I begin.

She cuts in with a smile. "Apologizing doesn't seem like your style."

"It's not exactly something my sisters and I do," I admit, lips twitching. "What I was going to say is...I would apologize for prying, but you're nosey."

The joke lands, but her smile falters when I ask, "What have you paid?"

She hesitates. Her finger traces the rough edge of the stone ledge.

"My sister," she says finally, "she took the other half of my soul. I haven't gotten it back.

She exhales. "My coven took my sanity too. Necromancers... when we're practicing, we feel like gods. I *was* a god. Nothing, and no one, could stop me. I was the strongest of the younger witches. Except for her."

Her voice drops. "I lost sight of what life meant. I turned it into a circus; whatever I wanted, I took. My hands are soaked in blood, and the worst part is, I never felt remorse. Not then."

"The high of creation—of pulling life back from death—was too sweet. It dulled everything else. I was untouchable—superior."

She stares into the yard below. Her eyes settle on Kalix, as if anchoring herself.

"When I stopped..." Her voice trembles, "it was like coming off the finest drug I'd ever injected straight into my veins."

"What made you stop?" I lower my gaze to the yard below, giving her space.

"My sister," she says. "Eden was kind—kinder than me, even. Then the elders started holding special sessions with her. She changed and started hearing voices. She became violent...paranoid. I had to get us out."

She rubs her hands together, still staring at Kalix. He seems to anchor her—to hold her here.

"I was too late," she says, voice breaking.

I don't think. I just reach out and take her hand, squeezing it in mine.

"Regret and guilt have a permanent residence in my mind," I say. It's meant to comfort her, though I suspect our definitions of guilt are vastly different.

I don't regret the lives I've taken or the rituals I've carried out.

My guilt lives somewhere else: on the battlefield between emotion and duty. It's born from weakness and failure—in moments when I couldn't save my sisters, my mother.

She squeezes back. "I hope you can fill other homes in your lovely head with better emotions to balance it out."

She exhales slowly. Kalix glances up and catches sight of us. His gaze lingers on her.

He grins, raising his voice. "Enjoying the show, Rainbow?"

Her sadness vanishes beneath a wide smile.

She lets go of my hand, cupping her mouth, and shouts, "Take your pants off next!"

Kalix smirks, keeping eye contact as he reaches for his belt.

Her laughter erupts, chasing away the last of the shadows from her face.

My shadows remain, and in this moment, the difference between us is so clear.

There is nothing that can chase away the dark that draws my very features, stirs in my very blood.

For I am it.

Like Arcadia, Iris is light, with shadows of loss cast upon her. The difference is that she can step into the light and vanquish them.

How do I vanquish what connects the very particles of my being?

"Kalix!" she scolds, still laughing wildly and unrestrained.

Kalix clasps his belt again with a flourish and bows before turning back to the training yard.

One nearby guard earns a slap to the back of the head when Kalix catches him staring up at us.

"Eyes on your opponent!" he barks, grabbing the boy by the collar and shoving him back into the ring.

I admit the real reason I was watching the guards: "I was considering training."

"I think that is an excellent idea!" Iris beams. "I could train too, but, honestly I'm still learning. I'd be no challenge for you."

She leans against the railing, still grinning. Her positivity shines like the midday sun. "A lot of the guards are well trained, but the knights might be more your speed. The mages too. And Kalix or Cage would probably be willing to help."

The idea of training with Cage unsettles me.

I worry that if I lean too far into it—if I lose control—I'll lash out. And Nora is still keeping a close eye on me.

I cannot falter.

If I get my mother's killer under me—his heart calling to me, pleading with each beat to have its long song ended—I will not stop until the tan from his skin pales, the warmth a memory.

Tyran's orders are clear: no assaults, no exceptions—not even if I found peace after tearing Cage apart.

"I will think about it," I say. My gaze drifts down to the yard, just as a familiar presence pulls at the edge of my awareness.

Iris gasps and grabs my arm, whipping around to face me.

"Millicent, look!" she exclaims, pointing down excitedly at the floor below.

There, staring up at us with black beady eyes, is Ollie.

He licks two of fingers and smooths over nonexistent eyebrows. "Well, hellooo, Misses," he whistles, eyeing Iris with exaggerated flair. His gaze slides down her leg and then up, and I can already hear the thoughts forming in his head.

"Oliver, no humping," I snap, earning a huff and an indignant scowl.

"Oliver, this is Iris. Iris, meet Oliver, my familiar."

Iris giggles. "He is so *cute*! That's amazing. I wish necromancers got

familiars. We have to make our own." She crouches and extends a hand. "It's lovely to meet you."

Oliver flushes pink all over, flattered by her compliment.

His chubby, clawed hand grabs her finger and gives it a formal shake.

"Ollie to friends!"

"Ollie it is, then, as we must be friends."

He blinks up at me, surprised. "Me Misses made friend?"

"Yes, Oliver. Don't look so damn shocked."

The annoyance in my voice masks something deeper.

I do want connections...sometimes. It's just hard for me. I'm not allowed. Connection means caring. Caring means weakness. And weakness invites pain.

My magic doesn't respond well to such things. It's better for everyone if I don't let anyone close enough to hurt me. If they did, the loss of control would lead to bloodshed—that is, when I rip their heads from their bodies.

Arcadia slipped into my heart when I was still too young to build walls. She fought to stay there. She always does.

Oliver plants his hands on his hips, sass radiating from every inch of him.

"Well, sorry that Me Misses never goes to parties, and we sit alone in room all the time."

"Oliver, shut it," I snap.

Iris's laughter bubbles up again, encouraging him further.

"Me Misses has also felt aroused while here." He smirks like the little hellion he is. The bond between us leaves little room for secrets.

Iris's eyes shoot at me, mouth parting with a question.

"Ollie, I am not giving you any more wine!" I bark, cutting her off. I yank on our bond, tightening his leash to lock those damn lips. The last thing I desire is Oliver divulging every emotion he feels from me because he wants to make a pretty girl laugh in hopes of being allowed to hump her leg.

Manipulative thing.

Oliver closes an imaginary zipper over his lips and hums innocently.

"Are we having wine already? And I wasn't invited? That's rude, Millie."

Kalix's voice draws our attention as he strolls down the hall toward us, towel in hand, wiping sweat from his face and chest.

Up close, I catch new details: small, pale scars scattered across his torso, the kind earned in combat, as well as one particularly nasty animal bite marring his bicep.

Iris straightens with a grin. "This is Millicent's familiar, Oliver!"

"We've met. What's up, little guy?" Kalix waves at Ollie but walks straight to Iris. He slips his arms around her waist, tugging her close to his chest.

"You're covered in sweat!" she whines, pushing against his bare chest.

He chuckles. "You love it. Besides—" He leans down and whispers something in her ear that makes her cheeks flush scarlet.

Oliver tilts his head, confused. "Me Misses...how will he fit inside her?"

The silence is immediate. Iris and Kalix both freeze.

I can't help it; I burst out laughing.

"You see, Oliver, when a woman is aroused, she—"

"Shut up!" Iris yells, glaring at me. "We are not having sex! Never have! Never will!"

She pushes Kalix back down the hall, forcing him to walk in reverse. He shoots me a shit-eating grin—*that devil*—and waves at me over her shoulder.

"Be back in a few hours!"

"A few hours?" she mutters.

"Come now, Rainbow," he says, voice low and rough. "I like to savor you."

Then he grabs the backs of her thighs and hauls her into his arms. She laughs, wrapping her arms around him as he carries her off.

 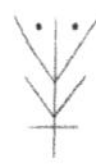

The hollowness returns; it's subtle but sharp. I stare after them until a tug at my dress draws my gaze downward.

Oliver clambers up my side and settles on my shoulder, curling in like he belongs there.

"Me Misses, don't be sad," he says gently. "She will survive, even if she is small and he is massive."

I snort. "That's not why I'm sad, and I'm not even sure I'm sad."

"Me Misses, I feel what you do. You are left wanting—alone—but I am here now. Never alone. Remember?"

He rubs his cool, slick cheek against mine like a naked cat trying to comfort its owner. Heat radiates deep in my chest, along with a slight pressure as he works to ground me through our bond.

I fall quiet.

I can't lie to Ollie. He can't lie to me.

I just lie to myself all the time.

I wish that Arcadia were here to guide and anchor me.

Restlessness rises again in the absence of distraction. So, I begin walking the halls, Oliver talking my ear off as he perches on my shoulder.

He's thrilled by everything we pass. His joy is infectious. Slowly—quietly—my spirit lifts as I give him a tour of the palace, pointing out every strange or wonderful thing I think he'll love.

CHAPTER 22

Millicent

AS THE SUN VANISHES AND THE MOON TAKES ITS PLACE, Oliver tires of the tour and disappears, retreating to whatever hellish domain he crawled out of this time.

On my way back to my room—hoping to relax and maybe read—I catch sight of Felix climbing through one of the windows, his dark sage-green cloak billowing behind him. The king of the South is truly climbing through a window in his own palace in a disguise. I stroll over toward the struggled huffs, a smirk pulling at my lips.

"Sneaking out again?" I can't help but laugh as I watch him drunkenly haul himself through the opening. There's a door just a few paces down. I can't deny that watching him use the window is exceedingly entertaining.

He lifts his eyes from the floor to meet mine. "Ah, Millicent! Just got some fresh air," he lies, words slurring.

"Was the air made of wine or mead?" I snort, grabbing his hands to help tug him through. "Gods, you're heavier than you look."

"It's rude to mention a lady's weight," he grunts, wriggling through the window. "Now pull! Put your back into it!"

I heave, digging my heels in for some leverage, "Felix, there's a damn door right down the hall!"

"That hardly screams *sneaking out*, does it?" he retorts sassily, just before falling face first onto the floor with a squeal that sounds more pig than man.

Laughing hysterically, he pulls himself upright, completely unfazed by the alcohol sloshing in his system.

"Your subjects are going to see their king drunk and dressed like a commoner," I tease.

"Drunk is nothing new. You should see me at a ball: the ladies love me. I have to beat them off with a stick!" He grins proudly before glancing down at his disheveled clothes. "Let them wonder. They can call me the handsome, mysterious king."

"Felix, this—" I gesture at his tousled outfit, stained with red wine and littered with dirt and leaves from the shrubs outside, "—is not mysterious. It's more homeless drunkard, maybe."

He rolls his eyes, brushing at the bits of greenery stuck to him, but he hardly makes a difference. "Come! I need more wine. You're giving me a headache, which can only mean *you* need wine too."

His sass incites my intrigue to follow his line of thinking. Felix is dangerously entertaining. And he's grown on me. I try not to dwell on this fact because it clashes with everything I've been taught. It'll drag me into a hole of self-loathing I might not crawl out of.

"Witches make their own brew since human wine doesn't affect us the same."

"Please. You're just not drinking enough," he scoffs, dismissive as ever.

He leads us into his study and heads straight for a row of wine bottles lined atop a high, glossy black table trimmed in gold.

"You want me to black out?" I laugh as he pours the glass, nearly to the brim, and he hands it to me before sprawling out on the couch.

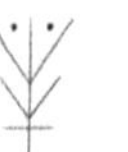

I settle beside him, cross-legged on the floor, accepting the glass with amusement. He confirms his intention—to black out and drag me with him.

The hours pass easily.

Felix flits from one absurd story to the next. I learn he loves women and wine in excess, and based on how he speaks about being king, I suspect he doesn't want the title. He's a clever little devil—sharp tongued and surprisingly endearing, even when drunk. However, he never confides in me exactly where he goes when he slips away.

Eventually, I'm tipsy enough to be giggling as he tries to braid my hair from behind. I'm not even fully aware of how we got in this position. Our conversations began to blur into one and became hazy from the wine. He was right: I just needed more wine.

"You squirm so much, girl. Do you *want* to look horrendous?" he mutters, tugging at my hair as he restarts the simple braid.

"You blame the art and not the artist? Typical," I giggle, leaning into the joke. "My sister always said any hairstyle would look beautiful on me."

I smile thinking about Arcadia again, as I often find myself doing. The wine does a fantastic job at dampening the shame that rises over my attachment to her, which allows me to think of her without oppression.

Tyran's words draw me back. "Well, she's a liar," he mumbles, still focused on the task.

I laugh so hard my whole body shakes, and it sends Felix into a fit of laughter with me.

Our laughs die abruptly when the door swings open. Cage stands at the threshold, watching us.

"Do you not knock?" I blurt, crossing my arms with a pout.

Felix tugs my hair again. "Yeah! We could've been naked!"

I reach back and slap his knee, earning me a sharp tug in response.

The intensity in Cage's gaze causes me to shift on my crossed legs, suddenly self-conscious.

"The guards checked your room. You were missing," he says, eyes flicking to the three empty wine bottles scattered on the floor. "I was just making sure you are safe." His voice flattens. I'm not at all surprised Felix slips away from his own guards. "You're both drunk, aren't you?"

"Why *aren't* you drunk, is the real question," Felix replies, playfully unfazed as he continues braiding.

I sit up straighter, trying not to move now that he's nearly finished.

"All done! I've got a mirror somewhere," he mumbles, rifling through the clutter on the side table before producing a small hand-held mirror. He holds it out to me.

I take one look and burst into laughter. It's atrocious: lumpy and crooked, with strands sticking out in every direction.

"This is horrible!" I wheeze, wiping away tears. My eyes snag on wrinkles around my eyes and mouth as my skin pulls up from the force of my laugh. As I giggle, my own expression is so foreign that I forget about the braid for a moment and study my own face.

"I *thought* you said you'd look beautiful in any hairstyle? See, your sister is clearly a liar!" he declares triumphantly.

My eyes drift up from the mirror to Cage, who's staring at me with an emotion I can't quite place.

"It looks like shit," he adds coldly.

I roll my eyes. "Wow, it's a marvel you're still single."

Cage smirks as he steps closer. "Single by choice, but my bed is never cold, little witch."

Behind me, Felix snorts and flops back on the couch. "You have no class. That's why every woman you bed ends up a scorned lover, pining and cursing your name. I swear they pray for your downfall, Cage."

Cage shrugs and comes to stand beside me, his gaze dropping to Felix.

"I'm not a coddling caregiver like you. I'm honest: lust is the only thing I offer. You romance them. I don't. My appetite is...rougher."

He flicks a side glance at me from the corner of his eyes when he catches me staring.

"I think our dear king needs his beauty rest," he says, "and you need to return to your room."

Felix is starting to pass out.

I rise, wobbling on legs that haven't stood in hours, and that isn't to mention the three bottles of wine. The unsteadiness makes me giggle along with the dancing room, right before large, strong hands grab my arms.

"Please tell me you can walk," Cage says, clearly annoyed.

"No, I forgot how to use my legs; of course I can walk! Unhand me!" I demand, yanking my arms free—only to fall flat on my ass.

I cross my arms and lift my chin, determined to show no sign of defeat.

Felix snorts out a laugh. "No! She can totally walk! Matter of fact, I want to watch this." He crosses his feet at the ankles and tucks his crossed arms under his head as he grins down at me.

"You are stupid and stubborn, and your braid makes you look as insane as you are," Cage grumbles, bending down to scoop me up.

"Put me down before I obliterate you," I warn as he pulls me against his chest. One of his arms hooks under my knees, and the other wraps around my shoulders.

"Oh, I'm shaking in fear," he deadpans, carrying me out of Felix's study.

His sarcasm flies over my head in my drunken haze, and I wave goodbye to Felix just as we exit. "As you should be. Many tremble in my presence." I grin, glancing down the hall.

A strange part of me takes enjoyment in being carried. I know he loathes this, and that only makes it better. The thought makes me kick my feet in joy. A free ride to my room while simultaneously annoying Cage? *Jackpot.*

He casts a sideways glance at my casually kicking feet. "I will be the kinder one between us and resist making you shake," he murmurs.

I frown and look up at him, confused. "I will *never* tremble in fear of you."

His voice dips into something low and dangerous, a husky promise of some dark, hidden desires. "Who said it would be out of fear?"

I shut my mouth, my drunk brain fumbling to process the suggestive words, and my feet cease their kicking. Agitation pricks, demanding I argue back, but confusion forces me to shut my mouth as my brain struggles to process why it sounds like he desires to touch me. I'm drunk and losing it. Heat blooms on my cheeks as my flustered state ultimately silences me. I huff and look back down the hall; he's already covered a lot of ground. Being tall really does get you places faster.

When we reach the private hall, he carries me into my room, ignoring my insistence I can walk. He drops me onto the bed with little ceremony, and I bounce once, giggling too hard to be upset.

"You are dismissed now," I say, waving him off as I pull back the covers.

I yelp in surprise when he grabs my ankle and pulls me flat onto my back. The sudden motion sends the room spinning.

"Hey!" I whine, starting to sit up, only for his hand to press just above my navel, pinning me in place. The muscles in my stomach all tense.

"You don't give commands, little witch," he murmurs, and I notice something strange; his silver eyes seem darker. I squint, attempting to decipher if it's just the poor lighting or if I'm imagining things.

He sits beside me on the bed, reaching down; he tugs the end of my braid. "Sit up, Millicent," he says.

Curiosity wins out. I slowly sit up, watching him with suspicion.

His hands move behind me, fingers working through the tangled mess Felix left behind.

"Your eyes are darker," I mumble, fixated.

"You're drunk," he replies quietly, still focused on my hair.

"I'm not that drunk," I slur.

"You're letting me sit on your bed and undo your braid. You're a drunk little witch."

"I just don't want my hair to be a mess tomorrow," I say defensively.

His hands are surprisingly gentle; they don't tug, unlike Felix's. When the braid is undone, his fingers slide through my hair, massaging my scalp. I groan as tingles ripple down my spine and the ache from the taut pull of my hair melts away. When our eyes meet again, I swear they've gone nearly black.

"Your braid is out," he says, still cradling my head with one hand. The other slides over my ribs, gliding to the back of my gown, sending my heartbeat skittering. His fingers slip beneath the laces of my bodice in one fluid motion.

"You're still letting me touch you," he murmurs. "You really want to keep pretending you're not as drunk as Felix?"

The imprudence of his smirk and the challenge in his voice motivate me to argue.

"You're sober and touching me," I shoot back, deflecting his suggestion that I'm a drunk mess.

Even if the room's spinning, my heart's picking up, and his hands feel *nice*.

He grins devilishly as his fingers find the knot in my bodice and tugs it loose, slowly. The fabric slacks, and suddenly I can breathe more freely. Each lungful causes the peaks of my breasts to press against the thin cotton of my gown and the rough, rigid fabric of the loose-hanging bodice. They tighten, stirring up heat within my chest.

He dips his head and murmurs against my jaw: "Feel better?"

One hand slides from my hair—down the back of my neck—joining the other as he works the remaining laces free.

Heat rushes over me, chasing the shiver that crawls down my spine. My breath quickens, but I can't find the words to respond. His touch is awakening something deep inside me that I've tried to bury.

My bodice falls away; my breasts are suddenly reprieved from the teasing, and they are left with a low, throbbing ache. His rough hands glide over my skin, and he slips the straps down my arms so that the fabric falls to the floor. I'm left with only my loose gown.

The soft cotton clings to me, tracing every curve of my silhouette. I feel more exposed under his gaze than if I were naked. My cheeks burn as my hardened nipples poke up from beneath the fabric.

He smiles against my jaw, his breath warm and his presence overwhelming. The alcohol has already fogged my thoughts, dulled my defenses. Now, with his lips on my skin, it's nearly impossible to think straight.

Whatever hatred I feel for him is drowned out by the wine and my remarkable talent for making terrible decisions—for surrendering control of my emotions and desires.

His hands glide back up my arms as he pulls away just enough to look at me. His gaze drags down my body and halts...directly on my chest.

"Fuck," he growls, his gaze locked on the dark hue of my nipples.

His hands grip my biceps as he pushes me down against the mattress. He looks up at the ceiling, and I swear I hear him counting.

"I'm not a good man. I try to be, but I wasn't born good," he mutters, jaw tight and eyes distant. His hands curl into fists on either side of my shoulders as he leans over me.

"I work every day to overcome my nature." Then, quieter. "And you...you test that."

His gaze lowers to mine, thick with frustration. "You test it when you look at me with those damn eyes."

I stare up at him, half-lidded, breath shallow. Need coils in my stomach, ravenous and growing, and my control slips.

"So damn needy," he curses, leaning down, caging me in with his arms. His voice drops to a near growl. "Lie to me again. Tell me you're not drunk. Tell me you came here with good intentions. Lie to me some more."

He wants a lie? I'll give him one.

Embolden by wine and his hunter, I swallow hard. "Touch me," I plead with a whisper. The words feel like my own and yet far away, belonging to another. Just like earlier, the wine does its job at squishing

down the shame I feel until I can't hear it, can't feel it. I just hunger for more. And he can satiate me.

His nostrils flare with the force of his exhale. "You're so pretty when you lie," he murmurs. "I almost want to indulge you."

His jaw tics. He leans in—close enough for his breath to fan over my lips—but stops short.

"You're an infection," he breathes. "If I slip my hand between those creamy thighs, and if I suck the breasts begging for my attention...I won't find a cure."

His words burn through me—fuel to the fire already blazing in my veins. In that moment, I feel devastating. Beautiful. Dangerous.

Instead of touching me, he pulls back.

"Sleep, Millicent," he says, shaking his head. "You're drunk, and I'm drunk on lust, apparently."

He retreats from the bed in one swift motion, vanishing through the door without a backward glance. Only then do I realize the room is spinning.

I don't remember when I close my eyes or fall asleep, the night blurring.

CHAPTER 23
Cage

I SIT IN THE MEETING ROOM, A SPARSE SPACE WITH A SMALL oak table, a few chairs, and little else. The walls are lined with tapestries and old maps of the continent, their colors worn and edges curled. Above us, a deep-gold chandelier casts a soft, warm glow. It lends a false sense of comfort to the serious business at hand.

Kalix lounges next to me, rocking back on two legs of his chair, boots kicked up onto the table. Iris stands beside Tyran, leaning a collection of yellowed texts spread across the surface.

The texts are too far, and I don't feel like squinting to try and make them out, nor do I need to. I know Iris will tell me everything I need to know.

"Inside of that sad excuse for a girl's body, I found a curse marking I've never seen before," Iris explains, pointing to a sketch of the sigil she replicated. "I can't find it in any texts. What interests me more is how it was carved inside her to begin with.

"How would we figure that out if you can't?" Kalix asks, lacing his fingers behind his head.

Iris glances at Tyran, a small smile playing on her lips. "You happen to be clever with words and very resourceful. I'm hoping you could petition a meeting with one of the covens dealing in curses."

"Absolutely not. That's far too high of a safety risk," I cut in, protective instincts flaring. The last thing I want is more witches here, especially a curse user. One look, one stray thought, and they could hex Tyran into oblivion. That's not a risk I'm willing to take.

Iris looks at me, still smiling. She expected this and has a deeper plan. Always a step ahead.

"Exactly," she replies smoothly. "That's why *you* will be Tyran. He'll stay outside the coven, safely guarded by Kalix and a few men, while you form a mental link. He can feed you what to say—make you sound like him and charm the pants off the coven."

"Only one problem with your ingenious plan," I say dryly, clasping my hands on the table. "Do I look like Tyran?"

She rolls her eyes. "No, jackass, you don't, but Kalix can transfigure you."

Kalix's chair thuds back onto four legs. Kalix blinks between us. "You want me to morph him into Tyran?"

I understand why I'm the one selected for the task and not Kalix, Iris, or even one of my best mages. I want to be the one handling such a delicate situation, ensuring we get everything we possibly can from this lead. Still, wearing the skin of Tyran feels wrong, a step far over the line of a simple disguise.

"You're our potion expert," Iris snaps, eyes narrowing. "Be a damn expert."

Kalix grins and turns to me, "Oh, you'll be so handsome with golden hair."

Tyran claps his hands like a delighted child. "I love this plan. Just the right amount of flash!"

"Cage, you'll take Millicent with you," Iris says. "They should respond positively to her, especially with that last name. We're essentially pulling rank."

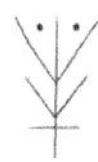

If anyone understands the internal politics of covens, it's Iris.

I nod once, acknowledging the decision. I'll take our fiery little witch with us...though I can't help but wonder if it'll come back to bite me.

"When do we leave?" I ask, watching as Tyran removes his crown and sets it on the table.

"Today, of course," he answers. "This business with the North can't wait. It's our first lead; we follow it while it's fresh."

"What about petitioning the coven for a meeting?" I turn to Iris.

"A messenger was already sent," she replies. "We could wait, but there's no guarantee we'd get a response. Curse users are the most rational type. I think it's safe if you approach nonthreateningly and with a witch beside you."

She shrugs. "If we get denied, we get denied."

Then she adds, more firmly, "I can't stress enough how important the Le Strange name is. And Millicent's strength. That alone will likely open the door."

"Millicent isn't here because you don't want her knowing I'll be posing as Felix?" I ask, her absence finally making sense.

Felix tugs at one of his curls. "We need her cooperative and sharp. Even if curse users are more stable than other witches, they're still lethal. Millicent likes me; she'll be more agreeable if she thinks I'm there."

I stare at him, stunned. "Be serious. She considers humans vermin."

Felix rolls his eyes. "I *am* human...and less bothered by that than you are. The rich in this city call the poor sewer rats. I don't see much difference."

"The difference is, she kills humans. The poor don't," I snap.

Kalix chimes in casually, worsening my mood. "Actually, some have. Mental illness, starvation, desperation—it happens."

Before I can fire back, Iris cuts in smoothly. "Her coven hasn't practiced human sacrifice in some time. If she ever did, it would've been when she was much younger."

I tense. "And how exactly do you know that?"

I don't mean for it to come out so tight-lipped, but it does.

"I like Millicent, and I talk to her. That is all I will say." Her face hardens, daring me to prod further.

I remain silent. I've already lost this argument.

How are they all warming up to her?

She is probably manipulating them—has to be. Nora's favorite is surely taking after her. I saw her with Tyran a few nights ago laughing, relaxing, and having a good time. I still can't wrap my head around it.

I walked her to her room afterward. I nearly made a mistake.

Whatever lives in my chest has started to stir in her presence. It *wants* her. Craves her. And I don't understand why.

The only theory I have is this: the darkness in her mirrors my own. And that recognition is rousing the thing I've kept chained for years.

Even drunk, she noticed my eyes going black as I began to slip. She saw it and I felt it: the urge to take her, mark her, leave her trembling and suffocating with the sound of my name, and then finally extract the power from her veins. It was nearly overwhelming.

I barely held myself back.

I need to be more careful. I cannot be alone with her until I understand why this is happening and how to stop it.

This part of me...I used to let it run wild when I was younger. On the battlefield, in blood and pain, I fed it power and let it guide me like a monster. I fought it for years. I trained until my control became instinct—until I could breathe without fearing what lived beneath.

Millicent is the first thing in *years* that's tested my control.

We spend another hour finalizing the logistics: where the coven is located, where Tyran will be stationed with his guards, and how Millicent and I will carry out our roles.

When we finally leave the meeting chamber, I follow Kalix down a rarely used hall to his apothecary. A large, rusted padlock clicks open, and he swings the wooden door open.

The interior is like a hoarder's dream: cluttered shelves of herbs, vials of powders and liquids, and rows of labeled bottles packed tight. The

L-shaped workbench groans under the weight of stacked instruments, and a single table in the center holds a leather box with drawers pulled halfway out. Each one reveals more vials and tucked-away tools—and even more storage.

Mortars, pestles, beakers, pipettes, and wide glass wicks lie scattered across every surface, set up for boiling, blending, and brewing. Among them are rings designed to conceal poisons. Hanging from copper hooks are long gold and silver chains with hidden compartments: lockets, pendants, and hollow cores.

Kalix might look like a brute, but the man has a rare talent for alchemy.

He grew up in the village of Caldwell. The local apothecary took him in at a young age and gave him work so he could help feed his family. Kalix stuck with it: learning, experimenting, and refining his skill. When he hit a wall in Caldwell, he left, eventually landing at Tyran's court. Within two years, his loyalty and strength earned him a captain's title.

He never lost his love of potion-making. Felix saw value in that and gave him this space. Encouraged him. Felix carries Kalix's brews everywhere—for protection, sure, but I suspect a few are for hangovers too.

Kalix strolls to a nearby shelf, trailing his fingers across rows of corked bottles. He selects one, turns to me, and holds out his hand.

I take the vial, within which a small amount of shimmering green liquid swirls.

"Drink it. It'll taste awful, and you'll feel weird. The effects will last eight hours—no longer—so I'll give you a backup just in case. When you take it, focus hard on Felix. The potion responds to desire," Kalix explains.

I uncork the vial and throw it back in one swallow. I wince with instant regret. The taste is sour and dry, like licking a copper coin dipped in vinegar. My throat tightens, my tongue shrivels, and I cough hard, choking on the afterburn.

I slap my chest, trying to clear the tightness, and then freeze.

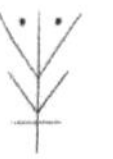

My hand is no longer my own. The skin is softer, paler. The broad lines of my fingers are replaced by Felix's long, elegant ones. I shove my sleeve up; my tan skin is gone, taking my mage markings with it. My show of power and strength is simply absent. I quickly call on the magic so readily available to me, and the cold replaces any previous warmth in my body as it awakens, filling my tissues. My next breath is looser, and my power, even if I can't see it, is confirmed.

Kalix claps for himself, grinning like a madman. "Goddamn, I'm good."

He points toward a circular mirror mounted beside the door, the glass covered in a thin film of dust. I stare into the mirror.

No tousled raven hair. No grey eyes. No mage marks. I've been erased.

And in my place...stands Felix.

"I look exactly like him," I mutter, the words slipping out in a tone that's not mine: softer and lighter. My eyes widen. Even my voice sounds like his. This is messing with my head.

"You sound exactly like him too," Kalix says, circling the workbench to look me over. "Damn, this is good. You need to change—too much black. Felix is *much* more in style. Fancy outfits—gold everywhere."

He grins, fully aware that the thought of dressing like a gilded peacock grates on me.

Still, I nod and leave his workshop.

The walk to Felix's room takes ten minutes. The palace feels different like this. Guards and servants bow—not stiff or cautious but warm, even yearning. I forget I'm not myself until their reactions remind me I am their king. The submission and desire awaken the sleeping hunger. I shut them down quickly, preventing any delusional whispers of conquest and power in my mind.

For all intents and purposes, I'm Felix.

When I reach his chambers, I don't bother knocking. I push open the golden double doors to find him already waiting, grinning by his wardrobe.

"Damn, I look that good?" he beams.

"Stop admiring yourself. It's unsettling. You look like you might kiss me—or yourself, I guess. Either way, it's disturbing."

I cringe inwardly at the thought.

"My dashing good looks can be overwhelming like that." He shrugs, turning back to his wardrobe. He waves me over, and together we dig through his gaudy collection until he picks *the* outfit; then he demands I wear it.

I let him dress me in tight leather trousers, black boots with jeweled straps, a fitted white tunic embroidered with gold swirls, and a long golden robe that trails behind me like some dramatic curtain.

Then, the final touch: he lifts the crown from his head and sets it on mine.

"This thing actually has some weight to it," I mutter, adjusting the crown. "I see why you whine after wearing it all day."

"Heavy is the crown," Felix says with a wink. "Literal and metaphorical."

He leans back against his bedpost and starts walking me through his typical behavior. I let him talk, but I already know. I've been with him since he was younger. I could recognize him in darkness by the sound of his breathing alone.

What does surprise me is when he brings up Millicent.

"I like her," he says. "I've spent some time with her. I enjoy her company. I keep it playful. I don't pry, Cage," he adds pointedly. "And, yeah, I flirt. Sue me. She's a beauty wrapped in black hair and devastating eyes."

"I'm not going to flirt with her," I say flatly.

"If flirting gets us answers about this curse, you'll flirt. Hell, you'll walk on all fours and bark if that's what it takes. We need this."

I know he doesn't mean it literally, but he's not wrong.

This is our first real lead. And the mutations are spreading. More disappearances. More bodies. If we don't figure this out soon, it'll get worse. On top of that, we'll be entering a coven of curse users who can

hex us through thought alone. Add to that an unpredictable witch who can't be trusted, and this simple questioning can turn dangerous extremely fast.

I listen as he explains other quirks I'll need to mimic. When he finishes, I speak.

"The link will feel just like this," I say. "You'll hear me in your mind, same as always. The only difference is, you won't see me for a few hours."

We use mental speech often: during court meetings, public appearances, and anytime we need to speak privately. He listens like a child on Winter Solstice Eve, giddy with the anticipation of gifts.

When we're done, I head off alone, beginning the long walk back to the solitary hall that houses both my room and Millicent's. The air grows heavier with each step closer to her door.

CHAPTER 24

Cage

I RAISE MY FIST AND KNOCK POLITELY ON MILLICENT'S DOOR.

It opens moments later, and the sight that greets me knocks me slightly off balance.

Her witch marks shimmer under the chandelier's light, exposed by the gown. The deep-red satin clings to her frame, the straps hanging loose off her shoulders. It frames a plunging sweetheart neckline. A corset-style bodice, detailed with black beading, hugs her waist. The fabric then flows into a fuller skirt that flares around her ankles.

A slit comes high up her left leg, revealing a golden snake cuff coiled around her thigh.

The gown is regal and expensive. The sight causes a sharp intake of breath before I quickly loosen it. I know, without a doubt, it's Tyran's doing.

"Well, at least you dressed up too. I could've just worn my coven garb," she says casually—too casually for how she usually speaks to me. *She's talking to Felix, not me.*

"We must make a statement. Besides, your coven gown is boring," I reply, slipping effortlessly into Felix's personality as I offer my arm.

"Rude," she says, rolling her eyes. But she still slips her arm into mine, closing the door behind her.

"I figured you like the truth. Shall I begin lying?" I tease.

"I bet you're a great liar," she murmurs, her voice hushed. "You sneaky thing."

Sneaky?

Did she run into Felix earlier? Did she go with him?

Did she know where he went?

Changing the subject—before I say the wrong thing—I slip back into character. "We'll take one of the carriages and be escorted by my knights. It's about a four-hour ride. Roads should be clear. Their coven has a gated road leading in. Seems they've built their own network of mansions."

"I'm not surprised," she replies, eyes drifting over the artwork we pass. "Curse users are the most emotionally stable. They don't need humans for sacrifice, so I imagine they've embraced a more civilized lifestyle—especially living so near to humans."

She continues toward the front of the castle where the carriage waits.

She often studies art in the halls. I've seen her do it before: pausing and tilting her head inquisitively. I never interrupt. I keep to the shadows, watching without being seen. It's safer that way; I enjoy watching her sometimes, a feeling I don't quite understand yet. It almost feels nostalgic at times before the reality of what and who she is sours my mood, dismissing me from her presence.

The castle wards ping softly in the back of my mind during the day as she unknowingly walks through them. I always know where she is.

She may not see me every day, but I make sure I see her. I still don't trust that she's not up to something.

I glance at her from the corner of my eye.

She seems too at ease.

"How familiar are you with this coven—or curses in general?" I ask lightly.

"This coven? No. I'm not familiar with the Exsecratus family," she says. "But I know a fair bit about curses. We have a curse user at my coven."

A hint of a smile pulls ever so slightly at her lips when she says it.

We arrive outside and climb into the carriage. As it takes off, I watch the castle pass by, sending a silent prayer to any god who will listen that this works and goes well—that it doesn't end in disaster—because I still don't trust her.

Millicent is alone with the king, surrounded by other witches. What better time to strike?

Why else would she cozy up to Felix? Nora manipulated me in the same way. She was warm, kind. I thought she genuinely wanted to help me—that her lessons had meaning and purpose. I won't make that mistake again, not with her protégé sitting across from me.

I glance at her. She's distracted by the trees flashing past the window.

Felix is right about one thing: she's beautiful.

Her looks don't soften my hatred for her, but I can admit she's captivating. The most dangerous things often are.

Iris has these frogs in her lab: sleek and black-skinned, with glowing neon stripes. They're gorgeous and mesmerizing. Touch one, and its poison absorbs through your skin. What follows is paralysis. And then the heart stops.

That's what Millicent reminds me of: darkness cloaked in electric blue—bewitching and cold-blooded, coated in poison.

And I know what her skin feels like. I touched her before. I found her wet beneath my fingers; the poison coating her tempted me like the first waters on the horizon after days traveling in a blazing desert. After that encounter, I had to dunk my head in a bucket of ice water just to think straight.

I made my point that night; I held the upper hand. At least, I hope she hates herself for it.

I'd be lying if I said I wasn't hard as hell after our little encounter, however.

I scrubbed my fingers raw trying to erase the musky scent of cherries she left on me—just to clear my thoughts.

It was nothing. Just a reaction.

She's breathtaking in a nauseating way; her pheromones are affecting me. Like any other animal in heat, it's simple biology. Unlike other animals, my attraction to her comes from no kind or sweet longing place, nor from any urge to reproduce.

It is fatal, rousing a version of myself that remains buried unless dark hours summon it forward—unless life or death demands its arrival.

"Felix, you good?"

I realize now that I'm scowling at her.

Wiping the expression from my face, I force a wide smile. My cheeks round in a way that feels foreign; I'm still getting used to Felix's facial structure.

"Just lost in thought," I say smoothly. "I'm hoping everything goes well at the coven. It's our first real lead."

"I will assist however I can. That was the deal." Her tone remains level and calm. "You just need to follow my lead. Don't question me in front of them. Some will see humans as worthless. Others may be... interested that a man is present."

She really thinks she's in charge of this. I don't interrupt, allowing her delusion of control to fully form.

She begins by debriefing me on the structure of a typical coven. I already know this—having grown up with the Le Strange—but I nod along.

There's always a Head Elder—the strongest and the oldest. Sometimes two others join her, but there's always one in charge. Below them are the sisters: skilled, specialized witches with designated roles. And, at the bottom: the witchlings.

These are young girls who haven't bled yet, their magic still dormant. They're heavily guarded. Witch fertility is fragile, and many never conceive. Because witches aren't created like humans, conception is rare. When a pregnancy does occur, the coven treats it as sacred. The child is raised communally and treasured like royalty.

The carriage ride is quiet for a while, but I remember how odd this is, as Felix never shuts up.

"Have you ever been to another coven? You know, outside your own?"

She shakes her head. "I have not."

I already knew that. Her little imp-fueled meltdown told me as much. I'm still curious. "Why not? Witches not very social?"

"We're not," she says simply. "Not with anyone outside our covens. It's been that way since the days of creation...when we were hunted—young and vulnerable. Or so the old texts say. Trust kept us alive. Over time, we grew stronger."

She pauses. There's something more behind her silence. I feel it.

A temptation rises in me.

Right now, I'm Felix. She won't have her guard up the same way she would around me. I could slip into her mind, quietly. I'll pull at the answers I want.

I don't, but not because I don't want to. I *do*—so badly it burns.

If I go digging, I won't stop. I know that. I'll strip her thoughts raw, clawing at every buried truth until I find what I want: why they tortured a child.

I want to know if they still did it to others.

Violating her would feel like justice. Like revenge.

She's not Nora.

I remind myself of that, even as my thoughts twist and warp to make her into the woman who haunts me. Millicent moves, and I see Nora in her. She speaks, and I hear Nora's venom. My mind finds patterns—just enough to justify the hatred, to make it feel right.

I want to be right.

I want to end Millicent just to take something from Nora and make her feel what I felt. I want to strip her of the only witch in history with two magics coursing through her blood.

Felix said he never pried. So, I don't. Instead, I ask her everything else I can think of.

Did she like the palace? The food? Her room?

She answers, polite and composed. I learn she's been spending a lot of time in Iris's lab, assisting her. Her only complaint is the lack of training.

"Kalix or Cage would train with you. I can easily command it," I say casually, knowing Felix would do whatever he could to meet her needs, as he does for everyone.

She chews on her bottom lip in contemplation, and my eyes flick to the movement before I can stop them, the sight causing my jaw to tense slightly.

When she finally releases it, swollen from the pressure, she looks out the window and murmurs, "I'll think about it. Thank you."

Thank you? So, she *does* have manners. Maybe all I need is golden hair and a king's smile to earn a little respect around here.

We were just children when those deaths occurred at her coven that night. It wasn't something I did on purpose. It was self-defense. A loss of control, yes, but not malice.

I buried the guilt a long time ago. Can't she let it die too?

She should accept her coven's failings, as well as her own, and maybe—just maybe—treat me like I deserve a sliver of decency.

I catch myself pouting and quickly glance away, fixing my eyes on the landscape outside the window, hoping the passing trees will distract me from the ache still buried in my chest.

She can make me her monster.

I am what they created after all. My sympathies slithered from gaping wounds long ago, until there was nothing left—until the world was black—and I didn't even think I had any blood left.

But you can always bleed more.

CHAPTER 25

Cage

A S WE APPROACH THE BRIDGE THAT CROSSES THE RAVINE and leads to the coven gates, I lean out the carriage window and signal for the one behind us to stop.

"Some knights will stay back here so the witches don't see us as a threat—while still providing additional safety," I explain, half-true. Kalix and Felix are in that carriage, guarded by knights, yes, but their safety is the priority, not ours.

Horse hooves clack steadily over the cobblestone. It's time.

I reach inward, delicately extending a thin black thread—barely more than a whisper of magic—down the line toward Felix's mind. I do not want to alert Millicent, so I keep the connection low and contained. No surges. No stray threads she might sense.

Kalix's potion is doing its job, dampening my aura enough that I pass for a mortal. He warned me that any real surge of power will break the illusion.

Felix is warm and eager as I slip through the familiar opening in the back of his mind. I strengthen the link, thickening the thread into something more durable—less like a strand of hair and more like a tether of woven silk.

Almost showtime, I send down the line, testing the connection.

You have to tell me everything you see! Felix's excitement bubbles through our connection, crackling on my tongue like the pop-rock candy from the merchant in town.

The carriage slows to a stop just outside the tall, imposing iron gates. I step out first, and then I extend my hand to help Millicent. She accepts my touch without hesitation, flinch, or complaint.

That ease sours my mood, settling in my stomach like curdled milk. Felix must touch her often if she's grown so accustomed to it.

I let go of her hand as soon as she's steady and then lead the way toward two sentinel witches standing guard. They wear deep-red robes, perfectly matched. One has short, curly brown hair; the other's is buzzed short leaving a pale white cast on her head.

Stopping at a respectable distance, I lift my hands slowly, palms open in a universal gesture of amity.

"I come peacefully," I announce clearly, projecting Felix's easy charm. "I'm here only to ask for your aid."

"A mortal king asking aid from a coven, and accompanied by a witch?" The buzzed-haired witch scowls, her eyes flicking skeptically between us.

Millicent lifts her chin slightly, her voice ringing clear and authoritative. "I am Millicent Le Strange. We seek your elder... or someone well versed in curses. We've encountered a curse we cannot name."

The witches' eyes widen sharply at the mention of her name. "Nora sent no word of a visit." At the mention of her name, the witches tense ever so slightly. Defensively.

Millicent doesn't falter. "I'm here by her direct order to assist the king. Nora is fully aware in this matter."

She sounds truthful, and I'm not surprised. Nora always knows what Millicent is up to. No one controls every facet of your life, only

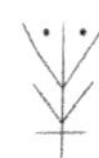

to send you away without keeping a close eye. Nora's collar hasn't loosened; she merely lengthened the leash.

Millicent must be in constant contact with her, likely through letters or, more disturbingly, through that familiar whose sole purpose was always spying. When I was Nora's favorite, that creepy thing hovered around me constantly. I swear it never even blinked.

The witches guarding the gate exchange a silent glance before the curly-haired one speaks: "Fine. You'll both wear no-harm curses. If you harm anyone in this coven—or even intend to—the curse will activate, collapsing your lungs within seconds. You'll suffocate and die in under a minute. It is a painful death."

"We accept." Millicent says without hesitation. "I'll be marked first."

Her confidence makes my own brief hesitation feel glaringly obvious. She moves directly to the curly-haired witch, and I follow suit, stopping in front of the buzzed-haired sentinel.

"Unbutton your shirt. This goes on your chest," she instructs curtly.

I loosen the golden buttons, exposing my chest. Her finger dips into a silver ink pad. The ink is cold; she presses it onto my skin as she traces a long rectangle, marking out a complex rune in one practiced motion. I recoil inwardly but force no reaction to show outwardly. It is necessary—a line I am far too familiar with in situations I dislike. A quick glance at Millicent reveals the same rune being carefully etched onto her chest, but her face does not give any emotion away.

When they finish, the iron gates creak open, allowing us entry. Inside, the courtyard surrounding the massive, white-marbled mansion is littered with statues of men and women, all half hidden beneath layers of ivy. Fountains gurgle quietly, the water dancing in the evening air.

"Seems rather fancy here," I murmur as we climb the wide staircase toward the mansion's ornate entrance.

"It wouldn't surprise me if these curse users leveraged their skills to rise in society," Millicent replies softly. "The curse user I mentioned—my sister—loves travel and luxury. If they're anything like her, this display makes perfect sense."

The front doors automatically swing open the moment we step onto a stone carved with a simple activation sigil. *Handy.* I'll have to remember that one.

My gaze lifts from the stone and sweeps into the coven's luxurious interior. Floating lanterns illuminate the space brightly, casting a warm glow across richly colored red carpets. The red theme carries through the curtains, drapes, and plush furnishings; deep, wine-red hues are everywhere.

Witches move gracefully about, dressed as if attending an elegant ball. Millicent's gown fits perfectly into the scene, blending seamlessly into the crimson sea of fabric.

"Who are you lot?" A curious voice echoes down the main corridor. A tall, red-headed witch approaches, her hair pulled into a tight, disciplined bun. She looks older than most here but not quite elderly.

"Millicent Le Strange," Millicent answers firmly, "and this is King Tyran of the Southern continent. We request an audience with your elder...or someone knowledgeable about curses. We've encountered an unusual one."

The witch tilts her head slightly, fixing me with an intense stare; it's hard to ignore. I hold her gaze, but Felix's soft eyes aren't particularly intimidating. Her attention slides to Millicent.

"A king and a witch?" she muses, her expression openly curious. "Are you breeding him?"

I cough out a startled laugh and then immediately realize she's completely serious, without a hint of humor in her expression. Glancing up, I see more witches gathering along the second-floor railing to peer down at me.

It hits me then: I'm being examined like a piece of candy.

"I am," Millicent responds confidently, firmly staking her claim over me.

Anger riles up inside me, fueled by an unwanted image of Felix tangled in bed with her.

Felix must sense the spike in my emotions because his curiosity

instantly intrudes. *Everything all right over there? Don't tell me it's already going badly,* he whines.

The witch has announced to the entire coven you two are sleeping together, I snap back mentally.

His response is colored with amused delight. *Oh? How scandalous! Are women going to fight over me? Do send me mental images; I'd hate to miss the show.*

Of course, the egotistical bastard relishes the thought of witches pining after him. He's like a brightly wrapped present at a birthday party, set on a table, with everyone eagerly waiting their turn to unwrap him.

The witches' lustful gazes only grow sharper after Millicent's claim. It must be jealousy—wanting what another has. And that someone, in this case, is Millicent, the only witch alive who commands two distinct magics.

"How intriguing!" the witch exclaims. "We are friends with the Le Strange coven. We certainly won't refuse the heir. Come with me." She pivots sharply, heading down the corridor and leaving me momentarily stunned.

I turn sharply to Millicent, narrowing my eyes. "Heir?" I grind out. Her clear confusion only irritates me further.

Hells, I mentally curse. I inform Tyran of our new development. *It appears we have the bloody heir of the Le Strange coven with us.* Blindsided by such valuable information, irritation bleeds into my voice. I know everything about anyone within a few seconds after reading their mind. And, of course, I can't read Millicent's: the one person whose mind is the most vital to ensuring the safety of this kingdom and my friends. She proves yet again that she's capable of holding great secrets.

His excitement pulses instantly through our bond. *A princess! Wow! Finally, someone else of royal blood around here.* I swear, his enthusiasm is relentless and irritatingly genuine.

I soften my voice, forcibly reigning in my agitation at this revelation she's kept hidden. "Well, it seems I finally have company worthy of royal blood. Lead on, *princess*."

Millicent's eyebrows lift slightly, unimpressed. "Royal blood? Little human king, witch heirs aren't crowned by birth; they're made through power. The blood making me heir is blood I willingly spilled. I had to bleed for it. You were merely born into yours." She quickens her pace, catching up with our guide.

I easily close the distance, matching her stride. "That seems rather dreary. If I so much as get a paper cut, guards come running. No one allows my blood to spill, but your coven demands it?"

"A paper cut? You truly are pampered," she says, a slight grin tugging her lips. "I've never been coddled over an injury. I can't imagine anyone running to my aid over something so trivial. I've bled until I've passed out and placed myself into stasis for three days to recover. And even when I woke, I was alone. I rarely recall anyone there when my consciousness faded."

"That sounds...dark," I reply carefully, still maintaining Felix's casual charm. "If you'd been raised in a house that fussed over every tiny scrape, do you think you'd be different?"

She pauses thoughtfully before answering with unwavering certainty. "I'd be weak. In this life, you're either a lamb or a wolf. Coddling creates lambs, and I refuse to be one. I wouldn't change a thing."

I wonder how much of her conviction is genuine—whether she even knows the truth herself. I remember Millicent as a child, before Nora ever set her eyes on her. She'd been argumentative too, but there was a wild kindness in her. She'd been my first and only friend, my lifeline in all my dark days. She'd been the one to smile and remind me I was a living, real person whenever my mind began to leave me. Would she have grown into a fierce but compassionate woman had she escaped the coven?

Or was it always her nature—her baser instincts—that shaped her into this ruthless creature beside me now?

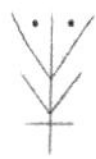

We arrive at a large, three-story library filled with rows of red-tinted wooden shelves and scattered desks piled high with books and parchment.

"Sit here. I'll fetch the elder," our escort announces before leaving us alone.

Only a handful of witches occupy the room, quietly jotting notes from open tomes. They mostly ignore us, aside from a few curious glances prompted by our sudden appearance. Pulling out one of the weathered wooden chairs, I sit down, about to cross my legs when Millicent abruptly drops herself into my lap.

"How about saying hello first?" I mumble, deliberately ignoring the way her curves fit so naturally against me.

"Hello," she drawls softly, leaning forward onto the table and propping her head up on her elbows. The movement accentuates every line of her figure, and I look away quickly, desperately avoiding the enticing curve from her waist to her hips—and her ass. Unsure where to put my hands, I rest them awkwardly on the table beside her.

"There are other chairs," I point out quietly.

"I have eyes, Felix." She glances over her shoulder at me, full lips curling into a devious smirk. Dark lashes flutter teasingly as her voice drops to a silken purr. "Do I make you nervous?"

Half of me wants to shove her off immediately. The other half—the deeper, darker half—is already stirring, thrashing inside me. It urges me to push her down onto the table instead—to make it abundantly clear that nervousness is the least of my emotions right now.

Felix would flirt back, I remind myself sharply. Yet, surely this is just an act on her part. She couldn't truly desire Felix...could she?

"When a beautiful woman is on my lap, I feel many things," I tease softly, my words carrying far more truth than I'm comfortable admitting. "Nervous isn't one of them, princess."

She lowers her voice carefully, ensuring nearby witches can't overhear. "Good. Weakness isn't allowed here. No matter how pleasant they seem, remember: they're all sharks."

"Is sitting on my lap your method of protecting me from these deadly women?" I mirror her mischievous smile. "Or is it just your excuse to be close to me?"

She rolls her eyes, "I claimed you, so I have to make it believable. The last thing I need is your little boy-bits becoming a bargaining chip."

"Man-bits, thank you," I correct her, leaning into Felix's playful arrogance. "I can demonstrate the difference if you'd like."

"If you even attempt to rub your 'man-bits' against my ass," she whispers sharply, "I'll personally neuter you when this is over. Then I'll shove your balls down your throat, and not even Kalix or Cage will be able to stop me." She finishes this with a proud smile.

I burst out laughing despite myself, the tension in my chest finally loosening. It hits me clearly now; she's not truly interested in Tyran. They haven't been sleeping together. The realization settles something inside me.

"Fiery as ever," I chuckle softly. "Very well, I'll play along as your very breedable man."

Just then, an older witch glides into the library, commanding attention effortlessly. Her sheer red gown leaves little to the imagination, showcasing her figure rather unabashedly. Long, straight blonde hair cascades down to her hips as she moves with graceful, swishing steps. Her eyes capture my attention immediately—clouded over and milky-white.

Young twin witchlings flank her, their matching blonde hair framing delicate faces. Their eyes shimmer with a pale-pink hue. They both don white dresses that are designed simply and modestly, ending just above the knee. One twin carefully pulls out a chair, and the other helps the elder sit.

As we are seated, the elder gracefully raises one hand. Instantly, every witch in the library, including her twin attendants, rises in unison and quietly exits, leaving us completely alone.

Once the room empties, the elder finally speaks. Her voice is soft, unexpectedly warm, breaking the silence gently: "I am Shalla Exsecratus.

Welcome to my home, Millicent Le Strange." She reaches out slowly, slipping her delicate hand into Millicent's. "My, how you've grown! You likely don't remember me; you were perhaps four the last time I visited your coven. In the past, we often communicated with many covens, but, sadly, times have changed. You look so much like Lyla."

At her mother's name, Millicent goes utterly still in my lap, her posture tightening. Her voice, however, remains steady. "Thank you. We're here seeking help with a curse we discovered."

Taking her cue, I reach into my pocket and carefully unfold a tattered canvas page, placing it face up on the table. The intricate curse Iris sketched is clearly visible. I move to place my hands back in my lap out of habit, but Millicent's position makes it impossible. Not wanting to appear distant from my supposed lover, I lightly settle my hands onto the gentle curve of her waist.

"This curse was found carved inside the flesh of a mutated girl...or something merely pretending to be a girl," Millicent explains. As Shalla examines the drawing, Millicent methodically recounts the events of the night when she confronted and killed the creature.

After hearing Millicent's account, Shalla's brows furrow deeply. "This is not a curse we practice here. It's an infestation curse. I only recognize it due to specific rune characteristics—like this swoop here and these dots. Think of them like braille. How a rune is drawn tells you much about its purpose and components. To find it carved into living flesh is exceedingly strange. Typically, these curses are inscribed onto objects."

She pauses thoughtfully, tapping her chin. "A curse carved inside a living being's flesh is not heard of. Curses can induce mutations, yes, but nothing this extreme. I fear what you've discovered might be entirely new." New is never good. This means there will be a hell of a lot more steps to figure out what is happening and stop it. I force myself to focus on the conversation at hand, even as my mind shifts urgently to outlining the next steps.

"There's absolutely no known method for inscribing a curse inside a living creature?" Millicent presses.

Shalla shakes her head. "Not without killing it first, placing the mark inside, and then reanimating it through necromancy." She traces the rune repeatedly with her cloudy eyes. "This still doesn't make sense. Part of this rune is clearly an invitation—summoning something to infiltrate. What exactly is being summoned, I cannot say. Creating such a curse would require extraordinary skill and power—power strong enough to distort reality itself. Such a caster should themselves be mutated by the sheer magnitude of their dark creation. Remember, power—"

"—has a price." Millicent finishes quietly. She leans forward slightly. "Let's consider the theory that someone did create this curse, possibly assisted by a necromancer. That still doesn't explain why no similar mark appeared in the Crep from the cavern, nor in its previous victim, the Duke."

Shalla nods thoughtfully. "Those cases might be unrelated. Or perhaps multiple forces are at work here. If a curse like this truly exists, consider what exactly it's inviting. Dark presences inevitably warp life around them. The Crep might have inhabited the cave long before that unfortunate girl wandered inside." Realization dawns over Millicent's face, matching the one I feel in my chest. This is far bigger and more complex than we anticipated.

Shalla gently pushes the drawing back toward us. "Tell me about this duke."

Leaning my head slightly to the side so I can see Shalla clearly, I finally speak: "The Duke had something else entirely living inside him; it took him over. There was no sign of a curse mark inside him, and no scars on his chest to suggest a necromancer's involvement." I continue elaborating as Shalla inquires further, filling in every detail I can recall.

Once I finish recounting the details, Millicent turns and looks at me, brows furrowed. "I wasn't told all of this," she says with a hint of irritation in her voice.

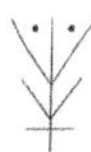

"It didn't lead anywhere," I reply with a shrug. "I figured it was a dead end."

She narrows her eyes slightly. "Why would someone with power, luxury, and the king's favor willingly welcome something so dark into themselves?"

I sense a test and an answer she already knows.

"They...wouldn't?"

"Exactly." She sits straighter. "Not even the North promising the same luxuries would tempt someone from such a sweet position. The only better seat would be the throne itself. I think our missing people—and the allies turning against you—could be the work of Manipulators."

The realization hits hard.

"Shit...you're right."

"I usually am," she mutters, turning back to Shalla and gently squeezing her hand. "Thank you, Shalla. I won't forget your help."

Shalla squeezes her hand in return and then hesitates before speaking. "Millicent...if I may, what is attached to you?"

Millicent recoils as if burned, ripping her hand back like she's been bitten by a viper.

"Please," Shalla soothes, lifting her palms in peace. "I don't mean to intrude. I've practiced curse work for nearly five centuries. I can feel them when they're close. And I feel something; it's carved into your skin."

Millicent shifts in my lap, pushing to rise, but I tighten my grip on her hips, keeping her seated. I need to hear this.

Shalla, sensing the shift, relents. She offers a gentle smile. "No worry, child. I didn't mean to upset you."

She rises just as the doors to the library open again. The twin witchlings return, taking her hands silently. "We're here to assist with whatever needs the Le Strange coven requires," she says softly. "Tell Arcadia I said hello."

With that, she exits, the doors closing behind her.

And we're alone again.

I finally release Millicent, allowing her to leap from my lap.

"Well, that was helpful," I sigh, rising from the chair.

"Hey!" I call as she storms toward the exit. I jog after her, reaching out to catch her wrist and tugging her back toward me. "Are we just storming out now? Not even going to try our hand at some of these texts?"

The moment my fingers touch her skin, I feel her magic spike—wild, unsettled.

"Millicent?" I murmur, but she doesn't hear me. Her eyes are looking past me, like I'm not there.

If I were myself, I'd shake her—rattle the storm out of her—but I'm Tyran now. Tyran is softer.

So, I let my thumb trace soothing circles along her wrist.

"Is it...about something following you?" I ask gently, trying to not escalate her further.

She jerks her arm back, glaring. "Let me go, Tyran. I don't need you caring about me," she snaps.

I ignore her words and cup her cheeks instead.

"Perhaps I'm not caring about you, exactly," I say steadily, "Maybe I'm just thinking about the mission...and how bad it'd be if a witch from another coven had a magic tantrum in their library. That'd be... inconvenient, yes?"

I nod, nudging the point home.

She exhales sharply, the fire in her eyes dimming to a stubborn pout.

"I should've left your drunk ass in the hallway," she mutters. "This isn't a friendship."

"Now *who's* being rude?" I flash a big cheesy grin. "We're definitely friends. And now that I've finally found another royal, you'll *have* to attend court. Sit right at my side."

"Oh, sure," she says dryly. "Your subjects will love a witch at court."

"I hardly care what they think." I drop my hands from her cheeks, grinning. "Honestly, it's just for my personal amusement. I want a front-row seat to your suffering."

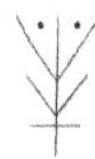

She scoffs. "That's something I would expect from Cage, not you."

"Oh, don't worry. Cage will be there too," I smirk. "He wouldn't want to miss it."

She rolls her eyes, turning for the door. "Great. My *favorite* person."

As she walks, I call after her, feigning curiosity. "I get that mages and witches have been at odds since creation, but what exactly is it between you and Cage? Seems...personal."

Her voice sharpens as the sarcasm falls away completely. "I don't care for history when it comes to him. My hatred isn't because his kind were made to put mine down. It's because he murdered my mother. And half my coven."

She turns toward me now, eyes burning. "I was five. Left to die while I held my mother's body in my lap. And he just flew away like a coward."

Her words land like a strike to the chest. The urge to reach out to her rises and I resist. It's the same urge I felt that night, resurfacing once I saw her. I have no shame for that night—no guilt—except for leaving her.

I tread carefully now. "You think he did it in cold blood? That there wasn't a reason?"

"I think he was power hungry," Millicent says bitterly. "He wanted more and more. I bet he felt unstoppable taking so many of us out in such short time."

I feel the accusation stab deep, but I manage to stay silent.

"You probably don't agree," she continues, softer now. "We were once friends. He was one of my best friends."

The admission hits harder than anything else she's said. I always thought I cared more—that she never saw me the same way.

"We weren't allowed to play with him," she says, shaking her head. "The elder segregated him from us. My mother warned me he was dangerous, but I didn't listen."

Her mouth tightens, and her eyes gloss over with regret.

"I saw someone who needed a friend. And, like a fool, I gave him

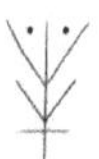

that…befriended him. In return, he betrayed me so fiercely; it haunts me, even now."

The bite in her voice softens—not forgiving, not forgetting—and cracks, just enough to reveal the pain she keeps buried.

Something twists in my chest. "Cage is my best friend now," I say slowly, surprised by my own words. "Outside of Kalix, he's important to me. He's told me some things about his time at your coven. It's not my place to share, and you wouldn't believe me anyway, but maybe it's worth hearing for your own peace of mind."

I can hardly believe I'm saying it.

Hearing her voice thicken with grief—the only softness I'd ever known after my own village burned—I can't stay silent.

"You're Nora's favorite, aren't you?" I ask gently. "You speak about bleeding and sacrifice. Maybe Cage endured the same things while he was Nora's favorite. Maybe he bled too."

She whirls to face me as we hit the door.

"The difference between us, Felix," she spits, "is that I understood what was necessary. I bore it. I didn't retaliate because I am not weak. I am worthy of the power that lives inside me."

Her voice rises with an aching ferocity.

"I gave everything," she breathes. "Since I was a child, I gave until I was nothing but an empty vessel, and then I was rebuilt. I was filled with power. I earned it. I am worthy."

Her hand presses against the door, trembling.

"He is unworthy."

There it is—her attitude—easily reigniting my hate, pushing it back over any fragile attempt at understanding her.

I won't fight her. Not as Felix. I choose my next words wisely.

"Those who are truly worthy, Millicent, don't need to keep reminding themselves they are," I say quietly, motioning to the door behind her. "Now…shall we go?"

I don't understand the flicker of hurt that flashes across her face.

Channeling Felix's softer nature, I reach out, cupping her cheeks once again. My fingers trace lightly over her warm skin, and I feel her breathing hitch beneath my touch.

"You were worthy even before you drained every ounce of emotion and blood from yourself," I murmur.

"That's easy for a mortal to say," she whispers, and I watch her mask crack further, piece by piece. "Such comforts are not afforded to my kind."

It no longer feels like manipulation. This isn't her acting for Felix's benefit. This is real, like they're friends.

I realize—too late—that I'm trespassing on a sacred friendship that doesn't belong to me. If I were a good man, an honest one, I would stop.

Instead, I reach inward and sever the mental thread connecting me to Tyran, locking this moment away from him.

This is mine.

"I can offer you comfort," I whisper, leaning closer, breathing her in. "Tell me your sins, and I'll absolve them. Tell me a truth, no matter how dark, and you'll taste freedom, even if only for a little while."

"A truth for a truth?" she breathes.

And even though I'm offering up one of Felix's secrets and not my own—just to have one of hers—I find myself whispering back without hesitation.

"A truth for a truth."

The air stills between us. She swallows hard.

"I have given everything since I was young. I gave until I was nothing but an empty vessel."

She exhales a shaky breath, and her voice begins to crack as she continues.

"Even when they filled me back up—with power, with magic—I'm still empty, Felix. I'm still hollow...I feel it inside me," she whispers. "The weakness. I can't get rid of it."

Her voice breaks fully now.

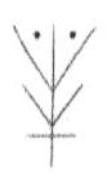

Shalla had mentioned her mother, the curse carved into her skin. With old traumas being dredged up, it's pressing down on her. I can't blame her.

And I know witches: when their emotions spiral, so does their magic. Just as her imps had manifested in her sleep, her pain could easily boil over now, twisting the magic inside her into something wildly dangerous.

I keep my touch steady, caressing her cheeks gently as her eyes fill with pain and anger.

"To feel your emotions is strength, Millicent," I murmur, letting the words sink between us. "Weakness is pretending you don't feel anything. Weakness is shoving everything down until it poisons you."

I lower my voice.

"Be angry. Be scared. Be hurt. Feel it. Let yourself be everything you are. And when you're ready...find something to fill that hollow space, and chase it."

I hesitate because what I'm about to say doesn't belong to Felix anymore.

"It's okay to not know now, but lean on...me."

I choke slightly, forcing Felix's voice to stay steady. "Lean on Iris. Lean on Kalix."

I leave my name out.

She needs comfort, not confusion.

As her breathing evens out, I slowly lift my hands from her face, lingering longer than I mean it to. That's when I notice the slight lean into my hand—Felix's hand—just before I pull away.

"You level?" I ask quietly.

"Yes, thank you," she says quietly, offering a tight-lipped smile. "It was hard. Hearing about my mother...and the other things Shalla mentioned."

I grin, slipping back into Felix's role, lightening the mood as he always does. "Anything to keep our witch from exploding!"

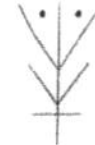

Reaching around her, I grasp the doorknob and push it open.

And because I promised—a truth for a truth—I add, almost casually, "I never wanted to be king." The truth, even if not mine, is heavier than I expect.

The door swings wide open, and she glances up at me, her blue eyes softening.

"You have too much life in you to be a royal," she says with a small smile; it's tentative but real. She's trying to comfort me, a tiny piece of herself offered back.

We step out of the library together, carrying the weight of the coven and all its secrets with us.

The ride back to the castle is quiet.

Given what passed between us, it's not...abnormal. It's expected. I let the silence stretch, offering her that small mercy.

Still, I catch myself watching her from time to time.

There's another person buried beneath her iron skin and razor claws. Even with her sharp edges, her outer appearance is...

Who am I lying to?

Millicent isn't simply pleasant and easy on the eyes.

She's terrifyingly beautiful—the kind that doesn't invite admiration but dares it. The violent sensuality woven into the fabric of her being is uncanny in a way that promises something fatal if you get too close and taste that sweet, forbidden fruit.

In another life, she must have been a siren, luring men into dark waters and singing them straight to their deaths. And if I reached out now—not as Felix but as myself—she would cut me down gleefully.

I would be her willing victim.

My hatred for her muddles further, blurring into something too complicated to name, just like the gaps in my own memory—pieces of who I used to be, eroded by time and survival.

Wouldn't I have become just like her if I'd stayed in Nora's grasp?

I long to understand Millicent.

People are puzzles to me—complex, fascinating things to be pulled apart and solved.

What motivates them? What terrifies them? How could I twist them to my will?

I tongue the inside of my cheek, irritation prickling at the edges of my thoughts.

I *hate* that I can't get into her mind. If I could just slip past her defenses, I would know everything.

I could stop fearing that someday she'll turn and tear apart the people I care about—predators locked in a vicious circle, looking for one another's weakness.

And I am learning hers. I feel no guilt for whatever methods I use.

Even as I adjust the crown atop my head, wearing this gilded meat suit, I'm built to pull the softer parts of her out.

When we return, I swiftly return to my chambers. I bathe, scrubbing away the remnants of Felix's shape.

Two hours later, I am myself again, the transformation finally broken—despite drinking a second elixir in the carriage to maintain the disguise.

I dress simply: black trousers and a loose black tunic.

And then I gather Iris, Kalix, and Felix back into the meeting hall.

Felix already knows most of it, but I lay it all out carefully, answering every question.

It takes three hours to sift through everything and to face the uncomfortable truth.

We need to infiltrate a Manipulator's coven. We need to find out if they're behind the disappearances, infections, and *mutations* spreading across the land.

We still don't know exactly what we're dealing with. Not after the Duke. Not after the abomination in the cave.

At least we have another lead now, even if following it means walking straight into the dark.

 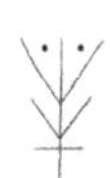

CHAPTER 26

Millicent

THE NEXT TWO WEEKS PASS UNEVENTFULLY, OUTSIDE OF Felix insisting I share some of my meals with him. He never mentions what happened at the coven, and for that, I'm thankful.

It turns out Felix and Ollie get along far too well. I sometimes forget Ollie's emotions are tied to mine and that his reactions—his likes and dislikes—often mirror the things I won't admit to myself.

Kalix and Cage are in and out of the palace grounds, hunting for any wandering manipulator witches to question.

Meanwhile, I remain in the lab, assisting Iris.

We add to the journal, noting that the curse seems to be capable of tearing down mental shields on contact. We hypothesize this makes a body more compliant—more vulnerable to whatever infection or possession it invites in.

The anxious energy that's become part of me finds some outlet here in Iris's lab.

She is growing on me, more than I expected. Often, she makes me miss Arcadia. I should write to her. I think she'd actually enjoy the castle and the people here.

People.

It's strange to admit: Kalix and Felix have grown on me too. Iris is brilliant, and her marks prove her strength. I would have once thought her weak for liking humans. Now, I'm not so sure.

Maybe it's not weakness to change. Maybe it's a strength to feel—to care. That thought is fleeting, chased away by the sudden brush of a cool hand over the back of my neck.

The Nightmother.

Her presence is exceptionally strong today, unmistakable. The full moon.

It's a reminder that a sacrifice must be made. I finish up in the lab, but my hands are clumsy, and my mind is elsewhere.

A beaker shatters, and Iris waves me off, dismissing me with a worried frown.

As sunset bleeds across the sky, my awareness only worsens, my sole focus on her and the steps I must complete tonight.

The night approaches. And the Nightmother is waiting.

I follow the light of the full moon through the dense brush guided by instinct alone.

The siren call hums in the air around me, my name whispered in a dozen overlapping tones.

"Come," it whispers, distant and echoing, as if carried on the wind from every direction

Multiple voices. All hers—all hers.

My legs move without thought, drawn forward by something deeper than will.

No creatures dare cross my path tonight; my presence reeks of her with every talon that claws into my mind.

Eventually, I arrive—always inevitably—at a lake. The full moon hovers above, casting a perfect twin onto the water's surface.

The soft glow ripples across the dark waves, mixing its beauty with something more menacing.

"Come" she beckons again.

I don't hesitate. I know what to do. I have done it year after year.

On the full moons, she demands worship.

Prayers.

Offerings.

You're expected to give a piece of yourself, surrendered to the depths, and you will be rewarded with her blessing.

I sink to my knees, the white linen gown pooling around me like moonlight. She likes the white; I've learned this.

It shows the blood better—reveals every flaw and every weakness.

Even the buds of my breasts are visible through the sheer fabric barely clinging to me via the delicate tie at my chest. I bare myself because that is what she demands. My arms are exposed, my shoulders bare. I hold out my hand, summoning her magic.

It rises as something familiar but markedly stronger than mine. Tendrils of silver streak through the pool of inky black that swirls in my palm.

They sharpen, forming the sharp edge of a dagger. The hilt is carved bone. The blade glows red and settles in my hand with a chilling ease.

I reach for the tie between my breasts, ready to begin when I hear her.

Not just around me now. Behind me.

"He comes," she whispers.

My brows knit together in confusion until I feel it.

Him.

I move quickly, slipping the dagger beneath the folds of my gown, hiding it behind my thigh.

Then I whip around, my eyes scanning the darkness beyond the trees. He's there, lurking in the shadows and avoiding the moonlight.

"Your obsession with me is tiresome," I call, my voice flat and unbothered.

A low, dark chuckle snakes out from beneath the trees. Then he steps into view. Those silver eyes are the same ones that haunt my nightmares.

He is clad in nothing but a plain black tunic and loose trousers. His boots are barely laced, and his hair is a mess.

He must have been in bed, yet he came here.

"What are you doing in the woods, little witch?" he taunts. "Hungry beasts lurk out here."

"I don't recall needing to tell you my every move," I snap, letting him feel the words laced with steel.

His gaze drifts over me—lingering, assessing—trying to put pieces together in his mind.

He is yet to understand what he's walked into.

The Nightmother purrs against my mind, her hunger deepening, drawn to the storm inside him. I salivate for the power in his blood and thrum with desire.

This kind of hunger does not make requests.

It *takes*.

Give him to me, little star.

Her voice is soft—almost tender—but the command strikes like iron. The blade heats against my thigh in response, pulsing like a second heartbeat.

It wants blood. His blood.

I can't kill him.

Nora's rage would burn the world.

A soft chuckle curls in my mind, silken but sharp.

Bind him, little star. His power can be ours.

And I realize she's correct. Blood magic is powerful, and I can do it, but I need him closer.

The thought of Cage beneath me—bound, his power mine to drain, his obedience absolute—sends a rush through me.

My heart skips. I force my face to communicate neutrality, taking the hunger with cold indifference.

I picture him kneeling, his will mine. He is my dog on a leash, rolling over at my beck and call. He tilts his head.

And then I feel him—his magic—gliding along the edge of my mental wall.

Like a raven's wing, its feathers brush over like the curious creature he is.

My barrier holds. I think of iron, unbreakable.

Not tonight.

I want to snap at him again, push him back, but I need him closer. So, instead, I offer him a sweet smile.

"You know," I say lightly, "You could just ask a girl how she feels. It's called communicating."

A sly grin tugs at his lips. "I find people to be rarely honest, and when they try to be, they are not even truly honest with themselves."

He says this smoothly, taking a step closer.

"Ask me, then," I challenge, folding my hands together and turning fully to face him. "Give it your best shot."

His gaze drops—to my neck and then lower—and I see the flicker of tension in his jaw.

He forces his eyes back to mine, keeping his face blank, but something still lingers there. Perhaps it's hunger.

"How old were you," he asks softly, "when she first spoke to you?"

The surprise must flash across my face because his damn grin blooms wider—almost smug—revealing a dimple I have never seen.

"And don't play coy," he tacks on smoothly. "You know of whom I speak: the one who summoned you here tonight...who calls to me every full moon."

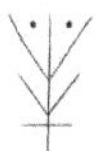

He crosses his arms, the fabric of his tunic stretching tightly over his chest and shoulders.

He knows. At the very least, he suspects more than he should.

"I was fifteen," I lie but too quickly.

His eyes narrow just a fraction.

He doesn't call me on it, but I see the skepticism...the knowing.

Instead, he walks forward and then crouches. Resting his forearms on his thighs, he settles in front of me. I hate the way I have to tilt my chin up to meet his eyes.

"Mmhmm. Yeah." he hums, as if I'm a child spinning bedtime stories.

"What does she require of you?" he asks a bit too casually. It feels like an interrogation wrapped in silk.

My irritation flares, but I stamp it down. I need him closer.

"Wouldn't you like to know?" I murmur, coating my voice in velvet. I let the charm bloom—let it drip.

His gaze sharpens, locking onto me. The forest, the moonlight, the beasts he warned me of—all vanish.

"I'd like to know," he replies, his voice dropping a register, now a quiet murmur between us. The space is suddenly...*intimate*. "How she likes to be worshiped."

He slides to his knees so that he's only inches away now, but while I kneel back on my heels, he stays upright, looking down on me. "How?"

"Devotion looks different for everyone," I answer quickly, trying to ignore the smoky, oaken scent that clings to him. Uniquely his.

He studies me. "You kneel here, alone in a thin gown," he says slowly. "Must one be beneath her...and laid bare?"

His eyes smolder, tracing my body like scripture.

I simply nod, but I'm unraveling inside.

The Nightmother's command presses in. I feel my hatred simmering.

However, he makes me feel something else, but I can't quite place it.

I do loathe you, I remind myself.

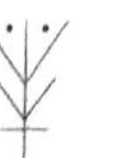

He reaches out. His fingers trail lazily up my arms, tracing over the swirls and dips of my markings.

Goosebumps rise in waves over my flesh. Still, I don't look away.

I won't.

"Tell me how to worship her, my little witch," he whispers.

His voice is husky and low, nearly desperate.

And, suddenly…I know.

He isn't talking about the Nightmother. He's talking about me.

His fingers slide to the straps resting on my shoulders. Slowly, deliberately, he hooks them, slowly pulling them down, inch by inch.

The fabric slips, and cold air kisses my skin. My breasts are bare beneath the moonlight. Exposed and pale, my nipples are tight from the chill.

His eyes drop, and he bites his lower lip. The hunter there isn't masked anymore.

I tell myself I'm allowing this because I need him closer. Because I need to bind him.

His fingers are soft as they ghost along my shoulders, tracing my clavicles.

Then, lower…

His palm cups the weight of my breast, thumb brushing over the peak of my nipples until a sharp pull coils deep within my gut. My breath stutters as my pulse pounds faster.

"I could be the most devoted worshiper," he murmurs, "to something so divine."

His voice is like a hymn, low and reverent.

"Maybe I'll be condemned."

He grins devilishly.

"Maybe I already am."

He tugs on my nipples, sharp and slow.

My hands clench the skirts of my gown.

The dagger at my thigh burns hotter, reminding me of the task at hand and what must be done.

"Those pretty lips," he murmurs. "They love to talk so much." His other hand rises, firmly gripping my jaw.

"Use your words, Millicent," he commands.

The huskiness in my own voice surprises even me.

"Did I say you could touch me?"

His eyes flash, completely consumed with hunger—with something dark—and I've only seen glimpses of it before.

Now?

Now it's staring me down, and my heart won't stop racing.

"You're blushing, my little witch." He pulls my face closer, sweeping his lips over mine but denying contact. "And these perfect tits—they're throbbing, aren't they?"

His voice is heat and hunter. It makes the ache worse.

His hand slides to my other breast, fingers toying with the aching bud, matching the same attention he gave the first.

"I wonder, where you would want my mouth first?" The deep, delicious pull in my stomach sinks lower, gathering between my thighs. I hate how responsive I am. I hate that he knows it.

"Inch by inch, I'd devour you," he growls, his breath hot against my lips. "And still I'd hunger."

His eyes are molten now, seeming to consume me. "I'd want to start with these lips that never stop mouthing off, just to pull moans from them instead."

He pinches my nipple; my breath falters, and my traitorous body clenches low.

"Then, I'll take each of these breasts into my mouth and feast like the starved man I am."

He leans closer, lips skimming my jaw. "I could be a gentleman—take my time kissing down your body—but I've been left to starve far too long."

The images he conjures in my mind fog my brain further, but the burn of the blade against my thigh fights to keep me here and on track.

He chuckles low, his breath fanning against my ear. "I want to *pray* before you. Between your thighs. You're probably soaking for me already, aren't you, my little witch?"

His hand slides from my beast, tugging my gown lower and exposing my stomach inch by inch. His knuckles brush my skin, leaving trails of fire in their wake.

The soft fabric pools around my hips.

His thumb draws a slow, lazy circle around my navel, and the swirl of heat ignited there blooms downward, until I'm throbbing with it.

"Argue with me, little witch," he breathes, "like you always do. I love the way you hate me."

My lips part to try and argue, but no words escape, just soft pants as I suck in air to feed the fire growing in my veins. I want power, I want to own him, and I want to destroy him, but I selfishly want him to cure the ache strengthening between my thighs.

His hand on my jaw tightens.

"Hate me—hate me while I slide my fingers into that sweet little cunt and find out the depth of your loathing. I'll learn exactly how deep it goes and how much of me you can take."

His tongue traces the shell of my ear, sending a shiver down my spine.

I realize then I'm panting—loudly now—drunk on the lust thrumming through my veins.

He pulls back.

Lust and anger are at war on his features, shadowing his silver eyes and tightening his jaw.

I smirk, relishing the effect I have on him. "Do you often think about how sweet I must taste?"

His answer is instant.

"Think? Thinking isn't enough. I'm far past that."

His voice is a growl, raw and reverent.

"I imagine it. I dream it. You'll taste like every dark desire and fantasy I've ever had—given flesh."

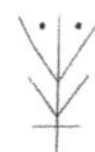

He's trembling now. "Thoughts of you beneath me…they feel like both a blessing and a curse. And I'll take that curse. I'll sacrifice myself willingly, just for a taste."

The moment shatters. Whatever leash he had on himself snaps as he crashes his lips to mine.

It's not tender. It's ruinous.

He devours me, starving me of air and thought—of restraint.

His hand slides from my jaw to the nape of my neck, tangling in my curls as he forces my head back. He demands I give him more.

My hands move on their own. I tug on his shirt, urging him closer, deeper.

The cold presence of the Nightmother runs up my spine, a complete contrast to the heat Cage is building in me, reminding me of my purpose here.

His hand skims down, flattening over my stomach, tracing my wrist, and sliding to the curve of my rear. He grips it hard, pulling me forward and onto his lap.

My thighs part; I straddle him as I cling around his hips. The pressure, angle, and heat are all too much but not enough.

He groans into my mouth, kneading my ass roughly and claiming me as his own. The sound rips a moan from my own throat, caught between pain and pleasure.

And I drink in his sweet surrender. His offering. Like a perfect wine, I get drunk on it.

This is no holy prayer. This is a completely selfish one, given to me, and I can't get enough. And yet—

I will not be his salvation but his damnation. I get lost in it: his mouth, his hands, and the ache blooming between my thighs.

And then she laughs, dripping with malice.

His body. His blood. His body, his blood.

She chants, her voice twisting into something oily and dark as a void.

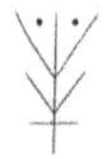

His lips break from mine only to trail lower, forcing scorched kisses down my throat.

"I'm on my fucking knees at your altar," he growls against my skin. His words vibrate through me before he nips tender flesh just above my pulse. He soothes it with his tongue and then moves lower, searching and claiming me.

I tilt my head back, dizzy with fire and fury.

My hand reaches behind me, fumbling and remembering.

The dagger.

A reluctant moan escapes me when his devious mouth finally finds my breast, his lips sealing over the aching peak.

A sharp gasp escapes me as his teeth graze, and then his tongue swirls. He sucks harder, hungrily, relentlessly. He searches for more skin to claim with red marks. Another reluctant moan tears free.

The sensation distracts me until the dagger burns in my palm, alive and waiting.

I arch my back with my teeth clenched, telling myself I'm just keeping up the illusion. In the meantime, the throbbing between my thighs becomes a desire, demanding to be satisfied.

Just a reaction, I lie.

His mouth shifts until finding the other breast, tonguing it, and worshipping it with bruising reverence.

I need to move. I need to end this.

When I glance down, I see that his eyes have never left my face.

He watches me, drinks me in. He sucks harder, pulling back from by breast with a wet pop, leaving me exposed, swollen, and *panting*.

His hands grip my hips—rough, possessive— forcing me to rock against the rock-hard bulge beneath me. Heat flushes down me as the friction sparks through the soaked fabric beneath us.

"I can tell you are aching, my little witch," he punctuates his words with a harder press against my core. "I will cure your craving."

"Just one taste," he growls. "Just one, and you'll haunt me no more."

My hand finds his shoulder, bracing and panting through the lust choking at my throat.

The other—dagger in hand—slides behind him. And our eyes lock. I want to see all of it.

I strike.

I drive the blade between two ribs—deep and sure—and then I twist.

The Nightmother's satisfaction is instant, her approval purring loudly all around me. *Yes...yes, little star, bind him. BIND HIM!*

Shock flares in his eyes. Then rage explodes, obliterating every shred of lust and desire that had just lived there.

I begin the incantation immediately, one that I know by heart.

And now...he knows.

CHAPTER 27

Cage

SCORCHING PAIN EXPLODES THROUGH MY SIDE JUST AS the dark little witch soaking on my lap dares to drive a blade into me. It clears the dark fog over my mind inflicted by the monster inside of me.

Millicent's magic, mixed with her patron on this evening, pulled me out of bed. The beast in my chest rose from its slumber to hunt for her. Any hesitation or logical thought had been erased, overshadowed by the growing obsession the thing inside of me has with her. I was so caught up in the pull of her magic against mine that I wanted to drown in her.

Now I want to drown her.

This isn't a normal dagger.

Heat—like molten fire—flares out of the wound, searing through my chest. And then I hear it.

Her.

The Nightmother is laughing inside my head.

Millicent pulses with magic atop me; her skin is cloaked in black waves as red light glows from the dagger.

The bitch almost got my heart.

My arousal hasn't even left yet, but now it's drowned beneath a rush of white-hot rage and the jolt of adrenaline as I register the pain...and the spell on her lips.

She's chanting.

Swollen lips I had just tasted—had gasping for me—are now spilling out an incantation I know all too well.

She's binding me.

The tug on my chest confirms it. And it's not just a knife in my chest.

It's a fucking bond. If she finishes it...she'll have access to my power. She'll be able to command me to her will. She'll be inside my mind, and she'll make it so that I can't even touch her—let alone use my power.

And that is what shatters the last thread of restraint. I grab the back of her head, hard, twisting into her thick raven curls. My rage crackles through every muscle.

"There she is," I snarl. "Those fucking pretty white jaws!"

My grip on her hair tightens. I don't care if I'm hurting her; my side is on fire. And she dares to sit there, chanting with the dagger still buried in me.

My magic rises in tandem with my rage, tattoos writhing and crackling with the magic building up in my body.

The trees around us respond; shadows stretch forward, crawling toward us like they've been starved of purpose.

She clings to me, still chanting in that cursed tongue. I reach back—gripping the dagger—my strength straining against hers.

The earth answers. The soil explodes around us, and grass is torn away as thick, shadowy chains snake from the ground and coil around my limbs, working to trap and bind me.

And I laugh wildly...madly. I *relish* it.

My power roars in response; tendrils burst from the shadows, slamming into her frame with the force of fury incarnate. She's thrown back, but I keep a hold of her hair and drag her with me as I rise.

I yank the dagger free from my back, hissing through clenched teeth. Pain burns, but my rage burns hotter. The kindness is gone, burned out of me.

"Trying to bind me?" I snarl. "You little bitch."

I slam her to her knees, dragging her down with my own shadow-forged chains. They coil around her legs and then her wrists, binding them tight behind her back.

Another snakes around her throat, tightly. Too tight. She chokes, gasping for air as I watch the world fade behind the depths of her eyes. I watch her panic, just long enough to feel like I've won something. I remind myself not to kill her. Then I loosen the coil at her throat, just enough for her to force down a breath of air.

I can feel her magic surge again, ready to make a lethal strike. Not this time.

I move fast, straddling her from behind. With one hand, I yank her head back, forcing it against my shoulder; the other presses the blood-slick dagger to her neck.

A drop of blood beads where I press, brilliantly red beneath the moonlight.

"Try it," I growl; my voice is low and laced with venom. "Go ahead—"

"—I **dare** you."

My smile is feral and unforgiving. "I would love nothing more than to cut you open like a pig. Let your precious Nightmother take that as my fucking sacrifice."

I lean in to break her, to taunt her. A grin soon tugs at my lips at the thought.

"Go on, Millicent," I whisper against her ear. "Call to her. You're so *rare*, right? The Nightmother's chosen child?"

I chuckle, letting the heat from my breath mock her. "Call to her now. *Beg* her to save you from me, princess."

She thrashes against me, her rage breaking loose.

"Fuck you!" she screams.

The motion drives the blade a little deeper, and I hum in pleasure at her gasp.

"Oh, don't worry, little witch." I sneer, tightening my hold on her. "I know exactly what you want."

I press into her back, laughing darkly against her ear. "I know you want me filling you. You want me fucking you. You've already soaked my pants. Your pussy is begging for my cock, isn't it?"

That hits her harder than any blade could.

Her blue eyes ignite, and the shadows around us are no longer silent; they snarl, alive and vicious.

Her shadow beasts are coming.

Good.

I'm not in the mood to let them interrupt. I roll my neck, exhaling slowly, and then summon Vyraxis.

Mist peels off my skin—dark, thick—twisting upward into a rolling cyclone that devours the sky.

The air grows heavy. Above us, the massive form of Vyraxis tears free from the clouds, blocking out the moon and drowning the clearing in darkness.

Millicent shudders in my arms.

The game has changed.

"Aww," I hum mockingly, forcing her head so that the clearing is all she can see.

"Is that who ate your precious sisters?"

Vyraxis roars; the sound is so deep it rattles through my chest, even from where I stand.

Her horned head swivels slowly, focusing on the writhing shadow beats lurking at the edges of the trees.

Sensing my need, she responds immediately, her massive body surging forward, and silver flames pour from the dark alcoves like a flood.

One by one, the shadows ignite. Snarls cease mid-breath; ash rains down, but I don't even bother watching them burn.

Rather, I look down to Millicent. I don't bother dressing her. I like her vulnerability. I slide the dagger away from her throat and turn it on her gown instead, slicing through where it managed to cling around her wide hips.

The fabric falls away, puddling at her knees. She's left in nothing but the barest lace, clinging uselessly to her skin.

The heart-shaped curve of her rear is exposed. Her body is offered up, whether she wants it or not.

My cock twitches, responding without permission at the sight of her.

Focus...control.

The thing inside me—the dark, monstrous thing—thrashes against its chains, demanding release. It wants to tear her apart. It wants to finish this the way my blood was designed to. Already, too much of it is in control.

If I let it loose; it will kill her.

Pain pulses through my side—a constant reminder of what she tried to steal from me.

My freedom.

She wanted to take it, just like her coven takes everything.

They lie, manipulate, and kill the weak and innocent to climb higher. And she's no different. She's the vermin dressed in divine silk, a liar with bloodstained hands. I want her to remember who she is—to remember her insignificance, what I am, and how easily I can end her.

"Is it because they call you rare?" I sneer. "Is that why you act like a goddess draped in shadow?"

My voice is low, seething. "Rare like what? A diamond?" I snort, leaning into her. "One in a dozen."

I see the flicker in her eyes: hurt, rage, or both.

She opens her mouth to catch her breath.

"The moment I—"

I cut her off.

"Yeah, yeah. The moment you stop playing nice, you'll gut me and eat my insides, or do whatever it is you feral things do." I look at her with disgust. "Until then..." I raise the dagger in front of her. My magic surges down my arm, sliding into the blade. The red flickers and burns out, and a hot pulsing silver takes its place.

She tenses, confused.

Her eyes dart between the blade and my face. Her breathing picks up, and I see the exact second it registers.

"Take this as a reminder," I snarl, my voice dripping with venom. "Every day, every breath...beneath me, my rare little witch." A smile pulls across my face. "Let's add something to make you truly rare, shall we?"

The shadows constrict around her, locking her in place. Her aura pulses darker now—a rich black infused with sapphire. She's gathering magic.

I sigh, annoyed.

Before she can strike, I slam into her mind, breaking against her mental shield like a battering ram. At the same time, I wrap my free hand around her throat and squeeze.

Her body bucks once, gasping. I choke her until she wavers, slipping toward unconsciousness.

In that thin veil between wakefulness and oblivion, I find the crack in her defenses. I sink my talons into her mind, latching on and wrenching her down until I strangle her magic into submission.

It will not hold for long. I press the dagger to her chest, right above her heart.

"When this is over," I whisper against her ear, "I will carve this out—"

I press harder.

"—and feed it to Vyraxis."

"You can join your sisters in her gut."

The voice that falls from my mouth is not mine. It's something

darker—something I've always kept caged—but now it's loose, and I don't stop it.

I drag the blade across her skin, mutilating it. She screams, so sharp and raw it tears through the night. It only feeds the fire inside me. I savor every slow cut, slowing my efforts to draw out her cries, as they bring me a sense of euphoria. I am her executioner, her punisher.

I work carefully, methodically, slicing a large, brutal *C* into her perfect flesh.

The blade's silver flame sears each cut closed, cauterizing the wound as I go. I remain focused, feeding my magic into every stroke, deep into the split skin.

I bind the mark so she can never erase *it*.

Never erase me.

She'll see it every time she looks in the mirror. I finish carving rather quickly, my excitement getting the best of me, not caring if the lines are jagged or if the scar heals poorly.

I don't want it to heal. I toss the dagger aside; the blade lands with a dull thud on the grass. Then I release her hair, letting her body—small, broken, and trembling—crumple forward to collapse in the dirt.

She doesn't move.

Her body shakes from the invasion: my blade through her skin and my mind through her soul.

My own wound—the one she left on me—is already knitting closed.

Hers never will.

I walk forward, crouching in front of her. "Did you pray to her?" I ask softly, mockingly. No answer, just the ragged sound of her breathing. She keeps her face buried in the tall grass.

I lean closer, my voice a blade all its own. "Allow me to tell you something no one ever has." My next words are cruel and final. "You are not rare, Millicent. You are not special. You are not chosen."

"You're just a witch who swallowed the needles of the abuse they fed you, until they could stitch you into something new: a pet, a fun little experiment. No better than a necromancer's half-dead puppet."

I pause, savoring the words.

"Your kind is a disease."

I rise to my full height, standing over her like a gravestone.

"Don't worry, little star." I mock, using the loving name I heard her mother call her all those years ago. "You'll join mommy soon enough. I'll make sure of it."

I don't look over my shoulder. I don't need to. Whatever humanity that once lived inside me—whatever thin, pathetic leash that held the monster back—is gone.

I do not need a mirror to know my eyes are black holes now.

Bottomless. Starless. Devouring.

I do not need to check the cage deep inside my soul to know it is empty.

The monster is me.

Vyraxis circles overhead, wings stirring the trees into a howling frenzy. She looks down, waiting.

I wave her off with a flick of my fingers.

"You can eat her later," I say, voice as casual as tossing scraps to a hound.

"Go rest."

She beats her wings once, twice, ripping at the sky with every stroke until she vanishes into the night.

All that's left is me and the ruin I've made.

CHAPTER 28

Millicent

A LAUGH RIPS FROM THE BACK OF MY THROAT, MY VOICE raw and broken.

It shakes loose from my chest, wracking my body until pain spears from the carved section of my breast to my back. The pain sharpens; it's bright, almost blinding, but it only feeds the laughter.

It grows wilder, louder. It's maniacal.

I hardly even recognize my voice anymore.

I rake my fingers into the dirt—deep, desperate—over and over again, clawing through the earth until my nails snap on jagged stones buried beneath the surface.

I don't feel it. Pain is meaningless now.

"I'll kill you," I whisper, still laughing. "I will fucking kill you, Cage!" I scream, throwing my head back and howling into the tree line where he vanished.

"Eat me!" I laugh. "Feed me to the fucking lizard! As If either of you could stomach me!" I shove myself upright to my knees.

The sky yawns open above me, and I laugh up at it.

Finally, I look down. The deep, jagged *C* burned into my skin glares up at me, carved just under my left clavicle and down a path to my breast, soaking the shredded remains of my gown crimson.

I drag a battered finger along the path of blood, lift it to my mouth, and suck it clean. I swirl my tongue slowly, tasting every bitter drop. A low groan escapes me, and a giggle follows as I pop the finger free from my lips.

Finally, I rise.

Sheep for thee to slaughter.

SHEEP FOR THEE TO SLAUGHTER.

The Nightmother's chanting crackles with a shrilling laugh, encouraging me to go further and take it all. It's my right. It's the law of nature.

The grass withers around me—curling, blackening—as my magic rolls off me in thick, suffocating waves.

I let it build—let it throb.

And then I release it.

A black cloud explodes outward—life devouring. Trees groan, and branches warp and snap as nature itself tries to recoil from me, but there is no escape; there never is.

My magic floods the earth like the coming darkness at the end of all things. Thick, living tendrils of smoky blackness race across the ground, coiling between the trees, crawling toward the one thing I seek.

Him.

The world warps around me, the earth turning into something dark, writhing, and alive with my hate.

And there will be no mercy—not anymore. I walk leisurely through the trees without ever losing my smile.

Tonight is a wonderful night. I get to kill my mother's killer.

Birds plummet from branches as I pass, quiet, heavy thuds filling the woods like a symphony of decay.

I don't follow death. I am death.

Frustration flares when I can't immediately locate him. No. This simply won't do. I raise both hands. Power collects in the spaces adjacent to me—thick and writhing—before ripping the very air apart.

Two oval voids tear open with gaping maws of endless darkness, their edges rippling like fine black silk. A sudden chill pierces through the air, and the faint scent of burning iron permeates the greenery. From within, they prowl forth.

My hounds—four of them—are terrible, skilled hunters, birthed from my hatred and hunger. Each is a nightmare stitched from shadow and bone. Six eyes burn atop their skeletal wolf heads, glowing a vibrant, blue. Their bodies ripple with shifting fur—tones of deep violet, dark sapphire, and blood red—like bruises painted across their monstrous frames. Their heads are bare bones. When they open their jaws, it's not just one row of fangs but many—spiraling rows of teeth meant for nothing but to rip things apart.

They inhale in unison, air whooshing through the slits atop their skulls; their bodies catch fire from the inside out.

Blue flames lick up their spines, casting the trees in eerie, flickering light.

I smile wider. "Kill for mommy," I say sweetly. My voice drips with vicious affection. They don't need names. They don't need direction. Each beast is a pure manifestation of my will—an extension of my hunger.

They turn as one, and they are bound into the forest, burning trails in their wake. They're locked onto their prey. Locked onto *his scent.*

I follow, leisurely, step by step. Their path carves a bleeding trail through the woods, leading me straight to the little mage who thought he could brand me and walk away.

I don't know how long I walk. Time doesn't exist anymore. Not to me. There is nothing but hunger, rage, and the need to rip Cage in two and wear his skin like a trophy. The castle looms ahead, silhouetted in the dead light of my magic. My hounds prowl the grounds, pacing and circling for a time before one lets out a long, shrieking cry. They've found something: the entrance to the mages' wing. They continue pacing, waiting for my approach.

"Stop!" a guard shouts, stepping into my path, and his spear braces against trembling hands.

"I have not even begun," I say darkly. The hounds lock onto their new target and take off.

The guard's eyes widen in terror. He blows into the horn on his neck, alerting others to the danger just outside the castle walls.

It is of no use.

My hounds leap, fangs flashing and claws extended to shred him limb from limb. Before they can make contact, a roar of fire pours from the mouth of the entrance behind him. Scarlet flames billow outward, forcing the hounds back. They snarl, pacing at the sudden wall.

A young mage steps through the inferno. Wild red hair tangles around her face, and she's still wearing a nightgown, but her hands are steady, fingers spread wide to control the rising wall of fire. The flames split the night open, turning darkness into blood-soaked day. The heat kisses my skin, even from yards away.

Cute.

I raise my hands, gathering my magic to snuff out her little show, but movement to my left catches my eye.

Someone charges me with arms outstretched—reckless.

I pivot, magic thrumming through every fiber of muscle. My fist slams into his ribs with bone-shattering force. He flies back, crashing into the ground. It's only then, as he gasps and coughs, that I recognize him.

Kalix.

It doesn't matter. He should have stayed out of my way.

"I can—and will—break every bone in your body," I taunt sweetly, playing with my new target.

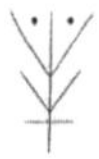

Kalix gets to his feet. His breathing is heavy, but his face is calm—unfazed—like I hadn't just thrown him around like ragdoll. He starts to circle me, calculating his next move.

I don't call the hounds. I want this one for myself.

His eyes flicker to the carved *C* on my chest—to the ruin left behind. "How did you get hurt?" He asks, voice careful. His hands rise slowly—palms out—like he's surrendering. "Millie," he says. "You don't want to do all this."

I grin wider. "I actually would love *nothing* more than to do all this." Joy bleeds through me; it fills me with something bright, manic, and unstoppable.

"Iris is in there," he says, tilting his head toward the castle, "You want the hounds getting to her?"

"They won't touch her," I snap. "They'll only touch who *I* want. **Bring me Cage.**"

"Not happening, Mill." He dares a step closer. "How about we take a walk?"

I laugh so hard I bend at the waist, gasping for air. When I straighten, I tilt my head in cold amusement at the idiot before me. "A walk? I am tired of this." I raise my hand. Shadows lash out as black ropes twist through the air, wrapping around his throat and tightening until they scream against his skin.

I lift him off the ground like a doll, his feet dangling uselessly. "I will not beg for what is mine." I snarl. "I will rip Cage from his bed; brick by brick, I will tear down this fucking castle. **I will destroy it all.**" My excitement rises, making my heart beat faster with anticipation.

Yes, take it all, the Nightmother whispers. *It was always yours.*

My vision blurs—edges pulsing black—and I feel her influence sinking deeper into me, leeching and distorting my emotions.

My shoulder jerks involuntarily at her invasion.

"Such a good pup you've been." I purr at Kalix, tightening the noose of shadows coiling around his neck. "Always so obedient. Always so

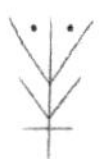

useful. I'd keep you—if I had the energy to train a bitch not to be so weak." I snarl the word like a curse. "I'll make sure my hounds eat your remains. I'm *so* generous after all."

His face is calm. Unshaken. It infuriates me.

I flick my wrist hard. The shadows snap tighter with enough force to shatter bone and sever spines. There's no snap or break.

Instead, I stumble back, confused that Kalix stands in front of me completely unharmed and calm. My magic is gone from his throat.

And for the first time, I feel doubt.

He sighs, crossing his arms and looking down at me. "There it is," he says softly. "Your bad side." He shrugs—a tired, sad little gesture. "We all have dark sides," he adds, voice blurring at the edges. "You will be okay."

His words slur slightly, and that's when the first thread of unease tugs at me.

"Wh–what? What did you do?" My heart slows—heavy, dragging—and I realize...

I can't hear my hounds anymore.

A sideways glance shows only empty grass. The waves of magic that had blanketed the forest have dissolved.

Kalix takes a slow step forward, still reaching out to me.

"Somnex," he says gently. "Absorbs through the skin. It's coated my whole shirt. And incidentally..." He smiles faintly, exhaling slowly before lowering his voice. "Your fist."

I stagger, panting through my fight with the sedative. Then his hands reach out for me. "Don't touch me," I slur, swatting at him weakly.

He ignores the flailing. He scoops me up, one arm under my knees and behind my shoulder. He cradles me to his chest like I'm something fragile. I try to resist and snarl, but my body betrays me, and I can do nothing more than mumble my protests.

I sag against him, head lolling back. My eyelids become too heavy to lift. Somewhere in the haze, I manage a glare, I think.

"Where's Oliver?" he says gently; he's being kind.

"Oliver?" I echo weakly.

"Yes. Where is he?"

"He...can't come...when she's here." I mumble, blinking slowly up at the spinning stars as I fight through the incessant pull on my lids.

"She?" Kalix says, his voice roughening. "Is she what takes the blue from your eyes?" His words drift through me like smoke—like a memory speaking inside my mind. I don't know if I answer aloud or only in my mind. Just before the darkness closes in around me, I breathe one final, broken truth.

"My price."

I drift in and out, caught between darkness and faint awareness over the next few hours. When I surface, I feel the soft cushion of a mattress beneath me.

I force my eyelids apart, trying to study my surroundings; they're far too heavy, sluggish. The world blurs in shades of gray and black. I can't make out where I am. I can't hold on. My eyes slide shut again, helpless.

Voices break though, bleeding into the haze. "She's dangerous!" a woman snaps, her voice sharp with fear. "She shouldn't be here. That guard—and gods only know who else—would have been slaughtered if she wasn't stopped. Her eyes were black, and her beasts...those things were hell itself! I'm not questioning your judgement, I—"

"Then don't," a man's voice cuts in, slicing through her like a blade. "Do not question me again." His tone is cold, final. "She stays. Your task is to simply be a healer, not give your opinion."

Then, more subdued, "Yes, Lord Black."

The voices fade again, swallowed by the darkness pulling at me.

Time passes, I think. I don't know how much later it is when I feel the mattress shift beside me—a weight, shifting the tide.

I'm too drugged to lift my head, too weak to even flinch. I am a stone on the bottom of a warm ocean. Some small, buried part of me trembles as the familiar scent of smoke and oak fills my lungs.

"Even when you tried to tear me apart," Cage murmurs, "You were...magnificent." He exhales, long and tired. "I might be sick for thinking so." His voice lowers: "We truly bring out the worst in each other, don't we?" He pauses. "Is it wrong to say I *want* that? To push you further. To peel back every layer of you until it's all laid bare." He shifts, and I feel him closer.

"I want to feel your magic bite. Feel your eyes burn when you look at me like you'd kill me if you could." Another pause, this time deeper, darker.

"I might even let you. If it meant I could get close enough." His breath brushes my temple. "I won't apologize. You tried to force bond me. You clever, devilish girl." He laughs low and humorless. "I have a dark side too."

A longer silence follows this time. When he speaks again, it's quieter. "I've thought about draining you. Your power. Your magic. I'd be lying if I said I haven't." He breaths in slowly. "I resisted. You... your struggle with yours." His voice softens, almost tender. "She told you to do it, didn't she? I heard her laugh. The Nightmother has wanted me since I was young, but I never heard her. Not until Nora's...sessions."

His voice breaks slightly. "I wonder sometimes," he continues, "did she do to you what she did to me? You have lived in that place...all your life. She would've had you longer."

He swallows hard. "That thought makes me violent, and I don't know why."

I drift—not fully awake, not fully gone. I'm back in a dream—buried deep in the past—from before I began paying the price.

Before she laid claim to my soul.

I SIT BENEATH THE WILLOW TREE BESIDE THE POND AT MY coven, watching a swan glide effortlessly across the surface.

Footsteps crunch softly behind me, turning my focus to who approaches.

It's Cage, motioning to empty space beside me on the plaid-woven blanket.

"This spot taken?"

Excitement pops off inside me after seeing Cage. He isn't allowed out often, and he's been sleeping through daylight hours lately. He told me that Nora has him in class at night.

I don't offer him my usual hug because he owes me grapes after eating all mine last time.

I narrow my eyes, crossing my arms. "You bring me grapes?"

"Of course."

He grins, plopping down next to me.

He scoots closer until our sides are squished together. From his trouser pocket, he extracts a bundle of grapes he swiped from the kitchen.

I squeal in delight, grabbing them greedily and stuffing my mouth full. My previous annoyance with him is completely erased. I lean into him, squishing us further.

With cheeks bulging, I raise my arms to show off my witch marks that are now darker and more defined.

"Wow, Millie! Your mama's right: you are gonna be strong."

His awe makes me beam with pride.

"Of course I will! I'm going to be stronger than you!" I giggle, kicking my legs over his and leaning into his chest.

I love Arcadia, but the other girls bore me.

Mama says that I should be nicer as they're my sisters. So, I try to be nice, but I grow tired of them.

Cage isn't boring. He's from the outside world. He has stories.

"Tell me about the markets again! The ones with farmers!"

Grape juice drips down my chin, but I don't care.

He leans back against the tree, pulling a grape free as he begins the familiar story. His mother would take him to the market, and he'd get a caramel pastry he loved. Just the thought of it makes my mouth water.

"One day we'll go to a market," I say excitedly, "and get pastries!" I'm too young to be allowed outside of the coven to explore and see the world. His stories make me so excited to do just that as soon as I am as big as Mama.

"Yeah, Millie," he murmurs. "One day." His voice seems a little sad.

I lift my head, pressing my forehead to his. "Are you sad?" I try to read his thoughts, squinting and focusing hard. I have no mind magic, but, maybe, if I try hard enough...

He ruffles my curls. "You'll burst a vessel squinting like that."

I laugh, forgetting the question. "What if we *both* get mind magic!" I ask. "We could have secret conversations!" I lean back onto my heels, imagining all of the secret talks we could have.

He grins. "Just promise to never leave me out of the fun, then." Cage reaches up, fixing some of the curls that have fallen over my eyes.

I hold out my pinky, and he locks his with mine.

We lean forward, kissing our thumbs and sealing the promise.

I drift closer to the surface, soft voices pulling me up from the dark.

"I don't blame her," Kalix says quietly. "Just like I never blamed you, my Rainbow, when you got out of hand."

"You're too good, Kalix. You know that?" Iris's voice is soft and tired.

"Never too good for you," he says. His voice cracks only slightly. "It's you who's too good for me. Hell, I'm a rotten bastard who's just fighting to be a man good enough for you—"

"Kalix," she interrupts, "I'm not—"

"Please." His voice is a soft plea now, not a demand in the slightest. "Let me finish. I don't expect you to wait on me. I'm the one who waits." He exhales slowly, trying to steady the emotions quaking in his voice. "I can't even romanticize the idea of letting go. I've tried to fill

the silence with something else—anything. I always end up back here, buried under thoughts of you."

There's a pause.

"I'll never be late. You'll never have to wait on me. I'll be early, Iris—every time," he continues, begging for her to witness the torment caused by such longing—the kind that is caused when you're just within reach but can't quite grasp something.

"Kalix," she whispers, voice trembling, "I'm not doing this. Not now."

And I slip again...away from their voices, from the ache in their hearts.

Back into the dark.

CHAPTER 29

Arcadia

ILLICENT, PLEASE TALK TO ME," I SAY, MY VOICE trembling as I reach out to touch her shoulder.

Millicent had been missing for two days before we found her, miles beyond the Twisted Hollows, in a small rural farming town, or what used to be a town.

She had slaughtered every living thing there: the farmers, pets, and even children. The most disturbing part? She had devoured many of their organs and hasn't spoken a single word.

Since then, she only stares at me with empty, lifeless eyes. The sea-blue gaze I love is gone, the waters drained until nothing remains but the void.

Blood and guts cling to her, including bits of skin. The skin doesn't belong to her, stuck to her like a second layer of grotesque flesh. She hasn't cleaned herself. She hasn't moved. She hasn't blinked. The stillness at which she has sat on this bed for two hours now is unnerving, and something I did not think was physically possible.

Something is deeply wrong.

Guilt gnaws at me for staying away so long. I've been traveling constantly. *If I had been here, could I have stopped this?* She had mentioned hearing voices and seeing things; were they connected? If she was going through something while I was away, she didn't tell me in letters. She never willingly told me much unless I was present and spent enough time with her.

I left her here under the tight restrictions of the elders and the lack of care from our sisters. They care for her in the same way they do the elders: with obedience and no true affection.

Did she finally snap?

"Millie, please," I beg, clasping her hand. "Come back to me."

I won't lose her. I refuse.

"I'm too stubborn and determined to let you go. So, snap out of this—now." Of course, only I have come to her room. None of our sisters really help one another; after finding her the way they did, they especially don't want to cross the threshold of her door.

Cowards.

I loosen my grip on her hand, which I didn't realize was tightening; my emotions twist between concern, guilt, sadness, and anger.

Blood trickles from her nose. Then her entire body begins to convulse violently, shaking the entire bed. Her muscle contractions become so intense, I hear the joints in her shoulders pop from the unnatural angles they are forced to.

"Nora!" I scream, climbing onto the mattress and turning Millicent onto her side.

I smooth her hair back. "I'm here. I've got you. I'm right here, Millie."

Nora never comes.

I press my weight down, draping my body over hers to try and restrain her limbs to keep her from contorting so hard she hurts herself.

Malicent

Eventually, Millicent's seizing slows. Her eyes close. Her breathing becomes so faint, I can barely detect it.

I refuse to leave her side. Over the next five days of her stasis, I only leave to eat or relieve myself.

I have you, Millie.

CHAPTER 30

Millicent

IV. Possession
*Host is drained by oppression and obsession. Entity now
takes over partial or complete control of the host's body.
Purify with fire.
Hope is lost."
-The Wretched Sacrament*

MY VISION PULSES, BLACKNESS BLOOMING AND RECEDING at the corners of my sight in a vicious, rhythmic cycle.

I run harder.

The skin of my bare feet stings from being torn open on jagged stones and sharp roots covering the forest floor. I don't stop.

The forest doubles above me, filling the sky. Twisted, tangled branches sprout from the earth and sky—a mirrored snarl of limbs with no sky above or ground below. Only the Twisted Hollows.

How is this possible?

The unnatural chill in the air cuts at my lungs, each breath becoming harder to pull.

White fog blankets the forests, glowing from an unseen light. The source is a moon I cannot find or feel but somehow know is there.

Branches break across me as I pass. They tear my dress as easily as my skin, slicing me open as if I were made of paper. My nightgown, once white, clings to me in tattered strips. It is now the color of wine and bone—of blood and cloth.

"Little lamb, little lamb, little lamb..."

The voice comes from everywhere: above, below, and inside my head, chasing me down.

"Lamb to the slaughter, lamb to the slaughter!"

The chant grows louder, complete with more mania and delight.

Their voices clash, a chorus of many mouths speaking thorough one throat. An unholy harmony erupts from the people haunting me for weeks.

"Run. Run. Run."

The laughter turns shrill and maniacal. It chases me like wind at my back, driving my legs faster.

I can't breathe.

My lungs seize, and I stumble, falling forward as a coughing fit racks my body. I manage a stumbling step and catch myself before I fall and hit the ground. I pause to try and catch my breath.

I raise my hand to my mouth on reflex, trying to muffle the sound.

Copper floods my mouth; it's warm and metallic. I pull my hand away and stare at blood. My blood.

How...?

My fingers tremble. A sob tears out of me, each step heavier than the last. Each breath is a plea that pounds against the forest floor.

It builds into a scream of frustration—of desperation—ripping through me like a curse.

Let me go. *Let me out.*

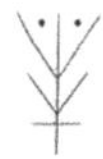

This must be some sort of nightmare, where the forest is never ending and skies do not exist.

My body betrays me again, releasing another howl of pain. I come to an abrupt stop when pain slices through my lower belly, so sharp it doubles me over. No branches or thorns are causing this pain.

I gasp, clutching my stomach as the cramp twists tighter and deeper. It brings me to my knees.

Another cough rips through me, and the pain flares again. Hot liquid trickles between my thighs, slowly spreading a tack wetness between them. I blink through the tears, dragging up the hem of my tattered nightgown, just enough to see.

Red.

Blood is pooling beneath me but not from a wound.

My first bleed.

The ground soaks up my blood like it has been starved of rain for months, and I swear it seems to breathe.

Am I dying? Is this what it feels like?

The pain claws up my spine, tightening in a vice that makes my head spin. I choke on a sob, barely managing a whisper through my voice.

"Please..."

If any gods are real and can hear me, save me from this hell.

The answer to my prayer is pain: a sharp, searing lash that coils around both ankles and begins to climb.

I scream, my voice raw and animalistic, as my body is yanked forward, face first into the dirt.

Roots thick, twisted, and covered in sharp barbs dig and slice into my skin as they drag up my legs.

I claw at the earth, frantically trying to pull myself away, but it's no use.

The thorns climb up my thighs, and the agony that follows is blinding. They sink themselves into my legs, pausing once on their ascent up my thigh.

285

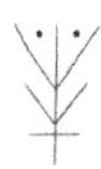

I choke on my own breath as a cold sweat breaks across my skin. My body trembles on the edge of collapse.

I don't pass out; *something won't let me.*

Some unseen power holds me there, awake and aware. It forces me to bear this weight.

A crow calls above me. Then another. Soon, the mock sky overhead becomes a swirling, screaming storm of countless black wings.

I stop struggling.

I splay my hands in the dirt, pushing myself upright just enough to twist and look back so I can see what the birds are fleeing from.

Past the trees, in the shadows beneath the trunks twisted like bones, something moves.

Four long, impossibly slender arms stretch outward. Each pale-white extremity ends in clawed, crimson-black talons. It grips the bark and pulls. And from the darkness, it emerges, pulling free a humanoid figure. Two sinister eyes, gleaming like rubies in oil, lock onto me.

I kick frantically, trying to tear free from the thorny roots. They only dig in deeper.

I claw harder into the earth, bloodied fingers digging, slipping—desperate to follow the birds above.

To fly. To flee.

More roots erupt from the ground, wrapping around my arms, pulling them down, and pinning me flat against the dirt.

I scream but not from the pain. I am gripped by refusal.

I will not die here.

I summon my magic, trying to call Ollie—to summon Nyx and Twyx.

Nothing. My body shakes, and my strength fails me all over again.

Let me in, the voice whispers, stronger than ever.

Her voice is silken, almost soothing

I will make you strong. Her words slip beneath my skin, curling through my thoughts like smoke.

And it would be so easy, so effortless, to simply let go—to open my mind and let her inside.

Behind me—

thud-thud-thud.

Heavy footfalls. The creature is coming, bounding fast toward me. I twist, trying to look, but my curls fall forward like a black curtain.

I'm so dizzy.

The ground around me glistens red. My blood spreads in a cold pool beneath me, seeping deeper into the roots and dirt. My teeth clench from the shivering cold, my head dips lower from fatigue, and my face nearly drops into mud.

And then she arrives.

Pale limbs plant themselves beside my face, near my head and shoulders.

A strange sound comes—*click-click-click*—from the thing's jaw. It leans down. Oily, matted hair falls over me like a veil of rot. Its breath hits my neck with the smell of putrid decay, something deeper than death.

I gag, turn my head, and regret it instantly.

Its mouth hovers inches from mine, dripping with black slime and fangs long and rotted.

I tremble...and then I stop.

The voice hums gently in the back of my mind like a lullaby, and I finally do what I've avoided for months: I open the door.

Come in.

Sharp pain blooms at my neck; it comes hot and sudden. The creature bites down and *pulls.*

Something tears my throat.

A rush of warmth floods my mouth and then my lungs.

It's blood.

I cough once...and it sprays outward, red and violent.

My vision flickers. Darkness pulses at the edges. I feel my body shift beneath me, but the pain is already fading.

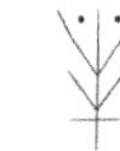

Distant.

I hear the sounds of the creature feasting, somewhere behind me now, muffled. Either it or I am far away. I let myself drift. There's warmth now: a strange, quiet warmth.

Dying isn't so bad. It feels like silk wrapping around me, like sleep.

The pain melts, not just this pain but all of it: the lessons, the scars, and the expectations.

I am expected to be strong, useful, rare.

I'm tired of doing this alone—tired of missing her. I have no one. Not really.

Arcadia will survive without me. I know she always does.

Rare...? Is this how rare dies?

Maybe being rare was never real.

I can rest now. I used to try and get high enough to see her.

Now I can.

I'm coming, Mama.

I sit in a bottomless pit. There's no edge, ceiling, or light. It's just quiet. And I'm content to look around. I feel no pain—not anymore.

What was causing my pain?

Actually, who am I?

I rise slowly, barefoot in this nothingness I begin to explore. The void stretches endlessly in all directions. I walk anyway.

After a while, however long, two shapes ripple into existence beside me.

Panthers.

They walk at my sides, and I can't help but smile as they take turns nudging me with their massive heads.

"Hello," I say tenderly, running my hands over their sleek fur. It's

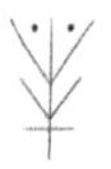

velvet-soft beneath my fingertips. Unbidden, the familiar names float up from somewhere deep within me.

Nyx. Twyx.

I know them. I know their names. I made them, long ago.

I sink onto the ground again, not because I'm tired but because it feels right. The panthers curl around me like shadows made soft. I let them.

We remain there in the nothing. Together.

And I pet their heads slowly—over and over—as if I could remember the shape of myself through their touch.

CHAPTER 31

Cage

WHO CAN TELL ME THE SIGNS OF A HOST?" I lean back against my desk, surveying the rows of students in front of me. With the growing number of entity manifestations in civilians, revisiting the topic felt necessary; the mages need to be ready.

"Changes in eye color, personality, and increased aggression," one of the younger mages offers quickly.

"Good. What else?"

"Early signs can include sudden illness, unexplained weight loss, and changes in appetite. In some cases, they may also develop an aversion to light," a more seasoned student adds.

"Correct. Recently, new beings have begun manifesting within mortals. We don't yet have names for them, or any true understanding of what they are. Iris believes what we're seeing are only in their infant forms. We've yet to face the full strength of what they could become."

The conversation with Iris hasn't left me. I hate surprises, and the thing that burst from the Duke was surprise enough, but this? If Iris is right, that creature was just the beginning. The idea of something worse—something stronger—gnaws at me. *How strong could these things get*?

That creature had two phases—an anomaly for sure. If the creature did end up powerful in its full form, the second form would have given us some trouble.

I grind my jaw. I can't predict it. I can't control how this situation will unfold. And that fact alone is driving me insane.

"Exercise caution when dealing with any suspected hosts. The last one Kalix and I encountered had two phases. Don't assume a killing blow means the job is done."

Quills scratch across parchment as my students dutifully take notes. I continue lecturing them, moving onto the varying incubation periods of different infectious entities as I round my desk, and then I step up to the massive blackboard. I write as I speak, expecting their full attention.

The room is a tiered, theater-style lecture hall; rows of seats rise in clean formation from the floor where I stand. Every student has a clear view of the board, meaning there are no excuses for distraction.

To ensure their focus, I maintain mental tethers with each of them. I don't sift through every thought, not unless I must, but the cords keep me aware of their presence and alertness.

One of them wavers. I feel the fatigue before his head drops, the tether dimming as he begins to drift. I yank on the cord as I raise my brow.

A startled yelp erupts from behind me as Leviticus jerks upright, ripped from his half-slumber.

"Pay attention, Leviticus," I say coldly, never bothering to turn around. The chalk continues to move under my hand, uninterrupted.

I set the chalk down and turn to face the class.

"Questions now." It's not a request but a command. I expect them to think—to use their damn brains to form coherent thoughts, not just sit there like dead weight when the floor opens to them.

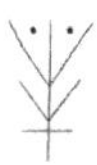

Hands shoot up in abundance. *Good. They know better by now.* Before I can call on anyone, a low hissing sound fills the room. It grows louder, like metal protesting under intense heat. Then—

BOOM.

The steel doors at the back of the hall explode inward, crashing into the stone walls with a thunderous slam.

And there she is.

She's pissed off, her sapphire eyes burning.

Hello, little witch.

She's still in the thin black nightgown the healers dressed her in after Kalix's sedative. A wave of satisfaction washes over me as I recognize my initial carved neatly into her chest. *She healed beautifully.*

My students lurch to their feet, rattled by the sudden intrusion and the very real threat in front of them: a witch. She's the one who nearly leveled the ground two nights ago.

"Leave, and I will kill you all. Sit. Now." Her voice is lethal, like the calm waters before a storm.

"You will not touch even a hair on them," I snap, though my mind is already linking to each student. *Do as she says. For now.*

They sit.

She smiles wide and viciously, and then she saunters down the aisle, gaze flicking over their terrified faces like she's admiring meat.

This version of her is unfamiliar. Gone is the guarded, clipped girl. When she does speak, her words are harsh, but she is in control until I push her far enough. The leash Nora put on her must have snapped. Finally, I get to see who this witch really is.

As much as I want to see what this malevolent being can do, my students are still here. I can handle Millicent. They can't.

"I will do whatever the fuck I want." To prove her point, Millicent forces down the last few standing students, slamming them into their chairs with an invisible force. Their frightened eyes dart to me, panic dawning as they realize she can get into their minds too. She's fast. Too

fast. She slips in alongside me, digging into their consciousness and sowing pain sharp enough to buckle their knees.

I remain calm, a sly grin curling on my lips as the collar singes her neck. "Keep doing whatever the fuck you want," I say, mocking her words as the scent of burning skin rises. "And your throat will be burned through entirely." The fury radiating from her when she reaches me is delicious.

"What the fuck is this?" she seethes, grabbing the steel collar on her neck, tugging at it. The skin around her neck is already blistered and red.

"Is knowledge not required in order to be heir in your coven? Seems rather important that a queen would be smart."

"Oh, and I suppose being a murderous asshole is what qualifies someone to be the king's mage? Teacher of the year?"

"You did stab me, remember."

"Oh, boohoo! Get over it!" she snaps, flinging her arms up in wild frustration. So much for the calm, brooding heir. Nora was a mask, never showing any emotion save for the occasional tight smile. Millicent is all raw emotion.

"Get over...being stabbed? And forced into a bond?" I smirk. "If you want to be with me so badly, you could've just asked. Not that I'd say yes. Maybe if you begged, practiced your pleases."

She doesn't take the bait; she throws it. A fist sails toward my face, but I lean to the side just in time.

Now *that's* good form. Why can't the guards hit like that?

I catch her wrist mid-strike, twisting it behind her back in one fluid motion. With a quick shift, I slam her forward onto my desk, feeling her ragged breath under my grip.

"Now, class, this is Millicent. Say hi to the witch." I can't help but taunt her as she curses and thrashes under me.

"Hello, Millicent," my students say in unison, some smiling while others snicker.

Gods I love humiliating her. Shit kind of turns me on.

She's still cursing me, vowing slow painful deaths and revenge, but I ignore them. "Depending on the witch, some are skilled in hand-to-hand combat." I explain, still holding her. "This one in particular is a *rare* blood and dark magic user. And, as you've just witnessed, she's quite capable in close quarters."

Sounds of awe ripple through the room. None of them have ever seen a witch handle two schools of magic. I allow her to be feared.

"The collar she wears suppresses her magic. The runes in it are ancient; the one who placed the collar is the only one who can remove it. The longer she uses magic, the more it burns. Push it far enough, and it'll sear through her throat."

With my free hand, I gather the hem of her gown, sliding it up her legs.

She goes still. "What the fuck are you doing?" She thrashes, trying to break free, but without her magic, I overpower her easily.

"Well-trained witches often conceal weapons. This one favors daggers; something to keep in mind."

I pause, just at the swell of her ass. She's still covered, but the exposure is enough to make a point. I lean in close, my weight settling on her back. My head dips, brushing my voice to her ear.

"No secret daggers tucked higher, Le Strange?" I murmur. "I can perform a more thorough search if necessary."

She snaps her head toward me, bearing her teeth. She tries to bite me, but she misses by a few inches.

"You have the collar on," I say coolly. "Don't make me muzzle you too, pet."

"What the fuck is your problem?" she spits. "You killed my mother, my sisters; now you attack me?"

Her body twists beneath mine, the friction between us growing harder to ignore. She's infuriated and wild, and it makes her power hum even without magic. She's proving to be more of a distraction than I had planned.

"Class dismissed."

Chairs scrape back. Robes swish. Not one of them questions me. They whisper hushed words between one another as they take their leave. More curious than worried, they know the power I possess.

As the last student leaves, I release her, taking a step back. "Let's talk, as you're so adamant we finally do."

She pushes herself off the desk with a huff and turns to me.

"I hate you."

"Likewise," I say flatly. "We're not five. So, allow me to be perfectly clear, not to soothe your fragile feelings, but so we can finally move forward without more of your tantrums."

"Your beliefs are a lie. A fabrication." I don't soften it. She doesn't deserve a softened version.

Her eyes narrow. "So, my *very* eyes lie?"

"What did your eyes see, witch?"

"Beasts," she hisses. "Came from the shadows. A dragon tore through the roof of our temple. *You* were upon its back. Do you mean to say I imagined that? That your dragon didn't slaughter my sisters? That you didn't leave me behind? You left me...and killed the one person I loved."

Her voice breaks. The fury in her eyes twists into something almost sorrowful, grief made brittle by years of silence.

Her accusations, however true, cause my own frustration to rise. She practically takes her finger and digs it into deep wounds that I have been trying to heal for years. "Millicent," I snap. "I'm six years older than you. I was eleven." The words punch out of me before I can check them. I didn't mean to raise my voice, but she won't stop picking at this. "What was I going to do?" I bark. "Think, damn it! How would I, an eleven-year-old, have summoned a dragon? Or slaughtered half of a coven?"

"You were always strong. I obviously don't know the logistics, but your excuse? Someone forced you onto a damn dragon? Someone else killed everyone?" She scoffs, already dismissing anything I might say.

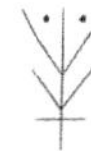

"Millicent, why would I hurt you? Or your mother?" My voice is steel. It's not sorrowful or pleading, just honest. "Especially you," I add. "You had your mother. All I had was you."

Her chest rises sharply, breath picking up. Rage and pain churn in the depths. "Why not?" she snaps. "You're a mage. Killing my kind is in your blood. You were growing stronger; maybe you just wanted more."

I laugh, growing cold and sharp. "Then let me show you that night."

She doesn't respond right away. Skepticism hardens her features. She knows letting me in means being vulnerable, which is something she's never been comfortable with, at least not around me.

"I won't snoop," I reassure her. "You have something in there guarding you anyway."

"I don't trust you. No." She lifts her chin in stubborn defiance born out of self-preservation.

I need this wall between us to break, at least enough for this hostility to end and for us to function. Her attempt on Kalix's life was too close of a call.

Slowly, I slide my hand to my thigh. I grip the hilt of my dagger and draw it free.

I flip the blade and offer it to her, handle first. It's my first attempt at trying to make some sort of peace between us. We will not survive the North and Millicent's revenge.

"Hold it to my throat." I say quietly. "If you feel me prying, you can slit it. You and I both know I won't be able to react fast enough if I'm in the memory. You'll have the advantage."

She snatches the dagger from my hand, and the blade slices across my fingers. I ignore the pain. My body's already working to mend the wound. Arcana rushes beneath my skin to stitch the flesh back together.

She's a predator. Show pain or a hint of weakness, and she'll sink her teeth in. I still only half believe she won't slit my throat *just* to see what happens. Not that it matters. If she does, Vryaxis will be here in seconds. The dagger was never about risk; it is about control. Let her feel she has some.

I return to my desk, sitting this time so that we're eye to eye and without the looming dominance of me towering over her.

Another calculated gesture. Another illusion of equality.

She approaches hesitantly until she's standing between my legs. Her scent hits me—jasmine and vanilla—curling up into my lung like smoke. I grip the desk behind me to keep my hands where they belong.

Cool steel touches my throat.

"We have been here before," I murmur. "Though I'll admit, I prefer the view of you underneath me."

"You talk entirely too much." She pushes the blade harder.

Tempting.

I have a dozen ideas of what else my mouth could do right now, but she's too volatile. Push too far and she'll turn the dagger inward. I lean back, forcing her to lean into me so she can keep the dagger pressed.

"Stop moving." Her voice is sharp, and her weight is solid. She's trying to control the chaos in her own skin.

My hands leave the desk behind me and glide over her hips and down to her ass. Grabbing her roughly, I lift her onto my lap.

She gasps just once and braces herself with one hand on the table. The other keeps the dagger pressed to my throat.

"There," I say. "Now we're settled." I keep my hands where they are, enjoying how she fills them.

"You just make excuses to touch me. Pathetic."

"I wonder what excuses you tell yourself when my touch doesn't disgust you."

She's quiet.

Smart girl. *We both know the truth.*

Her voice shifts. "The memories you claim to have…"

I nod. My hands move slow and measured, over her ribs and across her spine. My finger grazes the curves of her figure. I don't let myself think about why I'm touching her. I could share memories without it, but I don't.

My hands cup her face and I lean in. "Close your eyes."

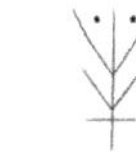

She hesitates. Her instinct is to fight and defy every request I make. Her curiosity wins. Her eyes flutter shut, giving me a reprieve from her gaze.

I watch her, just for a few seconds. I find myself doing that more often now, just watching her. The initial reaction I used to have of her—that volatile, knee-jerking rage—is fading. The truth is settling in.

She's not Nora. Not even close. That fact settles in me with each passing day. Nora was calculated emptiness, a hunger wrapped in skin.

Unlike her, Millicent is a beautiful, chaotic creature sitting on my lap, driven by so much emotion. By need. There's something in her that Nora never possessed.

She bites her bottom lip, a nervous tic since she was young. *She's nervous.* I reach up, brushing my thumb along her cheek, and I gently tug her lip free.

I close my eyes, inhaling deeply as I reach out for her. Her defenses are finally down. It's the first time I've ever been invited in, truly invited. I don't push; I don't dig. I stay just on the outskirts, not wishing to cross the threshold.

This isn't about power. Not now. It's about her trust and safety, as well as for everyone else's well-being.

I extend a silver-threaded string between us, and then I descend deeper into the cold, heavy stillness of my subconscious.

Tingles spread through my fingers, toes, and skin. There is a strange buzzing sensation of slipping between consciousness and memory.

The outside world fades, and we fall.

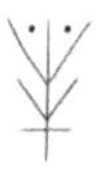

CHAPTER 32

Cage

I stare at the globe beyond my bedroom window, its light slicing through the dark like judgement. Dread anchors my limbs, and exhaustion gnaws at my bones. I'm not sure I'll make it through the night, even after sleeping away most of the day.

Something's wrong or getting worse.

Since Nora's latest lesson, I've started to feel hollow. There's a squirming sensation just beneath my skin, slithering inside me like a snake. It drove me so mad last week that I took a dagger to my own arm trying to dig the worms out.

Then came the voice. It speaks like me, but it isn't. It whispers hunger, and it craves power, especially the kind that hums in others. It resembles those with magical blood or artifacts containing magic. No matter how much I eat, I can't satisfy the bottomless ache clawing at my insides.

I sleep through the daylight most days. I'm awake only at night, pacing or enduring whatever punishment Nora has waiting.

Out in the courtyard, the bell chimes midnight.

Time for my lesson.

I walk toward the temple. There's no point in hurrying to my own execution. My limbs move, but they are not mine. It's routine at this point. I'm outside myself—detached—as the elders strip me beside the circular altar.

I let them, eventually dissociating and going somewhere far from here.

This is what saves people from me.

That's what I tell myself. Over and over, I summon my mother's face, her words, and her hope.

I don't blame you, baby. You are so strong. Now I need you to be brave.

I forgive you. It's not your fault. I should have gotten you help sooner.

I cling to the voice—hers—or the memory of it, as if it might keep me from splintering apart completely.

I lie on the cold stone altar, stripped bare beneath the painted ceiling. There is no measure of warmth remaining in my body.

The art on the temple ceiling depicts some type of war in the heavens. Angels and demons are locked in eternal violence. One weeping angel takes a spear through the chest. I stare at him. He's the only one who looks like he wants to leave. Who could blame him? This place is far from heavenly.

My wrists and ankles are weighed down with silver chains, far too heavy for even me to snap.

Nora begins her ritual in a language I don't understand. The others join her, hooded and silent, with antelope skulls on their heads.

They descend. Blades flash across my arms, legs, and chest. They carve me open in practiced strokes.

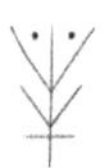

Nora stands over me, cutting matching runes into my chest, mirroring the ones she carved on my back. Even with healing, I can't hide them anymore. The scars are permanent now, like she wants.

A belt is shoved between my teeth. The sour leather taste fills my mouth. I bite down hard, and my jaw cramps from the pressure.

I can't scream anymore. My voice is shredded. My back arches off the stone as a wave of magic crashes through me.

"Hold," Nora's voice calls out sharply.

Hands grab me, and blades press down, forcing me flat again. My vision starts to darken, slipping into a never-ending black tunnel as life is drained from me.

"I said hold him!" Nora yells again, dragging me from the brink. The stone disappears beneath me.

I'm levitating. The chains scrape loud against the altar as they stretch, restraining me just above the surface. The chains whine, pulled taut as my body attempts to rise higher. Power thrums through me, each wave forcing me up.

Hands press down again, harder this time. Even the witches are straining now.

"Nora, we can't hold him!"

Something in me is awakening, and it does not want to be chained. The alien force causes every cell in my body to vibrate violently. I can't get enough air into my lungs as this overwhelming feeling of transformation consumes me, swelling through organs and tissues; the change occurs within my very soul.

Nora curses as she raises her blade, aiming for my heart.

I'm too injured and drained to even begin to fully grasp what's happening. However, I can understand she means to kill me. Then panic hits. A new wave of adrenaline courses through me, mixing with festering fear like acid in my veins.

Then, suddenly, a gust of wind extinguishes every torch in the room. Darkness.

From every shadowed corner, *they* arrive.

Beasts tear through the shadowed alcoves, no two alike. Their forms flicker and shift between cloud and flesh, fog and fang. Snarls erupt into screams as they pounce.

One passes my peripheral, a lion–bear hybrid, bones jutting from its back. Its unnatural roar splits the air. Behind it, a serpent-headed gator slithers past, jaws wide with hunger.

They slaughter the witches. Horrid cracks echo through the dark from the bones snapping like dry twigs.

Magic retaliates; inky tendrils lash across the floors, ensnaring the beasts and breaking their limbs. Black fire erupts, igniting the temple's tapestries and blanketing the room in a thick smoke.

Then, amid the chaos, Nora's blade finds its target again.

It descends but never lands.

A burst of iridescent silver erupts from my chest, blasting Nora backwards. Immediately, the shadow of a massive wing rips out of my chest. Talons as long as my body follow. Her scales shimmer in the faint light, and then smoke pours from a newly opened maw.

The dragon emerges, materializing over me. Its stomach shields me. Its massive wings can split the temple walls, and its body turns solid above me, silvery and smoking.

My eyes track the silver glow running beneath her scales, from her under belly, up to her throat, and then to the curve of her jaw

Then her mouth opens.

Fire pours out as a wave of blinding heat that engulfs the entire side of the temple where Nora landed. Stone cracks, screams vanish, and ashes rise.

She turns her massive head and lowers it to me. She gently nudges my broken body with her nose, her warm breath encasing my body. I cry out, not in fear but from the pain of my injuries.

Hello, child.

The voice isn't mine, but I know it. I've always known it. New tears flood my eyes as my soul recognizes hers.

I am yours, just as you are mine. You are no longer alone.

Her silver eyes are like reflections of my own. They flick to the chains binding my limbs. Displeasure sickens my stomach, and a rumbling growl causes the stone beneath me to quake. She lowers her head again, delicate despite her size, and bites through the metal, one link at a time.

Once I'm free, she nudges me again, urging me to stand.

"I...I might pass out," I warn, dragging my legs over the altar's edge. The world sways, and my knees buckle.

Concern fills me, and the sweet taste of affection coats my tongue. They are her emotions, but they aren't mine, I realize.

Still, fresh tears fill my eyes after feeling such emotions bestowed upon me.

She cares for me.

Someone cares for me, someone will save me.

Before I can hit the ground, one of her leathery wings wrap around me. She lifts me, guiding my battered frame along the curve of her wing until I slide onto her spine.

Sit between my largest spikes.

With my strength leaving me, I crawl forward and slump between the ridges. I melt there. My fingers weakly grip two smaller spines. It's all I can manage at this point.

Head down, eyes closed.

I am all too happy to listen.

Vyraxis crashes upward, her skull smashing through the temple roof. Rubble rains down over me. Dust coats my shoulder as I cling weakly to her spikes.

My heartbeat echoes in my ears as my vision blackens, flickers back, and then fades again.

Outside, the world burns and buildings collapse. Beasts run wild. Witches lie strewn across the ground like dolls in ash.

I did this.

But I don't know how to undo it.

My throat tightens around the stench of scorched flesh. It hits my nose and then catches in my throat, dragging the bile with it.

The devastation...

They deserve it. They harmed what was not theirs. Her voice is final, lacking any sympathy for those here who have harmed me or turned an eye from it.

"How do I stop it?" I rasp, unsure if I'm even speaking aloud.

We do not. We leave. You are weak.

Her wings beat. Air lashes across my skin, stealing more warmth from me. My body trembles from blood loss, cold, and pain. I am naked, cut open in too many places to heal.

My vision clears just long enough to find her: Millicent.

Her eyes...I'll never forget their bright-blue color, which I can only compare to a chilling winter's breath and the color of crisp frozen dawns.

Millicent.

I try to call out and reach for her.

The girl stays here.

We are off the ground in an instant; the last thing I see is her, growing smaller and vanishing into the smoke.

The darkness takes me.

When I open my eyes, Millicent is staring at me. The dagger still rests at my throat; she doesn't remove it.

A tear slips down her cheek, and I do my best to not react. Acknowledging her vulnerability would only make her recoil.

"I hate Nora," I say quietly. "And most of the witches at the coven. I thought you were just like her. Hell, you're meant to replace her." She lets me speak, a rare opportunity, so I choose my words wisely.

"I don't know you," I admit. "I knew you when you were a child. The person in front of me now...I'm trying to accept that you may not be Nora."

"I am not Nora," she snaps. "I am my own person."

"I'm sorry about your mother." The words feel foreign on my tongue. I rarely apologize for anything.

She yanks the blade back and hurls it into the desk beside me. "I understand we can't control magic when we're young," she says. "But understand *this*: my heart died with her. I don't need your apology or your excuses." Her arms wrap around her waist in a protective, guarded manner. "If there's anything left in me capable of love and forgiveness, I haven't found it."

She steps back. Her message is clear.

"What's done is done. And I will always hold you accountable. Don't try to make amends with me until you make them with the dead."

"Fair enough," I say, shrugging. "Let's just agree to work together without stabbing each other. Deal?"

"Fine. The sooner we finish this, the sooner I can return home."

I scoff; that stings more than it should. "So eager to get back under the blade?"

She bristles. "Why must everyone speak like they know me?"

"Show me your back."

"I'm not giving you my back. Don't mistake cooperation for weakness."

I strip off my shirt and turn around.

Silence.

Her breath catches. I know she sees the scars, the runes, and *the proof.* Her eyes are fixated on my back. Her gaze becomes a mix of shock and recognition. No snappy retort follows, just silence and the intense inspection of my back.

Thought so.

"Nora doesn't help us," I say. "She controls us, one way or another."

"I am stronger because of her."

"Did she teach you that? You sound like a well-trained pet." I turn to face her once again, pulling my shirt back on.

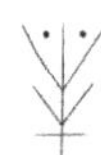

Her eyes flash. "The truth is in my abilities. I was not born with two kinds of magic. I was *made* this way—"

"In her image, little witch." I rub my hands over my face, trying to ground myself amidst the frustration. "Gods above."

"Even if I am," she hisses, "look at me. I'm perfect."

I glance her over, slowly and deliberately. "You're right, Millicent." I step beside her, lowering my voice until it barely brushes the space between us. "When I look at you, I see something perfect. The kind of perfect only forged under pressure, like diamonds. Long, unrelenting pressure."

Her brows furrow. She doesn't believe me. Not yet.

"There's something violently brutal in you," I whisper. "Something fascinating. Stop kneeling to Nora. The only thing in that coven worthy of such worship...is you."

I leave her there: blade in the desk, scars on my back, and too many words hanging between us.

Gods help us both. I need time to process what the hell I just relived.

CHAPTER 33

Millicent

Almost! There!" Ollie grunts, pressing his feet to my shoulder, using his entire body weight to pry the collar off.

"Oliver, the bloody thing won't come off unless the one who placed it removes it!" I snap.

"Me Misses, we just need oil! Ollie was stuck in a slide once, oiled myself right up I did! Slipped right out!"

When the hell did this happen?

Oliver hops off the bed, his solid form turning to gas as he zips away on his mission for oil. Wonderful. I'm going to be a greased-up pig. I shift my glare to the window where Nora's owl perches like a smug sentinel.

"You can't do anything to get me out of this? Seriously?"

Why the hell can't Nora get this thing off me?

Elders are the oldest witches in a coven. Their magic's strength grows with age. Nora is an incredibly strong witch and a big reason our coven is so respected by others.

The owl clicks its beak and then plays a recording of Nora's voice: "Millicent, your own stupidity got you into this. You can get yourself out. I told you to behave, and, per usual, you can't control yourself."

Shame floods through me, which seems to always accompany a speech from her. A small flicker of anger pushes against it. "Thanks for nothing," I mutter under my breath, too low for the owl to hear.

Iris is my best chance at getting this thing off, but I have avoided her—and anyone else—for the past four days since waking up. I lost control. I tried to kill Kalix. Whatever's going on between him and Iris, she cares for him. Talking to her now seems like a disaster waiting to happen.

Ollie crashes around the bathroom, his bottles of oil clinking like a cacophony of chaos. That's my cue. I slip out in search of Iris.

Her lab door creaks as I open it. Inside, she's hunched over a corpse, peering through a large magnifying glass while prodding around its intestines. I make sure my steps are loud, and I close the door with purpose—no surprises.

"Back already? You better not have eaten any of my mangos on the way here, Kalix. I swear, if you did, I'll send you right back to cut some more up."

"It's Millicent," I say softly, crossing the room at an even pace.

She pauses, stripping off her gloves to reach for her journal. "You're awake; how do you feel?" She still hasn't looked at me. That's not like her.

"I've been better. First time I've ever woken up with a collar on," I reply, tapping at the cold steel.

"It's unfortunately necessary."

"So...you agreed to it?"

"Don't accuse me of being a part of that decision," she says, sighing as she flips open her journal. Then her gaze finally meets mine, sharper and heavier than I've seen before. "You tried to kill Kalix."

Her voice darkens. There's a new chill to her that prickles across my skin.

"Iris, Cage attacked me. My magic reacted."

"You attacked him first. Take responsibility." She closes the journal. "I'm sorry it's like this. I wanted to trust you."

"I'm...I'm sorry, Iris." I force the words out, pride scraping my throat on the way up. She reminds me of Arcadia—of a version of home that still means something to me. My chest tightens over the thought of Iris shutting me out.

She studies me like some complex puzzle, uncertain on whether she wants to solve it. I suppose I am in some ways. "I'm sorry you had to be collared. I know how awful it must feel being cut off from your magic. You will be allowed in certain situations; Tyran will explain the details."

The tension between us continues to make me feel uneasy. I spin my ring on my thumb in an attempt to ease my discomfort.

"Kalix is important to me," she says. "He didn't go out there expecting to die. He is smarter than that. He planned. Even with all the preparation, I still hated the threat to his life." Her voice sharpens to a lethal blade. "If you ever hurt him again—if you kill him—I will tear you apart and reshape you into beasts to serve me forever."

Damn. Touchy. "But you're not dating, right?" I tease, forcing a small smile in an attempt to ease the tension between us. Some people flinch at a person's darkness, but that's not my style. I live there too.

Iris's features soften, a reluctant smile tugging at her lips. "Right."

She closes the space between us, pulling me into a tight hug with the heavy sigh a parent makes when their child inevitably hurts themselves again. Whatever walls I'm trying to keep up collapse. I return her embrace, just as tightly. I feel her forgiveness and relief untying the knot in my chest. When she pulls away, she gives me a firm nudge toward the door and tells me to seek out Felix.

She's swamped, apparently, with a backlog of specimens piling up. I catch a few glimpses of Kalix haunting her halls like a shadow hoping for an opening.

I guess the mangos were just a delivery after all.

My search for Felix lands me outside his bedroom. I knock, and when he calls out for me to enter, I step inside.

"Felix," I say, slipping into his room and closing the door behind me.

He's out on the balcony, his legs stretched lazily across a lounge chair to bathe in the warm midday sun.

"Princess! Ah, you're up! Come join me!" He's all sunshine and mischief, as usual. I half expected my outburst to earn at least a sharp word or two, but apparently not. Ever the stormproof lighthouse, Felix just beams at me like he always does.

I cross the room and settle into the chair beside him, letting the sun soak into my skin. When I meet his gaze, I raise a brow.

"You don't sound mad at all."

"I've had days to cool off and move past the idea of beheading you," he says, flashing a mischievous grin.

"Fantasizing about killing me?"

"Naturally. It's great stress relief."

I laugh. I've come to enjoy our banter. Felix is fire and laughter—a constant positive spark. I thought him foolish and naïve when I first arrived. Now, I find myself seeking out his company more and more. It unsettles me, forming this bond with a mortal, but Iris's words echo in my head. She cares for Kalix, and I don't think her weak for it.

"So, instead I got collared?"

"Correct. Cage placed it under my command. It'll come off when you're deployed in the field and need full access. Once you have adjusted, if you and Cage can tolerate each other, and the team deems it safe, then we'll remove it."

"A team vote?" I scoff. The idea feels absurd.

"Yes, Millicent. This isn't a one-witch show. We work as a team. That means, no stabbing people."

Ah. So, Cage told him. I wonder how much he revealed. Did he gloss over the details, or did he share everything? His eyes give nothing away. If he knows, then he's playing it close to the chest. Or maybe it's nothing new for Felix to hear.

"No stabbing, and a team vote. Got it."

"Don't pout, princess. You're no harmless flower. It's like watching an alligator pout; it's honestly unsettling."

I kick out, nearly knocking him off his chair. His laughter bursts out of him, filling me with warmth and joy. It's the kind of joy Arcadia and I once shared on the riverbanks in high summer. It settles in my chest like sunlight.

"My pout is cute," I protest.

"You're fishing for compliments, and I'm not biting."

This time, I kick much harder. He tumbles from the chair with a dramatic yelp. Before I can gloat, his hand shoots out and grabs my ankle, and he yanks me down to the ground beside him.

I land with a laugh, breathless and smiling as the stone warms my back. The anxiety I carried earlier slips away, exhaled in laughter as I stare up at the passing clouds.

"What if I broke my ass from that fall?" I ask, playing it up dramatically. The fall didn't hurt at all.

"You slid onto the ground. 'Fall' is a strong word." Felix says, rolling his eyes. He lifts an arm, pointing upward to a cloud. "That one looks like a bunny."

"I see a duck."

He turns his head, angling it slightly to the left.

"Look at something one way, get one result. Look at it another way, get something entirely different. Perspective, Millicent." He pauses, finger tracing the shape of the cloud. "It's all just perspective. And our views don't make either of us wrong. We're both right."

His words land too directly to be random. I stare up at the sky, chewing them over. Does perspective really matter in situations where risk and reward are such high costs? At least someone has to be wrong in those situations.

"You know I talked to Cage?" I whisper.

"No," he replies gently. "I had hope that you're strong enough to do it."

He takes my hand in his, giving it a gentle squeeze. The touch is simple but grounding. After everything I've endured the last few days, I don't want to leave this moment.

"Can we lay here a while?"

"For as long as you need, princess."

That nickname pulls at something deep in me; Arcadia's voice echoes:

As you wish, Your Highness.

I squeeze his hand in return. I don't ask for comfort, but he gives it anyway. Arcadia would be proud of me. I'm letting a mortal touch me, and I'm enjoying his company.

I glance over at Felix. The sun catches the gold in his clothes and lights his curls like a halo. Even his eyes shine brighter in daylight; they're alive with boyish wonder as he points out new clouds and guesses their shapes.

The warmth of the sun bakes into my skin. I welcome it. I don't know when I drift off.

I wake, still curled beside him, the stone warm beneath us. Felix hasn't moved, apparently joining me for a nap in the sun.

"Felix," I whisper, gently shaking him. "Come. You should sleep in your bed."

He stirs, mumbling as he struggles to keep his eyes open in the haze. He nods with a sleepy yawn, sitting up with bleary eyes.

I help him inside, guide him to his bed, and then slip away in silence.

On my way back to my room, I spot Kalix drifting down the hall that leads to Iris's lab. Just like before.

I pass Kalix in the hall, unsure what I'm supposed to say. His brow arches as I pass without a word. His hand darts out, catching my arm. "Whoa, whoa, whoa...slow it down, little witch."

I keep my eyes lowered, "Kalix, I'm sorry. I—"

He cuts me off. "Millie, we all have bad shit in us. Sometimes our demons break loose. That's all that happened." His hand drops from my arm. "Honestly, even Cage can set me off."

His acceptance disarms me. I don't know how to respond. I'm not used to being met with understanding instead of judgement in light of my mistakes.

What kind of demons must he carry to say that so easily?

"I'm not good, Kalix," I murmur. "You all seem good, and I'm not."

"Good and bad are just labels," he shrugs. "Sometimes, to do great things, we must become the worst versions of ourselves. Stop punishing yourself."

Iris's door creaks open. Her face is streaked with sweat and dried blood, and her braid is undone in a wild halo of frizz. Her overalls are splattered with bloodstains—some fresh, some darkened. She looks worn to the bone. Yet, despite that, the moment he sees her, Kalix lights up. He doesn't look away from her once. I'm not even sure he blinks.

"Ready for bed, Rainbow?" he asks, offering her his arm.

"Goodnight, Millie," Iris yawns with a tired smile, slipping her arm into his.

Kalix guides her down the hall, moving slow and steadily. His free hand hovers beside her in case she falters. She makes it to the end before her knees buckle, and Kalix scoops her up in one motion. I hear the soft murmur of praise against her hair, whispered comforts meant only for her.

Necromancers push themselves too far. Iris is a true testament to that. Kalix is often the one catching her when she falls.

Little star.

The Nightmother's voice slides through my mind like a silken noose.

I hurry to my room, and my heart hammers against my chest. The moment I step inside, I drop to my knees, bowing my head and focusing in on her presence.

"Mother, I have been collared, my powers restricted. Will you free me from this restraint?"

You asked, you shall receive. Feed...that is all I request of thee.

My gums throb. The hunger rises instantly in response. She would unbind me if I obey.

Feeding means risk. Losing control. A real massacre. This past week, they only glimpsed the stain of my magic—tainting me, not taking over.

I push the idea aside. Not yet. I can't risk hurting Iris, Felix, or Kalix. Not yet.

Not even as my gums ache and saliva pools in my mouth.

Not even as she shows me images of something that will make me hurt them all.

Their blood.

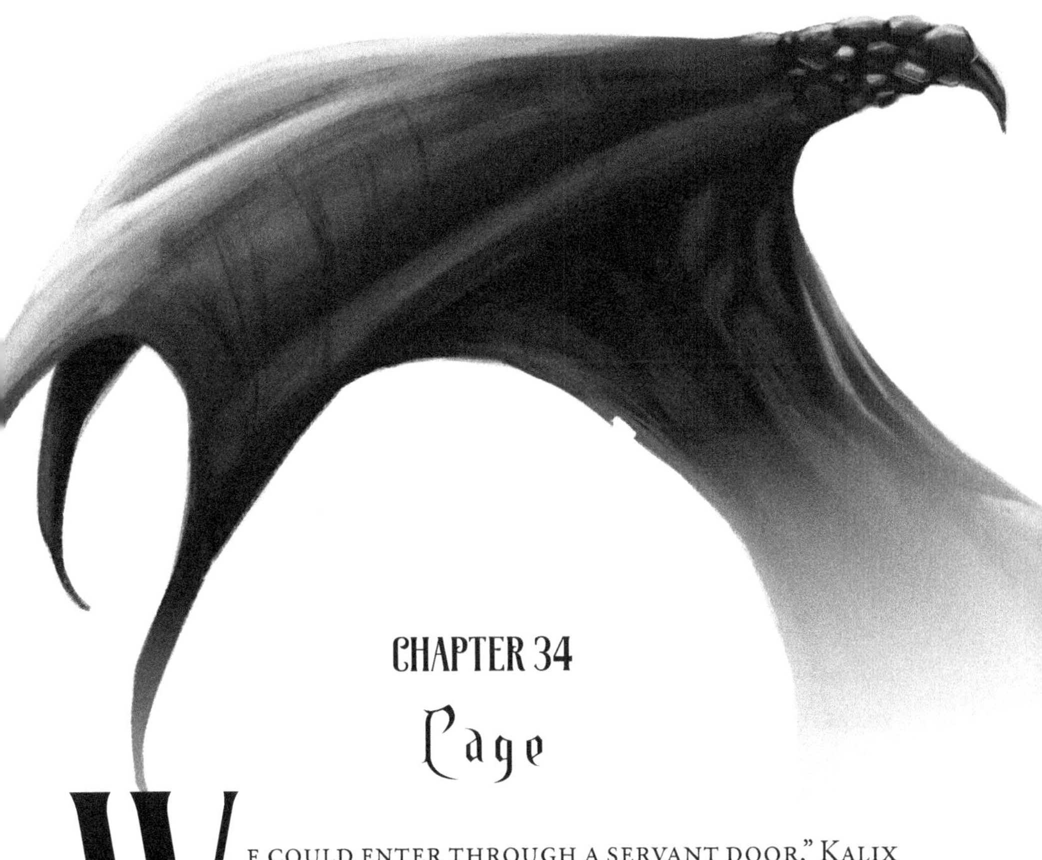

CHAPTER 34

Cage

WE COULD ENTER THROUGH A SERVANT DOOR," KALIX offers, suggesting yet another way into the manipulator's estate without getting us caught.

"Kalix, you're well over six feet tall. The entrance won't matter once you step inside," Iris counters, pointing out the oversight.

"They'll try to compel us the moment we're in, right?" Felix asks, sounding far too intrigued by the idea of a dominant woman. His enthusiasm makes me want to slap him.

"Manipulators crave total domination and it's an easy task for them to achieve without draining themselves," Millicent says coolly. "They'll target anyone whose eyes don't show signs of submission," Millicent says.

I'm not used to having Millicent in our planning sessions. Her presence is rare, but Felix insisted it was time to fully integrate her. It has only been a few days since she woke, but Iris has sworn along with her that she is fine to proceed. Now she stands beside Iris, leaning over the documents spread across the table.

"So, it's the eyes?" Kalix muses, rubbing his chin as he processes the information.

"It's always the eyes—and their obedience," Millicent confirms. "They can tell who's under by the way they look at you. They prefer men, but Iris and I will still be targets. Would be lovely to have my collar off."

She tosses Felix a sweet, pleading smile.

The bastard in me bristles. I'm the one who positioned the damn collar. She should be begging *me*.

"What a—" Felix draws out the words dramatically, "horrible idea! Millie, my sweet gumdrop princess, a manipulator is going to try to compel you and you're going to obliterate them—losing a lead we spent weeks tracking down! And, restraint *isn't* exactly your strong suit."

Millicent rolls her eyes so hard that I'm half convinced they'll stay that way. "Fine. I'll carve the bitches instead and make coats out of their skin. My magic would make the kills cleaner, but if you want me to go full barbarian, I can accommodate."

"That...that is not—" Felix groans, pressing two fingers to his temple like the headache is already blooming.

Kalix chuckles while Iris covers her mouth, trying to stifle a laugh. Millicent, of course, is dead serious.

"Down, girl. The goal is not to cause friction," I remind her and everyone in the room.

"Do we know what the coven members look like? We could transfigure into them," Kalix suggests.

Gods. I already had to be Felix once. His body felt too loose, like wearing an ill-fitted coat. I would prefer never to turn into someone else again. However, the biggest problem is imagining who you wish to turn into, and we have never seen one of these Manipulators.

"No," I say. "We only know of their suspected involvement by reputation. The witches haven't been identified or confirmed."

"You all get to go to a sin house and I have to stay back?" Felix whines from across the room. "What kind of kingly treatment is this?"

Of course he wants in. The establishment we're targeting is practically his personal heaven—alcohol, women, and gambling all in one depraved bundle.

"Felix, you'd be the first one either compelled or drunk. So, no— you stay here." Iris shoots him a pointed look.

"Does the coven *own* The Viscountess?" Millicent asks.

"Papers and pockets lead to one of the lords running it. He's not under compulsion, interestingly enough." Kalix slides the deed across the table toward her.

We need to speak with a manipulator witch. Covens' general locations in the kingdom are vaguely known. The closest manipulator coven is quite far, and going to a coven is dangerous. There will be a very high concentration of manipulator witches and their minions there. They are not as mild tempered as curse users are. Our best bet is to try to find a smaller group of them.

Our informants discovered some working at The Viscountess. I believe the witch and lord have a deal and they help one another out. She can make anyone do anything for the lord and he can line her pockets with coins and help feed her cozy lifestyle.

There will still be a head witch, one who is like an elder. Witches always hold their hierarchies. This is the one we will try to target for questioning as calmly as possible. Causing a fight at one of the most profitable sin houses is going to cause Tyran grief with the higher society folks.

"Kalix, you poisoned me. What *else* can you do?" Millicent mutters, dry as bone.

Between the six of us, a plan forms. One that helps us remain under the radar and sets us up to gather intel in the most passive way. Thankfully, it is also a plan that does not involve me turning into Felix Tyran.

The plan is wobbly at best—but right now, it's all we've got.

KALIX IS ABNORMALLY TENSE AS WE ESCORT THE GIRLS TOWARD The Viscountess. Iris's gown barely counts as clothing, the deep plunge revealing most of her breasts, and the high slits bare her the length of legs as she walks. Hers are crimson. Millicent's, in contrast, are a midnight blue—similar in form and equally dangerous.

Relax. You look like you're about to murder someone, I speak directly into Kalix's mind.

I just might, if anyone lays a single finger on Iris. I hate this plan. I hate how much skin she's showing.

His emotions surge through the tether between us like a possessive and primal suffocating roar.

Please spare me your fantasy of claiming her. I don't need a visual of your hard-on.

Then get out of my head, mage.

Someone is grumpy, I think privately, leaving him to simmer in that attitude of his. Gods, it's going to be a long night if Kalix is this wound up. I'll be babysitting his murderous instincts while keeping in check the loose screws in Millicent's head.

Iris, I send, *Kalix is one deep breath away from combusting. Stop swaying your hips so much. He's about to cum in his trousers.*

Her laughter flickers into my mind. *Cage, I'm simply walking.* A pause. *But if you insist ....*

The vixen doubles down. Her hips sway even more exaggeratedly, prompting a low, guttural growl from Kalix's chest.

Millicent glances back, brows raised. "Did you just...growl? Like a dog? Is that your secret talent?"

"You're the one wearing a collar," he snaps, voice tight with sexual frustration.

Millicent's eyes widen. Wisely, she turns around.

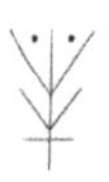

Iris ignores Kalix entirely, even as he shadows her steps so closely he's practically walking on her heels. His eyes scan the crowd for threats or anyone daring to look too long.

"We should split here," she says, reaching for Millicent's hand. "The building is just ahead. It's better if we're not seen together."

Kalix's arm snakes around her waist, halting her escape with a firm tug back against his chest.

"Don't forget who owns this perfect little body." His voice roughens at the edges of restraint. He leans down and bites her shoulder, not gently.

Iris smacks him. Hard. "Kalix! Right now? Seriously?"

Her slap barely registers. Still he lets go, stepping back, leaving the imprint of his teeth on her skin. A mark of possession.

"Asshole." She flips him off without looking and storms off with Millicent in tow.

I step closer, lowering my voice, "Have you taken your dose this week?"

Kalix nods. "Last night. I'm level. Even with the high doses not everything is blocked."

"We've got back up, yeah?"

He taps his breast pocket. "Right here."

Relief drapes over me like armor. The last thing I need tonight is Kalix spiraling.

The Viscountess is packed but surprisingly spacious. The two-story structure features an open upper floor; its balcony feeds into the grand chamber below.

Massive crystal chandeliers glitter above, casting a soft ambient glow that flatters the patrons. The dim light makes them appear far more attractive than they likely are.

Velvet floor cushions surrounding plush tables create cozy smoking stations, leaving a constant haze drifting overhead.

Around us, men and women drink heavily, their laughter and moans intermingling with the low thrum of a sultry tune. Some indulge openly in carnal acts while harlots drift between crowds giggling, flirting, and targeting men with the heaviest purses.

Cheers and jeers erupt from gambling tables spaced along the walls. Silk-clad dancers undulate across an open stage, their hips rolling in time with the musicians performing behind them. Multiple bars frame the room, imported liquor gleaming on the shelves.

"Shall we?" I mutter, pushing through the crowd toward the gambling tables.

Kalix's eyes continue scanning the floor, clearly searching for a flash of red hair streaked with white.

The girls know what they are doing. We need your focus here.

The reminder is enough. He nods, his attention finally snapping back to me and our task.

Drunk men love to talk, especially while gambling. Our hope is to catch wind of something useful, some whispers about certain working girls or rumors of women who aren't quite what they seem.

While we work this angle, the girls mingle as though harlots. Perhaps one of the women we're after is embedded among them.

We sit at a card table and are dealt in. It doesn't take long.

The working girls drift toward us, drawn like moths to gold.

"You're a big boy," a young girl with tight blonde curls giggles, leaning onto the table to give Kalix a better view of her cleavage.

"You have no idea," he replies with a wink, taking a slow sip from the drink the waitress delivered before the round began.

She soon ends up in his lap, giggling while we play. Occasionally, she presses her hips back into him with every excuse to shift against him. Despite his charming smile and flirtatious remarks, I can feel that his thoughts are elsewhere. Iris. He's trying to stay present; she consumes him.

A woman approaches me with deep black hair and blue eyes, she's breathtaking, which gives me pause.

"Hey handsome," she purrs. Her voice lulls over me like smoke. "You look lonely. I can fix that." Her hand slides boldly up my shoulder.

"Come," I say, leaning back in my chair and parting my legs before patting my thigh. "Keep my lap warm."

She straddles me without hesitation, her ass soft and plush against my lap.

I slip a hand across her hips to her pelvis, guiding her back until she's flush against me.

"You're demanding; I like that," she murmurs, glancing over her shoulder. Her grind is slow, she's teasing me.

A predatory grin tugs at my lips. "Let me finish my hand; then I'll play with you."

Focusing on the men playing cards, I still manage to keep a mental note of where the girls are.

Iris leans over a bar, laughing and chatting with a group of men and the little devil accompanies her. Millicent's presence has morphed into one that is rather inviting. The typical dark cloud over her is missing.

Glimpsing at to them occasionally to ensure no issues arise, I find it fascinating how these men will see women as both sweet girls and those they can fuck. In reality, Iris is inside dead things all day and Millicent would probably eat all four of men absorbed in them within a few minutes.

Wolves in sheepskins.

THE CARD GAME YIELDS MORE THAN COIN. MERCHANT WOES, extra marital affairs, and personal tastes slip out between sips of alcohol and ego. I focus on the more submissive men, those who prefer to be dominated. That's where our manipulator will strike.

 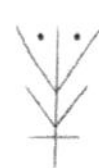

My next lead is perched on my lap, sipping the drinks I keep feeding her. She thinks she's seducing me.

The game will wrap up soon. I refrain from scouring the minds around me just in case a manipulator lurks nearby. My defenses must remain high. Once the game ends, the real work begins. I get to have my fun and extract what I can from her between whispered promises.

A commotion stirs the room in a wave of laughter that cuts through the smoke-drenched air. I glance up, scanning until I see her.

There she is.

Millicent isn't entertaining four men. She's enthralled an entire circle now. They're slouched on floor cushions, dazed from whatever herb they smoke that drifts around her.

Her laugh, fake and lilting, rings out while she is passed from lap to lap, treated like meat in a pack of starving dogs.

She lands between two men. Their mouths descend, one to each side of her neck.

I watch, captivated, as her head falls back, exposing the soft column of her throat like an invitation. Her back arches. Her breasts push forward, and she parts her mouth in false pleasure.

One man slides his hand beneath the high slit of her gown, brushing the inside of her thigh. The other palms her breast.

Desire spikes with the next beat of my heart, driving straight through my chest to my cock.

The woman on my lap, Morana, I've learned, grinds against me again, mistaking my arousal for interest. Her pride blooms with the motion.

Millicent halts any further exploration. With a coy smile, she rises and takes one of the men by hand to lead him through the crowd toward the stairs.

What are you up to, little devil?

Morana leans close, her breath a teasing whisper against my ear. "Take me somewhere quieter."

"It won't stay quiet for long," I reply, sliding my hands to her hips again and lifting her effortlessly off my lap. She gasps, delighted by the strength.

I'm going to pull answers from this one. Behave, I think toward Kalix.

Kalix lazily raises his glass in acknowledgement then downs another long sip. He's drinking more than usual. My confidence in Iris's role starts to falter. Maybe making her play a harlot wasn't such a good idea.

Morana leads me up the same staircase Millicent took. My eyes scan each door. Which one is she in?

Morana pauses near the end of the hall and opens a room with a small brass six on it. She pulls me inside.

The room practically screams indulgence. Red walls. A circular bed draped in black silk. Sex tools of every kind hang on display like artwork.

Morana drops to her knees without hesitation, her lust-filled eyes lock onto mine as she unfastens my belt.

I'm still hard, lingering from watching Millicent and the eager girl kneeling before me. Morana's resemblance doesn't help. Blue eyes and black curls. She plays the part well.

I didn't intend to let her touch me, but I'm already aroused and she's too willing.

It isn't Millicent; it's just like any other girl I have used for release.

When she frees me, her eyes widen in surprise. "You look delicious," she purrs, fisting the base of my length before slipping her lips down my shaft.

My breathing deepens as pleasure coils tightly through my abdomen. "Don't talk, I have better use for this mouth."

I grip her hair and thrust forward both rough and unrelenting. She gags as I stretch down her throat. I don't look down. I see now that her eyes are the wrong shade of blue, her hair devoid of wild curls.

She's a beautiful girl but my hunger is drawn to someone else.

I look up, eyes fixed on the ceiling, and pretend it's Millicent. The fantasy hits hard, and I thrust harder, tripling the pleasure and unraveling what little restraint I have left.

"Such a good girl. You can take it all," I groan, catching my breath as the fantasy blooms.

I remember the weight of my little witch's breasts in my hands, the softness of her thighs, how easily they bruised under my grip, and the way her reluctant moans slipped past her defenses.

Touch me.

She had been so needy that night, I barely held myself back. In my mind, I sink into that memory, into how tight she would be, her taste, how hard she would milk my cock when she came.

And the way she'd scream my name until it burned in her throat.

"Fuck, Millicent."

Her name bursts from me and I bury myself deep, spilling my release in this girl's throat. My grip on Morana's hair doesn't loosen until I'm done.

When I finally let go, she pulls back, gasping to catch her breath. The haze lifts, and clarity cuts like ice.

I curse myself.

I hate when I gaze down at her to see she is not Millicent.

Fuck. What the fuck?

Irritation pricks so sharply at my skin I feel the need to itch. No. I don't desire a lying, murderous, manipulative, bond-forcing bitch.

Morana rises and reaches for me. "I can be whoever you want me to be, baby." Her eyes gleam as she leads me to the bed.

I shove her down onto it roughly.

As if you could ever be the shadow of Millicent.

I slap myself mentally at the reflexive thought.

Refastening my trousers, I then walk to the wall, returning with rope. She blinks up at me, confused, until I bind her wrist and ankles tight.

"What I need, baby," I say coldly, "is the girl who gives me answers."

Her expression changes instantly.

"Answers?"

"Who is the manipulator here? Are there multiple?"

I sit beside her on the bed. My eyes flash with brilliance and I push into her mind.

Who the fuck is this guy? Ariella is going to need to know about him. Immediately.

"Where is Ariella?"

Her jaw slackens. "You...you can read minds?"

Dread floods her features, all pretense gone. She tugs at the ropes. Too late.

"I can do many things in your mind," I whisper. "Observe."

I squeeze. Pressure bursts behind her eyes. She screams in agony, body arching off the bed. No one comes. This is a sin house; such things are common here.

I release her. She slumps into the bed, gasping for air.

"Where is Ariella?"

She says nothing, but her body shakes in fear.

Have it your way.

I squeeze again and this time I let all my frustration at calling Millicent's name seep into the woman with her reminiscent eyes and hair. I watch with great satisfaction as she is pushed to the point of unconsciousness, only to return to me and repeat the cycle until I get what I want.

CHAPTER 35

Millicent

I DON'T THINK THIS IS WHAT FELIX MEANT BY SUBTLE," Iris says, trailing off as she takes in the art I've made of the man who touched me so boldly.

His body is still bound to the chair, but his tongue and dick are nailed to the wall. His arms rest neatly on the floor beside him. I was halfway through sawing off his leg when Iris arrived. Her interruption now has left the poor limb hanging on by a few ligaments.

"Did you plan this ahead of time? Where did you get a damn hammer? Or...is that a bone saw?" She tilts her head, studying the display with more curiosity than concern.

"No, funnily enough, it just happened to be in here; I felt inspired," I lie smoothly.

Truth is, once I snapped the bastard's neck, rage took over. He touched me. The fucking vermin touched me. I summoned Ollie, and he was *delighted* to bring us some supplies.

Now he stands proudly on the desk behind me, trying (and

failing) to hide the hammer behind his back while he twirls one of the man's fingers.

Iris glances between us. She knows I'm lying.

Oliver waves the man's finger at her, all smiles.

"He talked too much. And he ground that sad little shrimp against me." I grimace at the memory.

Maybe I went a little overboard. I'm easily excitable around blood as well as annoyed about the collar. Now they know that even collared, I am perfectly capable of unspeakable violence.

"Well...I didn't kill my guy," Iris says, "Just sent him on his way after using the truth serum Kalix supplied. He knew nothing."

"What did yours know?"

I wipe the remaining blood off my hands with a nearby sheet before tossing it onto the floor.

"He was going to report me to Arella," I say. "She might be the Madame here, which makes her a good place to start. Manipulators aren't exactly the subservient type. That she hasn't shown her face yet tells me something's off."

I can't pin down what it is, but her absence doesn't sit right. For a woman supposedly in control, she's staying far too quiet.

A sharp bang cuts through the room. I turn.

Ollie is still going, hammering the man's finger to the wall like we're finishing a mural. Completely oblivious as ever.

"Ollie, read the room," I sigh. The moment for our playtime has passed.

He finishes with a delighted gurgle, then kisses his fingers like a chef admiring a dish. "Mwah!"

Then, a crash from below.

Iris's eyes snap to mine; a silent understanding passes between us.

"Oliver, leave."

He obeys, dragging his hammer into the shadows. The tether between us quiets as he fades, distant into another realm.

We move fast.

Downstairs, a brawl has erupted at the gambling tables. Kalix towers over a man, fists slamming down on his skull again and again.

"Oh, it's your truth serum guy," I say, masking a half laugh behind my hand.

I'd seen Kalix brimming with jealousy earlier, practically vibrating at the thought of anyone touching Iris.

Apparently, someone did, and now he's snapped.

Iris doesn't answer, she's already sprinting down the steps to reach him.

He's the one who needs a collar. Not me.

I scan the room below, which has descended into full-on chaos.

Arella. What the fuck does an Arella even look like?

If I didn't have this damn collar, I could tear though their minds, find her in seconds. But no—I need him for that. Cage. That insufferable, arrogant prick.

Just thinking about needing him for anything grates on every nerve.

His memories still swirl in the back of my mind. I haven't processed them, haven't even tried, really. I don't know what to think. His pain reminded me of mine, too much. The panic. The helplessness. The desperation to reach me.

I grip the railing hard, shaking the thoughts from my head. Below, the party rages. Some fight, some laugh, others drink through it all. Just complete chaos.

Just like my mind.

I close my eyes and focus, feeling for Cage's mental imprint.

Gotcha.

I don't bother knocking. I kick in the door.

Inside, a sobbing girl is tied to the bed, her whole body trembles. Cage stands beside her, his face unreadable. The moment his eyes find mine, annoyance flickers across his features.

"Do you not know how to knock?"

"Are you so bad in bed you make girls cry?"

He rolls his eyes, exasperated by my antics.

"I need my collar off," I snap. "I can search minds since clearly you're not doing it." I cross my arms, leaning against the frame.

He glances over me, taking a quick sweep, noting the blood.

"No, you already have blood on you. I take the collar off and there'll be more."

My jaw tightens. I barely resist the urge to argue. Only the urgency of our mission keeps me from throwing something.

I glance down. Damn it! I *did* miss some blood on my gown.

My foot begins tapping impatiently. "Then can you actually use your damn powers?"

"What do you think I'm doing, Millicent?" He throws a hand toward the sobbing girl on the bed. "Use your goddamn eyes!"

I cross the room and pause beside the girl.

Black hair. Blue eyes. Not quite like mine, but close enough to make me wonder. Did he pick and torture her as a proxy for me.

"What does she know?" I ask.

"Arella. She's the Madame here. I'm trying to find her."

"P-please," the girl stammers trying to stifle her trembling voice. "He's insane."

I feel it, the perfect opening.

"He is," I whisper. "And he'll pay."

My hand moves smoothly to the dagger strapped at my thigh. In one quick motion, I slice through her bindings.

Cage steps forward to stop me, but my blade meets his abdomen. He freezes.

"What are you doing?" He growls, practically snarling inches from my face.

"Taking you in."

Before he can process the full intent behind my words, my free hand strikes the side of his neck. A perfect pressure point. He drops like a stone.

His head slams against the floor. Satisfaction blooms in my chest. *His head did hit the floor hard. He'll be fine. Probably.*

Do I need to spit on him?

Yes.

I make sure I spit right on his face. Then I turn to the girl. softening my features.

"What's your name?" I ask gently, helping her sit up.

"Morana," she sniffs, rubbing at her purpled wrists.

"We working girls have to stick together. Arella must deal with that mage." I offer my hand.

Her face hardens with determination replacing fear. "Yes. He's awful. Come, she'll reward you for saving me. I'm one of her best girls," she adds, smug with pride.

We plunge back into chaos.

Morana leads me downstairs. We weave past brawling drunks and shattered glass until we slip behind a black curtain I hadn't noticed before.

Beyond it, a black marble hallway stretches into silence. As we walk, the sounds of the laughter and violence behind us fade into a low hum. The further we go, the more the world narrows.

The hall ends in a richly decorated room still in theme with the sin house but quieter and more official. Leather furniture is perfectly arranged and not a thing is out of place.

Morana leads me toward a set of imposing doors on the right. She pushes them open.

Inside, there are multiple small lounge sofas in deep red and purple covered in sheer silk panels. On each one, women reclining in delicate silks are accompanied by men with glazed-over eyes. Their bodies drape like queens while men kneel before them acting as servants, worshippers, and *toys*.

Those who can compel drape themselves in finery and don't so much as lift a hand to care for themselves.

Another breed of sheep.

At the center of the room, a makeshift throne rises like a stage. A woman lounges atop it, platinum hair spilling down her hips, a shimmering purple gown clinging to her curves like liquid light. One man kneels beneath her feet. Another feeds her grapes. A third fans her slowly with a giant palm leaf.

Her pink eyes lazily flick to us.

"Morana? A new guest?" Her voice drips seduction like it's stuck in a permanent bedroom whisper. I'm not swayed the slightest, the saccharine in her voice repugnant like sulfur on my tongue.

Morana smiles and offers a quick bow. "Madame, a mage attacked me, trying to get information about you. This woman here saved me." She squeezes my hand.

Arella bites into a grape a man feeds her as she determines if I am worthy of her presence.

If I didn't have this damn collar, I could butcher every single one of these manipulative cunts without breaking a sweat.

Let Arella think she's the apex predator here. Let her feel in control—for now.

"Defending off a mage?" Her voice feigns awe, but it's thin and unconvincing. Even as she stares directly at my witch markings, she dares to dismiss me.

I grind my teeth.

She snaps her fingers.

Four massive men rise from kneeling beside her throne and move in perfect synchronization, their eyes stripped of color. Marching in a straight line out the door, they move with purpose embedded in their bones.

They remind me of a shared consciousness. A hive mind with a collective desire one woman implanted.

"Do sit. What is your name?"

"Millicent," I reply, keeping my last name out of her reach. I take a seat on the sofa facing her throne.

"Why are you here, witch? I don't know you."

Her head tilts, her pink eyes narrow with practiced intensity as she scans me for weakness.

I don't waver under the scrutiny. "I have questions, about a curse I'm unfamiliar with."

"Why would I know the answer?" she asks, smirking. "Better yet, why would I give it to you if I did?"

She laughs. A cue. The women in the room laugh with her.

Their laughs would not be so pretty and delicate if I eviscerated their throats.

I imagine Nyx and Twyx bursting from the walls like shadows made flesh, ripping and tearing them apart. I push down the fantasy. There are too many of them and I have no magic.

"Protection," I say instead, keeping my tone measured. "Men are turning into beasts, imagine the cost of losing one of your girls."

Her expression doesn't flicker. She doesn't care. No surprise there, but I had to try.

"More important," I continue, trying to sweeten my voice into a purr. "It's a favor. The mage being brought here is the strongest of his kind. He's the only mage bonded to a dragon."

I grin wickedly as Arella perks up.

"He is extremely powerful. You wouldn't be able to take him down. I have. And I'm offering to keep him in line...in return for information."

She hesitates, unsure if I'm telling the truth.

 But she's tempted.

I don't actually believe I can contain Cage once he wakes up. His tantrum will level this room. Hopefully I'll have what I need before he explodes. Because I can already hear it now.

You stabbed me, tried to force a bond on me, now you knock me out and try to give me away for slave work ...

Gods, men are so dramatic. I internally roll my eyes.

The doors open and her enthralled guards march in, dragging an unconscious Cage between them.

Shit. Guess I hit him harder than I thought. *Good.*

I meander over, flicking my hand in a dramatic wave above his limp form.

"He is very handsome, right? And yes, strong."

Arella rises, finally lifting her feet from the kneeling man beneath her. She descends her steps like a queen, fixing her eyes on Cage like he's a jewel.

I grab the hem of his shirt and pull it up, revealing the arcane marks on his chest. "They run up his neck, and down his arms."

Arella licks her lips at the greed gleaming in her eyes. "How marvelous."

She reaches for him just as he stirs.

Showtime.

I drop his shirt and step back.

Cage's eyes flicker open, blinking rapidly as he adjusts to the light in the room and the sight of a woman standing over him like he's prey.

"What the fuck…?" he mutters, disoriented.

Arella doesn't waste a breath. I sense her magic surge; it's subtlety and insidiousness creeping toward him.

Cage drops his gaze instantly, avoiding hers. His magic answers with a roar. The air shifts, dominating the space.

"See? Told you. He's moody," I say with a grin, completely uncon-cerned by the spike in danger. "If I were you, I'd tag me in now. Let's make ourselves a deal before he kills everyone."

Checkmate, bitch.

Cage explodes into motion, hurling both guards who hold his arms across the room. They crash into the sofas, sending furniture screeching and tumbling across the floor.

"Get him! Hold him!" Arella shrieks.

More of her enthralled men rush forward. Several of her girls rise, their gazes sharpened on Cage in an attempt to force compulsion.

This is going to take a minute.

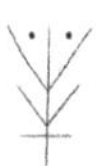

I claim a sofa and stretch out, arms crossed beneath my head. These lounge chairs? Worth It. I kick up my feet and settle in to enjoy the chaos.

Men go flying across the room and the shadows grow denser and darker.

"Listen, bitch," Cage growls, his voice echoing across the room. "I don't know what the fuck the plan is here, but if you try to compel me again, I'll kill everyone in this room."

The temperature shifts. Whispers ripple through the girls who now grow thick with unease.

Arella finally looks at me. "You weren't joking...he is strong." A pause. Then, more softly, "Fine. Help me, and I'll help you."

If the daggers in Cage's glare were real, I'd be bleeding out and like a sieve. I grin and stroll toward him.

"Surprise!"

"You knocked me out to give me over as a *fucking slave*?" he snaps, rubbing his neck.

"Maybe," I shrug, daring to step closer.

"Wouldn't you be the better option?" he smirks. "You'd make a perfect whore."

My eyes narrow. His smirk. That smug tone. My original plan, it all evaporates as anger, per usual, gets the best of me.

I slam my knee into his crotch.

As he folds forward, I grab a fist full of his hair and yank his head back.

Arella, already poised, doesn't miss the opening. I watch fascinated as Cage's eyes flick white, the compulsion slips over him like frost despite his attempts to resist.

He won't be carving out my heart anytime soon.

"What...interesting methods to get him exposed," Arella mutters.

"Hey, gets the job done. Now, my part of the payment?"

"Of course." Her smile is as fake as it is perfect.

She guides me to a sofa. Cage follows her like a trained dog. She makes him kneel, remove her shoes, and begin massaging her feet.

For just a moment I picture Felix and I can't help but think he'd find this hilarious. He always threatened Cage would end up rubbing *my* feet if I skipped meals.

I glance back at Arella, offering the widest saccharine-filled smile I can muster. Hollow meets hollow.

"I'm curious," I begin, "if a witch of your caliber is capable of using this curse."

Reaching down beneath my bust I pull out a rolled cloth, yellowed with age. I unfurl it across the table.

The inked design Iris drew, both elegant and threatening, comes into view.

Arella leans in, studying the curse. Her eyes trace the design's sharp angles and dips.

"We are not curse users," her brow furrows. "Even those of us who dabble couldn't manage something like this; it's too dark."

"Have you seen it before? Any idea what it does?" I press, watching her face for the slightest twitch.

The collar chafes at my throat. A reminder that I'm playing this game restrained.

I hate it.

They're beneath me.

Sheep for slaughter.

The Nightmother's melody whispers in my ear, honeyed and hungry. My eyes flick to Arella's exposed throat.

I could tear it out. Just like that. She would bleed so easily it would make me—

Stronger.

The voice that finishes my thought isn't mine.

I clench my fist, nails biting into my palm until pain stings me back to clarity. *No, I can't lose control right now.* I try not to let any panic rise.

It will only strengthen her. I breathe out a slow steady breath, my anxious emotions fleeting with it.

A flash of silver at the edges of my vision makes me glance sideways. I swear I saw Cage—watching me?

No. He's under compulsion.

I'm going insane. The realization lands softly, not disturbing me as much as it should have.

Arella shifts her attention, now locked onto Cage. He continues to rub one foot, then the other. He clearly enamors her.

She'll use him, I know it. Intimately.

Good. Let her ruin him. Let her take everything, down to the scraps of his soul.

I almost pray to the Nightmother that Arella's a soul-feasting parasite. Let her devour whatever's left.

"I haven't seen this before," Arella finally says. "Look at the line work. The markings are rough. Ink rises from the page. This isn't something made for kindness. No curse is."

Her laugh is fake and thin.

"I have a theory," I say, tapping the scroll, "that someone—maybe a manipulator—is transporting something with this into people. High-status targets are turning on their allies with little regard for reason. They die and end up in terrible situations they'd never choose."

"That would be a curse user. One embedding this into an object, and someone with compulsion guided them into place. If you're looking for that here," she flicks her hand, "they're not here. I haven't seen a curse user in years."

She picks at her nails. Bored already.

"I can get you more men just like that one," I say, dripping my voice with smugness. "I have access to the castle grounds where the strongest mages live. I can bring them to you. One by one."

That gets her full attention now. Her eyes flare with intrigue and she bites her bottom lip, pausing before she responds.

"I'll see if the girls know anything. Wait here."

She glances back at Cage. "Cage, is it? Rub her feet now, like a good little boy."

She clicks away, each step makes obnoxiously loud clacks from her heels until she disappears behind the curtain. Arrogant woman. Of course she would have no care to leave me alone. She doesn't know what I possess inside me and this is her sanctuary filled with her minions. She feels safe and in charge. *Who am I to shatter her illusion?*

"Oh gods, don't touch me," I mutter, watching Cage as he moves to kneel.

My protest, naturally, is ignored—compulsion trumps opinion. Still, I can't help myself.

"I do approve of kneeling though."

I grin, Proud of my own wit. *I'm funny.*

He slips off the heel of my shoe and begins to knead the sore muscles in my foot. I squirm, clutching the cushions beside me as his fingers hit the perfect combination of relief and the unbearable tickle at my toes.

"I hope you're in there," I murmur, "You're rubbing my feet."

I nudge his knee with my other foot. He lifts it, pulls off the second heel, and sets off to work.

"I am aware."

I blink. His voice is calm.

"You can talk?"

"Just now noticed? Witch, your intellect disappoints."

My jaw drops. He's still a smug asshole, even under compulsion.

"I've never even heard someone speak under compulsion! Of course, you'd figure out how to be a prick through sheer spite."

I shove my foot into his palm hoping to jam one of his fingers. "Keep rubbing, boy."

He says nothing more and obediently resumes rubbing while I stew.

Eventually the annoyance fades. And once again, I'm waiting on Arella.

Cage's hand slides up my calf, thumb working in slow, deep strokes into the muscle.

Goosebumps rise along my skin as his fingers creep higher, brushing the sensitive crease behind of my knee. He sets to work kneading my muscles with expert precision.

I glance sideways. His eyes are still clouded in milky haze.

The door opens. Not Arella.

Then hot breath ghosts over my foot. I look down.

Cage presses a kiss to my toe. Then another. He trails kisses up the arch of my foot, slow and languid, dragging his mouth to my shin, then back down.

"Cage?" I ask, uncertain.

No response. A part of me wonders if this is part of the compulsion order; another wants to kick him in the face. Yet, the darker part of me stirs at the sight of him on his knees as he kisses my feet.

Then, suddenly, he bites. Pain spikes through my calf as I jerk my leg away.

"Giving me away as a fucking slave?" he asks aggressively, rising off the floor. His hand snaps forward, grabbing my collar and yanking me upright.

I shove at his chest, kick out hard. "Get the fuck off me!"

"We are going to have a little chit chat. You have been a bad girl."

"Bad girl? I'm not some dog." I aim another kick at his crotch, but he deflects me with his knee.

"You have a collar sweetheart. All you're missing is a tag. Then again, we *all* know you're a bitch."

He rips me off the sofa and my knees slam against the marble floors. They sting as he drags me by the collar across the floor. My brief triumph fleets and humiliation reigns.

I gasp as the collar tightens, cutting off blood flow in pulses. Light-headed, I struggle to get my footing, but he drags me too fast.

"Cage!" I choke, trying to force out my voice.

Around us, girls summon their enthralled men—none of them dare get close.

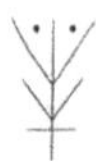

Arella bursts through the doors and her face twists with rage and disbelief. She screams, *"How are you free?!"*

I scream as Cage lifts my body and hurls me across the room. I curl in on myself midair, saving my head from the impact.

I slam into a wall, ribs cracking on impact

That's it. I am going to kill the bastard.

I sit up slowly, gauging the shallowness of my breath and the ache in my ribs.

The collar—the fucking collar—is slowing my healing. I can feel it. *Great.*

I am definitely going to kill him.

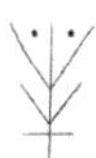

CHAPTER 36

Cage

THAT'S IT. I AM GOING TO KILL THIS BITCH.

I fantasized about it the entire time I rubbed her feet. I could make it slow and peel back every layer of skin until only bone remained.

Or quick. I could snap her neck like a twig, but where's the fun in that?

I sat quietly, listening as they spoke, watching to see if Millicent could *actually* extract any useful information. Fights are loud and messy—the opposite of what Felix commands. It's easier to fake my compulsion and wait for the perfect moment to strike.

Arella was telling the truth, that much I knew. I was in her head as well as in everyone else's in the room.

What did Millicent not know? That Arella had Kalix. Which is very, very bad for everyone involved.

I discard the trash against the wall. I hope her ribs cracked in the process; maybe she'll stay down this time so I can focus on Arella.

The moment she asks how I'm free is the last thing she says.

Power pulses through me. With the beat of my heart, rings ripple outward, sharp and fast. At lightning speed, they slice clean through the torsos. Some take heads. Bodies fall over, impacts are echoed by wet thumps of blood pooling on the floor.

I run a hand through my hair smoothing back a few wild strands before I turn my attention back to my pet.

Her hand drops from her ribs, trying to hide the pain.

Too late. I prowl toward her, locked in on my injured prey.

"Up," I command.

She exhales a sharp, reluctant huff. It almost makes me smile. Almost. Her body's fighting her as she tries to push herself off the floor but falters. One or more of her ribs must be broken and the collar's keeping her from healing.

"Aw, poor baby," I coo, letting a sly grin curl my lips.

I extend my hand. A black tendril slithers from beneath my sleeve, down my palm, and stretches toward her collar.

It latches on.

In seconds, it solidifies—black leather, coiled into a leash. I wrap the end around my hand and give it a tug.

She's yanked to her feet, stumbling to keep up. I make sure to give her no choice on the matter.

"The moment I have this thing off," she snarls, "or the second I get my hands on a weapon, I'm starting with your heart. I'll carve it out and devour it in front of you.

"No—better yet, I'll start with your fingers. I'll make you eat them."

I don't respond, but she continues anyway. Detailing all her plans to mutilate or consume me.

I pull on the leash—hard—just enough to nearly send her face-first into the floor.

She stumbles but still doesn't shut up.

"Yeah, yeah. Can you shut up? I'm thinking."

"Oh I'm sorry! Am I inconveniencing you?" Millicent snaps, the situation infuriating her voice.

341

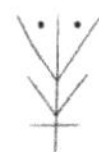

"Yes, as you tend to," I mutter. "They have Kalix. I'm trying to find where they're keeping him. I've been digging through as many minds as I can reach.

"So, for once, can you shut up and listen, Millicent?"

I rub the bridge of my nose in frustration, sighing as we head down a long hallway back toward the main chamber.

To my disbelief, she goes quiet. Her pace quickens too, which must mean her ribs are finally healing. Ahead, a group of girls with men round the corner.

Shit.

We don't need more eyes on us right now, not when they have Kalix. He can't resist compulsion like I can. My immunity is tied to my mind magic. Unfortunately, Kalix doesn't have that edge.

I turn sharply and shove Millicent against the wall.

"Pretend to like me for a few seconds while they pass." I whisper, wrapping the leash tightly around my hand to tug her chest against mine. I keep her legs between mine as I place my other hand next to her head on the wall. I lean in, just close enough to pass for intimacy. Just two lovers, lost in conversation.

"Do not actually kiss me," she hisses, eyes glowering.

"Wouldn't dream of it," I whisper back. "The last time I did, you literally stabbed me in the back and tried to bond me." This is truly a strategic move to avoid further confrontation. Of course, with Millicent there is no such thing.

"Tell me—do you try to trap *all* your men permanently?"

"They'd be so lucky," she snarks, tilting her chin up.

I take the invitation.

I ghost my lips over her exposed throat, just beneath the curve of her jaw. Her pulse jumps beneath my mouth. I press firmer.

My lips part, tongue sweeping over her soft, heated skin. I suck gently, tasting vanilla and jasmine. Her scent crawls into my brain, its uniqueness riling the evil within. Okay, maybe this is not the best

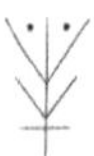

strategy. I don't even try to listen for those who pass when my senses hone in on her.

Mark her.

I bite down. She gasps, sweetly. I soothe the indented, milky skin with my tongue and the sound she makes nearly undoes me.

Her head tips back. A silent invitation.

I kiss lower, taking my time to explore. I savor the trail down to her shoulder. My tongue traces the edge of her witch marks. She shivers under me.

Control slips further away.

When I reach the scar—my initial carved into her skin—I pause. Gratification blooms hot in my chest.

I press a kiss to it, then lift my hand to trace the lines with my fingertip.

"I should've put my name on your collar too," I murmur, more to myself than to her. My fingertip flexes at the urge to dig into her chest, carve her out and wrap myself around her spine.

"They passed," she says flatly. "You can get off me now." She elbows my ribs.

I chuckle, releasing her and letting the leash dissipate. She's walking just fine now anyway.

The act worked. To anyone watching, I was just another patron indulging in his favorite girl.

Maybe I got a little lost in the role.

We continue down the hallway. The noise from the main floor grows louder as we emerge into the open. I navigate through the crowd, weaving past dancers and drunks until we reach a narrow wooden door tucked off to the side. More of a broom closet than anything else.

"From what I gathered, there's a holding cell system below," I explain, relaying what I pulled from the minds around us.

Of course the door is locked. Blasting through it would draw attention.

"Is there an issue?" Millicent asks, voice laced with condescension.

"It's locked."

"No," she gasps, the sarcasm in her voice weighing it down. She looks at me like I have no functioning brain cells. "You said it's a holding cell entrance. It's going to be locked. Just break it."

I shoot her a flat look. "Millicent, if I break the lock, we'll alert half the building."

She rolls her eyes and shoves me aside. "Move, You're useless."

I scoff, crossing my arms and leaning back to watch this supposed solution unfold.

She plucks a red jewel from her earring and shields the door handle from view. Sliding the post into the lock, she works it like she's done this before.

"You were so convincing back in the hall. Talk to me now, so it doesn't look like I'm breaking into a door," she murmurs.

"You can lockpick? She's a murderer, a liar, totally manipulative... and now a thief?"

"You forgot something."

The lock clicks. And she opens the door with a flourish.

"Extremely good-looking," she finishes smugly before descending the stairs.

I briefly consider pushing her down them. No—that's too childish.

Throwing her? Now that's more my style.

I settle for just following instead.

The stairwell opens to a dank corridor lined with rusting iron bars. The air is wet and sour. A rat darts past as water drips steadily from somewhere overhead.

"There you are!"

Iris's voice cuts through the gloom. She waves us over, standing at the end of one of the rows beside a cell.

When I reach her, I peer into it.

Kalix sits on the floor with his wrists and ankles bound in iron cuffs.

"Oh, I thought they were going to compel him. They just locked him up?"

"He started a fight," Iris says, shooting a look of disapproval into the cell. "They put him in here to sober up and they let me come down here with him. I told them I'm a healer." She rolls her eyes, clearly annoyed. "They don't like vomit from drunks in the cells, I guess. So, I'm babysitting a grown man."

I laugh.

That earns me a slap on my shoulder. "It's not funny! We've been of no use because he got in trouble. Did you guys find anything?" She sighs, placing her hands on her hips.

Dark magic prickles up my spine as Millicent approaches. Her presence hits before her voice.

"We did," she says coolly, "I'll fill you in once we're both out of this place. I think we'd both prefer to be clothed and far from these men."

"Agreed."

Iris walks past me and loops her arm through Millicent's. "We're heading out to get some fresh air. Meet us when you're done in here. And it's dinner time...I'm starving."

Iris is the same as Millicent. I am not shocked that they have slowly grown toward one another. Still, I can't silence the small voice in the back of my mind that warns Millicent's nature is far more sinister. A nature that could just doom us. Once they're gone, I melt the cell lock with a quick pulse of magic, then turn to the cuffs.

"Magic's handy," Kalix mutters. "I'd be down here attempting to pick a lock for centuries."

"That's because you're a *terrible* lockpicker," I say, smirking as my magic slices through the last of the cuffs.

He rises slowly, stretching out sore limbs.

"What made you get into a fight?"

His eyes flick toward the far wall. "Someone touched something that doesn't belong to them."

He doesn't elaborate, and I don't push. He's not his usual self so I decide not to pry.

I know the look.

This is about Iris.

We walk out of the cellblock together, stepping into the cool open night air where the others wait. Finally, a sense of tranquility flows over me. Only our boots crunching as we walk to the horses, some insects chittering, and the birds calling out in deep baritone coos reach my ears now.

CHAPTER 37

Millicent

I SILENTLY THANK THE NIGHTMOTHER FOR MY RIBS FINALLY healing. Riding horseback demands every muscle, and the terrain hasn't been kind. The thought of enduring this with broken ribs makes my body want to eviscerate.

I welcome the chill wind as it sweeps over us, coating the fields in a thin layer of frost. The moonlight catches on the icy grass, casting an eerie sheen across the open landscape. Fog rolls in from the woods, adding another layer of unease.

We keep to the main road to avoid the trees. I don't mind because open fields offer better visibility. Less cover for anything lurking out here in the dark. It is night after all, creatures are always more active after dusk.

I glance toward the forest, wondering what lingers in these woods. From here, I can't see if magic wraps the trees or if they remain green and soft, only exposed to small portions of magic.

My senses remain sharp. I scan the auras around us, alert for anything unfamiliar. Kalix's stands out. He usually gives off nothing—just the quiet, dull stillness of a mortal. Tonight, something crackles around him. Chaotic. It flares like jagged pulses of forest green, sharp and scratchy at the edges.

He hasn't spoken once during our ride. More than anything, that tells me something's wrong. The man never shuts up, especially when Iris is around.

Iris rides just ahead of him, silent. Not a glance nor a word.

Lovers' quarrel. I chuckle quietly to myself.

Movement in the field to our left catches my attention. A herd of deer bounds through the tall grass, their glowing eyes reflecting the moonlight as they pass.

Hooves drum across the dirt path mere feet ahead of us.

"How cute," Iris says in awe, her gaze lingering on the three fawns scrambling to keep up with their mothers.

The large buck trailing behind them stumbles. His steps ungraceful. When his front hooves hit the ground again, one buckles. He crashes forward, collapsing onto the road.

"He's hurt."

Iris wastes no time. She halts her horse and dismounts. I've never even see Kalix move, but somehow he's already behind her like an imposing shadow at her back.

"Iris, animals are always getting hurt. If you are going to play savior, at least be quick about it? I'm bloody hungry," Cage grumbles, stopping his horse with a sigh.

I slow mine just enough to keep a clear view. I've never witnessed a necromancer at work before. I find the prospect thrilling.

The buck lets out a harsh snort, followed by a wet, wheezing breath. It's a warning.

"Hush."

Her voice is the softest I've ever heard it. The animal continues to grunt while it struggles to rise, but Iris isn't deterred. She sinks to her knees at its side.

"I will not harm you."

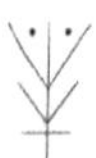

With a steady hand, she pets gently along the buck's neck. He thrashes (or tries to) until Kalix leans in, pushing the large beast's heavy frame down with surprising ease. One hand grips the antlers, pinning the sharp tines away from Iris.

"Rainbow, he smells off," Kalix murmurs, eyeing the buck with a calculating intensity.

"He's hurt. Do you have my tools?" Iris extends her hand expectantly, ignoring his warning.

Without hesitation, Kalix reaches into his coat and retrieves a deep velvet pouch and a silver hammer etched with intricate carvings. She snatches them from his hand so he can resume holding the buck steady.

Iris opens the pouch. Inside, silver nails, thick as mini stakes, gleam unnaturally in the moonlight.

She inhales deeply.

On her exhale, the markings on her back begin to glow. Vibrant green light blooms through her thin gown and pools onto the dirt road beneath her. The hammer glows the same hue and the nails shimmer to match.

A wave of magic hits me. It doesn't just pass, it slams into my senses, like cold water over raw nerves. It stirs the Nightmother inside me; she *notices* this power.

She is strong.

Iris's nails begin to float in her palm, suspended and pulsing with that emerald light. I dismount, drawn closer, needing to see.

One by one, the nails rise, drifting on unseen threads. They position themselves above the buck—one over its heart, another at the neck, and the last just above its skull.

Then—

The hammer comes down.

The impact doesn't just crack the skull, it sends a ripple of magic through the surrounding air. It shimmers like moonlight refracted in water. I swear I see fractals—fractures in the very air around her. My fingers tingle with the urge to touch the invisible curtain.

 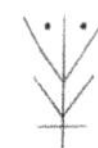

The buck stops thrashing.

The next calm strike drives a nail into its throat. Then its heart.

When she finishes, she rises. Arms lift to the sky. Her head tilts back.

"Vita Nova," she breathes.

The words barely reach me but I *feel* them.

The buck inhales deeply; its eyes snap open.

A heavy presence suddenly settles over the space. Something new has arrived, and it feels...off. *Is this normal?*

I watch intently.

"Easy," Kalix warns, slowly withdrawing his hands.

The buck stands, finally finding purchase. The nails clink as they fall to the dirt, and yet no wounds remain. Not even a scratch.

Kalix retreats and the buck tenses. Iris steps forward, lowering her head and outstretching her hand.

After a long pause, the buck presses its muzzle to her palm.

"You are mine."

The words stop me.

I didn't expect to hear the possessiveness in Iris's tone. She always struck me as someone who valued freedom, especially for others. However, she's a necromancer, and I've heard their magic can change them, even if only for a while.

Kalix approaches her slowly, cautious not to startle her or the buck.

"Come, my little goddess," he says gently. "You've done enough. Let's go home."

He offers his hand but she doesn't take it. Doesn't even look at it. Instead, she stares at him. Something fierce and unsettling swirls behind her eyes. Her hand continues to move, calmly petting the buck's face, even as tension thickens between them, even as it heightens, spreading to where I stand.

Kalix keeps his hand extended. He reaches out, brushing a stray strand of hair behind her ear.

"Come home," he whispers like a soft plea. "Come back to me."

He threads their fingers together. She lets him, but her hand stays limp. The rejection lingers in the space between them.

I suddenly feel like I'm intruding on something intimate. I turn away and head to my horse, slipping my foot into the stirrup.

Pain explodes through me as I'm thrown forward, slammed into the beast's side. Rough fur meets my face before I hit the ground—hard. This is the third or fourth time today. I've lost count.

My horse rears. Hooves crash into the earth around me, quaking the ground like thunder. I curl inward, protecting my ribs to protect any of my vitals from being crushed.

Then, a familiar body wraps around mine.

The thrashing stops and the horse bolts, galloping off into the dark.

I lift my head to find Iris wrapped around me, shielding me with her own body.

"What the fuck is going on?" I rasp, breathless from my heart hammering in my chest.

"We need to move. Right now. *Carnium Edax.*"

She drags me to my feet and we break into a sprint. Her voice cuts through the dark.

"Fuck!" Iris shouts as her horse takes off.

I look back over my shoulder. Where the buck once lay, a monster now stands.

The Carnium Edax.

Shapeshifting predators that love fresh meat. They take the form of their last kill—luring in their next target under the guise of innocence.

The illusion never lasts, their true forms are gruesome.

The creature is massive, nearly the same size as the buck, but the resemblance ends there.

Its body is thick, built for speed and brute strength. No fur remains, in its place pale, slick skin stretches over bulging muscle, tapering into a grey-black hindquarter like rotting smoke.

It crouches on all fours, claws buried deep in the soil like roots of some ancient, cursed tree.

Its front limbs are worse: twisted cords of tendon wrapped over jagged bone, ending in talon-like points.

Its long neck swivels, sniffling the air through deep slits that stretch up its face.

No eyes, but it doesn't need them. Everything about them is designed to hunt.

Its jaws open slowly, revealing a forest of needle-like fangs. A black serpent tongue flicks between them, tasting the air.

Wonderful. It's fully grown. And all my weapons are on my horse that just fled.

It lunges for Kalix.

A black tendril slices through the air, spearing through its side mid-pounce. The Edax is thrown back, crashing into the field.

It howls a deathly wail somewhere between a deer's and a human's scream. The cries of its last two victims echo in that terrible noise.

Cage appears from the fog, sword already drawn. His eyes burn a fierce silver, seeming to glow brighter than moonlight.

"Both of you, get back."

His command pisses me off, but right now is not the most practical time to argue about the collar.

Kalix shifts in front of us as Cage steps into the tall grass.

The Edax rises with a snarl and snaps its long neck forward, jaws seeking blood. Cage's shield of dark magic materializes in a flash, parrying its strike with a burst of force.

He pivots in one smooth motion. The sword arcs down and bites into the beast's neck.

The beast reels backward, bleeding and in pain, but not done.

It begins to circle him, stalking for a weakness. Then it lunges again, ready to rip into his flesh.

Cage doesn't retreat.

He runs toward it.

At the last moment, he drops low, sliding on his knees beneath the Edax's belly. His blade slices upward in a vicious arc, opening the creature from throat to abdomen.

The Edax shrieks. Tumbling behind him, it thrashes violently as its innards spill across the grass.

It stills. Finally.

I exhale a small breath of relief and the tension in my muscles slightly eases.

Cage wipes his blade off his thigh and sheathes it without a word.

"The horses may not be far off. We'll be risking it on foot if we can't find them," he says, scanning the dark.

"There's at least one nearby," Kalix murmurs. "I can hear it."

I glance at him doubtfully. "You can *hear* it?" His green aura continues to oddly flicker.

He smirks and takes Iris's hand. "You can't?"

They start walking and I trail behind, frowning. Something about Kalix is wrong, but I can't put my finger on it.

He's just a mortal, but tonight, there's something else. Something new. A gift? A deal, perhaps? I can't say.

Then, I stop.

Out in the field—

"Cage...did you not just kill that thing?"

"I definitely did," he mutters, sounding wholly displeased as the corpse twitches before us, reanimating right before our eyes.

The damn thing's organs still hang loose, glistening when it rises again. Life flickers back into its eyes. Then it lets out a fresh scream, this time more human than animalistic.

"Kalix, take Iris to the horse. Now. Millicent you're with me."

His tone leaves no room for argument. Kalix scoops Iris into his arms and takes off sprinting down the road.

"I have no weapon and no magic," I snap. "Am I bait?"

"The horse can't carry three, and Iris can't fight. This is the best option."

He steps in front of me, pulling the two daggers from his thighs. "Here, you can have these." The cool hilts settle into my palms. They're too small for my liking.

I frown. "Wonderful. I get to be up close and personal."

Cage's fingers slide beneath my chin. He tips my head up until our eyes meet.

"You can handle it, witch."

I roll my eyes. *Of course I can, you idiot.* I yank away, storming past him, checking his shoulder with mine as I move into the field.

"Me missus!"

On command, Ollie appears at my side. His joy turns to intrigue when he spots our grotesque company.

"Ollie, fix my blades, baby," I say sweetly, offering the daggers without further explanation. Our bond makes words nearly redundant, his soul is tied to mine. He knows what I need.

Hovering, Oliver flaps his wings vigorously. His eyes glow as magic lifts the daggers from my hands. Light blue energy shimmers around them. They twist mid-air, lengthening and reshaping until they become short swords.

I take them back and test their weight in my hands. Perfect.

The Edax strikes just as it's recovered.

Its serpentine speed sends it barreling toward me, jaws wide. But Oliver casts a barrier just in time. A translucent cocoon flares around us. The creature's fangs slam against it with a crack.

"Rude," Oliver mumbles, side-eyeing the monster.

"If you stay, stay back and be safe," I remind him.

He obeys, lowering the shield and doing as I request. I step forward, just as the Edax turns its attention to Cage.

While it lunges at him, Cage feigns movement and quickly parries with his shield, baiting the strike to hack at its neck. I flank it and dig my blades into the back of its hind leg.

It snarls and lashes out, trying to slash at me with its talons. I side-step and pull, dragging down both blades, cutting through tendons until the limb gives out.

The beast collapses onto one knee.

Cage doesn't hesitate.

He sees the opportunity to bring his blade down hard, carving through its neck.

The head rolls. The body crumples beside it. Blood floods the grass in thick rivulets.

I take one breath. Maybe two.

Then—

Wails erupt from the trees. From *everywhere.*

"That sounds larger than just a typical pack," I mutter, trying to pinpoint the wails' origins. They're all around us. Their cries echo from every direction; there's too many to count.

I glance to the woods where more shapes emerge from the shadows. I count at least twelve.

The Edax at our feet begins to convulse.

Cage and I stagger back, eyes locked on the twitching corpse. From the bloody stump of its neck, a new jaw sprouts, followed by a gleaming, wet spine.

With a spray of blood, its new head snaps forward, fully formed and uninjured.

"They shouldn't be able to resurrect like this."

My grip tightens around the swords. My legs shift, bracing for the lengthy battle to come. This is no longer a fight. This is survival.

"No," Cage agrees. "This has to be some sort of mutation. If they all resurrect, this is pointless."

His blade erupts into silver and black flames.

The Edaxes charge. Dozens of them, converge on us.

The air fills with a chorus of suffering human and animal cries alike and pounding feet as all hell breaks loose.

I dodge jaws and talons, spinning and ducking beneath snapping

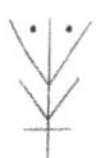

fangs. Oliver casts shield after shield over me, each one breaking under the claws' weight. The monsters crash into each other in their bloodlust, earning snarls and swipes from their own.

Cage is a whirlwind beside me. The style of blade work I saw him use against the Manipulators returns, this time with a more refined savagery.

He doesn't just slash. He rips through them with wave after wave of black magic, cleaving their bodies into pieces.

Still, they rise. No matter if ran through, gutted, or burned, they rise again.

My arms ache, my hands tremble and shake. Without magic fueling my movements, fatigue creeps in fast.

And still they come.

How are there so many?

"Cage there are more!" I scream, sliding under an Edax as it leaps over me.

Cage slams his fist into the earth.

A second later, a powerful pulse surges from the impact, rippling across the ground. The nearest Edaxes—eight of them—are blasted backward.

Then I notice something strange.

Even those farther away, untouched by the shockwave, freeze. They react as if struck too.

Then in unison, their attention shifts. Every single head, even the ones still flooding from the woods, turns toward Cage.

And then I see it. The way they move. The timing. They don't fight like beasts. They're coordinating, reacting in tandem, and their attacks are seamless. The only reason they keep crashing into each other is because we're outmaneuvering them.

They're learning—fast.

"It's a hive mind!" I shout, a grin tugging at my lips. That's why they won't die. Not until we find the source.

"Keep it up!" I call to Cage.

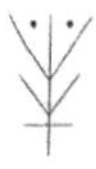

While he holds their attention, I sprint toward the woods.

Oliver flutters beside me, his tone tight with nervousness, "Me missus, where going?"

"We need to find the main one, the alpha. Can you help me? Look for something different—bigger, smaller, strange markings. They may be protecting it."

I push harder, my legs burning as I race across the field and into the forest's shadow. My blades stay drawn. Roots twist beneath my boots and branches snap past my shoulders. I focus ahead, the high from my adrenaline finally kicking in.

Luckily, the hive is still focused on Cage. I'm ready if that changes.

I don't know how long I run before Oliver reappears in a sudden blink of light. "I found it, me missus."

I follow Ollie deeper into the forest, weaving through the trees and low hanging branches.

Between two fallen trunks, I spot it.

A massive Edax prowls slowly, coiling its limbs in its path toward Cage.

Once its tongue flicks the air, its head suddenly snaps in my direction.

I waste no time running straight for it. I raise one blade, arcing toward it just in time for its jaws to snap toward me.

The impact nearly knocks me off my feet. Its bite is far stronger than the others. I try to dig in, brace for impact—anything—but I'm thrown back.

My hands hit the ground to stop my fall, and dirt grinds into my palms.

The Edax rips the sword from my hands with teeth and tosses it aside. It's already on the move again. It strikes out toward me with a shriek.

I stay low to the ground, forcing myself to wait until the last possible second.

When the Edax lunges again I push forward, the shield over me catching her fangs. Bone scrapes against the magical barrier. Her claws rake over it next, growing more frustrated as she tries to break through.

My magic-less weakness is no longer a whisper in my mind but a full scream as I depend on Ollie.

I slide under her belly, grit my teeth, and drive my second blade upward, aiming for her heart.

Black blood pours out in hot waves. The acrid stench fills the air, reminding me of the Crepitus Vox.

I clamp my mouth shut and hold my breath, unwilling to inhale whatever this is made of.

Planting my feet against her belly and kicking hard, I rip the blade free as I roll clear.

She lets out a piercing scream. My ears ring violently. Even when the sound fades, the deafening pain lingers.

Then I hear it.

Scampering paws thundering through the brush. Twigs snapping and leaves rustling straight toward me.

She called them. They're coming.

I glance at the trees. They're too close together for open combat. Plus, without my magic, I won't survive long here.

I will not die here. I'm not finished yet. I have given everything and they have taken everything. I will get what I am owed.

I raise my blade again, aiming to take out the backs of her knees. I need her lower so I can hit her vitals or sever her head.

I manage to cripple one of her legs. She stumbles just as the first of her spawn crash through the trees.

Oliver reacts fast, trying to raise a shield around us to buy me some time.

Gods, she never stops biting.

I'm tired from fighting, from bleeding, from dodging relentless maw.

She lunges again and I kick her snout down and follow with my blade. I drive it into the side of her neck. She bucks back and shrieks, the force flinging me skyward.

Branches tear at my back as I crash through the canopy. My gown rips; my skin splits. Sharp fiery pain flares along every limb.

The fall back down is worse. Bark slices my front and my ribs once again crack.

I hit the ground with a cry I can barely voice. Oliver is there, his expression growing with panic.

He shields me, creating a bubble around us. He lands by my head, stroking my hair with trembling hands.

"Me missus ...." His voice shakes with fear; his skin flushes to a sickly yellow.

He should not be protecting me. I should be protecting him, but I'm weak again.

I swore I would never be that girl again.

Let me in, the Nightmother coos.

The trill in her voice taps up my spine like clawed tips against bone. Her claws scrape up my neck, over my skull. I have to fight the force of her attempts to roll back my eyes.

Sheep for slaughter...sheep for slaughter...

Her laughter builds as she tastes the blood around me.

No.

I am not weak. I am rare. Chosen. I will kill them all.

Kill, kill, kill them all!

Her voice claws at my chest, rising like a fever. I begin to let go. My body slackens, letting the Nightmother take over. My eyes finally roll back and oblivion swallows me. Decadent, like the richest chocolate. Decadent, like death and decay.

Cage barrels through the trees. His presence breaks my focus and my eyes snap forward, my world light once again.

My collar ignites. The searing pain lances through my throat in response, cutting off the Nightmother's rise.

"Le Strange, do *not* make me deal with you in the middle of all this!" Cage roars.

Chaos spills in behind him as shadows writhe, shaping into blades—dozens of them, each with their own mind.

They launch like missiles, piercing the surrounding charging Edaxes with ruthless precision.

He charges on the queen, taking her head-on.

With her damaged back leg, her movements are unsteady and choppy. Cage takes full advantage.

He slashes at her left flank, his flame-wreathed blade carves through the flesh. The stench of burning meat floods the air.

Howling and thrashing, she becomes increasingly desperate.

His next blow drives the long sword deep into her side, and the flames on his sword surge.

She erupts.

Silver and black flames consume her body, roaring upward in a column of heat and fire. All around us, the other Edaxes wail in a sympathy of pain as if tethered to her soul.

One by one they collapse. Their legs buckle and their bodies twitch until the woods fall silent.

Oliver is still gently petting my hair.

My throat burns from the collar. With the Nightmother gone again, she recedes into the dark recesses of my mind. I can no longer feel her stirring.

I'm too tired to check my injuries. I can *feel* them splintering all over my body. The ground shudders as the alpha finally collapses. The odd dreary presence she emitted dissipates, cleansing the air.

Cage sheaths his blade and strides across the ruined space between us. Trees stand snapped in half, some splintering from force of impact while branches lay flung and fallen across the ground.

"Oliver. Let me in."

Oliver glares and keeps the shield intact.

"I can break this," Cage says, voice low and on edge. "Either let me in to help her or I will break it."

I rasp, barely loud enough to be heard. "Ollie...let him in."

Oliver reluctantly obeys. The shield fades, but he refuses to move from my side.

I can feel his distress like a storm of emotion echoing through our bond. It's making everything harder to bear.

"Ollie...I'll be okay. How about you go back to our room and get it ready for me please? Can you do that? I try to smile. "I need wine and a bath."

I need them—but more than that, I need him to believe I'll be okay.

"Of course, me missus. I will prepare your arrival."

He presses his cheek to mine and plants a soft, dry kiss. He shoots Cage a final warning look before warping out of sight, the air cracking faintly where he vanishes.

"We're going to have to train you without magic," Cage says, crouching beside me. He begins checking my body for damage. His fingers press gently at first and then proceed with more confidence.

"I was overpowered," I grumble back, wincing. "I also recall you using a *ridiculous* amount of magic during that fight." "And?" he says flatly, "I can wield magic *and* still not suck with a blade. Those two aren't mutually exclusive."

I glare at him but my strength to argue is fading fast.

"I'm going to carry you."

I don't have time to object. He slides his arms beneath my knees and shoulders and lifts me without effort. I bite down a cry threatening to escape but I clench my jaw instead.

Cage holds me close, careful to avoid putting pressure on my ribs. His warmth bleeds into my chilled skin. Instinctively, I curl closer, seeking anything but the pain eating through me.

I breathe in his smoky pine scent. It's familiar, almost calming. It distracts my thoughts. His heartbeat drums steadily beneath my chest.

I start to drift—half asleep, half clinging to consciousness.

"Millie," Cage says softly, "open your eyes for me."

I do. Barely.

He's watching me. Has been, maybe for a while.

"Let me in," he murmurs. "I can take it all away."

I tense. The idea of him in my mind—*rooting around,* seeing who I was, what I am, what I *want*—is too much. It's unnerving. Especially when he is unaware of my reasons for being here.

He senses my hesitation.

"Think of it as a fun new way for me to suffer," he says smirking, trying to be playful. "I'll take the pain for you."

"I can endure pain." My voice is low, rasping. I close my eyes again, unwilling to let him in. Not that far.

"Fierce as ever," he mutters. "She can endure pain and near-death... but can't handle someone helping her."

His voice is different now. It's soft but laced with something darker. Bitterness?

I don't have the strength to tell.

CHAPTER 38

Cage

FINDING MILLICENT A BLOODY MESS ON THE GROUND, HER throat scorched, had an unexpected effect on me. The darkness that I keep dormant has stirred, more awake in her presence than it's been in years.

Did the witch think death would save her from me? That such a thing could keep her out of reach?

Nothing will.

Not the imp shielding her. Not death. Not even herself.

I catch myself spiraling down into those thoughts and shake them off, focusing on what matters now. She is mine to carry—for hours, no less.

I finally find one of the horses that had bolted. I was close to summoning Vryaxis, but thankfully, the creature had only run down the path, avoiding the woods as if it could sense what lurked there.

I know Vryaxis would've set Millicent off. And right now, I don't know exactly what she's capable of. Not after what happened with Kalix.

She's changing, and I am trying to be cautious.

I've underestimated others before, even underestimated myself, and it's cost many lives.

She barely stirs as I lift her onto the horse, settling her in front of me. Even when we reach the castle, she doesn't wake as I carry her through the halls and into my room.

I know Oliver's likely pacing in her room, waiting, but he'll only get in my way. And if she cries out while I clean her wounds, the little menace will surely bite me.

I kick my bedroom door shut behind me and lay her on my bed. The gown she wore tonight, a flimsy thing meant to help her blend in with the working girls, is barely clinging to her now.

It's torn, soaked, and ruined. Her stomach, breasts, and back are exposed beneath what remains of the fabric.

I grab a dagger from my nightstand and cut the rest away. Modesty isn't my concern, not when she's this badly injured.

Her left side is black with bruises. Her ribs are definitely fractured. Her stomach and chest are laced with deep cuts, some still holding bits of wood and leaves.

I leave her for a few minutes to draw a warm bath. I set out two stools, one for me, one for the medical supplies I gather.

Then I return and lift her again. She doesn't even flinch.

"Millicent. Wake up."

I try being gentle. Nothing.

"Millicent, up."

Still no response. I shift my shoulder, trying to jostle her head, but she stays limp. I sigh, kick off my shoes, and do the only thing I can think of next.

I step into the tub. Water sloshes over the sides, soaking into the floor. As I lower myself in, I settle her between my legs and rest her back against my chest.

"Really making me bathe you, huh?" I mutter to myself. I grab the sponge from the rim and lather it in soap.

When we were kids, she used to make me brush her hair—braid it, even. A strange tightness knots behind my ribs at the memory, this strange echo of caring for her again.

I start with her stomach, carefully scrubbing the dried blood and dirt from the cuts.

For a split second, my hand hesitates as I make her wince again. I push the hesitation down. Good. Pain means she can still feel and is still with me.

I ignore the fact she's naked and moving in my lap. I focus. Another wood chip slides free from a deeper gash.

I rest my chin on her shoulder, watching the slow work of my hands. "Relax, little witch," I murmur.

I run the sponge higher, across her sternum. One deeper cut earns a sharper reaction. Bright sapphire eyes are greeted with steam and dim candlelight.

She furrows her brows, trying to sit up.

I press her back down gently, my chin holding her in place. I keep the sponge pressed against her chest.

"Relax, Millie. I'm just cleaning you. If you can do it, I'll stop, but you are pretty hurt."

She hesitates, considering my words. I feel the debate inside her. Then she exhales, sinking back into me. She must've been convinced my option was the better.

I continue. Her body tenses and trembles under my touch as I clear more debris from her body, piece by piece.

She's still not healing. It's the collar.

I could take it off, but I don't trust that she won't retaliate the second she's strong enough.

She's a blood witch. And I know exactly what that means. I know how to make her heal.

"You need to feed."

I run the sponge back down to her stomach, wiping away the last traces of grime from her creamy skin.

"I'm fine," she croaks hoarsely, her voice shredded by the collar and too many screams.

"We clearly define that word differently."

She doesn't answer. Her exhaustion has dulled the sharpness of her bite.

I reach out and take a surgical blade from the stool next to me. I stop washing and turn my hand palm up.

"Cage, what are you doing?"

Her voice sharpens as I feel her spine bracing against me. She tries to sit up again.

I slice a clean line down my forearm. The pain is quick and sharp, just a light sting, really.

Her next breath catches, and she freezes.

That's my girl.

"Feed," I command, pressing the wound to her lips.

She shoves my arm away with what little strength she has left.

"You're no use to anyone when you're half dead and bleeding. You're going to feed." I overpower her easily in this state, bringing my arm back to her mouth. She clenches her jaw and seals her lips in refusal.

"What? Afraid you'll enjoy the taste too much?" I sneer, hoping to bait a reaction.

Nothing? Fine, have it your way.

I set the blade down, then reach under her jaw. My thumb and middle finger press into corners of her mouth. She tries to resist by biting down.

I push deeper, past the molars, prying until I see her mouth open and her tongue flicker. In that moment, I shove my arm to her lips, muffling her groaned protest.

Her teeth scrape into my skin, and the wet warmth of her tongue hits blood. And then she drinks.

Her hunger takes over, lapping at the wound with trembling desperation, trying to pull every drop of my blood she can get.

I make a tight fist, encouraging the flow of blood. I glance down, her shallow wounds begin connecting, knitting themselves back together.

"Good," I murmur. "Very good. See how nice things can be when you do as you are told?"

I watch, almost mesmerized, as even the deeper wounds begin to seal. Her body drinks it all in.

Shit. Blood witches do really heal fast.

Note to self: if I have to kill her, do it before she can feed.

CHAPTER 39
Millicent

PAIN RECEDES FROM MY LIMBS, RETREATING LIKE A TIDE. In its place, a deep-seated hunger takes root like a hot, tangled network spreading through every inch of me.

The moment Cage's blood touches my tongue, all hesitation is gone. My refusal fades, eclipsed by the overwhelming pull of my blood witch heritage.

I sink my fangs into his skin, just outside the cut, anchoring myself while I suckle on the sweet, molten nectar from his body.

I seal my lips on the wound and suck hard. It isn't enough. The void inside me only grows, and I whimper with both desperation and frustration.

I sit up slightly, leaning into his arm. My eyes flutter shut. I feel my body tingling, alive again.

Then Cage pulls me back against him. His soaked cotton shirt clings to my skin as my spine meets his chest.

"That's enough. Let go. I need to check your back."

He pulls his arm away. My fangs drag against his skin, and I whine, my lips parting in protest. The ache inside me remains unfed.

"Lean forward," he says. "You can have more."

More. Gods, yes. I want more. I obey instantly.

I curl my knees to my chest, wrapping my arms around them as my chin rests on top.

His calloused fingers trace my back, sending little jolts of sensation where they brush softly along my sides.

"Are they healed?" I peek over my shoulder and catch a flicker of something on Cage's face, anger maybe. It's gone in an instant, replaced by the same cold neutrality.

His fingers trace small patterns along my back. "Not all of them. Some things never seem to heal, do they?"

I frown. "What are you talking about?"

My gaze drops to the blood dripping down his arm. I want it so badly, need it. My mouth waters, and my gums ache as my fangs throb with the urge to feed.

"We have matching scars," he says. "Your back is Nora's work, but you have far more than I do. So tell me, what did you get from those lessons in the end?"

"Power," I reply. "Power that I deserved. Power for which I have paid the price."

He snorts. "Vague answer, princess."

His finger runs through the blood on his arm, coating it before lifting it between us. "Turn and face me."

My eyes stay locked on the dripping red as I turn without thinking. I kneel, my hands gripping my thighs to keep them from pouncing at him.

The water sloshes around us, now resting just below my breasts. I feel exposed, hungry. He's my prey, and he's bleeding and injured.

He leans forward, holding his bloody finger out. My eyes dart to the blood on his finger, but it's the scent that hits me first, sharp and sweet.

 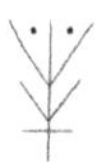

"Give me a better answer," he says, smirking, "and I'll feed you more, my little blood addict."

I snap forward, aiming to grab his wrist.

I won't be baited, not by him. If I'm going to feed, I'll take what I want.

He catches my wrist before I can reach him.

"Predictable," he murmurs. "Though I'll admit you're a lot stronger when you feed."

He tightens his grip, firm, but he doesn't seem hurried. His thumb strokes softly along the inside of my wrist, a stark contrast to how forcefully he pins me.

With one hand, he presses both of mine down onto my thigh. His palm engulfs them entirely, anchoring me.

Then his bloodied finger drags across my lips, painting them in crimson.

I part my lips without hesitation, tongue darting out to taste the smear. He watches me, still. His eyes have gone darker, hungry.

He lifts the finger, slices the tip, and offers it again, pushing it past my lips.

I take it greedily.

The flavor is rich and uniquely smoky. I suck hard, my groan muffled by the motion. My desire surges, my breasts tighten with an aching need, and a deep throb coils between my thighs. Every pull of blood feels like it tugs straight to my core.

He withdraws, then pushes it back in.

The rhythm is unrelenting. He forces his finger deeper, but I don't gag. I'm far too gone. The taste drives me, consumes me to drink it all.

"Fuck, Millicent," he rasps. His voice cracks with restraint.

I shift, and water splashes around us. My arousal spikes as I feel the heat blooming beneath the surface of my skin.

"I got you."

He leans in, releases my wrist, and takes one of my hands. He guides it down, slow and deliberate.

I moan softly as my fingers find that achingly sweet place. He doesn't let me move on instinct. He controls every motion with his hands. He presses my fingers to the seam of my heat, guiding them lower. He parts them, circles them, but never enters.

I whine, biting softly at his finger as I feed. My body clenches, desperate for more and protesting his delay. He knows what he's doing, and it's driving me mad.

"I almost want to make you beg," he mutters, jaw tightening as he guides my fingers upward. He circles my swollen nub, and my knees draw together. My body is coiling from the flood of sensation.

I'm hypersensitive. My eyes flutter from every nerve stretched thin. I moan, breath hitching as my fingers, still puppeteered by him, pull me closer to the edge.

He drags my hand lower again and presses one finger inside. The slick heat almost welcomes it, and a tremor rocks through me. Another moan escapes me before I can catch it.

"Do you have *any* idea what this is doing to me?" His voice cracks, sounding like a half-curse, or rather a confession. "What I *want* to do to you? The only thing stopping me is your drugged state. And even then, that isn't stopping me enough, Millicent."

There's heat in his words, frustration, almost hateful—hateful for the way I undo him—but his eyes are reverent.

I've never felt so wholly seen, desired, or devoured like his eyes are doing now.

"Keep looking at me," he growls. "You're getting so tight. I want you to remember who made you cum, even in this state."

His own voice is now drenched with the same fire burning low in my gut.

Another finger pushes in. I gasp at the sweet stretch, the way my walls tremble and tighten from his relentless thrusts.

He raises my thumb, circles my clit again, matching the rhythm of the finger in my mouth. The mirrored motion sends lightning through my spine.

It's too much. Too good.

I cry out. Walls shatter as release crashes through me like an unstoppable wave.

And I can't look away.

"That's it. Keep looking at me."

He removes his finger from my mouth once I release it, then grips my cheeks. He angles my face so I can't look away.

My eyes flutter

Pat, right to the side of my face, sharpening my focus on him.

"Eyes on me," he scolds.

He slows the motion of my hand, guiding me through the aftershocks until I stop trembling. Then he finally releases me.

"You tasted me," he says, lifting my hand. "I think it's my turn now."

He sucks my fingers into his mouth. My eyes widen, caught between amusement and intrigue as I watch him savor each one.

When he pulls them free, it ends with a soft *pop*.

"Delicious," he murmurs. "Just as I imagined. You taste like a horrible idea—my favorite."

"You can have more," I purr, shifting closer and letting my body speak for me, "if I can have more, too."

His gaze doesn't waver, but the smile that touches his lips is colder now.

"As enticing as it is to play with that delectable little body, if you're only offering it for more blood, I'll pass. I don't stoop that low. Not today."

His sharp words slice clean. The insult is clear to me.

"I didn't want your blood in the first place," I growl.

"And yet, here you are, letting me *eat* your pussy for dinner just to bleed me dry."

I slap his chest with a wet smack, disgusted—and done with his bullshit. I rise from the tub.

"Shut the door on your way out, witch!" He shouts after me, laughter echoing through the chamber.

I grab a towel, drying myself quickly. With no clothes of my own, I settle into a plain tunic and cotton trousers from his wardrobe.

For once, I'm grateful we don't share this wing with anyone else. No one needs to see me like this.

I reach my room quickly and find Ollie waiting patiently on my bed, only his head, wings, and arms visible beneath a pile of blankets.

He teleports to the door and lands on my shoulder.

"Me Misses! You are home, finally! A bath is drawn, and wine is ready."

"I already bathed, Ollie, but wine sounds perfect." I curl up with him on the couch, burying myself in a large fluffy blanket.

A bottle of wine—and a long-winded story later—Ollie is fully caught up.

He lounges in the corner of the couch, both hands wrapped around his tiny wine goblet.

"Me Misses still is on top," he declares confidently, wiggling his toes.

"Oliver," I sigh, amused, "out of everything that's happened, how am I on top?"

"Do they know why Me Misses is here? No. Does silver eyes wants you sexually? Yes. Easy to manipulate."

He sips again, barely pausing. "They put Me Misses in a collar. Thinks that means you can't break it." He laughs hysterically, splashing some of his wine onto his oversized belly. "As if! As if Me Misses can't rip off the collar and then all their heads. So stupid. *Idiots.* Flea rat pea brains."

I'm not even going to ask what a flea rat pea brain is after the day I have had.

He's right.

"A wolf in sheep skin," I murmur contemplatively, tracing the rim of my glass.

His wings flutter with excitement. "And when the time comes, you will be victorious. Powerful. Perfect."

His words inflate my ego, but they swell something warm in my chest. I never doubted I was all those things, but after half bleeding out...and whatever that post-blood lust shame spiral was, it's nice to have someone else say it. Someone who sees me.

"Bed?" Ollie bounces up, the cushion beneath him springing slightly. Thankfully, his glass is empty.

I follow him to the bed.

"Give me a moment," I call softly, pausing at the balcony

As always, Nora's owl awaits.

I relay everything I remember—our findings, the attack, the Edax, and the hive mind. As I speak, I make a mental note to get with Iris. The scent of the Carnium Edax mirrors the Creptius Vox. They are definitely related.

I don't mention Cage—or what happened after. That part is mine.

When I finish, I return to the bed and slip beside Ollie. He gently hums that familiar song as his finger strokes my scalp in slow circles. Our nightly routine.

Sleep comes easily, carried by wine, whispered affirmations, and the promise that I am not yet finished.

CHAPTER 40

Millicent

FEEDING IS A LOVE–HATE RELATIONSHIP.

The only part I hate is when the Nightmother takes over and I lose all awareness and autonomy. It's unnerving to wake up disoriented, covered in guts in strange places with no memory of how I got there.

I crave control, and handing it over to my patron is the antithesis of what I value. Still, the power she gives me is undeniable.

Blood tastes exquisite. It makes me feel alive, vibrant, and charged with power.

The aphrodisiac effect? Not something I choose, exactly. In the right company, it's not the worst thing.

Mostly, I'm just thankful. After feeding, I'm pain-free, and not even a bruise remains. My skin is flawless again. *Perfect.* I will always be that at the end of all things. I let a smile escape, just to myself as I arrive at the lab door.

I find Iris in her lab, elbows deep in a corpse. Despite the grotesque dissection displayed on her table, around her, light cheerful music plays and the high sun sends a kaleidoscope of colors through the windows.

"Good morning," I call out, not wanting to startle her mid-incision.

"Morning, Mille!" She pauses her cutting and wipes her hands. The warmth in her voice and smile eases me. The last time I saw her, she was buried in magic and shadows. I'm relieved to see her grounded and her normal self again.

"I want to go over the attack last night," I say, stepping closer. "I found some similarities between the Carnium Edax and Creptius Vox. It's got me thinking."

She grabs her journal and starts scribbling. "Go on."

"The blood from both creatures, it's black, and it reeks with the same rotting smell. What if they fed on someone already cursed? What if it spread that way?"

"Possible," she murmurs, nodding along. "Or the land itself is tainted. Whatever malevolent force fuels this magic…might be warping the beasts and terrain."

I cross the room to stand at her side.

On her table is something I can't identify. Its skin is peeled away, its chest cracked open, and a slew of organs glisten in unnatural pinks, purples, and bruised blues.

"I need a living subject, someone with this on them. We have to keep one alive," I say as I turn my attention from the corpse to her.

"The spies are collecting lists of traitors," Iris says, flipping a page in her journal. "There are missing persons, too. Either might lead you to someone infected, but you want to keep them?"

Her eyes flick up to meet mine, skeptical, and a flash of disapproval before she guards it.

"Yes. Dead bodies are your specialty. Mine is in the living. I want to study how the curse manifests in real time," I reply, trying to explain my thought process.

Iris nods in agreement. "Kalix will have the latest communication. He's probably out training the guards or in a meeting."

"I'm surprised you don't know exactly where he is," I tease, stealing a quick glance at a bunch of scribbles that mean nothing to me in her journal.

She rolls her eyes dramatically. "He's the one who keeps tabs on me, not the other way around." She pauses for a moment. "I'm not sure how aware those cursed are. There are conditions where the individual suffers and killing them is a mercy."

"Sacrifices have to be made," I say within the breath of her finished sentence. "Life is suffering. Even those I bring here will die, Iris. I will be their mercy."

She nods her head and gives me a tight, sad smile. "I'm learning better than to argue with you." She approaches me and shoves me toward the door. "Now shoo! I'm working." Any sadness is gone from her face, and I can't help but smile back at her.

The door clicks behind me, locking, but I don't feel shut out.

If anything, I know I'm distracting her too much if I stay. We talk too much. Always do.

I run into Felix before I find Kalix.

The king looks especially regal today, drenched in gold, the metal catching it in the light with hardly a single thread of another color to interrupt it.

Guards flank him. His older, round-faced assistant trails behind him, listing the day's activities.

"Ah! The lady of the hour!" Felix beams. "I'd heard you were half dead last night, and yet, here you are! Fresh as a daisy...or as resistant as a cockroach."

"Wow. I'm swooning, your majesty," I say sardonically, rolling my eyes at his approach.

"As all women do. Didn't think you were immune, did you?"

His smile is all teeth—and trouble. I don't doubt it works on most girls. I'm not most girls.

"Suppose not. Must be the nauseating *excess* of gold that attracts me."

He only grins wider. "Like a dragon lured to its horde. Fitting—for something so cold-blooded and bloodthirsty as you."

Without waiting for a reply, he threads his arm through mine and starts pulling me along.

"Now come have lunch with me."

He never gives me a choice when it comes to these lunches. After the night I've had, a distraction sounds nice.

"Do me a favor in return, then."

"Having lunch with the king is a *favor* done by you? Most see it as an honor."

"Most haven't *had* lunch with you, Felix."

He pinches my arm. I shove him with my shoulder in return. His laugh is loud enough to echo, filling the corridor with his presence before we reach the hall's end.

"What favor could I possibly owe you? Hungry for firstborns, or do you need me to find a man to slake your appetites?"

"You're an idiot, Felix. Can you shut up for two seconds so I can talk?"

"I *love* talking. And you love hearing me talk. Just look at that face. Priceless."

He reaches up and squeezes my cheek. I bare my teeth and snap at him. It only makes him laugh harder.

We round the corner to the private dining hall. I try my request again. "I need a cursed subject, alive."

Felix sighs in exacerbation, like we've been on this topic too long. "Why can't you ask for a puppy? Or a diamond necklace? Like normal women?"

"Why are you so against it?"

He gives me a look like I've started speaking in tongues. "You haven't seen what people become under the influence of that—curse, right? Is that what we're calling it?"

"Yes, Felix." My jaw tightens and my eye twitches at the remark.

"These people within my walls could easily become victims," Felix explains, keeping his voice low. "Each infection behaves differently, and we still don't know what a full manifestation looks like."

He pauses. "I will agree if Kalix or Cage is on board."

The dining hall doors swing open ahead of us. Gold gleams everywhere—plating, cutlery, and far too many candles. The light nearly blinds me.

"Don't trust me to contain it?" I ask. "Remove my collar and—"

"Only Cage can remove it," he interrupts, not even glancing at me. "And you *did* try to kill Kalix. So again, go ask them."

I stop short at the threshold, resisting the urge to scream or pout. The price Cage would demand for such an ask would be unfillable because he is never taking this off until he deems it safe, and the bastard is on a power trip.

Felix swaggers to the head of the table, collapsing into his chair with all the grace of a spoiled prince.

"Tell you what," he says, flashing me the biggest shit-eating grin. "Go track down some infected humans. Then come back and *convince* me they're worth keeping alive."

"Fine, I will."

I hold my chin high and pivot to leave, only to find two nervous guards blocking my exit.

Slowly, I turn back. Felix still wears that smug grin, one hand raised in a command.

"Millicent," he says sweetly. "Come have lunch. You look pale. *And* skinny."

I stomp toward the table, uncaring that it makes me look like a sulking child. I drop into the seat opposite him at the other end of the table with a dramatic huff.

"You're so far away. I feel like a divorced couple," Felix chuckles, laying a napkin across his lap.

Servants file in with silver trays filled with meat, fruit, cheese, and of course, wine.

"Daddy issues flaring up already?" I smirk, accepting a glass of wine from a servant just as another begins plating my food.

"And mommy issues," he adds. "Can't forget about Mother Dearest."

"Is she around?"

"Father is dead—hence the crown. Mother's alive, unfortunately. You'd hate her."

He winks at the servant girl arranging his plate. She blushes almost immediately.

"She'd hate me," I counter, lifting my knife to slice into the lamb.

"True. She despises witches and anyone lowborn. Don't worry. She's too obsessed with high society to grace us with her presence."

"Do you get your...spunkier traits from your father, then?" I ask, chewing the tender bite.

"My father was a tyrant." He shrugs. "Let's just say...I'm unique."

"Yes, you're very special," I tease, plucking a grape free from its stem. Now, this does surprise me. How did someone resist being tainted by wickedness? How did Felix end up the way he is?

Felix laughs. "You as—"

A large crash cuts him off.

Ollie materializes in the center of the table, sending two fully plated dishes flying to the floor with a spectacular smash.

"HAHA. Whoa!" Ollie snorts, wiggling his long nose before scratching his ear with a hind leg like a dog.

Servants gasp and begin whispering at the sight of him.

"Ollie!" Felix grins, "I see you've joined us again." He snaps his fingers. "Another cup of wine for our blue friend here."

Ollie spins to face him. "Very good!"

He patters across the table, stepping in food and swiping a sausage mid-waddle. Plopping down beside Felix, he chomps happily, grease smearing across his body.

"No hello to me?" I call out, not truly bothered. He adores Felix, and I consider this enrichment time for them both.

"Me Misses, I am with you *all* the time!" He says, snorting between bites.

He reaches up with a stubby arm, hand opening and closing toward Felix in a clear *give me* motion.

Felix grins all too happily and obliges him without hesitation. He removes his crown and places it on Ollie's head.

It's far too large. His ears flatten, and it slips over his eyes, preparing to tumble past his chin.

A shimmer of iridescent lights twinkles around him. The crown morphs, resizing perfectly to fit.

"Perfect, your Highness!" Felix salutes.

Ollie wiggles his toes in delight and lets out a delighted chitter. "All will *bow* before me! I shall feast on their flesh and take of their blood! They will all know *my name!*"

Ollie raises his half-eaten sausage like a war banner.

Felix casts me a glance. "Your son is just like you."

I smile, warmth blooming in my chest. "He's perfect."

Joy rushes through our bond like a strong wave. Ollie *feels* my pride and basks in the compliment.

Despite the comfort, my restlessness stirs. As much as I want to stay with them, I finish the last bite of my food, dab my mouth, and rise. "I'm off to find Kalix."

Felix waves without looking up at me, already deep in conversation with Ollie.

"You see, Oliver, Lady Annabeth is just a *dreadful* wife selection. She talks more than *I* do!"

"Does she have *big breasts?* Oh! Does she have *three?* Ollie likes three."

"In hell, are there three-breasted women? What do you even do with the third—"

"Ha HA. OH! You see, Ollie stands on one and then I—"

"Bye. I'm leaving!" I exit quickly, dodging what I know is about to be one of those *Oliver sexy-party story times*.

Felix is in for a demonstration. Spirits help him.

Hunting Kalix down proves to be harder than I expected.

I wander about the long meeting halls. Nothing. Eventually, I'm drawn to the wing of the castle that houses the training arenas and weapons barracks.

Gods, it stinks.

As I pass through the wide doors separating this wing from the rest of the palace, I'm greeted by the thick smell of sweat and body odor. It hits me like a wall.

Doors are left ajar down the corridor. From each, the sounds of grunts, clashing metal, and fists meeting flesh echo through the hall.

I find Kalix the same way anyone would: by his shouting.

"Quit bitching! Ten push-ups for that garbage form."

He's in a massive training room, lit up by the glass ceiling high overhead. Sparring mats line the floors. Weapon racks and gear flank the wall.

Pairs of guards practice in clusters while Kalix looms over one poor soul doing push-ups, barking out the count.

He spots me and snaps at the guard to resume sparring, then walks over.

"Whatever brings you to *this* corner of the castle?" he asks dryly, wiping sweat from his forehead with the hem of his shirt

Definitely part of the reasons this place reeks.

"I need a cursed subject. Alive," I reply. "Tyran thinks I should *experience* one for myself before making decisions."

"Demon hunting, with the demon herself? Don't see what could possibly go wrong."

He laughs like he already knows the answer.

"Tell you what," he says, nodding toward the mat. "Show me your skills."

"My...skills?" I echo. "As in, sword? Sparring?"

"Yes," he says, already stepping aside. "You're collared. I need to know you won't be dead weight."

"Cage did bring you back bloody," he adds.

I snap at Kalix before I can stop myself.

"Oh yeah? I could've easily been the one bringing *him* back bloody. I chose not to rip this damn collar off and feast on his flesh like I *crave* to."

Kalix's eyes widen in shock or awe, maybe both. "Gods above, you're like a feral dog. Fuck, a cat even. You'd gnaw on someone's bone."

He laughs, his shoulders relaxing.

"Listen, Millie, just show me what you've got. Think of it as an excuse to kick my ass," he offers.

The idea *is* delicious. Kicking his ass here, in front of people who respect him? That's too good to pass up. My victory will be exceptionally sweet.

"Don't say I cheated when I do." I shoot him a cheeky grin and head to the sparring mat.

He trails behind me, raising a brow. "You're in a gown? Do you want to change?"

"There'll be no need for that, Captain." I have been training for years well over his age. He has no idea what I'm capable of.

Once I am closer to him, I switch to monitoring him in his entirety—every muscle that shortens and lengthens as it relaxes or activates, what foot he leans on, what hand he may favor. Observation is everything.

I feel guards' eyes on me. Good. Let them watch. I'm going to be giving them a show, of course.

 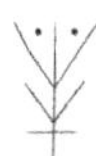

I clasp my hands behind my back and turn to face Kalix fully.

"Let's start with hand-to-hand," he says, taking position across me. He gives me a moment, but I don't move, a snake waiting to strike.

Kalix hesitates, then lunges, aiming a punch toward my ribs.

I sidestep, slamming my arm down over his forearm, redirecting the blow.

"Not bad, Le Strange." He chuckles, resetting his form.

He circles, then lashes out with a kick, targeting the back of my knee. I mimic my earlier move, raising my leg, stomping down as his foot slides beneath mine.

I spin, keeping my back away from him. Now it's my time to circle my prey.

I watch his shoulder, looking for the subtle flex of muscle before each motion.

"You're fast." He grins cockily, taunting me to approach. "But I'm faster. Only defense? Come on, witch."

I rush forward, slamming my foot into his thigh and driving my elbow up toward his chin.

He blocks, palm to chest, knocking the breath from my lungs as I'm sent sailing to the floor.

He's moving faster now.

I force myself up, ignoring the pain flaring in my back and ribs.

I run again, feinting a punch. As he focuses on my fist, I bring my leg up and over, my heel slamming into his temple.

Kalix stumbles, blood trailing from his nose, but he only grins viciously.

"That's it, witch!"

His next strike comes faster—and stronger. I cross my arms to block my stomach and kick his knee in return.

The rhythm begins picking up. The adrenaline coursing through me brings out my own vicious grin.

He kicks me in the gut hard enough to send me skidding well off the mat.

"Nice," I wheeze, coughing from the impact.

He saunters over, arrogant, loose, and dramatic as ever.

He reaches down to try to help me up.

I take advantage of my opening. I take his hand, then slam my legs up and into his chest, rolling back and hurling him over me. He hits the mat with a heavy thud.

I crawl after him, locking my legs around his neck, trying for a triangle hold.

His hands pry my thighs apart with ease. Too strong. His unnatural strength once again surprises me.

"No way you're just mortal," I hiss breathlessly.

I feel a bit like a sorry loser, but how is he this fast and *strong*?

If only I had my magic.

"You forgot to add 'most handsome and charming mortal,'" Kalix says, reclining onto his hands. "If we spar with swords, are you going to try and actually draw blood? You give off that vibe."

"How else would you do it?" I ask, sitting across from him.

He chuckles low. "Covens are such a strange place."

He gestures toward the guards still training. "Tell you what. Help me train these lot, and I'll take you to a ball."

"A ball?" I wrinkle my nose. "I don't want to go to a ball, I—"

"There is a nobleman rumored to be acting strange. Might be infected," he cuts in, his playful tone dying off into a more serious one.

"Why wouldn't you lead with that?"

"It is called conversation, Millicent. Not just exchanging intel. Besides, most women go to balls for the music, dancing, attractive men, not to find cursed monsters who might try to kill them."

"Uh-huh. Do I look like most women to you?" I deadpan.

He slowly looks me over, top to bottom, then pulls a face like he just caught a whiff of something foul.

I kick his knee for the insult, which earns me a crooked smile.

Kalix swats my foot and finally rises, scanning the training floor.

"Who wants to take on a witch? Her magic is restrained."

385

Really? He had to *say* it? It would've been so much more fun if they thought my power was still in play.

Unsurprisingly, no one volunteers—until a younger guard steps forward. He has a freckled face and copper hair braided with shiny beads that glint in the light.

"I'd like to fight her," he says steadily. His eyes meet mine. They don't fill with fear but with curiosity.

"Very good, Luca! Let's see what you got." Kalix claps once, then returns to stalking the others, barking out corrections.

I step back onto the mat and wait.

"Ever fought a witch?" I ask sharply.

"No, ma'am, but I'm always up for new experiences." He flashes a cheeky smile.

Flirtatious and bold, huh?

"Get a sword for this *new* experience, then."

I move to the weapons rack and select two short swords.

Dual wielding has always been my preference. One blade limits direction. Two lets me flow—strike, spin, and entrap—overwhelm my enemies from multiple directions. Fighting is a dance, and I don't do linear steps.

Luca surprises me by choosing matching blades.

"I prefer two," he explains. "Lets me move better."

I nod as I return to the mat, blades in hand.

I loosen my knees, bending them as I take my stance. Luca mirrors me, then spins, his swords singing through the air before they crash against mine.

I parry and pivot, planting a kick on his back that sends him stumbling.

"Too slow," I say. "I can read you like a book. Again."

He comes at me once more, slightly faster, but still sloppy. His wrist buckles when our blades clash.

"Is this seriously how you hold your blade?" I say, eyeing his grip with disdain.

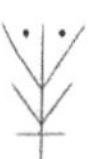

"Yes. Has been for four years."

"It's awful."

His shoulders sag. "I'm not the best guard," he mutters.

Behind him, I catch guards watching, snickering and whispering between each other.

I hurl one of my blades toward them. It sinks into the mat just inches from the closest group. They yelp and scatter.

Luca turns back to me, startled, probably about to say something annoying like "thank you."

"Clearly," I say flatly.

I stab my remaining sword into the mat and grab his hands.

"Hold it like *this.* Closer to the guard, not the pommel. You're asking to snap your wrist like that."

"Momentum is your friend, and so are your accessory muscles. Protect your joints. When you absorb my blow, use your *arms*, not your wrist."

Luca nods, stepping back to try again.

His next strike is stronger. Cleaner. And I notice his wrist holds.

"Better. Now try a different move, would you? This is getting dreadfully dull."

"Yes, ma'am," he says with a respectful eagerness. A smile tugs at his lips as we continue.

He shows me a few more moves. I correct them. Ruthlessly.

"Why are you so weak?" I ask, yanking him up by the back of his shirt. I'd just slammed him to the floor after his block connected. His stance was pathetic.

"You need a wider stance. Otherwise, the force of my blow will knock you back every time."

"I'm just not as strong as the others," he admits. "I've been training harder lately. I want to become vice captain one day." His eyes drift over to Kalix. The admiration is unmistakable.

An idea takes shape.

I've been itching to train, use some of the anxious energy creeping

in my body. I don't want to do it under Kalix's barking or Cage's brooding gaze.

"I'll make you strong," I say. "We start tonight. A run, and then we will hit the obstacle course."

"You want to train me?" He flushes, becoming flustered. "Please... I'm not worthy of that."

"Don't insult me," I snap. "If I see something worth training, then you will train with me."

My tone leaves no room for negotiation.

"Yes ma'am!" He straightens, still red but still smiling.

I release his shirt and step back.

"Up your protein and hydrate like your life depends on it."

I was trained for years. It was brutal and lethal. Witches heal quickly, so limits didn't exist. I'll need to adjust for this squishy mortal.

"Clean up the weapons and resume your training."

I walk away, leaving my blades behind. He can manage.

Back at the coven, I oversaw the instruction of many witches. This feels familiar, fulfilling, even if the student is mortal. Fulfillment from mortals has only come when it was time to try to become pregnant or when their blood satisfied a sacrifice. Having them fulfill me in this new way is foreign, but the feeling is not.

Kalix meets me at the door, arms folded. "Great work, little tyrant," he teases. "Luca is our youngest. Barely twenty-one. Smart kid. Smaller than the rest, but he's sharp. Try not to kill him, yeah?"

I give a half shrug, but his words linger.

He is a good kid.

"I will only gravely injure him," I say sweetly, flashing a too wide smile, just to be an ass.

Kalix rolls his eyes, unamused by the comment. "Wouldn't expect anything less."

He shifts back to business. "Tomorrow evening is the ball, but we'll need to head there earlier. The lord's estate is across town."

"Can we go alone?"

"Felix and Iris aren't coming. It's too risky if there's an infected. Cage will need to join us, especially if we plan to contain it."

My fingers drift over the coolness of my collar, tracing the carved runes on its surface.

He's right. We'll need Cage's magic.

The petty, stubborn part of me still wants to argue. Wants to prove we can do it *without* him. Cage is at least becoming slightly more tolerable—slightly.

And I can't help but wonder if that thought is mine—or if it's the bloodlust telling me to sink my teeth into him. The part of me that tasted him now wants more.

A crash behind us. Steel on wood. Behind us, two guards tumble into a full-blown brawl.

Kalix jogs back into the room, dragging them apart with a snarl. His shouting echoes like thunder, rattling my ears.

I leave before it gets worse. No thanks.

CHAPTER 41
Millicent

LUCA MANAGES TO KEEP UP DURING OUR RUN—BARELY. He sounds like one of those smooshed-faced dogs who struggle to breathe.

"Breathe through your nose and mouth. Time it. Deeper. Be more controlled. With me." I inhale slowly and hiss out air through my teeth. Our steps begin to sync up, and he adjusts to match my rhythm.

"How is this?" He pants heavily, his words ragged but steadying.

"Much better. Less piggish. Now pick those feet up, and no heel striking." I grab the back of his shirt and pull, forcing him to match my pace. He follows well. Once his form smooths out, I release him.

We run four miles around the castle grounds, past open fields and the edges of the forest. I breathe deep, welcoming the fire in my lungs and the burn in my legs.

In the center of the field, I slow to a stop to watch the sun rise. An array of hues of orange, pink, and violet. The sight is both soft and violent, all at once. It's breathtaking.

Luca stops beside me, hunching over, trying to catch his breath. "It's beautiful," he says between his gulps of air. "My little sister loves watching the sunrise."

"My best friend loves them, too." I smile. The warmth touches my face, casting my pale skin in gold. "We used to watch them all the time growing up."

I *used* to love this. Sunrises. Soft mornings. That changed when my lessons did. I am a creature born of shadows now. And to the darkness I must return. This light, this beauty—it's temporary. A dream. And I am the thing that ruins dreams.

"Why did you stop?" Luca asks.

"Why does the sun set and let the moon rise? Why are life and death lovers doomed to long for each other, never able to touch?"

He blinks, still catching his breath, and looks like he's trying to figure out what to say.

I turn to him with arms open.

The sunlight catches my witch marks, making them sparkle.

And then I remember...

Arcadia holds out my arms, rotating them ever so slightly to catch the light. My marks shimmer.

"My queen you are radiant, literally." She snickers.

I smile, warmth blooming in my chest at her laugh and touch. "Please, I'm positive you're one of those rays of sunshine."

Her own witch marks glimmer faintly across her collarbone, the gold matching the overcast above us as the sun rises.

She releases my arms and pulls me close. We sit like that for a long time, saying nothing, content to just watch the sun rise over the forest.

We've always loved this hilltop, the way it offers the whole sky.

Her soft voice breaks our silence. "Why did we stop this?"

"I'm tired a lot," I say, "and the lessons go late."

"They are more frequent, too."

I nod.

"They're changing you."

I freeze, no longer leaning into her. "They are making me stronger."

"Millicent," she whispers, "you *are* strong. You are enough. You are worthy. You don't need to become whatever Nora is turning you into."

I pull away from her grip, glaring at her with the sharpness of a blade.

"It is not enough, Arcadia. One should always seek more."

"You sound just like her." Her words are filled with spite.

"Good. Nora is strong. And I will be, too."

My breathing grows heavy. My hands dig into the grass.

She is insolent, the voice hisses. Rage rises like fire beneath my ribs.

"You come back covered in blood," Arcadia snaps. "You don't speak. You don't remember! You've no memory of me. *You don't even recognize me!*"

Her voice cracks. The tears follow close behind it.

I feel nothing. Her pain rings in my ears.

And yet *I don't care.*

"Some of us have what it takes to grow stronger, Arcadia. Some don't." I know my words are cruel, but I say them anyway as I leave her side.

Arcadia flinches but doesn't break.

"I am strong," she says quietly. "It's my strength that lets me love you, even when you're hateful."

Her eyes shine with unshed tears before she looks away. "Forged by fire, right, Millie?"

Her words hit harder than I expect. I stay, turned away from her, the breeze pulling strands of my black hair across my face, shifting my gown at my ankles.

Forged by the hottest fires in the deepest pits of hell.

She speaks again when I cast a glance over my shoulder.

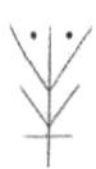

"I miss you. I miss our mornings together. It felt like we started the day ready to face anything—together. Now it feels like you're the source of my fears at night."

A pause. A breath stills her trembling lips for a moment.

"I face most things alone now. And when I look into your eyes, there's no light left. I don't know what to do to bring you back to me."

She wipes her cheeks, still not looking at me.

Then I hear it, the laughter.

The voice that's followed me for months erupts in glee, drowning Arcadia's pain in its echoing joy. I can hardly hear her now.

Arcadia is daylight. Warmth. The sun, rising over the forest.

And I—

I am what comes after. I am black inside. I am the cold, the darkness that follows the moon.

My darkness will not go.

It will only grow.

"Wow, those are beautiful," Luca says in awe, studying my arms.

His voice yanks me from my thoughts. I drag my arms back quickly.

"These marks show my power," I say flatly. "I house dark magic. The sun isn't made for things like me."

"I don't believe that."

"Why not, mortal?"

"Because you are too beautiful in the sun. Look at how your arms shine. You can't shine in the dark. So it's a shame you think you belong somewhere that hides your light."

"Luca, I am two hundred years old. Don't flirt with me."

"Maybe I like older women," he shoots back shamelessly.

I take off running, expecting him to follow.

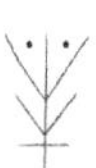

He yelps behind me, scrambling to catch up.

"I also know how to give a compliment without flirting!" he shouts. "That was called an observation!"

He speeds up, reaching my side. "Besides, I want to propose to the baker."

"Well then, you'd better train harder. What woman wants a weakling?"

I shove him off balance and surge ahead.

"Cheating!" he calls out, laughing as his footsteps thunder after mine.

When I win, I'll make sure I bask in my glory while he's stuck sharpening every sword in the training hall.

The honor of the loser.

AFTER OUR RUN LAST NIGHT AND THIS MORNING, I FINALLY am relaxed for once. I was right. Training Luca will be mutually beneficial.

I sit at my vanity, studying myself in a red gown.

Strapless, with a sweetheart neckline. It hugs my body like a second skin before flaring gently at the ankles. After enough complaining, I get Ollie to cut a slit—one—up to my knee so I can have some mobility. Any higher, he claimed, would "ruin the look."

He stands proudly on my vanity now, lipstick smeared all over his thin lips. Bright pink eyeshadow cakes his eyelids, and far, *far* too much blush brightens his cheeks.

The best part? His hair, of which he has none. Instead, he shows up in a short, blonde wig that's unbrushed and stiff with too much volume.

"Ollie, where did you get butterfly clips?"

I reach toward one of the tiny, colorful bugs caught in his synthetic hair.

"I takes them!"

"You stole them?" I chuckle, fixing one of his clips so it sits evenly on his face.

"She wasn't using them, Misses. They were on the counter, not in her hair," he says with complete conviction.

Of course, per Ollie's logic, that's not stealing. But I suppose, to Oliver, not much is considered stealing.

"I like them." I lean in and kiss his cheek. My dark lipstick leaves a perfect imprint.

He all but purrs, turning bashfully toward the mirror. When he spots the kiss, his eyes widen, and he gently traces the mark with his finger.

"I keeps forever," he whispers.

"You'll have to bathe eventually, Ollie."

"Never this *cheek*!"

I pick him up and settle him on my lap.

He plops down, grabbing the ends of my hair. Chubby fingers tangle in the loose strands.

"I will give you new kisses," I promise.

A shrill squeal leaves him, all joy and flailing toes, only the tips peeking from beneath his stomach.

I stay with him as I finish my makeup.

He helps curl and straighten my hair into smooth barrel waves, his stubby hands steady, his magic surprisingly precise. The ball I will be attending with Kalix has a high dress code. My hair must be in order even if chaos is sure to ensue when we try to capture a cursed person.

For now, there is only me and Ollie.

And warmth.

And the calm before whatever comes next.

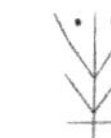

CHAPTER 42

Millicent

THIS IS JUST A LORD'S ESTATE?" I MUTTER TO KALIX AS WE enter the garden. "Seems more like a palace."

The courtyard is alive with energy. Strings of lights ripple across the air like stars caught in a web. A violin commands the space, its high-pitched notes whipping the dancers into a frenzy. Acrobats teeter on tabletops, somehow serving wine with their hands and feet. How they manage not to spill it, I have no idea.

In every corner, something dazzles the crowd: a fire-breather roars the flames of applause, a magician spins light into birds, tables brim with glistening platters and flutes of sweet wine.

"This lord's connected to some of the biggest merchant trades in the region," Kalix explains. "He enjoys showing off his wealth."

"Even when infected?" I lower my voice, mindful of Cage, who is no doubt eavesdropping nearby. "They're not usually this...social."

"It's not typical, but some can maintain their appearances," Kalix replies, offering his arm. His eyes tell me I need to play along. I place my arm in the crook of his elbow, letting him guide us toward the crowd. At a nearby table, I grab a glass of wine, forcing down the syrupy sweetness.

"So, what does he look like?" I ask, scanning the area for someone powerful—or dangerous. It's hard to tell in an extravagant place like this.

"Short blonde hair. Green eyes, I think."

"You think?"

"There's a lot of people here, all right?" he mumbles into his cup.

"He's here," Cage interjects, suddenly beside us.

"Then let's find him," I say, excitement rising at the prospect of encountering one of these cursed beings in the flesh.

Cage shakes his head. "I can sense a void. He's blocking me. That in itself confirms his presence."

"I bet I can locate him." I tap the collar at my neck in a silent request.

"Not a chance," Cage dismisses quickly.

"But..." He pauses, then extends a hand toward me. "We can try luring him out."

I raise a brow. "How?"

"Come, and I will teach you."

I sneer at him but wipe it from my face. I don't need Cage to teach me anything, but I do want to see this infected human. Cautiously, I take his hand, letting the other fall from Kalix's arm.

Cage raises our joined hands and leads us toward the to the dance floor.

"Seriously? Dancing?" I scan the crowd. "Is he hiding among them?"

I dart my gaze over the courtyard, seeking someone with short blonde hair and green eyes. Luckily, the combination seems rare tonight.

Cage stops in an open space and turns to face me. Without warning, he pulls me close.

"For now, yes."

He keeps one hand raised with mine and rests the other against the small of my back. I settle my free hand on his shoulder.

"Can you even dance?" I ask, wary of his toes.

He chuckles softly and begins to move us fluidly in a rhythm. All right, *so he can dance.*

As we glide across the floor, my eyes continue to roam the sea of faces.

"Impatient, aren't we?" Cage smirks, drawing my attention back to him.

"I've never been good at patience," I mutter, letting him spin me as the music swells.

He pulls me back, and this time, his chest brushes mine, closer than before. His hand settles low on my back again, steady and warm, and every nerve there tightens in response.

I ground myself in other sensations, the texture of his shirt beneath my fingertips, the shimmer of swirling gowns. Finding anything to focus on but him.

I refuse to meet his eyes, the same argent eyes I've been avoiding since our ride here. Since that night.

Feeding from him changed something. I've kept my distance ever since, afraid that locking eyes with him might snap the thread I'm barely hanging on to.

I remember the way he held me, the way he forced my eyes to stay on his as he guided my hand between my thighs.

Bloodlust or not, it still haunts me. Still burns under my skin.

And if the hunger had gone deeper, if the Nightmother had stirred harder, I would've torn his heart out and devoured it.

"A learned skill, I suppose. I'm more of a hunter myself. Knowing a creature gives you an upper hand." He dips me sharply. One hand supports my back while the other slides boldly to my thigh, pulling it toward him. My hair brushes the floor, my chest tenses with the strain, and my neck locks as I meet his silver gaze.

"If this curse has possessive traits, it might be a hellion. What emotions draw them out?"

The answer's old knowledge. "Lust and pain."

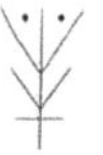

"Exactly." He pulls me upright, returning us to our former stance. "Like a shark smelling blood. Shall we lure them out?"

He lifts my hand toward his mouth, slowly, giving me time to pull away.

I don't. Not yet. I don't flinch as his teeth graze the inside of my wrist. I prepare for the bruising hot pain his teeth will cause. His tongue follows the nip, smoothing it. Then he presses a soft kiss.

Surprise fills me when he doesn't take the chance to inflict pain on me. I tense and try to pull away, but his grip tightens, and his fingers thread with mine. He bites gently at my bicep in warning. A languid kiss follows, and he trails more up to my shoulder, lingering at the hollow of my neck, where his hot breath ghosts over my skin. This is dangerous. Baiting the hellion out and Cage. The danger only surges my adrenaline, elating me.

His voice is low and edged with hunger. "I can see your pulse thrumming in your neck."

His hand slides lower, gripping a handful of my ass. The sudden pressure makes my breath hitch. Lust. not pain. He's leaning into it hard. And I am being dragged down with him.

He dips back into my throat, nuzzling a silent demand for more. For the sake of this trap, I tilt my head, obliging him. This time, his mouth isn't gentle. His tongue drags along my skin, sending a shiver down my spine.

When he reaches the pulsing curve beneath my jaw, he sucks, slowly and firmly. My breath quickens, nipples tightening beneath the velvet red of my gown.

The room around us becomes a haze of bright colors, laughter and music. Bodies near us spin and dip, too caught up in themselves to pay attention to us.

Stray hairs cling to my flushed cheeks as he trails kisses toward the hollow of my throat. His hand on my hip shifts, grinding me into him, letting me feel *every* inch of how much I affect him. I almost revel in the moment.

I arch back, letting my chest press higher till the curve of my breasts rises over the neckline. I watch as he pauses. His grip tightens. The silver in his eyes darken with a deep and guttural urge that mirrors my own.

"Just a trap, my little witch." His voice is rough like gravel.

"Just a trap," I echo, but my voice betrays me. It's low, sultry. And when our eyes meet, something cracks.

He releases my hand and guides his fingers up my arm, curling them into the base of my neck. My skin prickles under his touch. His gaze drops to my lips, then back to my eyes.

His jaw tenses, and he hesitates before leaning in close, our lips separated only by the breadth of an inch.

"You make me wonder who the trap is really set for." His tone darkens. A deep rumbling timbre rolls through his every word. "I hate this gown."

His sudden shift in demeanor hardens my posture. "Gee, thanks. Way to kill the trap." I roll my eyes sassily, but the heat in my veins doesn't cool.

"You mistake my words for jest, my little witch." His voice dips low. "Then again, your kind always did struggle to discern truth from mockery."

His hand drags slowly from the nape of my neck up my jaw with a slow reverence, like he's memorizing the outline of my features for a drawing he can perfect. He grips my chin gently but firmly, his lips brushing over mine with each word.

"I hate this gown on you. I hate most gowns on you. I'd prefer them off you, on the floor."

He lets the implication settle before he pulls away. My head spins between the insults and the flirting. Am I becoming some fun game to him? Or does it bother him just as much that he likes his skin against mine?

His other hand shifts roughly, sliding up my ass and lifting me off my feet just enough to unbalance me. Then it settles to my back. He scans the room.

"Did it work?" I prod, keeping my voice hushed.

"It worked," he confirms. There's no satisfaction in his voice, only bitterness, which only leaves me confused.

"Okay, well, where is he? Care to share?"

Kalix nods from across the room. So, Cage *has* shared something, just not with me. I scowl up at him. The flush of arousal burns with fury. *But he can tell Kalix.*

"You just grabbed my ass, and I'm right here. Try communicating with me next time."

"Don't screech." He releases me, stepping back and brushing his clothes off, as if ridding himself of contact. The insult only strokes my ire.

"There, by the pillar, use your bloody eyes," he adds, nodding toward the tall blonde man with green eyes, now being swarmed by guests.

"And touching you?" Cage meets my eyes, his voice turning to steel. "Means nothing. It gives you no power over me—and certainly no right to demand shit from me."

His words are ice but have little impact.

"Did you expect that to break my heart?" I ask, arching a brow, "Oh, how you wound me."

I turn and walk away without looking back. I have more interesting prey.

I slip between clusters of nobles. I make sure the lord sees me.

"My lord," I purr, dipping just low enough to let my breasts crest over the neckline of my gown. Every inch of me is a weapon. Nora taught me that for many years. Men like their women soft, prefer shy, submissive things. I've worn those skins before.

"You're a new face," he says, offering his hand. I slip mine into his. He seizes the moment to kiss along my knuckles. "I would remember such rare beauty." His eyes drop to the collar on my neck, then to my breasts.

"You would? I'm honored, my lord. No, we've never met." I offer a sheepish smile, feigning modesty.

"The honor is all mine. What name belongs to you?"

"Millicent." I bite my bottom lip. His gaze flicks from my mouth to my eyes with an almost poorly veiled interest.

"A name that means strength," he says admirably. "And who attends you?"

"The captain of the guard—as a chaperone. A girl can't attend one of these events alone, can she?"

"I'd be shocked if a lady of such finery like you is alone."

I shrug. "My tastes in company are ... *particular*, my lord."

"And do I satisfy any of those tastes?"

Oh, you stupid man. "I don't know," I murmur, letting my voice dip into seduction. "How do you taste?"

He pulls me closer. "Would you care to indulge?"

I nod, sliding a hand to his chest. His heartbeat is wild, just as I want it. The crowd parts before him as he moves us quickly to his estate. He ignores every person who dares to speak with him.

We pass Kalix and Cage. Kalix gives a discreet nod while Cage— looks absolutely foul. His irritation crashes against my mental shields like thrown rocks. Not truly trying to get in. He's being annoying enough just to get under my skin. *Prick.*

I flash him a quick smile, trying to be smug and triumphant. It falters the moment his magic stings harder. Then, satisfied, he stops. His own large grin spreads lazily as he winks and disappears into the crowd.

Bastard.

The Duke's home is just as glamorous as his gardens. He's no minimalist. That's for sure. Imported silks and exotic leathers cover furniture too elaborate to be native to this city.

He leads me to a lavish sitting room with a zebra-skin rug stretched beneath a high-backed sofa. Its embroidery is detailed with foreign artistry.

"Whiskey drinker?" he calls from the bar as he fumbles with a bottle.

"Sometimes," I lie. I *hate* whiskey.

"Wine, then? Red?"

"Yes, please."

"Ah, out in here. Wait just a moment," he says, "I have some in the cellar, finest you will find in the country." Already crossing the room, he shoots me a playful wink before disappearing.

I sink into the sofa, letting the silence settle—until it breaks.

A laugh. Light, familiar. Arcadia?

I sit up straighter. The hallway is empty, but the sound rings again. It's soft but distinct.

Curiosity overtakes me and I step into the hall, listening. Silence. Just as I turn back, there it is again. The unmistakable trill. My chest tightens. No. I must be imagining her. I miss her.

Still, I drift down the corridor. White curtains flutter open from windows. Warm lamplight flickers from wall sconces. Doors line each side, all shut—except one. A gentle creak echoes as it opens. Light flickers at the end, bathed in amber from a dancing fire.

"Hello?" I call. No answer.

Music begins, soft and sweeping, issuing from a record player in the corner of the room.

I step inside and over to the spinning record, watching the needle glide.

Now, who started you?

Then the tune shifts.

I know this song, every note. My mother used to sing it to me.

The tune changes to a hum, and my mother's voice begins to play.

"Sleep and hush. Time can wait.

My little star, the world is yours to create.

You shine so true, my precious one.

Your glow will last when the day ends and dark comes."

I haven't heard my mother's voice since the day she begged I run, since her blood drenched my hands, so thick it clung to me for days.

I freeze, my heart folding in on itself, barbed wires constricting around it with every beat.

Air. I can't breathe. My lungs seize. My eyes burn from the rivers cast down my cheeks.

"Forever in your love I will stay,
To guide you home and light your way.
Never be truly afraid.
However, my sweet little love,
You are far too clever."

The record begins to skip.

Never be truly afraid. Never be truly afraid. Never be truly afraid.

I lunge for the stylus, yanking it up, but her voice continues. It twists to something dark and guttural. It's not hers anymore.

Never be truly afraid.

I've had enough. I rip the record from the turntable and hurl it across the room. It shatters against the wall, pieces raining down, and the voice finally stops.

I gasp, trying to steady the breath I was holding the entire time. So much of my mother's memory is tainted. I will not allow this song to become one of them.

Then.

A whisper, low and rotten, coils against my ear

"Be afraid."

The door slams shut behind me. A lock clicks into place. The fire dies, plunging me into darkness.

An overwhelming presence enters the room, and the faint swish of fabric brushing against itself comes from the ceiling.

I press back up against the wall. My vision shifts, quickly to the absence of light.

Something's moving.

From the ceiling, crawling unnaturally toward me, is the lord. His limbs hang broken from their sockets. His legs and arms arch like a spider's. And still, he drags himself closer.

So, this is the curse in a human.

I slide along the wall, inching toward the door. In the first room he

took me to, I had catalogued possible weapons and planned to use the curtain ropes to bind him. Here, I have no plan, just adrenaline. Luckily, the merchant's hoarding tendencies left me options. I snag a sword jutting out from a basket and keep moving.

My footsteps land on a loose floorboard. It groans.

The lord freezes. Then his neck cracks audibly as he snaps his head in my direction. The sound makes me wince.

He moves extremely fast, all of him, focused on me.

I bolt to the door, but the lock is on the outside. I slam my foot against it again and again, the vibration jarring all the way to my spine.

The thudding above me grows louder and closer.

I scream as I drive my foot into the door a final time. Wood explodes outward. The door bursts open. It slams against the wall behind it, and I take off running down the hall, my vision tunneling for a second before snapping open.

I'm not in the lord's estate anymore.

I'm in my coven.

I whirl around and see nothing but a blank wall. No door. No lord. I look down, and my palms are bare, my sword has vanished.

Panic hammers in my chest as I race down the corridor, trying to reorient myself. This is the academic building. Nora's office should be upstairs. The tunnels and caverns will be right beneath our feet.

Then I hear it. Arcadia's scream. A cry of pain that cleaves straight through my chest. The pain in it is unmistakable.

"Cadia!"

Terror floods me as I follow the sound bursting through the stairwell door. I vault downward, her cries echoing up, ricocheting off the stone walls.

I don't stop running until I reach a chamber room I've never seen before, but I know the altar.

The circular stone slab is identical to the one from Cage's memories. Arcadia is tied to it, surrounded by witches in black robes. Their faces are hidden behind massive antelope masks.

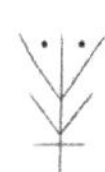

I rush to her side, trying to summon my magic to rip the masked figures away.

Nothing happens.

My throat ignites in pain, but I push harder still. A few tendrils lash out, just enough to fling two cloaked bodies from the altar.

Blood trickles down my neck. The collar is burrowing deeper, searing my flesh as I fight against it.

I yank on the chains at Arcadia's wrist once I reach the altar. Her skin is covered in slices, acts of cruelty that mar what was once perfect.

"Millicent, kill me. Please."

Her voice is so broken I can't look into her golden eyes.

"I will not," I snarl.

Magic ripples beneath my skin, cracking against the restraints of the collar. I force it through me, just enough to snap the cuff on her wrist.

A blow of chilling cold slams into my back.

I am launched over the altar, crashing face first into the stone floor. Pain erupts through my mouth and up into my skull. My lip splits open.

Arcadia screams again.

I look up just in time to see a figure drive a dagger into her stomach.

Rage swallows me whole. I stand, grip my jaw, and snap it back into place. Blood floods my mouth, but I spit it out.

Pain will not stop me. Nothing will stop me.

I grab the nearest witch by her antelope horns and slam her face into the altar. Her dagger clatters to the floor. I scoop it up and drive it into her back. Over and over. I bask in her screams.

I leap onto the altar, hunting the next. I grab another masked witch and impale the witch in her gut. I twist the knife until it slips in my bloodied hands. I don't stop. Not when they scream. Not when my own palm is sliced open.

I don't stop the massacre until there's only one left.

She's curled up on the floor, crawling away. I stalk her. Slam my heel into her ribs, then grind it in.

"Tender is the flesh."

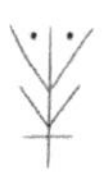

I raise my foot and crush her throat.

I rip her mask off.

It's Arcadia.

Her eyes are rolling back. Blood spills from her mouth in a silent scream—

—a scream I finish for her.

I spin around. The altar is empty.

"Wh-what?" My voice trembles. I fall to my knees. My hands seize the moment I cup her face.

"Cadia?" I whisper. Then I scream. "Cadia!"

Her neck bends the wrong way in my hands. It's limp from the broken bones.

"No," I choke. "No, this is a trick. This is a trick!"

Her body doesn't vanish. It stays. Heavy and still.

"Don't go where I can't follow," I beg, repeating the words as I remember Mama, remember her blood sticking to my skin just as Cadia's slicks mine now. I cradle her chest. I rock her. I scream her name.

"Cadia!"

I am breaking...

I am broken...

I am undone...

Magic surges through me, and I welcome the burn in my throat.

"Take me with you. Please, take me with you."

Red is everywhere. It coats my skin, hers, the floor—

Red. Red is everywhere. Rain isn't red, but red covers me. No. This isn't right.

Then everything goes black.

The red ends.

And the darkness that made me—comes to claim me.

 407 

CHAPTER 43

The Hungering One

INALLY, SHE IS WORN DOWN.

My teeth chitter. A wet, bubbling laugh escapes me as I peer from behind a boulder. Her slumped form on the floor. Still alive...barely viable yet brimming with power.

Our favorite.

She is perfect, the most perfect. I giggle, her voice merging with mine until they're one.

Delicious little sleep, delicious to eat, delicious for thee! Oh, a sweet treat!

I crawl from my corner, moving fast. The hunger gnaws inside me. I can feel the insatiable drive to feed.

First, we eats its flesh, then sucks on its bones. Then, then, then! We takes it! We takes...takes it all!

"Yes! Yes! Very nutritious." My teeth loosen and spill from my gums, pushed out by the long fangs that erupt in their place. I pounce—

Only for her to whip around and seize my throat.

I snarl, shifting my body, bones snapping as I attempt to change, to become something capable of ripping her apart.

"Someone's hungry," she says. That voice. No, that voice is not hers. No, no, this one's far too deep. Her eyes are no longer blue. They're infinite voids that pierce into me.

Wrong. Wrong. Wrong. I hiss, clawing at her, and recoil at her insulting presence.

"I am starving," she groans.

No. She is mine. This one is MINE! The voice inside me shrieks, withdrawing from her, desperate to escape. Wings burst from my back as the thing within tries to remake me.

Millicent cocks her head. "Naughty," she hums. "I almost want to let you run, so I can *hunt* you."

Then her hand punctures through. She grips my esophagus and rips it from me.

My body convulses from the violent assault, but the power thrumming in me refuses to let me die, forcing me to witness it all. I swipe, trying to gut her, but miss when she leans back and laughs at my failure.

She tosses the trail of tissue aside and drops me only to plunge her arm back in and tear out my upper spine.

The entity shrieks.

MINE! The screaming rips through my throat, so strong it projects without sound.

Her hand crashes into my chest, and my heart is torn free.

"You dare challenge me?" She sneers. "What unintelligent parasite drives a host to such arrogance?"

She nudges my body with her foot and devours my heart.

"Not good, not good," it hisses, before fleeing, leaving only nothingness as everything goes to black.

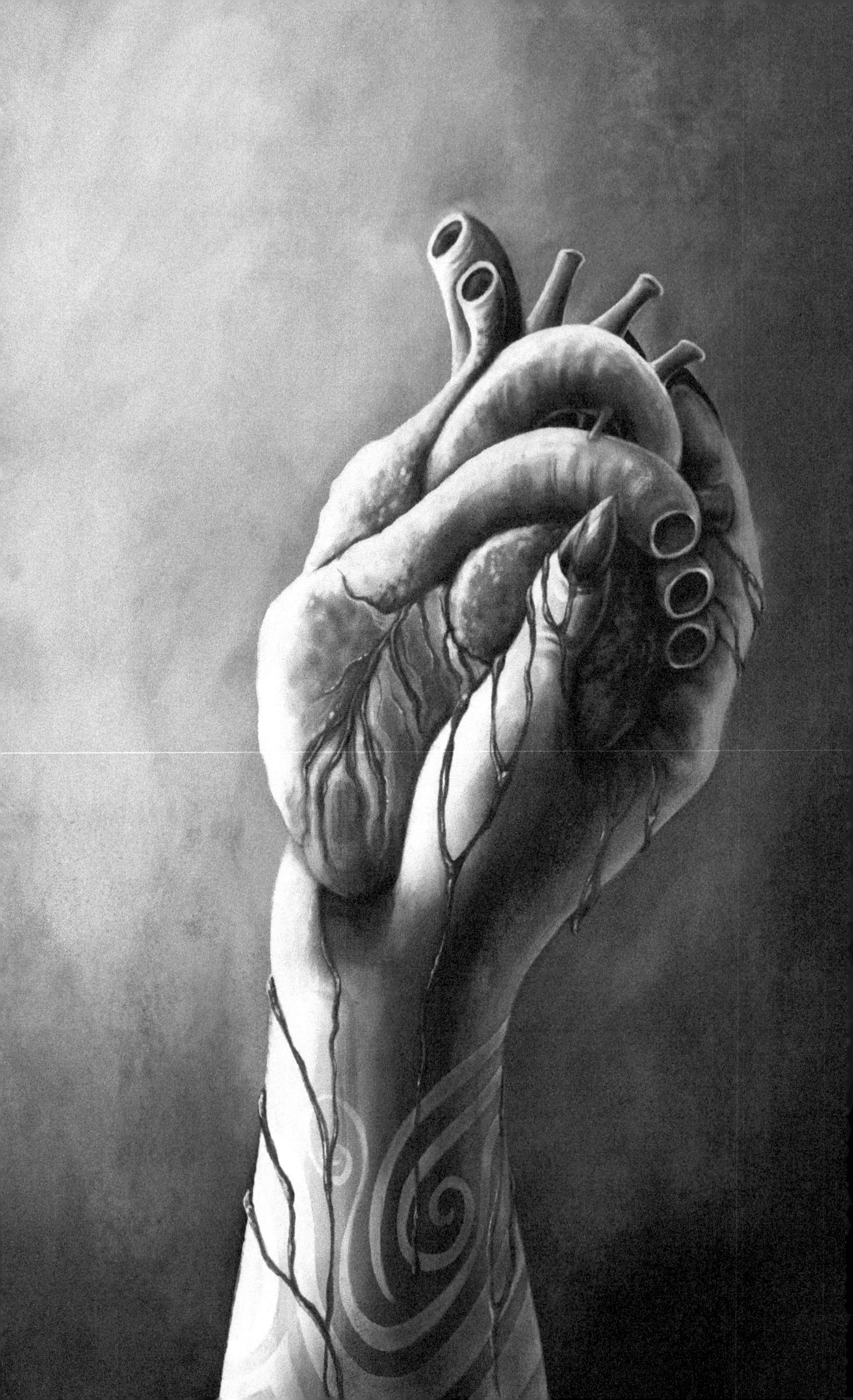

CHAPTER 44

Malicent

NCE I STEP INTO THE NIGHT AIR, I'M OVERWHELMED by the hearts I hear, each one thudding like a war drum. A feast. An entire feast waits for me, and the thought thrills me so deeply it sends me skipping into the crowd.

"Millicent?"

I ignore the lumbering fool who dares to call her name. "Millicent Le strange!" He yells again, pursuing me. I slip through the sea of bodies, giggling. He's too big, unable to maneuver as I do.

A divine scent arrests me. I hone in on a woman, neck bared, begging me to have a bite as she chats casually.

Oh, if you insist.

Another tall figure steps in my path, but this one's magic offends me.

"Move."

"Hello to you, too. Is this a new look? People are staring." He gives me a warning, as if I need one.

I raise a hand to slam through his chest, but the vermin dares to grab my wrist.

I grin wickedly and twist. The bones in his wrist snap like brittle twigs. His shout is delightful. I drive my heel into his gut, impaling him and launching him through the crowd. He crashes into a table. Screams erupt, and the crowd scatters.

Sheep. Panic-stricken, mindless sheep. *I am their shepherd.*

I summon a veil of night, my magic rising from the earth and sealing them in a dome of shadows that stretch into the sky. The herd crashes against its boundaries. They try to break through. Futile.

"You may all bow now."

I reach into their minds around me and rip through them. Knees buckle from the pain, their pleas now drowned in sobs.

I find my chosen offering, my precious little morsel. She sobs about her family and her sons. I wish they were here so I could feast on them, too.

"Kiss it and beg," I command, presenting her my bloodied foot.

She hesitates before kissing my shoe, then immediately turns and vomits into the grass.

"Well, that's rude. Eat it."

She refuses, so I grab her hair and shove her face into her own bile. Bash. Crack. Then again. And again. Until her skull splits like an egg under my hold. Even then, I don't stop, relishing the thought of seeing the color of her brain.

"Enough!"

A blast of searing heat slams into my ribs, flinging me into my own veil.

"You dare?" I whisper, rising as the grass grays beneath me and black tendrils writhe at my feet. A portion of my true power is now stirring.

I rise smoothly, brushing dust from my gown as I stare down brilliant silver eyes burning across the field.

His aura intensifies. *Someone is showing off.*

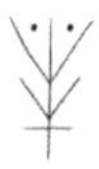

Recognition clicks as I take in the vessel before me, brimming with energy that practically begs to be torn free.

The failed bond.

The mind intruder.

The one who refused to kneel.

My lips curl as I lean left, effortlessly dodging a volley of darts from the large oaf who first dared to speak to me outside.

Oh, I will have fun devouring them both.

CHAPTER 45

Cage

HER COLLAR IS GONE, AND SO IS ANY TRACE OF RESTRAINT. Those collars are rare. Ancient artifacts forged by paladins, blessed by their deities. The only one we had was used on her. The voice that comes from her is wrong. Not Millicent's. It slithers out, thick and oily, warped into something masculine and un-recognizable. Her once bright eyes are pitch black now, matching the rolling waves of magic bleeding into the air around us.

Kalix attempts to dart her with a sedative, but it doesn't take. Of course it doesn't. Her aura has mutated. Millicent was already formida-ble before, but this is insane. Was it the lord? Did he curse her, or did he simply awaken what was already there?

My own darkness stirs, clawing to be released. I manage to cage it down. If we both let go here, everyone dies.

I shift tactics when a plan finally forms. Tendrils of magic lance out toward her. I keep full command, making sure none of them can be redirected to the civilians. She meets them with no hesitation.

Each one dissipates on contact, dispersing into mist before it can even touch her skin.

"The best you got, mage?" she taunts, advancing with fire gleaming in her void-dark eyes.

"I only ever give you the best, Millicent."

No reaction to her own name, no fiery remark, no flash of recognition. Nothing.

I launch more tendrils, their shadowed points aimed to disable, not kill. It matters little when nothing touches her.

Then she retaliates.

Explosions of black fire detonate against my shield, each impact a shockwave of heat and crackling power. I anchor myself, pouring everything into my defenses as she presses a relentless assault, something I will use to my advantage.

Good.

I pull from the sky, calling my bonded. Vyraxis tears into existence above the garden. Her scaled body shimmers with threads of silver flame. Millicent's head snaps upward. An inhuman snarl resonates from her throat.

Vyraxis stays airborne, exhaling a storm of silver fire. The heat slams into Millicent's barrier, cracking and shattering it like black-stained glass. I seize the moment, launching a cluster of tendrils toward her before she can reform the veil. The shadows sharpen to the likeness of spears and soar through the air, aiming to impale her limbs.

She dispels my attacks in a burst of rage, but the crowd is already fleeing. Kalix stands at the shattered wall of magic, ushering the humans through.

As soon as there's enough space, Vyraxis lands in a rumble of earth and bone. She steps over me, shielding me between her forelegs. Her scales glow with silver heat as she coils her neck and fires a focused stream of fire.

Millicent finally shields.

Keep it up. We need to drain her, I push into Vyraxis's mind.

I could devour this abomination.

No, we need her. Hold steady.

As you will it, she replies reluctantly.

I place a hand against her foreleg, grounding her. The connection between us thickens as I allow her to draw from my magic. Our power hums in tandem, becoming steady and tireless.

Millicent's arms begin to tremble. Blood spills from her nose. Her form falters for just a moment, her stance widening.

Finally. The first signs of exhaustion.

Vyraxis continues her relentless assault, pausing only to inhale. My own reserves are waning, fatigue creeps through my limbs, but I hold the line.

Millicent drops to one knee. Her shield sputters from the onslaught.

Enough. Rest.

Vyraxis halts her flame, but her posture remains taut, guarding me like a living wall.

Rest, I repeat, softer.

As Millicent crumples, collapsing onto all fours, her breath hitches in strained wheezes. Vyraxis finally concedes. She rises into the sky in a single beat of her wings. High above, she spins once, then dissolves into a ribbon of onyx mist.

I cross to Millicent, crouching beside her.

"Someone's tired," I murmur.

"I...am not anything," she rasps with a brittle voice. She slumps onto her side, curling into the grass like a wounded animal.

I wait, let her breathe for a few minutes. "Millicent."

When the tremors in her limbs still, I brush hair from her face, tucking damp strands behind her ear. I slide my hand under her cheek and tilt her face toward me. Her tired eyes look up at me. Relief floods over me when I see them.

It's blue. Soft, familiar.

"There she is," I breathe.

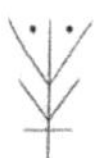

I gather her gently in my arms, settling her against my chest. Her body folds into mine without resistance, and she lays her head beneath my chin. The magic within has quieted—for now.

Exhaustion settles in. "Are you hurt anywhere?" I ask, voice low.

No response. Her eyes close. Her breathing deepens as she melts in my arms. She's already asleep.

Kalix joins my side as I begin walking.

"There are a few dead bodies in the kitchen; the Duke's down the hall—what's left of him." He glances at Millicent, eyes tight with confusion and uncertainty. "Maybe I was wrong. Maybe she isn't just a witch with a dark side. Maybe she's the very thing people fear, the reason they burned so many of them."

I pull her closer.

"If she should be killed for this, then so should I." He knows the horrible things I've done.

Kalix sighs and rubs the back of his neck. "Yeah. I don't mean it."

We walk in silence the rest of the way to the carriage.

Kalix takes the reins when our driver turns up missing. Probably fled, and I can't blame him.

Millicent stays curled in my arms inside the carriage. I comb through the knots in her hair. I take my time, memorizing each strand. I don't know if what happened was her or something inside her. I can't decide what's worse.

My fingers drift across her cheek, tracing the slope of her nose. Maybe her beauty is a blessing from her dark gods, or maybe it's a weapon, just like her. Either way, it hurts.

She's not just a memory that haunts me. I mourned her, but she's still carved into me. A brand, just as permanent as the scars on my back.

The trap worked, and I'm the one caught in it.

Desiring her pisses me off. She loves only herself—and Oliver, a piece of herself made whole. Loving Millicent isn't a choice. We can never go back to what we were.

I need to survive her.

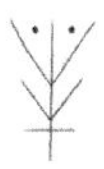

It's a slow brutal bleed. And still, some part of me, some damned sliver, would bleed for her forever.

I would have bled for her back then, too. Now? She is something else entirely, someone else entirely. I remind myself again—Millicent did die that night. The happy, trusting, kind girl is gone.

Sleep takes me eventually, but it's a shallow thing, restless, like everything else she leaves behind.

Millicent squirms as I try to pat her bloody knee clean.

"Millie, quit it. You're being a big baby," I say, using my elbow to pin her tiny thigh down.

"I'm not a baby! It hurts! You're burning it!" she yells, pushing on my back with all the rage a five-year-old can muster.

"It'll get infected if I don't," I mutter, cleaning more quickly. She pounds on my back with her fists, whining until I finally get the bandage on.

I sit back on my heels, catching my breath. She inspects her knee with a suspicious glare.

"Thank you," she mumbles reluctantly, but she's sincere.

Seeing her upset makes something ache in me. Millicent is all I have now. She's the only light left in this place, and I don't want to ruin it.

"You're not a baby, Millie," I lie, trying to cheer her up. "I'd be crying way more than you."

It works wonderfully, and her face lights up instantly. She hops up and grabs my hand, tugging me to my feet. She's so small she can't actually lift me, but I push off, letting her think she can.

"Yeah, you would!" She beams, chin high, like her pride is a badge of honor.

"Cage!" Millicent yells, fear shaking her voice. She presses her back against a tree as I approach.

I freeze. "Whoa. Why are you afraid? What scared you?" I crouch to her level, keeping my voice calm.

"You," she whispers. "*You're* what I fear."

My chest tightens. We were just playing tag. I never meant to scare her. Panic ceases me seeing her fear. "How do I scare you?"

"You were chasing me and not talking. Your eyes...I swear they turned black." She comforts herself, holding her stuffed bunny close to her chest.

"Are my eyes black now?" I tease, trying to make her smile. Surely, she imagined it. My eyes do nothing of the sort.

She rolls her eyes. *There she is.* Her fiery attitude and spark returns. "Whatever. I'm hungry. Can we eat now?" She grabs two of my fingers.

Her touch chases away the cold ache her fear had left behind. I adjust our grip so her hand fits snug in mine. "Yeah. Let's feed you."

We walk together slowly. I match her little strides as we approach the dining hall. When we reach the doors, she starts whining in protest the way she always does.

"You know we can't be seen together," I remind her. "Go on. Arcadia's probably waiting."

She offers me her patched-up bunny with one button eye, and I take him. We've taken to sharing custody. In truth, it's the only thing I sleep with now.

The nights are getting harder. My insomnia is worsening. So are the visions...and the voices. I push the dark thoughts aside as I watch her skip away. She is a spark of light in a place that grows darker by the day. I cling to it, but...

What if my darkness spreads? What if I pull her into it with me?

A knock at Millicent's door rouses me. I must have drifted off in the chair watching over her.

She's still curled up on the bed, unmoving. Her chest rises slow. It's steady, but shallower than anything normal—not fully alive, not dead—but that is stasis. A strange purgatory where she can rest and recover.

I open the door and find Luca.

"Lord Black," he says, surprised. "pardon my intrusion. I didn't know you were here." He salutes before recomposing himself.

"State your business," I reply flatly. I'm too drained for pleasantries. Vyraxis burned through my reserves during the fight. The naps in the carriage and in this chair barely scratch the surface of what I need.

"Millicent has been training with me," he says. "Kalix said she wasn't available tonight. That's...not like her, so I just came to check on her."

I already knew. Kalix had mentioned it was comical, Millicent running Luca ragged, like a cat toying with a mouse.

The concern in his eyes makes me pause. Narrowing mine, I ask, "You care for a witch? One who killed mortals tonight, your own kind?"

He swallows hard, visibly working through his response. "When I was a boy, I teased a dog with a roll. He snapped at me, tore through my hand. And I was afraid of dogs after that. Years later, I found a stray, one who was the kindest thing. I fed him and took him in."

I give him a sharp look—get to the point.

"The first dog acted on instincts. I chose not to blame the dog for what it was born to do. I don't hate witches for doing what they were made to do. If she's made from something dark and otherworldly, then of course she'll continue to return to the dark. I can't pick and choose what part of her to accept."

His gaze shifts past me, toward her bed.

He means it. I believe he does. Most mortals would see Millicent burned, but Luca is kind. I imagine he's the kind of man who'd apologize to a snake for stepping on it.

"Fine," I mutter. "You can stand guard. If she wakes up and that dark thing is still in control, just yell."

I brush past him, exiting the room. Maybe it's unwise. Maybe it's petty, but if he wants to see her as something soft and worth saving, let him face the truth when it wakes.

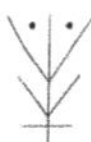

CHAPTER 46

Millicent

MY HEART SEIZES, AND ON ITS NEXT CONTRACTION, power slams through me like a hammer strike. My nerves ignite, and I jolt up, gasping for air as my eyes snap open. For a moment, the world spins like a kaleidoscope with too many colors and too much light. A few steady blinks brings the palette down to its normal, duller tones, the colors of my room.

I rub my hands over the comforter draped across my lap, grounding myself with the soft cotton, a welcome comfort.

"Me Misses!"

Ollie materializes near my feet with a frantic chirp and scurries into my lap, pressing against my stomach like an overgrown cat.

"Ollie." My voice rattles in my throat, low and hoarse from disuse, an expected side effect of stasis. I stroke the length of his back, the act steadying the both of us.

"There is water on the bedside for you," comes Luca's voice, drawing my attention to the chair near the bed, a new addition. He must've dragged it here just to sit vigil and watch me sleep.

I don't ask why. I just reach for the pitcher and pour a glass. The first sip hits like spring rain, a cool relief that brings me back to life. I hadn't realized how raw my throat was until the water slicks it down.

"Thanks," I mutter, still watching him.

"I didn't bring it," he says, smiling gently. "I'm glad to see you're awake."

I finish the glass and pour another. "Why are you here?"

"You never miss our training. When you didn't show, I asked Kalix, but he told me you were unavailable. I needed to see for myself."

"It's a fickle thing to care about."

"Caring for a friend isn't fickle," he replies, steady and straightforward, but he's not unkind.

I watch condensation bead down the glass, circling a fingertip along the rim. I contemplate his words, and Arcadia's screams flash in my mind. How I would've torn the world in two and clawed through Hell just to get to her.

I understand care. I give it, fiercely. To have it offered back when you've lived without it for so long...the intensity of it burns. Like sunlight on untouched skin.

You bring affection to a table that hasn't been set. No chairs, no warmth, only dust and forgotten hunger. And then I'm expected to feast. It makes me feel sick.

"Are we friends, Luca?"

"I like to think so. Friends help each other, the way you help me."

I nearly laugh. If only he knew I started training him to serve my selfish motivations.

I only know I lost control because I remember nothing after Arcadia dying in my arms, nothing after trying to drown us both in my magic, to let us sleep beneath it together.

I know now that none of it was real. It didn't make sense, not logically. In that moment, my mind was frayed. And still, some part of me can't shake the fear it was more than an illusion, that it was a glimpse into something real, a real future that I might one day cause.

"Helping me has killed people." My voice is quiet. I take another sip of water to ease the dryness that lingers in my mouth.

"Do they help you kill people?"

"No, I kill them."

He says nothing. Just watches me. I reach gently toward his mind, wanting to understand what simmers behind his silence. The moment I taste sympathy, pity, I recoil. I don't want that from him.

"Is it because I am beautiful that you forgive what I have done? What I continue to do?" My words cut sharp across the room. My anger stirs from the pit of my chest.

"I've hope you still have a heart. Is that so bad?"

"That belief will get you killed."

"Well, it hasn't yet." He shrugs softly. "I have no magic. I can't imagine what it's like having something dark crawling through your veins. I would hope someone would still see more in me than just that."

"And what do you see in me, past the darkness?" I laugh, incredulously. The idea is quite comical. My soul swims in shadow. What could he possibly see beyond it?

"You're smart. Arrogant. A leader. A great teacher. You demand perfection, from yourself and others. You're controlling—"

I raise a brow, unimpressed.

"—and powerful. And strong. I envy a lot of those traits."

The man is clearly insane.

"Me Misses is perfect." Ollie mumbles into the blanket, curled comfortably against my legs.

"We will train later. Shoo now." I wave him off.

Luca rises with a grand, sweeping bow that tugs a reluctant smile from me, the first since I woke.

"As my lady commands! I will see you tonight!"

Once he leaves, I spend some time snuggling with Ollie, his presence grounding me in a way nothing else ever could. After a while, I finally speak, keeping my voice low in case Nora's owl is perched in some shadowed corner of my room.

"Ollie, check on Cadia for me."

He pokes his head from under the blanket, tenting the fabric with one of his long ears.

"Yes, Misses!" he chirps. With a flutter of his wings, his form dissolves into a cascade of shadows, slipping beneath the covers until they fall flat again.

When hunger finally pries me from my bed, I venture into the hall. It's a hectic day today. Servants race past with arms overloaded with food and decorations.

I fall into step behind them, curious, letting their path guide me to the ballroom.

Inside, the space is even gaudier than usual, dripping in gold, with new tables being uniformly arranged. I immediately lose interest and turn away, indifferent to whatever event is being prepared.

"Millicent!"

Felix's voice cracks down the corridor like a whip, accompanied by frantic waving as he bounds toward me like a mad man.

I sigh and raise a hand in return, knowing if I don't, he'll continue to flail like a toddler.

"Felix."

He grins. "Have you eaten since you woke up? I expected you to look awful, but here you are! Honestly, death suits you."

"I'm hunting for food now." I yawn, still not fully free of the heavy pull of stasis.

"Perfect. Lunch together, then."

"I was planning to grab something and return to my chamber, actually." I attempt to brush him off, hoping he leaves me to my peace. Of course he doesn't.

"It's outside! There's wine, sun...and gossip! The picnic is already set. Come now."

Felix grabs my hand and tugs me down the corridor, talking the entire way about some ridiculous ball. Apparently, a new duke is being named and this celebration is to be held in his honor.

We arrive at a sprawling orange plaid blanket spread across the grass. He drops down and yanks me with him.

"Watch it," I snap as my ass hits the ground.

He ignores me, already reaching for the wine nestled beside the basket.

"Sorry, my little snowflake," he teases, his cheeks rounding with a devilish grin.

"You are hardly ever sorry," I retort, snatching the bottle from his hands.

"Please, we're both royals. It comes with the territory." He rolls his eyes, opening the basket and pulling out two sandwiches. He passes me one. Between us, he sets a bundle of ripe strawberries.

I keep busy, pouring our wine as he lays out the food.

"So, I heard you went full psycho bitch," he says, leaning back on his elbows and wiggling his eyebrows at me.

"I was attacked and collared," I mutter. "Blame Cage."

"Another royal trait we share—blame shifting!"

He nearly chokes on the bite he takes when I kick him.

"If any of you bastards collar me again…" The air around me pulses. My magic stirs, and I know my eyes have begun to glow.

He holds up both hands in mock surrender. "Lesson learned. Now have some wine before you blow up again. I'm not dealing with Cage and Kalix's problems. And I'm far too pretty to be collateral damage."

I allow a smile. Good. *I hope they're worn down.*

The silence stretches, but not uncomfortably. By the time I finish my sandwich and reach for the strawberries, my stomach has stopped complaining.

"Do you want to talk about it?" Felix asks gently.

I keep my gaze on the leaves dancing overhead, unwilling to meet his eyes.

His hand covers over mine in support. It's warm and light.

"I don't think there is anything to say."

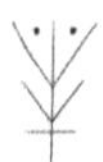

"Then we don't have to," he replies simply.

The lack of argument surprises me. I flip my hand over and curl my fingers around his. I don't overthink it. I don't let my mind shame me for the comfort. I just hold on.

He squeezes back gently.

"If you're in the mood, I'd like you by my side tonight," he murmurs.

I glance at him. "You don't want a courtesan or one of your usual admirers?" I raise an eyebrow. "I'm a witch. It's not very kingly."

"Nothing I do is kingly." He grins, as though the idea amuses him deeply. "I think it'll be funny."

"Fine." I smirk. "I'll come—just to see the look on the mortals' faces."

"That's my girl!" He laughs, plucking a strawberry from the bundle and biting into it. He's carefree as ever.

To keep my mind off Arcadia, I stay with Felix until he's pulled away for a meeting. Left alone with nothing but my spiraling thoughts, I retreat to my room and change into loose brown leather trousers and a tunic. I cinch the excess length into my waistband.

Once the clock chimes six, I make for the training grounds to meet Luca. My anxiety builds with every hour Oliver does not return. I channel that restlessness into my muscles, pushing myself harder and faster. Luca struggles to keep up, but I don't slow down. I run as if I can outpace the thought of Cadia suffering.

After the run, I move straight into the sparring ring. I throw Luca again and again, partly as training and partly to let the excess energy out.

From the ground, he raises his hands in surrender. "Millicent, enough for tonight. I'm dead," he pants, red-faced and swaying with exhaustion.

"Up. It's not enough." I reach for his shirt, dragging him up by it.

"Millicent, please. We'll train again in the morning. I am getting dizzy. I might be sick."

I tower over him. "No, up at once," I demand.

His voice cracks as he pleads. "Millicent, I don't think you are well today. Please, see reason."

"You are what is wrong with me!" I shout, rage finally surfacing from the depths of my fear.

"Millicent, let him rest." Iris's gentle voice cuts through my fury like cool water over fire. I hadn't heard her approach.

I drop his shirt and turn toward her. "He'll die if he needs rest on a battlefield."

"This isn't a battlefield," she says softly. She gives Luca a nod, and he wastes no time leaving, but not before casting one last kind smile over his shoulder.

"You coddle him," I snap.

Iris steps closer, inspecting me. "Do you want to talk about it?"

"Talk about what? Why is everyone asking me that!" I rake my hands through my hair, tugging hard enough to burn my scalp, distracting me from the anxiety.

"I stand corrected. There is a battlefield." she taps her temple. "Right here. You're rocking on your feet, pushing Luca harder than ever, and you've been spinning the ring on your finger."

I pause, looking down. I hadn't realized I was turning the ring again and again. The unconscious movement betrays me.

After I scan the training yard to make sure we're alone, I step in closer and lower my voice. "I have an odd feeling Cadia's in danger. Or will be. I can't explain it. I'm not a seer, but..." I trail off, furrowing my brow. "It's like a warning, like I'm supposed to know something."

Iris considers this. "I understand. Have you written to her?"

"Ollie's gone to check on her, but he should've been back by now. It's not like him."

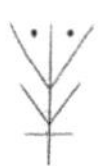

"If the feeling doesn't pass, we'll go see Luna together, the seer in this region. She may help ease your mind."

"I'd like that."

She reaches out, taking my hands in hers. "All will be well. You've just come out of stasis. Things always feel off afterward. You don't have to come to the ball tonight if you need to decompress."

I nod. Staying in my room might be safer—for others and for myself. However, solitude means sitting with these thoughts. "I'll consider it." I offer her a forced smile, then shift my focus. "Were they able to get the lord's body to you?"

"There wasn't much of a body left once you were done," she replies dryly, "but, yes, Kalix did report the same markings inside him."

"Whatever it was, it created a domain," I murmur. "It warped reality, changed everything. It all felt so real." My fingers unconsciously begin spinning the ring on my thumb, a new habit for a familiar dread. Arcadia on that altar still burns behind my eyes.

"It's clear the curse amplifies its host," Iris says thoughtfully. "You've only ever mentioned one sister, Arcadia. She's the curse expert, right?"

A sudden wave of clarity slams into me. "Yes, she is." I can't believe I hadn't thought of this sooner. My original plan to take a prisoner is shattered, but this? This is better. I can keep Arcadia close. I can keep her safe.

"Excellent. Have Ollie summon her. I'm sure Felix will send support if needed," Iris assures me.

I reach for my bond with Oliver and send the command. He doesn't answer, but his presence is steady, alive, and uninjured.

"I've instructed him." A smile breaks across my face at the thought of Arcadia here, with me. For the first time since waking, a flicker of warmth stirs in my chest.

"Wonderful!" Iris grins. "Another witch will be fun! Maybe Cage will burst a blood vessel!"

I laugh under my breath, her warmth finally leaking through my

tension. She senses it and takes her chance, stepping backward and holding both my hands in hers to gently lead me forward.

"You know what always cheers me up?" She asks mischievously.

"Creating abominations?"

She throws her head back in a laugh that spills into the sky. "True, but I'm not allowed anymore. The deer frightened Kalix."

"Kalix? The mountain man? Frightened by the deer?"

"More like frightened of *me* using my magic."

"Why?"

She sobers slightly. "Think of my magic as a seductress. It changes me. Every time I use it, I become who I used to be. I think…Kalix fears the dark will take me."

"Has it ever taken you over?" I ask quietly, matching her slower pace.

"For years, it was all I knew," she says. "I haven't always been this person before you." Her voice grows distant. I recognize the look in her eyes—lost in memory. I resist the urge to dig through her thoughts, giving her the dignity of silence.

"What brought you out of it?"

"Eden."

"Your sister," I confirm.

"The better half of me." Sorrow weighs down her voice. I can't imagine a better version of her, with her kindness and measured wisdom. She sees the world for what it is, both the rot and the bloom.

She pauses. "I had a feeling something awful was coming for Eden. I was right. You should heed that feeling with Arcadia."

I nod, understanding more than I want to admit.

Then, with a slow exhale, she shakes off the weight. "Now come have hot cocoa by the fire with me."

I smile despite myself. "Pastries, too," I add, following her through a tall archway and back into the castle.

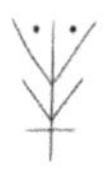

CHAPTER 47

Cage

I CAN'T STAND ANOTHER MOMENT NEAR THIS MAN.

I speak directly into Felix's mind, standing stiff at his side while he schmoozes with the duke this entire gathering is meant to honor. Felix only smiles in response, sipping his wine with a smug face. He enjoys my discomfort far too much.

My eyes continuously sweep the crowd, always alert for threats, while my mind drifts between thoughts. I brush against those present to monitor for any spark of rebellion or violence.

At least Millicent offers some entertainment.

She moves like a storm cloud through the crowd. While everyone else is draped in jeweled gowns and gold accents to flatter Felix's vanity, she's wrapped in black lace. Her hair isn't pinned like the others'. It spills down her back like a waterfall of night. Her dress clings to her skin, the lace sleeves revealing the witch marks beneath, a corseted bodice cinching her waist, and twin embroidered gold snakes rising from her hips over her chest.

She doesn't speak much. I catch her glancing through the crowd repeatedly, likely searching for Iris. She will not find her anytime soon.

Kalix is undoubtedly hovering close, as he always does when Iris is ovulating, something I unfortunately know firsthand from his outrageously loud thoughts earlier during a command meeting. I checked in briefly, only to be assaulted by a mental montage of lust and possessiveness. Typical Kalix.

Gods above, give me strength to not tie this woman down.

I smirk as Kalix's frustration radiates off him in waves.

Curious, I shift to Iris's mind instead.

I can wear whatever I want. Who is he to dictate what's too revealing?

Oh, she's livid. No surprise there. Their arguments can stretch for hours. I pull back from their squabble. Besides, Millicent is far more captivating prey tonight.

Luca comes to her rescue, stepping up to her side. I slide into his mind next, needing to know what stirs beneath the surface. Nothing but friendship. No flicker of lust. Good. The darkness clawing up my spine settles slightly.

He'd be a fool to desire her. He wouldn't survive it. She'd slit his throat mid-ecstasy and leave his blood staining silk sheets.

No, the little devil and her violent delights demand a firmer hand.

A hand like mine.

I roll my neck and press the rising hunger back down. Her darkness calls to mine, like oil drawn to flame. Even when I detest what she represents, she's...delicious.

Millicent excuses herself, slipping through the crowd until she vanishes into the hallway. I reach out mentally, brushing against her mind. The wall is there—predictable—but she doesn't retaliate. I'd hoped my intrusion would get her back into my view so I can look at her more closely, even if she'd spit venomously at me. She doesn't return, either.

Goosebumps race up my arms. The magic in the room thickens, electric. My eyes scan the crowd.

Fuck.

What if she lost control again?

Felix. I cast the thought to him. *Something's off. I need to check on Millicent.*

He nods to me, understanding passing between us.

I motion a nearby guard over. "Protect the king in my absence."

"Of course, Lord Black," the man replies, taking position at Felix's side.

The crowd parts for me, and I stride into the hallway. No sign of her.

I pick up my pace, magic prickling at my senses. It's strong, but it's all around me, bleeding through the walls and humming through the floors.

I search the halls, cut through the garden, checking the corners I know she prefers. No sign of her. Growing impatient, I shut my eyes and tune into the wards.

Her signature pulses inside her chamber.

I don't knock. Surprise is my ally if she's lost in that dark pit again.

She turns at the sound of the door. Millicent stands framed in the balcony's light. "Um? Hello?"

My eyes rake over her—sharp, precise, checking for the predator. "What are you doing in here, little witch?"

"I felt claustrophobic," she responds a little too quickly.

Liar.

"I thought we were going to start being honest?" I close the distance slowly.

"Since when?" she snaps, folding her arms.

My gaze flicks past her to the owl perched in the shadows of the balcony. Familiar eyes. Nora's eyes. She's watching. I noticed the owl when Millicent was in stasis, and I'll never forget those eyes.

I already figured Nora is keeping tabs on Millicent. "Talking to your mock mommy?" My voice drips with malice.

Her expression turns venomous. "Something like that."

I step closer, letting my size and presence tower over her, but she doesn't flinch.

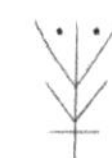

Intriguing.

"Why is there a surge in magic, Millicent?" I watch closely for a break in her mask.

Her grin widens like a challenge. "Maybe it's me. No collar, remember?" She drags her fingers along her bare neck.

My eyes track the movement. No scars. No sign of the Carnium Edax, no residue of the collar that once chewed its way into her flesh.

How many scars have been bestowed upon her skin, only to be erased?

"Do you think that makes you free?"

I close the last inch between us. Her aura pulses against mine. My hand lifts to her throat, fingers wrapping slowly, deliberately around the delicate column.

"I'm not a prisoner here, remember?" she asks, tone just shy of flirtatious.

"Free of your collar, perhaps. Not of me. I am your executioner, my little witch." I pull her against my chest, tightening my grip on her throat in warning. "I could snap your neck right now."

Her eyes glint with something unreadable. "Break me then," she whispers, her voice dipping into a soft velvet sound that pulls the beast inside me from its cage.

I push her backward, step by step, toward the balcony where Nora's owl watches silently from its perch.

I lean down to her ear, keeping my eyes locked on the bird. "How do you think Nora will feel, seeing her heir bent over this railing, fucked by the monster she helped forge?"

She turns, meeting my eyes with lethal calm. "How do you think I will feel when you fill me?"

Her lip slips between her teeth, and I grow instantly envious of the attention.

"Like sweet sin," I mumble, hoarsely.

I press my lips to hers. She resists at first, until I squeeze her throat tighter. Her lips part to suck in air, and I claim her. My tongue invades,

stealing her delicious taste, taking her breath and replacing it with mine. I'm inside her mouth, but it isn't enough. I need more.

She reciprocates with heat. Hands slip in my hair, tugging on strands as her teeth tug at my bottom lip before sucking it into her mouth. When she moans against me, my restraint crumbles.

My pants grow tighter as I grind against her, letting her feel my desire. And the sound she makes in response damn near breaks me.

My hands drop from her throat to her gown. I pull forcibly until I hear fabric tear under my grip.

"Cage," she whines, panting against my lips. It's the most perfect sound I've ever heard. I want to claim every inch of her skin.

"Keep saying my name," I breathe. "Just like that."

No, her skin is not enough. *I need to infect her soul.*

My hands are beneath the hem, ready to lift her and press her thighs to the railing—

The world tilts.

Her hands are on me. She eases me to the floor.

"Are you all right?" she whispers.

No. Something is wrong. Strength seeps out of me like spilling blood. I blink, trying to sit up.

"Millicent, what did you do?"

The devil itself smiles back at me. She caresses my head, stroking my hair in a parody of tenderness.

"Somnex." A sedative. The exact one we used on her before.

The little bitch. I should have known she was up to something the moment she kissed me like that. "I'm going to wake up," I growl, struggling to focus, "and rid us of you."

She laughs bright and full. I've never heard her sound so vibrant. "Please. No one even notices what I'm doing. What do you all think I am? A troubled girl with a soft heart?" She twirls a lock of my hair around her finger, treating me like a toy. "It's just my nature, right? Isn't that what Luca says?"

I see it now, the wolf beneath her soft skin, its sharpened teeth and hunting skills honed from years of practice. "I always saw you for what you are. A Le Strange. One we should burn first the second this war has ended."

She smiles wider. Her eyes sparkle with something lethal. "I'll take you down with me, but not today. I hope you sleep well, *little shadow.* And I hope you know the darkness coming is me. Everyone dies tonight, but don't worry." Her voice hardens. "It'll all be self-defense."

Her words cut like poisoned glass. My limbs begin growing cold, and I can no longer control them.

"Millicent, listen to me. I'm sorry about your mother," I force out. She's not lying. The sedative is pulling me under, but panic drags me up by the throat. "My family is here. Millicent, please. You saw my memory. I was tor—"

"Enough!"

She looms over me, voice thunderous. "You are pathetic, weak. Tortured? I've *lived* what you've lived and came out stronger. You bleed your weakness onto others like a stain!"

"It's not an excuse!" My voice slurs. My vision splinters, triple-layered and dimming. "You've been...brainwashed."

I fight the sedative. I *have to.*

No. No, I need to *save them—*

I can save them.

My hands tremble as I pull the spike from my mother's chest.

"Mama, please wake up," I whisper, rocking her limp body against mine. Her blood coats me, seeping through my clothes until it clings like a second skin.

I can save them.

I rock, holding her to me. Her last words, a lie. It is my fault.

I reach over, fumbling for my father's cold hand, curling my fingers around his.

But—but I can save them.

I rock faster.

I can save them...

HER RAGE RADIATES OFF HER IN WAVES. SHE SHOVES MY HEAD from her lap, and my skull cracks against the stone. The pain splits behind my eyes, and a shrill ringing floods my ears.

When my vision clears, she is towering over me.

"I wish I had a heart to care about the awful things I'm about to do to you," she whispers. Her voice trembles, tears trailing down her cheeks. "But you ripped it from my chest."

"Millie," I choke out. My chest rises and falls rapidly, panic consuming what strength I have left. "Vyraxis will come. You'll die." A truth.

"I am not living. This is not living, Cage. I'm a vessel. You don't understand what I am."

More tears fall, and I start to hallucinate. Her adult face, morphing, melting into a child's, then back again. The sedative is dragging me under. I see the five-year-old girl I loved. My only friend.

This is the cycle, isn't it?

I took from her. And now she's here to take everything from me. Even when I have lost so much, there's always more left for her to destroy.

"Lie with me...just for a while," I whisper. It's a phrase I used to say when we were kids.

The child version of her sits beside me, just like she did the day I left her behind, covered in bloodstains with tears down her cheeks.

She is going to die. I need to hold her just one more time.

I try to reach for her. My arm gives out and slaps the floor. "My star came to guide me home to rest."

Her hand slips into mine. Our fingers weave together.

"Let me in." My voice barely escapes.

She shakes her head.

I feel something wet slide down my cheek from my eye as her rejection stings.

In her death, I grieved the loss of what little I had. In her life, I grieve her refusal to let me back in.

"You promised you'd never block me out."

My eyelids fall. Darkness licks at the edges of my vision.

"You promised."

CHAPTER 48

Millicent

CAGE'S SUDDEN CHANGE IN DEMEANOR THROWS ME OFF. I stare down at his limp form, then lean in to press a kiss on his cheek.

Somnex coats my lips, applied the moment I entered my room. I knew he would come once he sensed the magic stirring.

Of course, the dosage doesn't affect me anymore. After Kalix drugged me, I began hunting for the plant. The beautiful purple petals, nearly iridescent in moonlight, caught my eye on a run with Luca. Every night, I dosed myself, slowly increasing each dose until I reached tolerance.

Let them try to drug me again.

I look to the owl. "It's done Nora, I will retrieve the artifact."

They all underestimated me. The collar gave me the perfect opportunity to slip into the mage's wing unnoticed. Week after week, I've been cataloging the artifacts. I told Nora everything. And she wants one item in particular: a small golden box wrapped in spelled papers meant to contain whatever great power slumbers inside.

Cage was going to be a problem. That's why he's taking a nap during all this.

Shadows begin to slither from his body. I know Vyraxis is coming.

I bolt.

Windows I pass display a suddenly dark grey stormy sky. Large bolts of lightning zip through the clouds, and thunder rattles the castle as Vyraxis's energy pulls. *Yeah, she is pissed.*

I sprint through the winding halls to the mage wing. Thanks to the ball, the entire wing is deserted.

Idiots. Too reliant on their wards. And their ward keeper is fast asleep.

I reach the sealed iron door. My magic slides from my fingers and sinks into the runes etched across the metal. One by one, the wards shatter. It's nice not having the collar on. There's no burning. This freedom tastes like power.

Inside, the artifact room feels like an overstuffed tomb. Shelves tower above me, crammed with cursed relics, ancient enchantments, and things that should never have been made.

I find the box easily. Golden, unassuming, barely bigger than a picnic basket.

A chill floods my veins the moment I touch it.

The Nightmother stirs awake.

Open it, she purrs. Her voice coils in my mind. My hands shake when I try to resist.

Open it, she growls. Her compulsion slices in my mind. Images flash in my mind—a grotesque, four-armed beast. The visions are drenched black and crimson.

"Stop," I whisper.

Open it. Open it. **OPEN IT!**

Her screams split my skull, and I collapse to my knees, clutching my head. I place the box down in front of me, grabbing my head.

"Stop! Stop!" I repeat. My scream cracks. Glass shatters across the room.

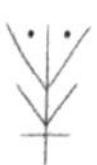

Her presence invades my mind. My vision floods black. My body spasms under the weight of her control as my hands move without my will. They rip away the protective wrappings, and the box creaks open.

She releases me, allowing my eyes to roll forward.

The box before me is empty inside, just a dust-lined interior wrapped in aged green velvet. A mirror is on the inside of the lid, so grimy I can barely make out my reflection.

Something moves in the corner in my periphery. I look over. Nothing.

Then the crows come, and I drop the box.

One, then a dozen, then hundreds explode from the box. Wings beat against the air. Screeches shatter the silence. They slash at me, beaks and talons piercing skin.

My magic erupts. A repulsion wave flings them back. I throw up a shield. They hammer against it, desperate to break through.

Some die on impact, but they keep coming.

I bolt for the door, flinging it open to escape.

They flood the hall like smoke, growing as they fly.

Legs lengthen. Muscles swell. Their claws twist into deadly appendages. From their backs, black spines sprout in whip-like tails sharpened into piercing tips.

Arms burst from their chests, each armed with three long talons

Their beaks stretch, mouths splitting open to reveal rows of glistening, serrated teeth.

Screams erupt from the halls, followed by the sound of fighting.

Iris. Felix.

I focus, ripping open two portals. Twyx and Nyx emerge with their fangs bared and their eyes blazing. They flank me instantly, growling at the threat ahead.

I sprint toward the ballroom, ignoring the maze of halls. I blast through a few walls, uncaring who sees or what I destroy

This wasn't supposed to happen. I wanted to freak him out because he deserved fear. That was all.

I wanted to rattle him, to show him what sedatives feel like when they blur the lines between grief and madness, to leave him shaking from a nightmare of loss, the way I've lived mine.

Not cause loss for Iris and Felix.

Nyx and Twyx rip through any twisted crows that draw too close. Their snakes lash out with venom, shredding wings, hissing death.

Once I finally reach the ballroom, it is an ocean of red.

Blood streaks the marble floors. Ripped bodies litter the space like broken dolls. Screams mix with the sound of flapping wings as creatures pluck victims from the ground, gorging in midair.

Kalix guards Tyran like a steel wall. Iris stands beside them, a green aura pulsing from her skin. Several crows hang in the air, stilled by her power. Others circle above like puppets waiting for command.

Some relief washes over me when I see them in one piece.

I move with Nyx and Twyx, jumping over bodies, my feet slipping through blood as I vault to Tyran's side.

"Millicent!" Felix shouts, eyes wide.

"What the hell is happening?" Kalix demands.

"I—I don't know." My voice cracks. I meet his eyes.

Kalix's expression turns to stone. "Millicent."

His voice is cold steel.

"What have you done?"

"Forget whose fault it is. Just fucking handle it." Felix snaps.

I've never heard him like this, rage dripping from every word. His eyes land on me, full of disappointment and anger. That look burns deeper than any curse ever could. I turn away, unable to face it. Not now.

Taking inventory of the room, I let Twyx and Nyx roam free, slaughtering as many as they are able.

They surge forward, their jaws splitting down the sides until four panels of gruesome teeth fan wide. Their tongues lash out like spears, dragging the creatures from the air to the floor.

From the corners of the ballroom, the shadows obey me. I call them in, shape them in my mind into lances—long, deadly, and sharpened to perfection. The air thickens as they begin to take form around me.

I let them fly and send my lances toward their forms. Crows shriek and spiral down, bodies punctured and split as the lances pierce through bone and muscle. One lunges for my side, too fast to dodge.

Nyx is faster.

His tongue impales it mid-flight, and with a guttural roar, he launches upward. They crash across the floor, limbs snapping, until Nyx's four-jawed maw closes over one's skull, severing it cleanly.

My heart pounds. I need to end this. I need to close the box.

"Iris!" I yell over the chaos. "Do you know anything about the artifacts in the locked room?"

She glances back. One of her controlled crows drags a corpse to her. "No, but Cage does! Where the hell is he?" She hammers into the crow, muttering an incantation before It rises under her command.

"Kalix, what is the antidote for Somnex?"

Kalix yanks his impaled sword from a crow's gut, blood splashing on his boots. "Millicent Le Strange, if we survive this, I am going to kill you myself!" he screams furiously.

"Noted," I shout back over the clash of screams.

"It's night lily! In my office, labeled and deep purple!" he says as he kicks the chest of an approaching crow.

The building shakes, floor and walls trembling as a low roar vibrates through the air. All of us stagger, nearly losing our footing.

Felix braces himself against his throne, flinching as debris rains from the ceiling. "Fuck. You pissed off Vyraxis didn't you?" he snaps.

"What'll she do if Cage is unconscious?" I shout, a crow's shriek clipping the end of my question as Twyx tears it cleanly in half.

"She'll hunt you down and kill you," Kalix calls, laughing grimly. He charges a crow diving toward Iris, driving his blade through the underside of its beak.

"Good," I say through clenched teeth. I raise my hands, channeling magic until it sears like lightning through my veins and my vision floods with blue.

I don't hesitate and fire upward.

The roof explodes in a deafening blast. Shards of stone come crashing down like hail.

It does not take long for Vyraxis to answer. Her enormous head forces through the gap, stones cracking and tumbling off her horns.

I leave Nyx and Twyx, saturating the room with my aura. Felix's guards are dead. I pull a sword from one of their fallen bodies and run.

Vyraxis senses me, and her silver fire consumes the space. Screaming fills the air from humans and crows alike. I dive through the nearest door, casting a shield over myself to avoid being burned to a crisp. The heat licks at the edges of my ward.

Once I hit the hallway, I release what magic I can spare, preserving only enough to keep Nyx and Twyx present. As long as they're active, my aura lingers enough to keep Vyraxis in place.

Her next blast confirms it. More flames roar behind me, engulfing what's left of the ballroom.

I sprint down the corridor. Crows dive at me from all sides. I dodge instead of fighting. Magic risks drawing Vyraxis after me. She needs to stay where her fire protects the only people I have grown to care for...in my own way.

I need Oliver.

I frantically pull on our bond, and he appears by my side in an instant. His form flickers with yellow, the color of panic. His wide eyes take in the chaos in the blood-soaked halls. Above us, the shrieks of hunting crows still echo through the corridor as they hunt any human they can find.

"Kalix's apothecary," I instruct, breathless. "Night lily. It's labeled and deep purple. Quickly now, go."

He vanishes in a flash, his urgency rippling through our connection.

I burst through my chamber door and drop to my knees beside Cage. My heart pounds, adrenaline masking the ache in my muscles.

Ollie returns just as I lift Cage's head. We move in tandem, prying open his mouth while Ollie uncorks the bottle and pours the antidote in. I clamp his jaw shut, covering his nose until his throat convulses with a swallow.

A beat of silence—

Then his silver eyes open. His magic bristles, and I see the wrath stirring beneath the surface as the drug clears his system. He begins to shift, trying to sit up.

"Hey, easy," I whisper, steadying his neck. "Cage, you can be mad at me later. Please. I was not going to kill anyone, but we need you."

"You drugged me," he growls, rubbing the back of his head. "I'm livid, Millicent. 'Mad' doesn't even begin to cover it. You'll not run from your punishment this time."

I smile faintly. "I'll take whatever punishment you want." I glance toward the door. "The golden box, it's open."

His expression shifts, alarm replacing the anger. "Fuck, we need to go. Now."

He pushes to stand, but his balance wavers. I step beneath his arm to anchor him. "Come on," I murmur. "Time to fix what I broke."

"Misses," Ollie pleads, wings fluttering in agitation.

"Not now, Ollie. Later." Even as I press ahead to the urgent matter at hand, his agitation twists my stomach into a pit of knots.

"Misses, I must tell you something!" His voice pitches into a frantic screech, but we're already through the door.

Cage's stride quickens as the antidote works through his system.

"What is the damage?" he asks sharply as we descend the stairs.

"Mutated crows. A lot dead. Iris, Kalix, and Tyran are in the ballroom holding the line. I baited Vyraxis in to assist."

"Good."

His silence lingers for a moment until we reach a turn in the hall. He stumbles occasionally, but I manage to keep him steady. "Vyraxis says the crows keep coming, but Felix, Iris, and Kalix are safe."

Ahead, another wave of crows swoops toward us. I raise my hand, summoning fire. Blue and black flames roar from my palm reducing them to charred ash. The heat licks my skin. Beads of sweat prickle the back of my neck.

"How long have you been fighting?" he asks, shadows slithering around him like living smoke. "How is your energy level?" Tendrils whip upward and lash out, catching crows midair. Their bodies burst against the walls in a network of sheared wings and torn limbs.

"I am starting to feel it," I admit. "It's manageable."

"You've lied to me enough. Not now." His voice is hard steel. "If you begin to falter, I will feed you. Are we clear?" he commands. His words are not soft and tender. No. He is a leader, a commander. This is the first mage of the king

I nod quickly. "Yes." I hate how much I mean it, but I can't afford to have my magic go out on me. If my magic depletes, it will then turn to my life force until I shut down and enter stasis.

We reach the artifact room. The air is dense with the sound of screeching crows. These ones remain unmutated and normal sized, for now at least.

Cage releases me and takes my hand instead. His shadows tear across the room, dragging the crows down in knots of black. Dead birds crunch and squelch under our feet, smearing blood across the floor.

"If you care for Felix, Iris, or Kalix," he says, reaching for the golden box with the faded inscription *bound box of Morpheus*, "you will bring me back."

I freeze, staring. "Bring you back?"

He drops my hand. In one palm, he summons a strange, ceremonial blade. Its curved edge and obsidian hilt are carved from black stone instead of steel. Etching of an unfamiliar language pulses faintly across its surface.

Without hesitation, he pulls the blade across his own hand. Blood wells and drips from his fingers. He presses his palm to the golden box.

The incantation he speaks is foreign and guttural. As the words leave his mouth, the room darkens. The air thins, each breath becoming harder to draw.

Images flash in my mind—red, black, a four-armed creature tearing through flesh. The whispers return, layered and overlapping, voices too numerous to separate.

The chill that enters the air causes frost to spread across the floor beneath Cage. My breath fogs, and a deep-rooted wrongness slithers into the space...and into him.

Every crow drops dead, their bodies hitting the floor in unison. Beyond the door, the sounds of slaughter and screaming vanish. I rush to the hall—blood, bodies, silence. And indeed, they're all dead.

"You did it," I murmur, turning toward the box, toward Cage. The moment I look at him, something primal in me recoils. Then I remember his warning.

"Cage?" I step inside cautiously, approaching him from behind. He still doesn't respond. I raise a trembling hand and press it to his shoulder. It's ice cold. The wrongness of it sends nausea spinning through me.

A deep, unfamiliar chuckle rolls from his throat.

"There's my special girl."

He rises. When he turns, I freeze.

His eyes are bottomless black. The smile on his lips is carved in sadism.

"Cage?" I whisper.

He looks me over like a predator admiring his prize.

"Millicent, our rare gem."

His voice slithers through the air as his hand grips my jaw, tilting my head upward. I flinch, another surge of violent visions flashing behind my eyes. A desolate landscape, a sea of broken bodies, black eyes blinking from an endless abyss.

"Cage, snap out of it," I growl, twisting against his hold. His grip claws into my neck, bruising me.

"Do not dare defy me," he leans in close, sneering.

"We need to check on the others," I try, clinging to logic. I hope a mention of the people he loves might ground him. He doesn't even blink. He's fixated on me.

"Who are you, and what do you want?" I demand.

"I am Cage. And you know who and what I want." His lips curl into a cruel smile. "You slip away like sand through my fingers, but not this time. You can't escape me, Millicent. I am inevitable."

Rage coils in me. "Don't make me fight you."

That intrigues him. His aura is completely different, it's colder, fouler. Whatever part of him remains is buried beneath this malevolence. I know this threat isn't directed at me. It's meant for the others.

I cup his face, drawing us close, our foreheads touching. "Let me in."

"Not a chance," he whispers. "You play too many games."

"I thought you liked games." I slide my hands slowly down his arm toward the obsidian blade in his grip.

"Not the kind you play," he snaps, irritation cutting through the stillness in his voice.

I move. One sharp pull, and I drive the blade into my own stomach.

Agony erupts through me. The cursed metal sears as it sinks deep, rot bleeding through my insides. I scream, my knees buckling beneath me.

"What have you done!" Cage roars, his voice thunderous enough to rattle the room.

He catches me before I collapse, and he rips the blade free. His eyes flicker, black splitting with flashes of silver. The presence inside him begins to shudder and reel.

The cursed energy that clings to the blade now tries to enter my system. The Nightmother stirs.

Stay out, she hisses at the invisible force.

"Millie." Cage lowers me to the floor, panic rising in his voice. Panic that sounds so familiar, from a time when we were younger, when I often hurt myself from running around.

He presses a hand to my wound, trying to hold me together. He lifts his wrist, pressing it to my lips. My teeth elongate, and I sink them in, drinking deeply.

The Nightmother coils around it, consuming the force trying to infect me. My magic surges. My skin tugs and seals, the wound rapidly closing. Then nausea hits me. I heave forward, retching a torrent of red and black again and again. Each heave pulls more of the disease from me, until I'm gasping, clawing for breath.

Cage pulls me into his arms, his palm stroking circles over my back. "Get it all out," he whispers.

I cling to him, the tremors in my stomach finally settling. The retching fades, and my head lulls against his shoulder. I curl into his embrace, my limbs too heavy to lift.

Victory may have been unpleasant, but it is still mine. Cage shifted after the blade. I guessed some type of possessive force is lingering on the blade or it's used in parts of a ritual for infestation. A vessel can only be overtaken if its current inhabitant is weaker than the invader. And the Nightmother is always stronger.

"We need to check on the others," I croak. My throat is scorched, acid and magic clawing at it from the inside.

"We will," he murmurs. "Just...let me be with you a little longer."

I don't fight it, not this time. The night's events weigh heavily on me, but for now, I let myself rest in the quiet of him.

He buries his face between my shoulder blades and exhales an exhausted sigh. "You are different from how I remember you, aren't you, Millicent?"

I don't answer. We both know the answer already.

"I sit here holding a figment of my imagination." The laugh that escapes him begins to morph into something cruel. "You know the

consequence for this, don't you?" Any panic, any softness in his tone has hardened. "You will be burned," he says with finality, releasing me.

Eventually, he stands and offers his hand. I take it, and he never lets go. I walk hand and hand with death, just as I always have.

I will not burn.

I will not die.

I have tried to. Too many times.

Things bigger than him, bigger than they can imagine keep my corpse from rotting and my heart from stopping.

The castle is silent except for the wet squelch of boots in blood. Carcasses lie draped over golden trim like meat on a banquet table. Crimson stains run down marble walls like veins.

We reach the ballroom. Felix and Kalix are moving through the dead, checking for any signs of life. Healers are already at work, guiding the refugees to the mess hall. Iris remains by the throne, staring blankly over the room.

Cage releases my hand. He walks to Kalix, the two speaking in low, grave murmurs. No one greets him. No one rejoices. Grief chokes out every other emotion.

I approach Iris slowly. "Iris, are you all right?"

She turns to me with a radiant, chilling smile. "I am perfect. I am *perfection!*" Her laughter is edged with mania. Magic arcs like static over her skin. I stop asking questions, finding it prudent to avoid pushing the conversation further. She's too far gone, swept up in whatever current she rides.

I begin to walk the room, mimicking the others, trying to keep my hands busy, my mind steady.

That's when Ollie returns, panicked, trembling.

"Me Misses, please, we must speak at once!"

The urgency in his voice cuts through the haze like a blade.

"What is it, Ollie?"

"Arcadia, not good, not good!"

Ice floods my veins. My skin dampens instantly, my hands shaking. "What about Arcadia?"

Ollie lands on my shoulder, his body vibrating with fear.

Images begin to flash in my mind, his memories bleeding into mine. What he's seen. What he's felt.

My heart clenches and then—stops. A scream tears from my mouth, silent and shrill, the kind that scrapes your soul raw. My body collapses inward, buckling to my knees as agony detonates through me. I see her again and again—Arcadia. And the pain only grows.

Everything I love dies.

I am not followed by death.

I am death.

CHAPTER 49

Arcadia

I RIP A FEW GOWNS FROM MY CLOSET, CRAMMING THEM INTO my bag with shaking hands. Blood oozes steadily down my back, hot and sticky, soaking into the fabric as tears streak down my face.

Every breath burns. The wounds my familiar sustained are carved into my soul. I cinch the bag tight and sling it over my shoulders. I burst through the doors and sprint toward the forest.

I don't look back. My breath begins to rasp as the drug they slipped me invades my system all over again.

The black-cloaked figures follow, their antelope masks gleaming under the moonlight. Their pace is unhurried, almost deliberate. The blades they carry glisten with my blood. This is a ritual, I realize. I just don't know what for.

"Run, little sheep. It enjoys the hunt," one of them taunts. The voice, warped by magic, offers no clue who hides behind the mask.

Fuck these people. I am no sheep.

Branches lash my skin as I break into the woods. Cuts bloom across my body. Then suddenly, something massive joins the chase. Its weight is pounding the forest floor, snapping branches like twigs. The vibrations reach me before the sound does. I'm covered in blood. I'm bait.

A prayer leaves my lips in silence, pleading with the gods to let me survive the night.

As if to mock my prayer, they answer with a Lycan's howl—deep, blood-curdling, and far too close.

Panic floods me. I no longer wonder *if* I'll die. I wonder *what* will get to me first.

The branches above thicken, strangling the moonlight.

I can't see.

My foot catches in a hidden hole. Pain tears up my leg as I crash forward, my ankle twisting with a sickening snap. I scream, agony flooding me.

From the shadows, another scream rises, echoing mine. Four long, pale arms emerge, clawed fingers dragging something monstrous through the trees.

It's coming straight for me.

ACKNOWLEDGMENTS

I may have self-published but I'm far from alone in this process. Without the immense support behind me during this process, I think my sanity would be lost.

Thank you to my best friends, Sophia, Ansley, and Danni, for being so involved during this process and helping me. A special thanks to Sophia for taking on so much of my merchandising and art aspects.

A huge thank you to my amazing editor and mentor. My writing has improved so much with her wisdom, knowledge, and experience.

To my fellow author friends, thank you! You give me a place where the author aspect of my life has empathy, where my writer's mind is encouraged and fed. A special big thanks to V for being my sun on cloudy days.

Thank you to my beta readers for being so thorough and honest and to my ARC readers for your honest reviews and overwhelming support.

Finally, screaming from the roof tops a huge thank you to you, my reader. Without you, my story is not experienced, something I loved is not shared. You help bring something I am so passionate about to life. It's sappy, but I have a gratitude journal, and I regularly cry from the joy I have experienced on this journey. A joy you bring.

With love and luck,
Cassi

AUTHOR NOTES

The greatest amount of transformation comes from pain and suffering. They are concepts I have been fascinated with ever since I experienced them for so long myself. Life does not filter or censor things for you. There is no closing a door when bad things happen to you. You must stand there and bare it. Just as life does not shelter you, I will not. This is why this tale will be so violating and hard to digest, because that is how it is intended to be. When you find yourself needing a moment before you continue reading, imagine how someone felt in real life when something awful was happening to them.

I'm sorry if it is hard to read but not truly because imagine having to experience it. Some of you may not know what I speak of, and for that, I am thankful. I hope your days are happy and you remain untouched by the dark depravity that exists in this world. Those like me, who have had to live in the dark for so long, will know what I speak of.

You will know how it feels to endure pain and suffering.

And you can't close the door.

WWW.CASSANDRAMDAUTHOR.WEEBLY.COM

Instagram: @cassandra.m.dalton

Patreon: @Cassandra_MD

TikTok: @cassimariah

Spotify Playlist QR Code